"Patrick Wensink's *Fake Fruit Factory* is a comedy machine, pumping out madcap action, large-scale disaster, and one strange character after another. Also, fake fruit."

—*OWEN KING*, author of *Double Feature*

"There are plenty of bastards in this world, but Patrick Wensink isn't one of them. Well, maybe. He is our Terry Southern and Paul Krassner and possibly one day even our own Jonathan Swift . . ."

—*SCOTT MCCLANAHAN*, author of *Hill William* and *Crapalachia*

"I like Patrick Wensink's work so much my heart had to issue its own cease-and-desist order."

—*GARY SHTEYNGART*, author of *Super Sad True Love Story*

"The greatest book about competing burger franchises since *The Grapes of Wrath*."

—*AMELIA GRAY*, author of *Threats*

"A small town rallies to beat ever worsening odds against its survival in this madcap comic novel."

—*KIRKUS*

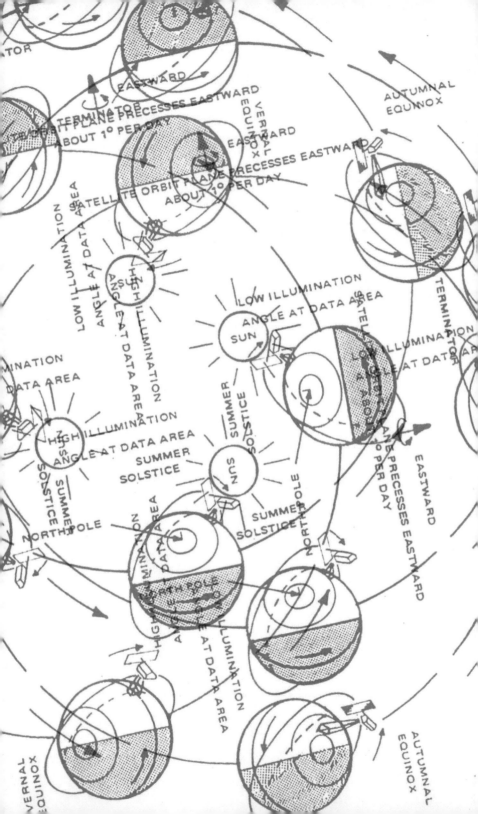

FAKE FRUIT FACTORY

A NOVEL

PATRICK WENSINK

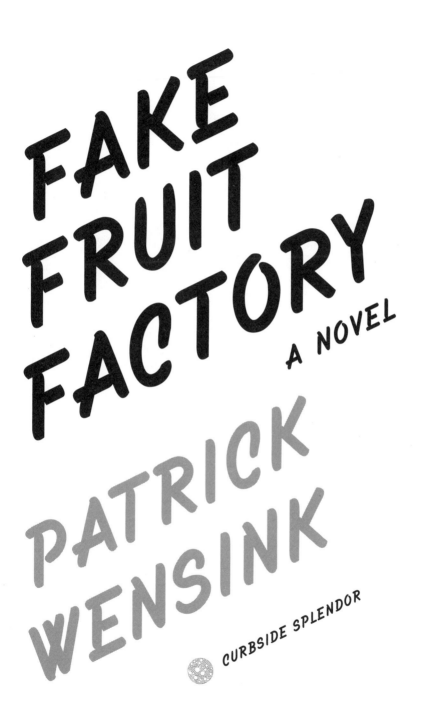

CURBSIDE SPLENDOR

CURBSIDE SPLENDOR PUBLISHING

The stories contained herein are works of fiction. All incidents, situations, institutions, governments, and people are fictional and any similarity to characters or persons living or dead is strictly coincidental.

Published by Curbside Splendor Publishing, Inc., Chicago, Illinois in 2015.

First Edition
Copyright © 2015 by Patrick Wensink
Library of Congress Control Number: 2015939311

ISBN 978-1-94-043056-0
Edited by Todd Summar
Designed by Alban Fischer

Manufactured in the United States of America.

www.curbsidesplendor.com

FOR DON AND NORMA WENSINK

"All thoughts are prey to some beast."

BILL CALLAHAN

PART ONE

WEDNESDAY, 9:02 PM

A speck of pepper.

On any map detailed enough to include Dyson, Ohio, it's a speck of pepper. But most maps ignore it. Most maps neglect the flat Midwestern fields of wheat and corn swaying for miles in every direction. Most maps turn their nose up at Dyson's lack of a university or major historical attraction or building taller than three stories.

Dyson is a village, technically speaking, and, technically speaking, villages aren't worth the mapmaker's time. Dyson's crumbling downtown isn't worth his time. Its few thousand people aren't worth his time. So, every citizen's job and family and dog and cat and mortgage problem all get housed on a tiny, unmarked dot of pepper. And that little spot of spice never causes so much as a cartographic sneeze. So, like all sneezes, Dyson is forgotten in an instant.

Today, that will change. Today, that pepper will be sprinkled under the nose of every newscaster, politician, and overly-concerned citizen in America. Today, but not quite yet. Right now an important council meeting is wrapping up.

Inside Town Hall, the gavel crashes down like murder. Meeting adjourned. It ends but nothing is solved.

Now comes the hard part for the mayor—now comes all the talking.

Bo hates how people still do impressions, like he's said something adorable. His voice really isn't anything special—maybe a little high and nasal—but, still, why are people compelled to parody it like parents quoting their kids? Bo is on the long side of twenty-eight, but in the mayoral world he may as well be sucking his thumb and sleeping in a bassinet.

It is one of the smaller challenges he's discovered since being sworn in last year. That mimicry wears thin fast, especially today. Sometimes it seems everyone is good at being Mayor Bo Rutili except Bo Rutili.

He is slim and anxious. The mayor looks like the kind of guy who's afraid of germs—which he is. When he's stuck talking to a citizen, Bo scratches deep at a razor-bumped neck. He's digging away right now.

"Why do small towns still exist? Why don't we all just move to the big, exciting city?" Joyce Camden tells the mayor, doing her best Bo impression. *"The Dysons of this world are going broke, being swallowed by sprawling neighbors and dying from old gays."*

"Old *age*," the mayor says, politely forcing a smile. "I said old age, Joyce."

"Oh, good. That seemed really insensitive." Joyce grins the way she always does with a few cups of coffee under her belt. "Still, I thought that was such a brave thing to say," she says in her own voice. "You're still a little guy, but you're right. Dyson needs to adapt or die. Well, I, for one, am not going to let our little slice of heaven disappear."

Dyson Town Hall is cramped and not equipped for such a robust turnout. A few hundred people constitute a serious crowd in a community this size. Plastic buckets dot the hardwood, catching whatever drips from those ugly ceiling spots. The walls were once white, but have gone smoggy with decades of cigarette haze. Framed photos of proud years gone, of civic leaders, rotunda bands, and egg hunts are all left to fade and dust.

At the meeting's start Bo began a long sweat that still hasn't stopped thanks to the germs. The touching, the talking, the back-slapping. Dyson's mayor would much rather be locked in his office solving this crisis than endure more socializing. Shoulders and elbows and necks all rearrange like a Yahtzee shaker. In the slick grease of the crowd, Bo thanks Joyce and quickly examines both palms.

The mayor stuffs those hands in pockets when Chief Grover claps his moist shirt back. "Good for *you*, Bo." His breath is strong enough to remove grass stains. A familiar Rutili impression begins: "*I will not address the issue of some mysterious ghost strangling chickens and destroying crops. That is an issue for the police.*" Dyson's top cop, burly and hairy and intense, tugs his gun belt as hundreds of keys jingle. "That was just the right response. People talking about some monster roaming the night, it's not *healthy*. Young man, you stubbed out that rumor like a cigar. Your parents would be proud."

"I said *thug*, not *ghost*. I don't believe in ghosts," he says loud above the clatter of voices.

"Awwww. Good for you." The Chief musses Bo's hair like a brave puppy.

The mayor takes a long breath and reluctantly shakes hands, building up sauna levels of sweat. *This*, he thinks, *is the hardest part of the job.*

Bo weaves and glad-hands, gliding between the dense pack. Stiff fluorescent lights convert his usual apologetic expression to something hard and dark. His thin arms and legs sliver through a crowd bold with fresh coffee smells. The mayor finally finds the cramped restroom.

"*Now, I have a lot of faith in the Destination: Dyson program*," Garrett Queen performs his Rutili impression in a floppy, feminine voice while filling a urinal. "Economic time bomb is more like it."

"That kid is a one-man kamikaze." Queen's urinal neighbor, Skeet Brown, shakes his head. He speaks in a sad growl. "It kills me to see this place die. So many good memories. Mark my words, when this town goes under, and it is going under big, it'll be Bo Rutili's fault—"

Bo clears his throat, looking in the mirror and adjusting a striped tie. Harsh lights shine bits of scalp through thinning brown hair. Bo's face is childlike, but his eyes stay hard and dark. He exhales stiff disappointment to inhale stale urinal air—searching for optimism.

"*Hey*, it's little Bo Rutili! Hi, Bo. Hell of a speech. Right up there with Lincoln at Gettysburg," says Skeet.

"Thanks for coming tonight, fellas," Bo says with a genuine smile, reminded that nobody agrees on politics. "If we all work together and make sacrifices, we'll never have to leave Dyson. Don't forget, Skeet, I have a lot of good memories here, too. So does Garett. Everyone does."

Bo shakes hands with the two men and sighs as the weight of Dyson's few thousands lives saddle up on his shoulders for a ride. The ride is barreling down a steep, loose hillside. Bo is struggling for footing. He would kill for a handrail.

Garret and Skeet shuffle out, grumbling something like an apology.

The mayor takes a silent moment to think about all the filthy palms he just shook. He should be calculating ways to funnel money into the town's bank account. Instead, Bo squints at his skin. His neck always stiffens at these moments, picturing microbes and germs throwing grabby little parties on his flesh.

Bo doesn't bother with the faucet. Soap and water aren't the cure. A warm panic grows in his chest. Bacteria, viruses, fungi, protozoa, helminthes—they are all around. He knows only one thing will cure this anxiety.

Rushing from the bathroom, Rutili thinks the entire town is waiting for him.

"Bo," councilman Wendell Dixon says. His skin bronzy, his body positioned to roadblock the mayor. But Dixon, the town's lone lawyer, is clueless to what a germy cesspool things have become. "I need a minute, stat. The council is a little concerned about where ten million dollars will come from—"

Bo sidesteps, pretending to wave to a far-off visitor. Nobody can capture the young mayor's attention. Some begin to express shared optimism, but don't get in a full sentence before he vanishes. Some just focus in skeptical stares, like Donna Queen, who delivers a sarcastic patty-cake clap, saying, "Bravo. Nice work up there."

Bo's feet rush down three flights of wooden stairs, beyond the endless chatter of citizens until he takes jittery steps into the black evening air. The night swirls with chirping insects and lime green firefly blinks. Bacteria, viruses, fungi, protozoa, helminthes. The mayor can't stop aching with germs.

Luckily, he finds peace from a bottle of hand sanitizer inside his car. His stiff neck softens. That warm chest cools. He watches with calm relief as the Disinfectant Police break up the party. Bo stares at those hands, measuring long breaths.

"Where are we going to get ten million dollars?" he asks the tingling palms. That massive number stares back in his mind. Ten million. All those zeroes. It's the number that will save his town, but also the number that will swallow it whole. "The state said no, the federal government said no. And I'm not asking Donna Queen. Good God, she'd love nothing more than to—"

The passenger door opens and the dome light spreads through the dark cabin, exposing Bo massaging his sanitized fingers. "People are talking, babe," Marci says. She slips in and buckles up.

Bo breathes easy and loose. He slides the sanitizer into the armrest. Marci has beautiful brown eyes that work in tandem with cheerful cheeks. Those features are packaged with a tight ponytail pulled into a doorknob the color of dark beer. She is so plain. Bo takes a lot of comfort in that plainness. She is one of those girls you admire while she jogs down the block—but you forget in the next minute. Occasionally, though, certain things draw attention to Marci's plainness: smudged makeup, a funny birthmark, shirt tags always sticking out.

"I'm sorry, sweetie. It was a great speech." She gives Bo a brief kiss. "But Donna Queen, that piece of work, is starting to get people talking."

"Let them talk." He turns on the engine. "There's one way to save this town—my way. Everyone'll see."

"Donna's saying things like you're not ready to be mayor." Words spill messy from her frustration. "Burying little seeds about how someone like you shouldn't have even been elected. And worst of all, she does it in this awful little voice—"

"Donna's a fine business owner and a friend of the town." Bo sounds weak compared to his public speaking voice. Every sleepy syllable balances between optimism and exhaustion.

"She is a friend to *no one*—oh, don't forget your seatbelt—a friend to no one but herself. If Donna's stupid bank wouldn't foreclose on every store in town, maybe we wouldn't need to find some magic plan to bail Dyson out of debt. God, I mean, ten million dollars?"

"Well now, the video rental store, the civil war reenactment store, and that restaurant that only made club sandwiches didn't utilize sound business models. If those owners couldn't pay their mortgage it's not . . ."

" . . . *The Queen Bank's fault.*" Her Rutili impression is slower and dumber than the genuine article.

He really wishes the entire town would move on from this fascination with his voice. He's not even sure anyone knows they're doing it anymore.

Marci grabs his hand with a loving squeeze before he pulls down the gearshift. "Sorry."

"Your shirt tag is sticking up," he says, nodding toward it.

"Thanks." Marci finds the back of her neck. "So . . ." She breathes long. "So, when are you going to decide?"

"What?" He watches the road.

"You know what. Tomorrow, right? God, I'm actually nervous."

"It's hard." He points the car up Main Street. Main is probably the first place he'd take visitors on a tour if Dyson ever had visitors. "I need you to keep quiet about everything. I shouldn't have told you that much."

"Sweetie, the town needs ten million bucks or it will grind to a stop. People can't hide an ingrown toenail around here, let alone *this*. If it helps, you were actually the third person to tell me."

"Something like Destination: Dyson is good. It's strong. It's my best idea yet. This'll boost us up. I'm really proud of myself." His throat clears. "But I shouldn't be talking to you about it. It's not fair to the other contestants."

They entered the heart of Dyson. Downtown, everyone calls it. Two blocks of brick buildings, each about three stories tall. At night, with the windows dark and the streetlamps glowing, Bo is always captured by an intense loneliness. Like falling in a dream.

Tight brick storefronts on both sides of the street are as empty and lifeless as Bo's monthly visit to the nursing home. Black's Pharmacy has had newspapered windows for as long as anyone can remember. Dyson Hardware went out of business when Home Depot opened a few towns over. Falafel Junction also shut down. Its owner never quite understood why even Dyson's more adventurous diners kept their distance. He never understood that most townspeople thought chicken schwarma and babaganoosh sounded like venereal diseases.

Downtown Dyson's decorating taste doesn't bring him much pep either. Not with all the twinkling red and green lights spun around lampposts. Not with all the cheerful wooden Santas. Not with the snowman a few blocks away at the park. The calendar is flipped to July, so Dyson's December spirit just makes everything darker and more depressing for the mayor. It only reminds him of the town's outrageous tinsel budget.

Beyond the only two stoplights, toward the edge of town, his car pulls into a driveway. The rented bungalow needs new shutters and paint. The shrubbery is in charge now.

There is an emotional humidity, a thickness in the air. *Don't ask. Don't ask. Don't ask,* Bo thinks, hating to let Marci down.

"Do you want to sleep over tonight?" she says in a sweet, suggestive way, her eyes glowing green and black from the dash instruments. Bo's groin awakens.

With her thirtieth birthday approaching, those eyes are surrounded by phantom lines. Marci's first grey appeared just as mysteriously. But when Bo actually spends a few delicate seconds looking her over, Marci is still as beautiful as their first date five years earlier.

Marci is graceful and charming and kind.

"I'd love to, but . . . budget stuff. There are all these proposals for revenue boosting to organize. Tomorrow's the Destination: Dyson meeting."

"I know. I'm going, remember?"

"Someone's got to come up with an idea that'll turn our economy around or—"

"Dyson will be a ghost town." Her impression is kind, but irritated. "I know."

A concrete wall of silence—a full minute's worth—urges the mayor to shift in his seat.

Marci burrows a hole through that wall. "Just tell me one thing before I say goodnight and let you wallow all by your lonesome."

"Anything." More silence and thickness follows, stiffening Bo's chest with anticipation. He hates disappointing people. Bo bites his tongue until the pain is a tickle. *Don't ask about marriage, please. Not again,* his mind begs. *Please.*

Marci smiles and strokes his cold hands. "Is there really a mummy killing chickens and destroying crops?"

WEDNESDAY, 9:19 PM

"What were you doing at twenty-eight?" Donna Queen asks her husband Garrett.

"I don't remember. Probably smoking dope and playing records backward." He looks across the car to his wife. Her collagen injecting, face lifting, tummy tucking, and breast augmenting make her look just as close to twenty-eight as the subject of their conversation.

"Exactly!" she says, listening to a few seconds of the radio before hitting SEEK. "I had a good job at the bowling alley at that age." She switches to another channel. "But I wasn't responsible enough to *run* Dyson. Not like I am now."

Garrett counts the station jump for the tenth time since leaving Town Hall. Their previous car was actually a van so cheap it didn't even have a tape deck. Digitally skipping channels was impossible before Donna bought some sports car made in Germany. Now filled with some echoing memory, Garrett runs his fingers over his bare skull, recalling that scrolling orange tuner bar and the raw crackle between stations. He wonders what that old radio is up to now.

"Bo's an awful mayor, but not as bad as Packwicz was." That old fool is the one who got us into this mess to begin with." Garrett thinks about comparing Bo to one of those poor infants with some genetic deformity passed down from a previous generation—cataracts or a bum pancreas or something—but knows it will surely piss off his wife. He just rubs his snowy white mustache and waits.

The radio station jumps forward without static. Halogen headlights glow blue across empty Main Street. The engine sounds like hot breath.

"Well, this quote-unquote mayor isn't making anything better. Honestly, how did a majority of voters think a *child* could govern us?"

"Donna, stop with the radio, please. Just ask me to change it." His voice tries to soothe her temper.

"Fine. I hate radio, anyhow."

Out toward their house in the country, the Queens pass at least a dozen FOR SALE signs. Some days Garrett thinks everyone is leaving Dyson but them. He knows Donna can't or at least won't. He stopped begging to move years ago.

Garrett reminds himself how blessed he and Donna are and decides to help her get over the hump. "You can't hold this in forever. The election was eight months ago. You have to forget it. Bo beat you fair and square. It was a clean campaign."

Her mouth snaps, intense and predatory. "The only things clean are Bo's ears, because he's still wet behind them."

Garrett's tone shifts to that of defenseless prey with shaky legs. "Now, I don't think much of him either, but we're stuck for the next three—Donna!" His hand slaps hers away from the radio button. "We're stuck for the next three years with Rutili."

The Queen Estate, all fifty sprawling acres—including the trout pond, memory garden, and movie theater—is another few minutes outside of town. Their car buzzes past Marci's driveway and the Mayor's idling car. She points in their direction.

"Does sleeping with the manager of that stupid museum count as grounds for impeachment? I mean, it is adultery. Bo and that tramp aren't even engaged. Not to mention it's probably a conflict of interest with his Desperation: Dyson contest."

"Donna, knock it off." Garrett swats her hand—her diamond bracelet and rings glitter like nuclear stars in the dashboard light. "It's called Destination: Dyson—"

Kl-blunk!

Tires squeal and the scent of Donna's perfume is replaced with fleshy scorched rubber. When the car rolls to a rest, the pair breathes heavy—her fingers tight around the wheel, his pressed deep into the dash.

Both sit wide-eyed in silence until their lungs settle and they finally blink.

"Was that a deer?" Donna asks between huffs.

"I hope so." Garrett's cheeks are the white of his mustache.

"No, no, no," Donna repeats quieter and quieter and quieter.

"Don't worry, it was a deer. You hit a deer. It definitely wasn't a person," Garrett says. "Let me go check. You stay put. Don't worry. It was a deer."

The door slams and her shaky fingers stab at the radio until she calms. Her husband's figure disappears from the red brake light haze to the outer dark of blackness.

She looks at the radio numbers and taps the button. Her head whips around and doesn't see anything. She hits SEEK twice more.

In a moment, Garrett comes back into view. He walks to the front of the car, lowers to his haunches, and inspects the dented hood. Silence is broken by the pounding, bending grind from peeling something off the fender.

He returns and says, "Well now, I don't know what it was, but it's gone." He closes the passenger door.

"Thank God," Donna says. "It must have gotten scared and run back to the woods."

Garret stares at his closed hand, fist held awkward.

"Right?"

"Donna, a deer doesn't wear bandages." He unrolls a strip of tattered brown gauze that looks like it came from a museum archive.

WEDNESDAY, 9:31 PM

Edna Rutili sits in her living room, radio so loud the windows shiver. With an air conditioner running and two near-deaf ears, it's almost impossible to hear Cody Kellogg read the news.

"Well, Dyson, it looks like Blue and Grey for All Occasions has closed its doors for good." The disc jockey's voice is as rapid and growly as Boots' purr. "The competition over in Findlay, Civil War Warehouse is picking its teeth with our proud little establishment."

The cottage-style home is swamped with dust. The pale snow settles on every shelf. It piles on outdated calendars carefully stored in closets. Edna's fingerprints smudge a trail across picture frames. Some days she walks the house and wonders how she ever found the space to raise a family, plus two grandsons. Things didn't feel so small back then.

Boots circles Edna's lap, swabbing a tail, letting his happy purr rumble the woman's brittle legs. The cat is shorthaired and grey with a white line running down its stomach that it loves to roll over and show Edna. To her, this cat is more than a responsibility. This cat is love and calm and a snapshot of her time on earth. There were days when she'd feel like God, thinking about how a cat's life was only a flicker of her own ninety-four years. It made her nuzzle Boots more and appreciate it.

She almost never misses a chance to get in close and nuzzle.

However, Grandma Rutili doesn't notice her best friend's plea for attention right away. She is half-listening to the radio and half-admiring the pictures of those two grandsons lined up next to the chair. Both grown up to be fine men now. Well, at least the one. Her wrinkled finger runs across the image, carving another dusty pathway.

The house has been this way for years. She doesn't even bother to pull the plastic winter sheeting from the windows anymore. It's an airlock with a musty, sweet aroma of lavender.

"All ceremonial sabers and uniforms are fifty percent off this week. However, shop owner Ed Lee gave WDSR an exclusive, saying that next week will be a clearance sale like none other. Now, he made no promises, but told us there was a possibility of muskets and gunpowder being buy-one-get-one-free. Don't quote me on that, but hey, let's support a local business while we still have a few left."

The radio pauses with the ruffling of paper. "Oh and also," Cody Kellogg's voice sharpens into a rude instrument, "I'm supposed to tell people to eat at Donna Queen's Pizza Pad. So, you know, if you're desperate and hungry I guess it's open."

Edna tilts her head at the news of the Civil War store, scratching Boots' ear. *Everything comes to an end*, she reminds herself and decides right then—surrounded by pictures of her family, with her best pal on her lap, proud of being Dyson's oldest citizen—she wouldn't be sad if she came to an end.

WEDNESDAY, 10:42 PM

The smell of deep fryer grease battles cigarette smoke.

The bartender, Murray Kreskin, points to the television. "Get a load of this." He leans over his bar to the closest customer. Unfortunately, it's Old Man Packwicz.

Packwicz's weak, limp face hangs like a stroke victim. His shirt is buttoned wrong and his grey hair broom bristles upward. He focuses on digging trenches across the mahogany bartop with a quarter.

"Packy. Packy, you hear me?" Kreskin is brutishly large, but neat. His dark hair is always combed and trimmed. Those massive hands with carefully clipped fingernails pour drinks. That neatness only makes the thin cigar between his teeth and the large tattoo on the back of his left hand stand out stronger.

Packy doesn't hear him. Nobody does. Murray is convinced customers never listen unless he is telling a joke.

The bartender rubs wet hands across a tidy white apron; dark bitters and golden whiskey streak his belly. Murray turns off the jukebox and points a remote at the corner television, its volume growing louder over a sea of bobbing heads and cigarette fog.

The Kreskin Inn is little more than a long wooden bar dominating a shoebox room. A few tables line naked brick walls. Visitors tend to stand around when they don't get a stool.

Most nights Murray thanks God his old man didn't go into corn farming like all the other geniuses in town. Exactly why Murray Kreskin Sr. opened a tavern is lost to time, but his only son is grateful. While every other business in Dyson slips through the cracks, Murray's cash register brims with money.

It always has.

Not like Donna Queen or anything, but something comfortable.

Unlike other businesses, nobody drives twenty minutes to Findlay for a shot of bourbon. "A depression or a gold rush," his father repeated millions of times. "People always have the thirst." Murray Sr. was philosophical like that, and folks around town took him seriously. Murray Jr.'s endless broadcast of knock-knock and "a pope, a rabbi, and a minister" jokes don't demand nearly as much respect.

Murray's patrons stop talking and gaze toward the blue television glow. This report is pretty tough to believe. Tonight, Dyson is on the national news. (The town did, however, once make the local news several years back after historical documents uncovered a story about Abraham Lincoln stopping there to use the restroom in 1859.)

The bar's television cuts to a commercial and the room dies a little. Nervous silence fills the normally rowdy bar—a place where country songs and fists often fly through the air together—until one man wanders back. "Wouldn't that be about perfect? A satellite," Troy Gomez says, flipping Murray a pair of fingers. "Two more beers." He pecks a ball of lint from a vintage Rolling Stones shirt. The album with the crotch.

"Yeah, but the news says there's only a small chance it'll come down. Nothing to have a heart attack about," Murray says, running his hands up and down his suspenders, eyes turned to the television. Kreskin may be the only man in America still sporting suspenders, but those straps belonged to his father and that puts a rare smile on the bartender's face every morning.

"You think they'd build spy satellites to stay in orbit. That's their job, isn't it? Fly around space and not crash land."

"Crash in our backyard, no less." Murray shakes his head and snaps off two beer lids. "But like the reporter said, it ain't gonna happen. It's a tiny, tiny, microscopic chance." His thick fingers pinch tight.

"The other channel said the same thing happened in Australia a few years ago." Troy has gained weight since high school and wears an outdated black goatee on his chin. The female regulars know him mostly as that kid who'll never buy you a drink or offer his seat, no matter how packed it is. Dyson has more popular stray dogs tipping over garbage cans than Troy Gomez. "I heard NASA narrows it down to a few hundred square miles usually. But nobody can predict where a satellite and all its crap will hit once it enters Earth's atmosphere."

A hot, damp sweat builds on Murray's neck. He's a little stuttery. "Ease up. Nothing's going to happen." Murray dries a mug, scrubbing hard with a soft white towel. "Anybody die in Australia?"

"Maybe. They didn't say. I mean, that satellite was the size of a Volkswagen, and then it busted into a bazillion pieces. It scattered across Australia. But get this: a couple chunks landed in some podunk Outback town, and they sent Uncle Sam a ticket for *littering*."

Murray laughs from his toes to his mustache, the way he does whenever a punch line hangs. The greatest joys of his work, besides simply staying afloat, are the jokes. His thighs quake, his doughy breasts shudder, and a fantastic wash of peace floods the whale-bellied bachelor.

"Man," Gomez says with a happy-go-lucky grin. "I hope a satellite wipes this stupid town off the map. And I hope it starts with my idiotic fruit factory."

"Hey," Murray's voice grows big and bold. Veins burrow from his neck. "I worked there one summer. Not to mention, that factory puts food on your table and beers in your hand." He reaches under the counter. "You have no respect for this town, you know it?"

For the second time, the room hushes and goes motionless. People listen to Murray Kreskin, he just doesn't realize.

The kid fidgets, worried about Murray's famous temper and nasty habit of sending Louisville Sluggers across foreheads.

"Murray, man, settle down. I didn't mean it like—"

"Get out of my bar." He fumbles with something low and hidden.

"Now, come on, just take it easy." Troy's eyes dart down to where he can't see.

"Get out of here," Murray says and comes up with a moist white towel. It whip-cracks Gomez's face. The kid instantly holds his hands over his mouth and nose, cursing. "Don't make me add you to the Shit List," Murray yells and lifts his tattooed hand.

"You're crazy," Troy calls, his lip bleeding, but not much. He skitters toward the door. Ripples of laughter are all around him. "You're a fat idiot. All of you are fat idiots!"

The burst of catcalls is thin and lonely. Part of Murray knows everyone wants a distraction from the ugliness onscreen. Nobody wants to swallow the news that Dyson is as good as dead.

Potentially dead, at least.

Probably not dead, but still microscopic chances are chances, too.

"Hey, Packy." Murray needs someone to admire his aim. "You see that?"

"Yeah, a satellite," the former mayor mutters, a pile of termite shit next to his quarter. "Maybe Mrs. High-and-Mighty can buy a missile to shoot it out of the sky."

"No, Packy, I put Troy Gomez in his place. I'm like Indiana Jones or some shit. Did you see it?" The bartender's smile shrivels.

Packy's voice blooms loud and shaky: "Or better yet, maybe the whole great big satellite would drop like a comet onto Donna Queen's Estate, right on top of that bitch while she's pruning her memory garden."

THURSDAY, 1:11 AM

Marci's sister, Pearl Krupp, slips off a Kreskin Inn work shirt and dances into a robe. She is whipped, but not too tired for a late night bowl of ice cream and some Ornette Coleman.

Her Tinkerbelle haircut—dyed something like blonde—and spider-thin arms are a blur, pirouetting around the apartment. All the day's drink orders melt away with scoopful after scoopful of mint chocolate chip. Every customer's pick-up line evaporates from the hot force of wiggling sax and sharp drumbeats. She turns the stereo up to Edna Rutili volume levels. She doesn't care what hour it is. She needs this.

This is the only time Pearl is comfortable in her own skin. Every moment would feel so free, she thinks, if not for this ridiculous job holding her back or those disgusting skinny arms or that embarrassing commercial she filmed so many years ago.

Someone is sure to hear the pounding jazz, because Pearl's apartment complex is a block of one-bedroom places. She rents the cheapest one, the slab in the dead center. She shares the white walls with people on both sides. There are tenants below and above, too. Pearl decorates the place like the FBI is on her tail—no pictures on the walls, double mattress on the floor, and folding camping chairs for furniture.

A pile of mail waits as she spins across the kitchen and clatters an empty bowl on the counter. She finds a surprisingly small number of bills, an expected amount of crap, and one hand-addressed envelope.

DEAR PEARL KRUPP,

THANK YOU FOR SUBMITTING YOUR APPLICATION FOR OUR PROGRAM. TO BEGIN, WE WOULD LIKE YOU TO KNOW WE RECEIVED OVER 11,000 APPLICATIONS AND HAD TO NARROW OUR SEARCH TO THREE.

THE GOOD NEWS IS THAT YOUR ESSAY HAS BEEN CHOSEN BY OUR PRODUCERS AS ONE OF THE MOST INTRIGUING. WE WILL BE SENDING A CAMERA CREW FROM "America's Boringest City" TO DYSON TO SEE HOW BORING YOUR TOWN REALLY IS.

YOU ARE PROBABLY WONDERING HOW YOU CAN ENSURE DYSON WINS AND GETS THE EXTREME COMMUNITY MAKEOVER PRIZE. THE GOOD NEWS IS: NOTHING! IF DYSON IS HALF AS UGLY AND SLOW-PACED AS YOU CLAIM, THIS WILL BE AN EASY CHOICE. WE'LL SEE YOU IN SEVEN DAYS.

SINCERELY,
Rajula Magbi

After holding the note to the light, and realizing, yes, Rajula's signature is real pen, Pearl's legs get weak. Her body collapses in joy, which lasts only about a second. Those rainbow bursts of happiness are quickly replaced with something doctors classify as that *Son-of-a-Bitch* feeling of cracking your head on the countertop.

Rajula Magbi's letter twists to the floor.

After a few minutes of cursing and skull-rubbing, Pearl reads the note again. "You've got to make this count." Big breaths punctuate her words. "I'm good enough to make this count, right?" A familiar plague of dread soaks her excitement to something dark. The recurring dread left over from when she shot that commercial. "Right?" She checks the postmark date and realizes it probably should have arrived days ago. The U.S. Postal Service decided to discontinue daily mail routes in Dyson and now letters come sporadically at best. "Oh, God, no."

Rajula should be arriving any time now.

THURSDAY, 8:12 AM

Summer morning sunshine warms the sidewalk. Mayor Rutili, on hands and knees, holds a tape measure in front of his store, the Dyson Drop. Chamber of Commerce bylaws state that a business' advertising sandwich board must supply at least three feet of space for pedestrians.

Sweating slightly, Bo counts the inches from the door and nudges the wooden sign a few ticks further. Since becoming America's fourth-youngest mayor, he's tried leading by example. He never exceeds the speed limit, always sorts his recycling, and makes sure this sandwich board is precisely thirty-six inches from its storefront, though his is the only business in town using sandwich board technology.

Inside the shop, Bo frowns and works a few dabs of sanitizer into his palms. The grimace isn't from germs, but from the promise of today's town meeting. The Destination: Dyson Committee is reviewing five proposals aimed at throwing a life raft to the sinking community. Bo's ulcer-delivering frown arrives because Dyson's budget only has enough cash to complete one project. That single submission will be responsible for boosting the economy and saving the entire town, a town on the brink of collapse after years of irresponsible spending before Bo took office. Dyson needs this ten million dollars.

No government means the roads will crumble, utilities won't function, public safety will be nil. Without government, a town dies.

The mayor sits on a decorative wine barrel next to a long wooden display rack filled with glassy green butt ends of cabs, merlots, and pinots. The shelving's finish resembles a few dozen different shades of chocolate. Large picture windows cast light onto his display of gourmet Swiss waters.

This is by far the nicest looking business in town. It is the only new store to open in the last decade.

As usual, the store is empty. Bo doesn't really know much about wine. He just likes the idea of a wine store. The sophistication and history of it all. Once a month a salesman from the alcohol distribution company visits, tells Bo what is selling well at other shops, and Dyson's mayor buys it on the same blind faith that steers his dreams of rescuing this town. Cute little wine and coffee shops don't know where to stash all their money in big cities like Findlay. But the taste for thirty dollar California Shiraz hasn't caught on in Dyson. Bo's attempt at giving his citizens some class and culture by opening the Dyson Drop smells more and more like a failure each day.

Inevitably, thinking of failure leads directly back to his hometown. *The Christmas City . . . how did Dyson come to this?*

Lately, Dyson's pulse has looked about as flat as the endless miles of farmland that surround it on all sides, like some island in an ocean of grain. Calling Dyson the Christmas *City* was a stretch-and-a-half from the starting gun. The state designated it as a village because Dyson counts fewer than five thousand inhabitants. It will never be a city, no matter how hard it tries.

Dyson, the mayor thinks, must be the cracked sidewalk and rusty hinge capital of America. Not dead, not run-down, just fading. It is the type of town where everyone has their baptism, wedding, and funeral at the same church.

In the silence, Bo imagines what this country was like when his parents were born in the fifties; back when America was dotted with small businesses that supported tens of thousands of similar villages, towns, hamlets, and burgs. Even in the eighties, while boyhood Bo pedaled his bike around the streets, Dyson's modest industries churned out paint cans, hubcaps, door knockers, and shoelaces—little things people never thought about. The farming was solid, too. All those jobs and taxes kept the town self-sufficient. Independent.

Now, paint cans, hubcaps, door knockers, and shoelaces mysteriously arrive on store shelves, forged by countries Bo can't find on a map. Unable to make ends meet, most farmers sold their land years ago. The result is Dyson's clock winding to a stop.

Sitting among the sunlight and quiet, this ghostly business day reminds Bo again of childhood. When he was young, Grandma went to the town's butcher for meat, went to the local eye doctor for glasses, had her car fixed by a Dyson mechanic, dined at Nagel's Kitchen on Main, bought her two-by-fours from the lumber yard. Everything people needed was in their community.

Bo runs his tongue over a tooth Dr. Staples, whose office was once two doors down, filled after several summers Bo spent visiting the candy store that sold Tootsie Rolls and suckers for a penny. *How did Ethel's Candy stay in business?*

The answer is: it didn't.

Since before Mayor Rutili's reign, people started driving three towns over to Findlay to buy their chocolate taffies in enormous ten pound bags at Costco. While they're there, visitors pick up meat, eyeglasses, lumber, tires, and dinner under a single, warehoused roof.

His fist clenches to the point of pinkness. It always does when giving himself a pep talk. "Hey, you single-handedly revitalized downtown with that inheritance money. You're not whipped yet. This plan is going to work. I know it." These talks always burn brightly in his gut. He feels alive and eager.

Beyond the Dyson Drop, nothing looks very revitalized.

Nobody stopped to tell the mayor he shouldn't put that inheritance toward renovating the old hotel. Bo's friends were mum to suggest that the cash wouldn't suddenly create a market for gourmet espresso bars and wine shops. After opening, the mayor quickly learned that nobody cared if a Nigerian roast comes from fair trade farms, because the town's lone gas station sells seventy-five cent coffee.

Actually, one person did mention the black plague of risks involved. But somehow Marci's concerns went ignored. The prospect of sparking a little gentrification hummed too loudly in his ears.

Destination: Dyson is going to work. One of those plans will bring money. He walks to the window, looking up and down the street. The glass scalds to the touch. From here, this revitalized downtown is nothing but a short scar of boarded doors and paint-peeled storefronts. Each FOR SALE, FOR LEASE, or FOR RENT. *Sell some wine, too. Probably unload my entire stock when tourists pour in. That's what we need, some trickle-down money. If I can bring people in to buy wine, then other businesses will see some action, too. Just need to bring in those visitors.*

Last month, Bo's Destination: Dyson announcement made the front page of the *Dyson Gazette*. Frankly, it had to be front page news. Not that there weren't car wrecks, mysterious rumors of mummy vandalism, or high school baseball scores to report, but the front page is all that remains. Since Bo was a child, the newspaper gradually trimmed itself from a sixteen-page weekly edition with a splash of color, to one sheet of printer paper the editor runs off from a home computer.

MAYOR CALLS FOR YOUR IDEAS, the headline read.

Bo asked the people of Dyson to start brainstorming. After his cabinet reorganized its budget, there was enough money for one event or attraction aimed at saving Dyson. One last shot at survival for the town. "One desperate shot at survival," Donna Queen quipped when she read the paper. The article sighted successful small town draws that rescued similar economies: Gilroy, CA's Garlic Festival; Bisbee, AZ's popular Dirt Mount Rushmore; Buford, GA's annual homage to marching band mayhem: Sousa-Palooza; and Lakeland, MO's Museum of Horrific Medical Mistakes.

PATRICK WENSINK

Unfortunately, Dyson's citizens proved even less creative than Bradford, MA's Shhhhhhh! Festival: a three-day event centered around sitting in the school gym and being quiet.

The bell above the door clangs.

"Excuse me?" a woman calls.

Bo pops his knuckles, wishing Dyson had a team as talented with dirt as Bisbee's. Calling Dyson *Christmas City* just doesn't cut it.

"Hello?" she says.

The mayor rocks out of his trance and notices a stunning woman. Her black hair and eyes are a few shades darker than her skin.

"Welcome," he says with a smile. "We're sampling a terrific pinot grigio today."

"Sorry, I'm working." Her lips form a perfect crescent moon until they blow a stray lock of hair from her face. Bo studies her—short and trim in a casual skirt and pink blouse—while her eyes run a curious lap around the store.

"Bottle for the road?" The way she stands off balance, with a hip bopping out, makes something dry roll down his throat. Normally, he doesn't notice the customers, his mind being too flooded with Dyson's agonizing problems. That, and there usually aren't any customers.

"No road for me. I'm staying in town for a bit." She extends a tiny hand. "Rajula Magbi. I'm with *America's Boringest City*. We do . . ." she rolls her Pepsi sparkle eyes, " . . . little stories, pieces, about small town life." She makes an *oh, forget it*-type wave with glossy fingernails.

"Really?" Bo pretends he didn't help Pearl Krupp draft a proposal.

"Sorry, I just need directions, and this looked like the only store open. Dyson's kind of like Wall Drug. Ever been there? It's a ghost town in North Dakota. Very cute. Very boringest city."

"Can't say I've been."

"You're not missing much. Actually, this place is quieter than a ghost town." She makes that wave again. "Anyway, where is Town Hall? I'm dying to speak with the mayor."

31

Cody Kellogg can't get enough of his own voice. He sings in the shower, reads to ladies at the nursing home, and has spent the last thirty years as a disc jockey.

Even while wandering his apartment, Cody consults an invisible audience. "The time is 3:18 in the afternoon, so let's double check the stock." He speaks to an open briefcase like a microphone. "Trench coat—check. Briefcase—check. *Special* cargo . . . "

As mega conglomerates purchase more stations and wire computers to spin the music, Cody "Razzle-Dazzle" Kellogg finds himself at one of the few independents left in America: WDSR.

Walkie-talkies have longer ranges than WDSR's tower, which stands atop the grain elevator. On clear nights, Cody's voice manages to reach most of Dyson. The station is online, too. But Cody checked the site's hit count one month and the visitors numbered fewer than their radio dial number.

Sure, broadcasting on WDSR means a steep pay cut, but it keeps him talking, which keeps Mr. Razzle-Dazzle—as listeners back in Memphis knew him—happy.

Cody's wardrobe is so out of fashion it's almost hip. A sprig of chest hair peeks from an open shirt collar and his eyeballs are sunken into his head from insomnia. Three decades of graveyard shifts have shredded his sleeping habits to nothing. This all-day caffeine lifestyle makes his every movement sluggish and cool.

Taking all that into account, his apartment always surprises visitors. Most picture his home covered in wrinkly clothes and Chinese takeout containers. However, the DJ is impressively clean. Cody's clothes neatly folded, his bed made before work, every magazine alphabetized, and the bleachy smell of cleaner in the air.

He paces the room, running over the list again. Cody slips a tie around his thin neck. Years of junk food and one of the world's most powerful metabolisms could land him a side job as a skeleton at the Dyson Lion's Club annual haunted house.

"Okay boys and girls out there in radio land, old Razzle-Dazzle's gonna put the olive in this martini for you."

He crosses the apartment to the refrigerator. From its top he plucks a black pork pie hat, the kind his father, a mildly successful pianist who was never really home and never really that interested in Cody when he was, wore in the forties. A cool fog brushes his skin from the open refrigerator. He removes a strand of raw sausage from the icebox and keeps pulling. He loops the sausage around his elbow, like an extension cord.

Cody gently coils the meat into the briefcase. He drops a few bundles of parsley on top, arranges some cherry tomatoes, and sticks a gift bow in the middle—a centerfold fit for meat market porno.

Cody clasps the case shut. "All right, ladies and gentlemen, lovers and night creatures, Razzle-Dazzle guarantees this next one's sure to be a smash hit. Buckle your belts."

THURSDAY, 3:20 PM

Children scurry around the tiny museum, ripping posters, juggling exhibit fruit, constantly jumping, and reminding Marci of the lawless mess in her chest.

Unlike the brats, she thinks, *her mess could all be fixed with an engagement ring.*

The air conditioning is busted again, and the museum has become a steamy underarm. She takes long sips from a water bottle while speaking to the group.

These kids aren't from Dyson Elementary because Dyson Elementary's windows are boarded over. Filthy nests of squirrels inhabit its classrooms. Dyson's youngsters are now bussed a few towns over to a consolidated school since the elementary couldn't afford to stay open.

These children came from some summer camp program.

"Hey, who buys this crap?" one red-haired boy asks, halfway through Marci's speech about raw materials combining to make plastic goo, which is eventually poured into molds shaped like bananas and bunches of grapes.

Her hair is pulled into its doorknob ponytail. A constellation of summer freckles fill her face with a kind aura. But tired, slumped shoulders speak differently. She takes another swig and lets coolness dance down her throat.

"I'm glad you asked. Plastic fruit was very popular in the 1950s. That's when FruitCo saw its biggest sales." Lesser speakers would simply shake this jelly-faced punk until he paid attention or stopped breathing. But Marci's patience is unrivaled. She sticks to the script: "Families use delicious fruit collections for centerpieces or as a decoration around the house. For a while, Broadway used *only* plastic fruit in its plays and musicals. The 1949 smash hit, *South Pacific*, was our biggest single sale ever. Over six thousand pineapples alone! So to answer your question, *everybody* loves plastic fruit."

The FruitCo Imitation Fruit Museum is housed in a three-story, red brick building that once held the Dyson General Store and, later, Conrad's Television Repair. Both shops soon rendered as obsolete as Dyson itself.

"It smells like my lunchbox," one girl complains.

Located directly across from the Kreskin Inn and mirroring its cramped architecture, the museum is little more than a long hall with exposed brick walls and creaking floorboards. That manufactured smell of plastic is everywhere, and sticks to Marci's clothes and hair.

"Tastes like that cheap Halloween candy," another says, toothing a fake apple.

"Boys and girls, how do we show respect?" The elderly teacher snaps to life after what Marci assumed was a nap. "Now, Miss Krupp," the teacher says, "can you tell us *why* Dyson is the imitation fruit capital of America?"

"Well." She lifts her chin high and spreads proud arms with the gusto of a conductor. "We are not just the largest producer of lifelike fruits and vegetables in the country, but the *whole* planet."

Once again, this data fails to draw Fourth of July fireworks types of "ooh"s and "ahhh"s. A little audience participation would go a long way right now.

But Marci never gets what she wants.

"And why is that?" the teacher says.

The taxidermied look in everyone's eyes is familiar. Nobody cares. Everyone is counting the minutes until they leave, including Marci. She draws the symphony to a close and slumps those shoulders deeper. "Because the other factories went out of business. Dyson's the only one dumb enough to keep making it."

The teacher's mouth forms a disappointed circle.

Fully deflated, Marci waves toward the door. "Just go and—" she sighs, "take your stupid free carrots."

"Ewww," the red headed boy says. "Carrots taste like dirt."

"Ma'am," she snaps at the teacher. "Please." The class shuffles out, each with a bright orange souvenir.

Lately, everything feels deflated. Wasting time with kids is exactly like wasting time with Bo. Nobody is listening.

When the room empties and the overhead lamps buzz, she fixes trashed exhibits. A hollow hunger clings to her gut and reminds Marci of reaching out to her boyfriend all those times: listening to him talk without pause, blindly encouraging his career, even missing her family's Hawaiian vacation because he needed help running the mayoral campaign. Marci has offered Bo her deepest secrets—how nothing makes her happier than reading a long-forgotten inscription in a used book, how nothing makes her sadder than short funeral processions—only to get, in return, the details of the latest plan to rescue Dyson. No matter how much she pours into their relationship, Bo is never more grateful than an elementary class.

"Your love and your job have been complete wastes of time," she whispers. There is a sudden urge to cover her lips. She's been waiting for life to come to her, but life is apparently running late.

She rearranges exhibits depicting plastic fruit's thrilling evolution. Mannequins dressed like cavemen carving cherries and pineapples from stone, colonial mannequins sanding down wooden bananas and peaches, space-suited mannequins with plastic fruit hanging from fishing lines.

Marci carefully dusts a caveman when her sister walks through the entrance.

"You're supposed to be working on your costume with Gomez," Pearl says before the door even closes.

"Jesus. What happened to your head?" Marci marvels at the plum-colored lump above her sister's eye. She is amazed because it doesn't seem to spoil Pearl's looks. Those cool sunglasses help a lot.

"This? Nothing. I just collapsed from happiness last night. I'll get to that." Her voice is trimmed to the bone. It's always fast like this when criticizing her big sister, which is about every other sentence. "You and Gomez? Destination: Dyson. Hello?"

Marci sounds as if she were peeking around a corner: "I don't want to chance running into Bo. I'm hoping absence will make his heart grow . . . you know."

Pearl is four years younger than Marci. Though they share the same bulbed cheeks and small nose, debate around the Kreskin Inn voted Pearl as the cute sister. Most of the time, people forget Marci is even around, like wallpaper. That plainness Bo enjoys so much.

Marci often takes comfort knowing Pearl's face requires more and more makeup than it used to. All those cigarette clouds at the bar, probably. Marci hates that comfort. But guilt usually flutters away when she focuses on the bigger crisis of perpetual singleness.

"What are you two fighting about now?" Pearl says. "Let me guess, Mr. Mayor took you for another romantic dinner at the old folk's home?"

Marci rolls her eyes and shakes her head.

"God, it's like you're dating Mr. Magoo."

"What does that mean?"

"Mr. Magoo, the cartoon. He was a little guy who couldn't see well."

"Where do you get this stuff?"

"I watched a lot more TV. You were playing varsity volleyball or studying and I was watching cartoons usually."

"Sounds about right."

"Point is, Bo is like Mr. Magoo. Neither one can see anything right in front of their face."

"Yeah. Okay. Sure," Marci says.

"What's going on? I can tell when you're blanked out."

"I'm thinking . . . maybe . . . about giving Bo an ultimatum."

"Well, duh. You're about the last person in town to think of that—"

"You know, marry me or—"

"*Marry this* charming *community?*" Pearl grumbles her best Rutili impression. "Sheesh."

Even when Bo wasn't around they impersonated him. Most folks in town didn't even realize they were doing it anymore. It stemmed from before he was mayor. Once, Bo stood up at a town council meeting to voice his opinion, only to be mocked by Donna Queen. She delivered the first Bo impression years back. When he got red-faced and asked her not to treat him like a child, she simply did it again, like a teasing bully in the lunchroom.

Small towns like Dyson—being light on entertainment, high on gossip, and brutal with modesty—jumped on the exaggerated impressions. The squeakier and cuter people made Bo sound, the harder he fought.

Until he stopped fighting.

One day he just nodded along as folks repeated him word-for-word with puppet voices, unaware how he felt. His teeth grind and his eyes ache from straining when he listens to people talk like that. But since he stopped making a deal about it, the people at least move on with whatever it is they are talking about. Cute little Bo impressions have become part of the town fabric, a hitch in the local accent.

"If you're so unhappy, move back to Findlay like everyone else in your class. I've been telling you that for years," Marci said.

"Believe me, I'd like nothing more," Pearl countered. "But I can't, not just this minute. I got this letter in the mail yesterday. Oh, my God, I'm so insanely thrilled."

Marci doesn't hear Pearl's elation. Her attention span is the size of a fingernail clipping. Especially when Pearl rambles about herself, making excuses why she can't leave Dyson quite yet or begging for a compliment.

At this moment, Marci is staring at the framed picture of FruitCo's founder, Gerald Rosinski.

"Of course you know Rajula Magbi," Pearl says. "Everyone knows Rajula."

The photo, faded brown and beige, was taken in 1931, the year Dyson's plastics empire began. Gerald looks so proud. His charming dark eyes make Marci's heart plump to the size of a fake pineapple. *Historically dashing*, she calls it. That dark mustache and snug brown herringbone suit would be freakish now, but look so handsome in retrospect. During the daydreamy hours spent without visitors, Gerald becomes Marci's make-believe husband and takes *her* off to Tahiti for a honeymoon instead of his actual wife. Even though Gerald and his bride died en route, Marci often wonders what it would be like to call a successful, loving man like Gerald her husband.

Her sister is lost amid a storm of chatter. Marci perks to life. "Do you think it's true?" she cuts directly into Pearl's excited story about *America's Boringest City*.

"That Rajula had her boobs done? Yeah, totally. I mean, I'll let you know once we're pals and hanging out at Hollywood clubs, dating drummers, snorting free blow." The sunglasses are off, and Pearl's stunning eyes pop wide open, fully believing every word.

"No, that story about Gerald Rosinski." Marci runs a light finger over the picture frame. "Do you think it's true?"

Pearl snugs against her and clutches both hands. The cute sister checks over her shoulders for a clear coast. "You know you're not supposed to talk about *the treasure*," Pearl says with a haunted voice.

THURSDAY, 4:22 PM

"Joyce, come on. How long have we known each other?" Chief Grover hikes up a sagging belt, weighed down with a gun, keys, a baton, and a pouch of chewing tobacco.

"Bert, I know you're a good guy." Joyce Camden's pale face is weathered and wavy with crow's feet. She slips a cigarette between her lips, briefly holds a lighter underneath, but tosses both into the grass by the driveway. "For Christ's sake, think about all the stuff you let me and my girlfriends get away with in high school. You were the only man I could trust then, and you're the only man I trust now."

Joyce's house isn't much to look at. One story and white, with the black shutters chipping down to the primer. The shingles are discolored and faded. It's nearly August and she hasn't taken in the Easter egg yard signs.

"A lot's happened in fifteen years, but if you would have brought this story to me back then," his lips jab out a low whistle, "I still wouldn't believe you." He pulls up the belt again and tries to calm a shaking foot. His voice grows tender and quiet being so close to Joyce's skin. Chief Grover tries breathing its familiar scent, but only detects the neighbor's fresh cut lawn. "Look, this is my job. I gotta take stuff seriously. Back then, hell, I was just as wild as you. But the world is different. I could lose my job. Today, every little detail is scrutinized in police work. There's no wiggle room."

Bert wakes up seven days a week and puts on a pale brown uniform. He eats meals in it and only removes the outfit for bed. He is Dyson's sole policeman and feels responsible for every citizen's safety at all times. He loves that responsibility, which is partially why he never rests. He gets a little antsy when downtime arrives.

Grover's hair is fading from black to grey. His body is bulky, but strong. His eyes constantly shift between suspicious slits and caring ovals.

Clouds roll overhead, trapping heat and humidity. Joyce paces the driveway a few steps. Her fingers repeatedly flex into a ball only to jackknife open. Joyce has trimmed down since retiring from the spotlight.

"Did you test it? C'mon, it's just some prank." Her hollow stare always bends the cop to merciful weakness.

Tall with a thick layer of loose skin, he hikes up that belt until it jangles like shattering glass. Chief Grover hates the way his heavy gun makes the belt slip, but the hundreds of keys stiffen his posture. The sound reminds Bert of his important role. There is a confidence knowing he is trusted with keys to so many important locks around town. The jangle is an icepack atop feverish anxiety.

Chief Grover drags himself to the patrol car and pulls the toxicology report. A two-page form regarding the contents of a bag of white powder Joyce provided. First thing it mentions is that the clear plastic Zip-Loc tested positive for the drug PCP.

"Where'd she get it? If you don't know, I'll take Haley down to the station and ask there. Get official and whatnot."

"You know Haley." Joyce paces the lawn for the lost cigarette. "She's a great kid. An honest kid. Would a liar show her mom a bag of dope?"

"Joyce, there is no way in hell I can file a report saying Haley was given narcotics by a . . ." His voice fizzles, staggering for the word. "Let's say, a suspect dressed for Halloween."

"They're called *mummies*, Bert." Joyce blows off a blade of grass and lights the cigarette.

THURSDAY, 4:32 PM

Grandma Rutili's door gently swings open. A Civil War general—dressed head-to-toe in Yankee blue wool, saber dangling to his side with dull, shining medals at his breast—carries in a steaming Tupperware bowl.

"Mrs. R? You home?" He broadcasts throughout the house. "It's Ed Lee, from down the street. My wife made some chili. Hello?"

Ed is balding under his military hat, flat feet constantly throbbing, and that lush black beard itches whenever the weather turns brutal like this. However, he has optimism on his side. So much so that upon learning of his Civil War reenactment store's closing, Lee just shrugged, smiled, and offered Donna Queen a second helping of coffee cake. "Well, it's been a good run," he said.

Ed holds the bowl to his beard and blows away steam. The beefy air tickles his nose.

His heavy boots march carefully through the house. It seems every free inch is covered with a gift or memento from Edna's life. A few weeks before, his saber had absently swung into a decorative 1976 World's Fair plate and caused Edna to sob.

"Oh yeah, I also brought over a box of those infantry hats the neighbor boys like fooling around with." His voice dampens, "You've probably heard, but we don't need them at the store anymore."

Ed pokes his head in the front sitting room packed with glass cats. Down the hall to the kitchen a cuckoo clock chimes. *There is something peaceful and lonely and alarmingly magic about growing old*, Ed thinks. *I'm going to like it when I'm Edna's age.*

He follows the sound of a radio blasting and walks into the living room at the rear of the house. The den is lined with cross-stitches of birds and trees and Bible verses.

"Edna, there you are." He walks up to the recliner.

Edna's cat, Boots, snuggles into his ankle.

"Now this is hot, so let it sit for a few minutes before you . . ."

He faces the stiff woman, a gentle grin across her blue lips.

"Oh, boy."

THURSDAY, 4:49 PM

"You picked an exciting time to visit, Rajula," the mayor says, turning left at a forty-foot snowman anchoring the city green space. Christmas Park is a desperate mess of holiday spirit: plywood reindeer and sleigh cut-outs, thousands of plastic snowflakes spinning from power lines, wooden elves scattered. But that enormous snowman is the sun around which everything orbits. "We weren't expecting you."

"I sent a letter saying it would be today." Her delicate voice fills Bo's rust-nibbled Taurus like her flowery perfume. She faces away from the mayor, eying the window.

"Ah, yes, our mail is," he swallows deep, *"unpredictable."* The steering wheel stings Bo's palms with summer burn. A dog-walking woman in a sweat suit waves. The mayor gives a friendly return.

"What's with all the shamrocks hanging from the light poles?" Rajula sniffles and rubs her nose with a thin purple handkerchief.

"You mean our mistletoe?" Bo realizes he never dabbed any sanitizer after shaking hands with the reporter. Even more surprising, he doesn't care. Up and down his core, a string of lights buzz to life with the urge to see if those palms smell as good as Rajula Magbi. "Yep, one hundred percent mistletoe. Care, ah, for a kiss?" That mangled delivery sparks the desire to ram the car into a light pole.

"Those are shamrocks and it's July," she says. Everything about Rajula's manners are proper and reporterly.

Bo is so thankful she ignored the *kiss* line that he gives a ringmaster yelp, changing the subject: "Welcome to Christmas City, USA."

She scratches something into a notepad. "Excuse me?"

"Well, probably not for much longer. Our last mayor had the idea to celebrate everyone's favorite holiday three hundred and sixty-five days a year. We hung lights and decorations. Heck, see those silos over there?"

"Yeah. Kinda hard to miss." She bends her neck to get a look at three large concrete tubes stretching above the trees. She can't take her eyes off the cockeyed circle and radio tower on top. "What is it?"

"Dyson's tallest building, seventy feet high! It's our grain elevator. All the farmers sell and store their grain, wheat, and dry corn here. Then it's sent out by train to feed the world. But every year, after harvest, we dress the elevator up like a big white angel. That's its halo on top."

She click-clacks a pen. "Honestly," Rajula's voice is direct and professional, "that's a little depressing."

Bo swallows a deep breath, eager to impress, conscious that staring at her legs isn't the answer. "Well you know, the old mayor figured everyone celebrates Christmas. Maybe it'd bring tourists."

"Not everyone." She blows a scrap of black hair from her eyes. "I was raised Hindu. Plus, I mean, aren't there any Jewish people in Dyson?"

"Good point." He nods. Bo wishes he had studied the Destination: Dyson proposals last night so he could wow her right now. Instead, he was weak and spent the night at Marci's. "But like I said, things are changing. They always are in a vibrant community like ours. Before Dyson was Christmas City, we were called," his throat clears, "Saint Patrick's Central."

He brakes at a stop sign and the old rotors squeal. He takes a long look at the reporter, hanging a cool grin off his lips.

"And before that, we used to be famous for a president visiting."

"Yeah, I saw the sign on my way in. He, what, used the toilet or something?"

"So, Christmas is actually a step up."

"Clearly."

Bo's cheeks have gone hot with nerves. "Okay, full disclosure, the mistletoe are actually just upside down shamrocks." His stomach giggles, cheeks burning holiday red.

"Let me guess. You realized not everyone celebrates Saint Patrick's Day either?" She scratches more into the pad.

"No, it was actually pretty popular." He waves to an elderly man on a bench. "We had visitors from all around. Hundreds of people dressed head-to-toe in green. But you can't imagine the toll it took. I mean, the responsibility of filling the streets for a parade on the seventeenth of every month was brutal. Not to mention all the green beer. Combine that with tourists looking to party and you get trouble. It was like a monthly Mardi Gras. The fist fights, people getting sick in the streets, sandwich boards placed wherever the hell anyone felt like it." He laughs uncomfortably. "What a nightmare."

She scratches more notes.

"Eventually, our police chief asked the old mayor, a guy named Packwicz, to stop. Which was good. These days, people kind of wonder if that mayor wasn't all there." Bo taps his hairline.

"Vibrant . . ." She dabs her nose with the hanky. "Look, I don't need a full history. Our show just sort of finds an interesting quirk about a town and we tape a few minutes of footage. Interview people like Pearl Krupp. It's no big deal, nothing to get worked up about."

Rajula Magbi gets a taste of the enthusiastic, electric voice that charmed Dyson in the previous year's election. "Sounds like a lot of fun to me," Bo says. "You get out there and see the real America."

For the first time that day, the reporter smiles. "Like I said, it's no big deal. I mean—" She tries to remember the point. "Yes, it is fun. I forget that sometimes. I thought this was just a quick gig until I got back on my feet. I was reporting from Iraq for three years. When I started, I said I was just dipping back into domestic journalism. *America's Boringest*

City is important to me. I'd like to return to hard news. But for now, I want to turn this reality show into something decent."

"I think a lot of people would call it decent."

Magbi laughs. "A lot of people call it shitty. And they're right. The producers edit everything to make it look like I'm making fun of these towns. I'm not." Something in her voice streamlines with pride. "I just negotiated for more control, so starting with this episode, we're going to do something proper and nice and fun."

"That sounds like a dream come true."

She laughs into her handkerchief. "Not to everyone. See, this idea sounds dumb to the network, so I avoid the topic. Okay, the way I figure it, Baghdad is nothing compared to how all these little towns are collapsing. I grew up in a little community in Missouri and it kills me to see this new generation of ghost towns. It's depressing. Industries shipped off to wherever, small businesses folding up, and, sorry for saying this, but I hate watching proud towns whore themselves out, inventing tourism. God, my hometown celebrates something called the Museum of Horrific Medical Mistakes. It's sad."

Bo parks the car and relieves the magnetic urge to smell his hands. "I couldn't agree more." His eyes lock on hers. The mayor paces himself, realizing he nearly upset the connection he feels right now. Bo speaks up, "I remember my grandma took me and my brother on a vacation to Arizona and Nevada when we were kids."

"Your grandma? All by herself?"

"She sort of raised us. My mom and dad died when I was young. Grandma loved us like crazy. She gave us everything my brother and I wanted. Even a cowboy vacation, which is what she called it."

"That's cute."

"We visited a ghost town, an actual ghost town. Not like Tombstone where they play dress up with cap guns. It was called Ryolite. It was just sun-bleached planks of a saloon and the concrete skeleton of a jailhouse. I couldn't stop asking, 'How did this happen? How do entire towns vanish?'" There is a bloated silence. "But now I'm starting to understand everything comes to an end."

Rajula pinches her bottom lip with white teeth until it morphs into a hesitant smile. Her tongue massages her mouth, waiting for the mayor to speak again.

Don't kiss her. Don't kiss her. Don't kiss her prints across tickertape in Bo's head. He digs fingernails into the steering wheel.

"You picked the perfect time to visit." His throat clears. "After tonight's Destination: Dyson meeting we're going to make medical mistakes look like a medical mistake." Bo slams his eyes shut. "That didn't come out right."

"It's okay. Relax." Her soft hand grabs Bo's. Her smile is full.

THURSDAY, 7:39 PM

"Aw, forget it," Old Man Packwicz says, tossing pen and paper over the edge. "Who needs a suicide note?"

The pen spirals past the rest of the grain elevator. He counts to five, estimating how long it takes for impact. "Just hit the ground already!" he shouts into the stiff breeze.

Meanwhile, the half-finished suicide note catches a gust and flutters above his head. As a parting raspberry, he planned to leave all his possessions to Donna Queen. The idea of getting one final cheap shot almost filled Packwicz with enough happiness to reconsider killing himself. But when the pen ran out of ink it reminded him of all the failures since that lotto mess.

Now, a seventy-foot swan dive sounds easier than sleeping in on Sunday.

Wrapping fingers around the guardrail, he looks across the bushy, ripe treetops and roofs that form Dyson's skyline. From here, with dusk's orange sun melting into the shivering cornfields, his hometown looks fantastic. He loves Dyson more than anyone.

Upon first meeting Packy, most people think it's kind of strange that a fifty-year-old is nicknamed "Old Man." Packy actually looked his age until about two years ago. Now he acts, roughly, like someone born before electricity. This was all thanks to Donna Queen and a Powerball ticket.

Most folks would just say it was bum luck and continue being mayor, but Packy turned the screws of misery deeper and deeper into his skull until jumping off a grain silo added up to a fun evening.

Old Man Packwicz swings his legs over the railing and presses his body tight to whatever feels stable. A hearty breeze flaps his pant legs and shirtsleeves. He takes in a huge breath—someone nearby is grilling steak. Without any guardrail for protection, the town below tugs at him.

This freedom knocks some internal gyroscope off its axis. Packy's vision wobbles before he closes his eyes. Sharp needles of breath escape as one finger unhinges its grip. Then another. And another. And another.

"Don't panic. Don't panic. This is for your own good," he says. Tears work down his face.

His left hand is completely free. Packy opens one eye and leans over the edge. It's clear he isn't going to have any more luck letting go of this guardrail than he did letting go of how Donna royally screwed him.

He wishes he had more guts. If he had more guts none of this would be happening.

At that moment, an electric hum fills the air.

The hum slowly cranks into a raw buzz.

The drone grows like a platoon of wasps zeroing on his ear. Next, a thick click ripples through the guardrail and a harsh yellow light throws itself over Packy's shoulder.

Old Man Packwicz briefly forgets his pancake-making plans and turns around, looking up to see the angel's halo burning against the purpling sky.

Even though it isn't Christmas season, the halo is on a timer and lights up automatically each night. Up close, the neon bulbs are brighter than most people imagine. Packy folds both hands into a visor.

Climbing the ladder to the top, he planned to say something viciously clever before leaping. Something like: "Thanks for the help, Donna," or, "Wish I could stay for dessert, but I gotta run."

Instead, he loses balance and tumbles backward, still blowing tiny needles of breath, watching the halo get smaller as he nears the blacktop.

Deep inside, Old Man Packwicz is happy—he never thought he would actually jump. *Maybe I did have guts?* he thinks.

THURSDAY, 7:54 PM

"Skeet, the folks at home are dying to know," Cody Kellogg says, tapping his foot faster than a heartbeat. "*What*, exactly, are you supposed to be?" That voice echoes across the large meeting hall's wooden floors and mixes with whispering white lights. Blinds flutter from a serious draft.

Rufus "Skeet" Brown earned his handle, like most people around town, in high school. He buzzed around defenses, stinging them for three pointers so often a nickname was necessary. As an adult, the name still applies, though only he knows about the buzzing mosquitoes of pride that fill his chest after scanning acres of freshly farmed corn. The brown, tilled dirt and the massacre of dried stalks left behind. Skeet loves the feel of a job completed. He always keeps himself busy with one project or another, or often several at once.

"Kellogg, you're not on the clock tonight. Knock off that Casey Kasem bullshit and wait for my presentation like everyone else." Skeet shakes his head with a warm smile for his best pal.

Skeet looks less like a successful farmer and more like an unsuccessful stunt man. His body is thin and hard and his face is creased with lines worn deep from endless sunburns. His head is quite noticeable, being disproportionately large. His body is wide at the crown and comes to a thin point at his feet like a capital V.

"Let's take a guess," Cody says, shifting his sore butt. City Hall's chairs remind him of countless bus stop benches he's waited on while zipping from radio station to radio station around the country. "Delores from Kansas City says: 'lion tamer.' Is that correct?"

Skeet tugs at his costume's tan canvas lapel. He adjusts the pith helmet. "Is that the best you've got?"

"Stevie from Cedar Rapids says: 'big game hunter.' How 'bout it?"

"By God, he's a Rough Rider if I've ever seen one," Ed Lee says, still dressed like Ulysses S. Grant and still blocking the image of his dead neighbor from his mind. Lee's greying eyebrows arch with excitement. "Teddy Roosevelt, right? You're missing the mustache and about a hundred pounds, though. Did he vacation here as a boy or something? I don't see the connection to Dyson. How does Teddy boost our economy?"

The mayor encouraged the final round of Destination: Dyson Committee presenters to "bring their ideas to life." For some reason, nobody thinks bringing an idea to life means more than a costume and a PowerPoint presentation. Ed Lee went the extra mile and brought a bag of fun-sized Snickers bars.

"*This* from a guy dressed for a war that didn't come within a thousand miles of Dyson," Skeet snaps, running a finger through Ed's golden shoulder tassels. "You of all people should know this ain't Appomattox."

"Alright, folks." Cody's voice has lost a great deal of its bourbon and ice bite over the years. But its ragged charm is pure Kellogg. "Looks like a spirited debate." He dramatically rubs his hands together. "The folks at home are dying to hear both sides of this epic battle."

They nag and nitpick for a few minutes, more out of boredom and nerves. These three have never said a believable unkind word about one another.

Town Hall springs to life when the double doors open. It seems Marci Krupp and Troy Gomez have also prepared for their big pitch.

"Now that's more like it," Cody howls, admiring their costumes. He slaps a knee and playfully thumps his neighbor's belly.

"More like *what?*" Marci says, waddling between the doors. Her bulky costume splits folding chair rows the way Moses handled inconvenient bodies of water.

"There's no mystery what you two plan to say," the DJ's voice sprays with buckshot force. "Let me guess." Raspy, joyful chuckles punctuate every few words. "Something about *eating healthy?* Are we the *Food Pyramid* City now?"

Troy Gomez was born burning.

"Idiots," he snaps, annoyed by anyone who doesn't instantly recognize his importance as the head of America's leading manufacturer of plastic fruit, even dressed like an enormous carrot with a gnarly goatee. "We're plastic fruit and vegetables. You know, Dyson's biggest export." Gomez says the last two words with emphasis, jabbing his fingers like "biggest" and "export" are bullets. Troy Gomez always carries the spirit that got him face-whipped at the bar. His lip has nearly healed. "Plastic fruit put this town on the map!"

Skeet leans forward, calm and amused. "Is that so? I always thought we were famous for our Christmas spirit."

"I heard it was because we all had a little Irish in us," Cody says. The pair struggle to keep faces straight.

"Or maybe," Ed Lee giggles, "Now we're the underwear capital."

The room falls silent with confusion.

Ed keeps grinning the optimistic smile he's worn since the shop's foreclosure, waiting for someone to get the joke. "You know, like Fruit of the Loom."

Everyone gives Ed a twisted look and waits until Troy Gomez side-steps closer. "This stupid town has no respect for the past. None for what my family has done for Dyson. But once I give my plans for the Fake Fruit Parade, you'll be sick for a week." A sneer fills the opening in the carrot's face. "I'm going to paint it black."

A general, *huh?* spreads through the group.

"*Idiots*, it's a Rolling Stones song."

"Not like that it's not," says Cody.

"Troy, just relax," Marci says, trying to find a way to sit while inside her apple costume. She keeps one suspicious eye on him, because *their* idea has quickly morphed into *his* idea.

"Yes, Troy, relax," Donna Queen's voice slices through the hall like a tornado siren. She walks in, wearing leopard print. Her diamond-spangled fingers snap off sunglasses. "You're all doomed. So just join the lineup of losers here." Under hot fluorescent lights her once coffee-colored hair is a shade of cream and sugar.

"Donna," Ed Lee stands like a soldier in ranks. "You're not on the schedule tonight. I didn't know *you* were presenting."

"Cool it, I'm not." High heels stop sharp. "I just have a teensy-weensy comment before the meeting starts." Her lips form a tight porthole where white teeth elbow one another for a view. Ed has seen that smile before—it's the same one she used when his Civil War reenactment shop was served papers. His bowels go uneasy, recognizing that grin.

"Donna," Cody stands and says. "You might need another nose job. It looks like that one keeps getting stuck in everyone else's business."

The near-empty room erupts with argument. Six voices chase each other, weaving a heavy curtain of chatter.

The ruckus stops when the doors open again.

The mayor, looking a little frazzled and clumsy, holds the door like a butler. A thin brown girl walks in, sporting some long fine legs that capture the attention of everyone but Marci and Donna.

Bo says a few words to this exotic beauty. She wipes her nose with a purple handkerchief and he disappears back through the door.

"Alright, creatures of the night," Cody's radio voice fills the silence. "I must run to the little record spinner's room. Be back after a few messages from our sponsor." He grabs his briefcase and dashes through the doors.

THURSDAY, 8:03 PM

The back of Murray Kreskin's shirt is dyed in gentle reds and blues from neon beer signs above the cash register. His forehead is pasted to the bar, hands slapping repeatedly into the hardwood. The owner lifts his massive frame, sucks a gallon of air, wipes a few tears, and looks square across the bar.

After a moment Murray bursts into laughter again and repeats the process. "Birth Control to Major Tom," he says, trying very hard to re-member the setup so he can claim the joke as his own invention. "Gar-rett, where do you come up with these? I swear, my heart can't take it."

Garrett Queen enjoys the rush of cracking up Kreskin until he sub-tly glances at the tattoo on Murray's hand. The last thing he wants is to be caught looking. He tries without luck to discreetly read the names scrawled across permanently inked lines. "I thought you might like that one," Donna Queen's husband says. "Just a gin and tonic for me, Murray."

"Coming up."

The Kreskin Inn is filled with its usual collection of elbow-to-elbow drinkers this Thursday. So when a man in a black suit, black hat, and matching mustache cuts through the crowd, a lot of conversations drop.

Some think he graduated with them. Some say he looks like one of the Queen Bank's toughnecks, probably passing out foreclosure paperwork. Some say to show a little respect; clearly this is the new priest in town.

"Evening," Murray greets the stranger, his brain still pirouetting from Garrett's zinger. "Nobody drinks without telling a joke, house rules." He gives the man an enormous, warm smile.

The gentleman, as thin and tall as City Hall's flagpole, squeezes pale lips together.

Murray detects embarrassment and nearly tells him not to worry about it and come up with a winner on the next round.

The man in black steps close—a stiff phantom through neon fog. "Why doesn't anyone eat dessert at the NASA cafeteria?"

"I don't know," Murray puzzles. "Something about freeze-dried ice cream?"

"Because when you order pie," the man's voice is as precise and exciting as a talking calculator, "you only get 3.1415926."

Murray clears his throat and wipes both hands on the apron. He is relieved Papa isn't alive. His father had no enemies except the humorless.

"I suppose that'll work. What you drinking?"

"Nothing, actually."

"Just polishing your standup routine?"

The man cocks his head the way people do when holding a conversation in broken languages. "No, I'm looking for Chief Grover. The police station appears deserted, and your tavern was the only business open."

"Ain't my job to keep track of the law, it keeps track of me, you know?" Murray gives another smile. He pickpocketed that joke from a guy last week.

The man in the dark suit squints into the red-blue haze.

Murray rolls his eyes. "Hey, Bonnie," Murray shouts down the bar. "Bonnie's the dispatcher."

"I see," says the talking calculator.

"Hey, *Bonnie*." Murray's face grows tense. "Swear, nobody listens," he says under his breath. Then big and loud, "Bonnie! Where's Grover tonight? This fella's looking for him."

A woman carrying a lot of stress in her cheeks walks over, stubs out a cigarette, and sips an orange daiquiri. "You don't want to know, mister. I swear to God you don't."

THURSDAY, 8:06 PM

Old Man Packwicz groans.

Both eyes open and see the grain elevator's angelic rooftop glow. This isn't Heaven and the weather is too cool for Hell. This is still Dyson. "Here's one *more* thing I can't do right."

The gentle rise and fall of evening traffic hisses around him.

Packy's senses funnel back and soon discover he is lying on something firm. "Just my luck." Packwicz runs his cold fingers behind him.

The last thing he remembers is catching his foot on some cable as he fell toward his death. He didn't remember seeing any power lines or phone cords as he climbed up, but he is clearly not much for planning.

Another painful growl fills the space around Packy, but not from his own throat. Crossed somewhere between a dying diesel engine and a sleepy grizzly, it rumbles beneath Old Man Packwicz's stubbornly beating heart.

Packy aches to his feet about the same time as the guy underneath him. Standing tall and broad, covered head-to-toe in disintegrating bandages, the mummy puts a ragged hand to its head.

Packy looks for a set of eyes behind this Halloween costume, but only makes out a pair of black pits. Confusion brings an encore of nervous falling sensations.

Something snaps inside him. Packwicz gives King Tut a shove.

"Some of us have nothing to live for, so if you don't mind, we'd like to commit suicide in peace."

The mummy lifts its hands the same way people around town say they are sorry after stealing the last open gas pump.

"You got it so good. You probably don't know what it's like to *hate* everything. To know life could be so different if only you didn't call in sick to work one stinking day. That kind of *pain* . . ." The former mayor shakes his fist. " . . . eats you from inside. There's no joy in life because fate's too busy kicking you right in between the zipper. Think you can fix that, Stretch?"

The mummy taps a finger to the spot where its lips should be, thinking.

They stand on the backside of the grain silos. Cars will never see them. Only a single security lamp, hanging above a nearby trailer, spreads its peach light over the botched suicide.

"Go ahead. You can't do anything but screw up my life further."

The mummy flips up its finger, as if to tell Packwicz, "just a second."

The enormous figure turns its back and Packy watches its arms move rapidly. *Worst case scenario*, he thinks, *this punk tries to rob me. Maybe even shoot me in the head. Heck, this could turn out alright.* As usual, Packwicz is prepared to die. He puffs out his chest and prepares to crawl toward the light in a tunnel.

The mummy turns around and presents Packwicz with a plate of food. The old man grabs it with shaky hands.

The mummy places a metal fork on the plate. It shines under the lamp.

"Are you sure you don't just want to shoot me?" Packy says, looking down at gooey brown lumps. His broken, black heart kicks to life because it smells like mom frying bacon early in the morning. He never went to school hungry or unhappy. That was his favorite meal, and his loving mother blackened a few strips each day when Packy still shopped in the children's department.

But *this?* This looks like a slice of bacon blew its nose on the plate.

The mummy drops a little paper card next to the lumps. "Foie Gras," spelled in dramatic calligraphy.

The mummy presents its palm, as if telling the jumper, "Enjoy, good sir. My name is Ramon, I'll be your server this evening."

The stack of bandages pats Old Man Packwicz on the head like his mother used to and casually staggers away, sending a message that it absorbs suicides and serves high-priced bird guts every day about this time.

THURSDAY, 8:08 PM

"So, Cody, you're saying *what*, exactly?" The mayor stands over his empty maple desk looking into the disc jockey's suitcase.

Bo's lamp gives his office a hazy red opium den vibe. It is filled with the raw, fleshy smell of a meat shop.

"I'd say you're the lucky winner tonight. My message is pretty clear." Cody tries covering his desperation with a confident voice, but poor posture and sweaty sideburns never lie.

Bo's hands are folded together, fingers awkwardly spidering. "Listen, I need to get in there and judge the proposals. *We* need to get in there. Your pitch for the Portuguese Heritage Festival sounds really exciting." The mayor coughs. "Honest."

"Bo," Cody looks down on this kid, this man-boy, inexperienced in the way politics *really* work. "This is my proposal. And you can count on plenty more *proposals*. My uncle owns a chorizo factory in Baltimore."

"This looks like sausage."

"Bingo. Chorizo is a spicy sausage invented in Portugal. I'm half Portuguese. My people were on top of their shit. This stuff is delicious. And you'll have all you can eat, assuming . . . " His hands cycle through the air, turning invisible gears. " . . . you know."

"Is this a bribe, Cody?" Bo's cheeks puff, embarrassed for him.

"Call it a gift. A young fella like yourself probably doesn't get many square meals."

"Let's go back into the meeting hall. And I think you should bring that with you."

"Think it over. Those other idiots can't match this offer. What, a lifetime of plastic fruit? All the muskets and Civil War crap you can carry? You accept a gift from those bozos, people will catch on." Cody's sleepy eyes grow lively with the final threads of hope. They are a complex mix of browns; Bo had never noticed. "But with me, you *eat* the evidence. Everybody wins."

"I'm not that kind of mayor." Bo whisks past Cody and out the door. "Best of luck with your presentation. We're going to do good things in Dyson."

THURSDAY, 8:53 PM

The graveyard is filled with opera and headstones.

A booming voice saturates every dot of air. Images of massive Italians in tuxedos, standing atop Europe's finer stages, would instantly fill the head of anyone who just happened to be hanging around their favorite tomb tonight.

A flashlight beam carves through the darkness like those powerful, perfect opera notes. The yellow light slashes with every limp after Chief Grover stubbed a toe on Seymour Calvin O'Dell's headstone a few songs earlier.

The Chief lugs up his jangling belt and puts the finishing touches on a powerful combination of notes, raising one hand above his head in triumph. His vocal chords sizzle from the abuse. Crystal goblets should fear for their lives.

The Chief's eyes and nose are moist.

"Why do you do this to yourself, Bert?" he asks the fog and emptiness of this darkened cemetery. "Why does anyone do anything that only causes pain? You know singing that shit always ends like this, yet . . ." His eyes and nose grow twice as wrecked, remembering why he gets so upset.

Remembering the fame. Remembering the paychecks. Remembering the love.

The moon bucks against heavy cloud cover, casting delicate strings of silver light on the grass and granite.

He inspects a few more headstones, ignoring the names and dates to focus his beam on the soil. "Nothing," Grover says with disappointment at another untouched plot.

"Nothing."

"Nothing."

Grover inches down the row, bursts a few vibrato-swelled lines into the sky and catches his face go lemon sour. "Stop it." He tugs that belt a few more times, but the sweet wind chime of banging keys doesn't fix heartache. "You are sick. Why can't you stop? Why are you always punishing yourself?"

Dyson's top cop bends into the circle of light and grabs a handful of fresh dirt. He's seeking recently vacated graves. His stomach grows queasy upon finally finding some raw soil.

The name on the tombstone is a man who died last week. "Sorry, Ralph. I doubt you're who I'm after. I'm looking for someone who's been here a lot longer than you." He doesn't actually know if this graveyard has any suspects. Bert seriously doubts anyone in Dyson has ever been mummified. But still, it's his duty to be certain and that responsibility is one of the few things in life that make him feel alive.

A distant rustling spins Chief Grover around until the erratic flashlight falls on a tree blowing in surprisingly strong July wind. An urge pushes inside his stomach where the atoms of ache collide to create an operatic Big Bang. But his throat and lungs push back. An elevator is pling-pling-plinging up the floors in his body. Whenever it reaches the top floor he is powerless to keep those tragic arias indoors. The symphonic rush of pain is too strong whenever he realizes how powerless he is.

His dry gums smack together, gulping air. The elevator is one floor nearer. Bert Grover grips the cold top of a headstone and opens wide. He hates himself even before singing a note.

"Hello there?" a monotone voice tears through the breeze.

A single violent note escapes the Chief's lungs. He checks over his shoulder to find a bluish beam bobbing in the night.

"Chief Grover?" The voice grows clearer.

Grover hikes up his belt, collecting thoughts, drying eyes, and switching the gun's safety.

This new light comes into view; a tall, thin man in a dark suit smiles. "You're Chief Grover, I hope?" He is older, but with a youthful face. "Boy, is it me or is it getting dark early this summer? I remember being a kid, it stayed bright 'til ten."

"Who are you?" Bert squints through the light, but can't read the man's eyes. "What in God's name are you doing here?"

"That's some great singing. *Faust*, right?"

"Yeah," he says with genuine surprise.

"Berlioz . . . that guy. What a genius. You still sound great, by the way. I have a CD of you two in Paris—"

"Oh, I just . . ." Grover grows soft and slow.

"Hope you didn't really sell your soul to the devil." There is a lush pause, filled with the invisible scrape of wind. "Look, sorry to sneak up, I searched all over town first. Someone named Bonnie at the bar told me to look out here. My name's Derrick Eggleston. I'm a representative from NASA."

A moist summertime breeze flaps the Chief's pant legs and fills his nose. "I'm sorry. I don't see the connection."

"I wanted to consult you first, because if there is a panic tomorrow, you should be warned."

"*Panic?* Mr. Eggleston, you're going to have to catch me up." Grover realizes a dark graveyard isn't the place to hold a meeting. "Let's go back to my car and chat."

"Probably wise," he says, gently grabbing Bert's shoulder. "Hey, by the way, I'm dying to know—what are you doing out here in the dark?"

"Do you know anything about mummies?" Bert says, instantly wishing he hadn't.

THURSDAY, 9:10 PM

The room's laughter evaporates, but Skeet is already deep into a dream about carving architecturally straight rows. Dreams about an enormous red combine. Dreams about plucking thousands of ears of corn. If he didn't summon those little starbursts of pride, Skeet might collapse in front of Dyson's decision makers here in Town Hall.

"Okay, let's settle down, everyone," the mayor mutters into a microphone.

Skeet changed his truck's oil earlier that day, and now, with the dark stains on his hands meeting nervous sweat, the smell of 10W-30 comes to life.

Troy Gomez waves his arms, rolling around the floor in a hard plastic carrot suit, powerless to lift himself. His face burns red with delight, "Idiot." The rest of the crowd grumbles and whispers and giggles.

Only Marci Krupp, leaning against the wall, sweating in her apple outfit, keeps a straight face. She knows Skeet might be on to something, but doesn't want to speak up and risk losing her chance to win Destination: Dyson.

"I think this committee agrees," Mayor Bo Rutili says. "Treasure Hunting Days isn't really the best image for Dyson."

"But it has *everything*," Skeet's voice is bold and defiant. "Mystery, physical activity, it's open to the public, and best of all, the huge prize won't cost the city a penny."

One of the board members, a curly-haired mother of three, speaks. "Rufus Brown, you should be ashamed. Everyone knows the Rosinski Treasure is something kids made up on the playground. To assume that a wealthy man had his fortune converted to gold and melted down into . . . into . . . "

"Yes, melted down into fruit shapes as a wedding gift to his wife, go on." Skeet struts forward, recovering from the embarrassment, ready for battle in a tan canvas scavenger uniform.

"Well, to think that something like that was *lost* after their tragedy at sea, it's ridiculous."

"Also," Wendell Dixon says. His stiff lips are unamused, his lacquered hair caps off a set of suspicious eyes. "This entire proposal runs the risk of being seen as a hoax. We're talking lawsuits when people learn there is no treasure." His eyes and hands are full of smug, superior gestures.

"All those in favor?" Mayor Rutili asks, raising a gavel.

Skeet's legs buckle and he considers dropping to his knees. The silence stings. It reminds him of the heartbreaking moment of that final buzzer sounding at the state basketball championship. Dyson was down by three and young Skeeter missed by an embarrassingly wide margin.

"All those opposed?" is followed by a chorus of "nay."

"Next, representatives from the Imitation Fruit Museum and Fruit-Co will explain why Dyson should sponsor their proposed Rosinski Imitation Fruit Festival."

"Whoa, whoa, whoa." Donna stands, raising a hand, sending disco ball reflections. "I've been sitting patiently for an hour. I want to say my bit."

The mayor shuffles papers and looks down, but doesn't actually read anything. "It appears you are not on the agenda, Mrs. Queen. Please wait until the end of the meeting. If we have time, the committee will hear you . . . If we have time." Much like scrubbing away germs, using his elected power to punt Donna Queen's ass makes the mayor feel electrically alive. It rarely happens, but when she stands there and accepts Bo's authority, his jaw fights a grin.

"Get real. This'll only take a second." She *clip-clops* to center stage like a show horse.

A little shaky, Bo speaks, "Mrs. Queen, please follow our rules. Everyone gets—"

"*Everyone gets a chance to speak when it's their turn,*" Donna mimics. "What a drag, am I right?"

A fair amount of *here we go again* sighs fill the committee.

"Look ladies and dudes, this whole Destination: Dyson idea is a waste of dwindling city funds. I have a plan that's going to make Dyson the biggest thing since, since . . ." Like Skeeter, Donna also earned a high school nickname; "Human Thesaurus." She earned it through a legendary inability to finish thoughts. "Forget it. If you really want to save the city, I have the answer. Anyone who wants to do that *and* make a truckload of money, come see me. But, if you enjoy embarrassing yourselves in dumb costumes, you know, whatever . . ."

Far away from Dyson, in a city offering exotic delights like public transportation and foie gras served by French waiters instead of mummies, a man tries desperately to recall necktie knots.

"I don't know, only a couple days," he tells the girl sprawled across a silk bedspread. "Give or take a few." His room is dimly lit by a lamp and yellow shade. The art on the wall is simple and Asian. The girl watches the tall man. Her features are soft and her skin smells like baby powder.

"That's not too long. I'll still miss you." She watches him struggle in the mirror, looping and pulling at the checked tie. Nervously, she slips the tip of her black hair between her teeth. "Why so fast? She just died yesterday."

"They're efficient, I guess."

"How old was your grandma?"

"Beats me. Do you know how old your grandma is?" The man is so tall in fact, his pants and shirts have to be special ordered.

"Eighty-six, smarty pants."

He smiles into the mirror, eying the woman. "She was *old*, Sloan. Ninety-something?"

"Here." She lifts off the bed. The woman wears a purple satin robe and a medal of some saint she can't remember. Her warm chest settles across his shoulder blades, torquing her arms around his neck until only an elegant Windsor knot remains.

His heart rides a slingshot whenever she's near. Is it love? He doesn't know, but he has to figure out sooner or later, what with that little secret kicking around Sloan's belly.

"You're nervous."

"Yes," he says.

"Family is nothing to be nervous about."

"It is when you haven't seen them in years."

"True. But you're coming back for a good reason," Sloan says.

"Reconnecting with him is a good idea in my head. Telling my brother that I really would like to apologize and start having a relationship again . . . that's just not." He clears his throat and sighs. "People just don't talk like that back home."

She kisses his ear and whispers in a humid breath. "You'll be brave. I know you will. I love you."

"I wish you were coming along. I might need your help for the funeral."

"Well, maybe. What's in Dyson?" Sloan stands on her toes, nuzzling his neck and kisses it.

"My brother, a bar, and way too much fake snow," he says, centering the tie in the folds of his collar.

She makes a face. "We've been together, what, a year? You've still never told me what happened between you two."

"I'm kind of the black sheep. It's a lot of things, not just one."

"Gene, how could you be the black sheep? How could someone as handsome and smart as you be the black sheep?" Petite Sloan tugs him close for a deep kiss.

"Well, for starters, he's only twenty-eight and already the mayor."

FRIDAY, 8:10 AM

"No offense," Rajula says, checking her phone, squinting at the fresh morning light hitting the tangled sheets. "But I've had better compliments."

"Oh, no. This is nothing." The embarrassed mayor loses focus, rubbing sanitizer over his genitals. "You should see what I do after someone I don't like."

"Thanks," she says, slipping naked legs through last night's skirt.

"I'm sorry, I'm sorry. Don't think I'm an asshole, but with the town's financial situation, my mind's a little . . . " His fingers flutter above his hair.

The ceiling fan takes lazy swats around the stuffy room. It reminds Rajula of a Syrian apartment she once rented while on assignment—its windows had been painted shut for years. But that place smelled like a pastry shop compared to whatever is coming up from the green carpet here.

"So, I didn't know there was a need for a hotel in Dyson?" she says over the sound of the splashing sink, taking a long look around. The paint peels away, revealing a ribcage of boards along the wall.

Bo admires his work hanging above the bathroom sink. Another swarm of germs successfully sizzled. "There used to be a big need for hotels. We were a popular railroad stopover until the fifties. This was called the Denmark Hotel, thirty rooms. Booked solid most nights. The Three Stooges slept here once. I bought the entire building a few years ago, but I never remodeled the top three floors. Just the coffee shop and the wine store."

"So, what is this?"

"I keep a couple rooms furnished. Someday I'd like to turn them into apartments. Once Dyson gets back on its feet. I live downstairs and I let another guy crash below this room."

"Mayor, wine expert, slum lord. How do you find the time, Mister Rutili?" Rajula blows that pesky sliver of black hair from across her eye, buttoning a clean blouse.

"Eh," he shrugs, slipping on his pants. "I don't charge him. I don't charge him. It's Packwicz, the old mayor I mentioned before. He's having a rough time He needs someone to help him. I feel for the guy."

"Why?"

"Like I said, he was a mayor. I'm a mayor. We share that. Plus, I've known him since I was a kid. He's a good person, his mind has just gone a little foggy. I want to see him get better."

"He doesn't work?"

Bo shrugs. "He worked at the bowling alley, but he just . . . stopped. He quit. Don't mention that on your show, please. Or, well, really, any of *this*."

"Don't worry. I won't tell your girlfriend. It was fun."

"God, she's been ignoring me lately. Are we still dating? I don't know what's up with Marci. I mean, you think a person would be really excited about winning the contest that's going to save this town. It was my vote that put this Rosinski Fruit Festival over the top. But, jeez, Marci just waddled past me. Maybe the apple costume was bothering her?

She has psoriasis, maybe it was acting up. But then, part of me is just like, *forget her.*"

Rajula's eyes catch the light as Bo walks into the room—doubting, questioning. She watches the mayor's face until it slackens to sorry status. "Bo, you just scrubbed your dick clean. Now you're talking about your girlfriend? I can't wait to see the next romantic trick. Is your mom hiding in the closet?"

Bo scratches his chin. He isn't the impetuous type, but quickly discovers he doesn't feel anywhere near guilty about sleeping with Rajula. He feels bad about everything from the pollution his car creates to that time he said the F-word in church. But there is a natural comfort Bo finds with this reporter.

He sits on that bed, gives Rajula's leg a squeeze, and lets his anxious chest slow to a crawl for the first time in a day. The fan's breeze falls cool across his skin. "My mom's dead. I thought I mentioned that? That's where I inherited the money for the hotel."

"Sorry, I was just trying to be funny." She flops backward and the springs chirp. She is familiar with this dance. She bites her cheek. Ever since Mark, her college sweetheart, Rajula does everything short of shoving men through windows to keep them away. She actually did once. But that's another story. All charges were dropped.

"Actually," Bo lifts a finger into the air. *This beautiful woman gave you an opportunity to act normal. Don't mention Grandma. Don't mention Grandma.* His temples throb, holding it back. "My grandma just died, too. Yesterday. Now it's just my brother and me."

"I'm sorry."

A grey cat leaps onto the bed and meows at Bo. "That was dumb. I shouldn't have said anything." He pets the animal until it hushes.

"I'll tell you what." She leans across the bed and gives Bo a full kiss. A perfume of clean hair, a little sweat, and morning breath fills Bo's sphere. "Let's grab a coffee, go our separate ways for the day, and worry about our own problems. My crew is arriving soon. Sound good?"

"That does," he says. The cat rubs aggressively against Bo's arm.

Rajula zips closed a shoulder bag and a purse. She checks her hair in the mirror.

"You don't strike me as a cat person," she says.

"I'm not."

"You're not?"

"I don't even know what cats eat."

"There's a cat on your lap right now."

"It's my grandma's. Her name is Boots. *His* name is boots? God, I don't even know. Somebody had to take this thing."

"Look at you," Rajula teases, sweetly. "Mayor, slumlord, animal adopter. You never fail to surprise." She kisses him quickly and aims for the door.

"Seriously," Bo says. "What do they eat?"

Rajula makes a face. "Try cat food."

An hour later, Bo no more than flips the OPEN sign and the Chief enters.

"Close up shop, Bo." Grover sounds sleepless. "Wine can wait."

Bo runs a boxcutter through a case shipped from a vineyard in Oregon. Foam peanuts fall across the floor, highlighted in the dense orange morning. The cat dives into the mess.

"I've got a pot brewing, Bert. Smell that? Have a seat. You should try this caramel pumpkin latte I've been tinkering with for October."

"I'll do it for you then." The Chief spins around the OPEN sign. He twists the door's lock. "Where've you been? I tried getting you all night."

Unamused, Bo says, "Chief, I already heard. A little bird told me at the meeting last night." He leans back, kicks his feet across the counter.

"And you're just sitting here?" Grover's lips pop a few times, unable to speak, shocked. It's disappointing that the mayor is handling this first tragedy—easily the biggest catastrophe in Dyson history—by brewing some drink only wealthy assholes in Findlay drink.

"Bert, let it go. It's your imagination." The mayor smirks.

"My imagination?" The Chief's voice booms. It is the intimidating voice Grover uses when he catches spray paint vandals. "I really doubt I'm imagining there's a man waiting for you at your office. I really doubt

I'm imagining you two should chat. I really doubt I'm imagining he's from NASA."

"NASA? What does that have to do with you wasting taxpayer money at the cemetery?"

"That? That's nothing compared to this fella. His name is Eggleston and you should hear it from the source before the whole town finishes the job Findlay started."

"Which is?"

"Destroying Dyson."

FRIDAY, 8:55 AM

Cody "Razzle-Dazzle" Kellogg flips up his sunglasses, watching the antenna cable flap against the radio station's aluminum wall in the painful morning light. The long black wire climbs from the studio, in what used to be that trailer's master bedroom, up seventy feet to the radio tower.

WDSR is a tightly budgeted affair. The station completely converted the used, single-wide trailer from a family residence to a place of business. The living room is currently the reception area, the child's bedroom is the station manager's office, and the kitchen is the break room. No matter how many Elton John posters they hang, it still looks like low-income housing.

Normally, the antenna wire is strung tight as the suspenders running down Murray Kreskin's back. This morning, however, that cable is begging Cody Kellogg for a quick game of double Dutch, slapping against the blacktop and using the powder blue aluminum siding for a drum.

Cody approaches the wire with snakehandler's caution. He's gone on the air with a thousand hangovers before, but he's never fixed antenna wiring with a pounding headache. Actually, he's never fixed one, period. Isn't this someone else's job?

The cable teases his grip. The wind picked up overnight, making its every move unpredictable. Cody gets low, ready to wrap his arms around it and reattach the bracket along the side of the building. However, a voice stops him.

"Kellogg," the nighttime disc jockey says. "What are you doing, trying to commit suicide?"

"I don't think the cable could kill me, Keith," Cody says, retreating
from wire wrangling duties and stepping toward the open door.

"No, but I will if you don't start your shift. This commercial is over
in forty-five seconds. You're late again."

"Blame Skeet. He's the one who kept saying 'one more shot.'"

The cable flaps high and grazes Kellogg's skull, knocking off his
pork pie hat.

"Lorette told me. Sounds like you, him, and Ed Lee dried up the
bar last night." The nighttime man steps onto the concrete where Packwicz had his mummified encounter only a few hours prior—grazing
that antennae cable as he fell. "Sorry to hear the Portuguese Festival got
canned. Better luck next year."

"Thanks. My feelings don't hurt so bad anymore. The bender was
Skeet's bright idea. Said it'd make us losers feel better, but I think I'm
getting too old for that kind of shit." Cody snaps his fingers, struggling
for words. "Hey, do you want some chorizo? I have more than I know
what to do with. Tons, actually."

"No thanks, I quit smoking years ago." Keith plucks the wire with
one gentle hand and smiles. "Get to work. I'll take care of this."

"You're a good one."

Inside WDSR's tiny booth, Kellogg spins a few CDs without intro-
ducing them and blows steam away from his special hangover cure: a
mug of green tea. Cody looks over the day's schedule—pretty standard
except for the live interview at noon.

Without warning, his mouth heats up as something queasy and ne-
on-colored brews in his stomach. The nausea is either from the thought
of interviewing his sworn enemy or the gallon of alcohol still sloshing
inside him.

He coughs and swallows a burning mouthful of tea while eying the
Gazette, circling articles to paraphrase along with the weather in ten
minutes. This morning's headline, taking up nearly the entire sheet,
reads like awful violence and fear. He stops the song midway through.

These moments are rare, but when they come, Cody worships the power of radio—the honor of being the voice of reason in someone's life. Days like this he lives out fantasies of being a fast-talking, hard-hitting newsman.

There is a delirious bubbliness when he speaks: "*Miiiiiiiiiiiister Razzle-Dazzle, Cody Kellogg, with you now folks. Shake out of your slumps, pull the car to the side of the road, and do not operate any heavy machinery. WDSR has some exclusive news that is certain to not only flip your wig, but burn it to a crisp.*"

Cody's once-nauseous stomach now flaps with butterflies rivaling the first time he laid lips to a girl. This crashing satellite news, if played properly, will bring Mr. Razzle-Dazzle to national attention and finally catapult him out of Dyson.

FRIDAY, 9:47 AM

"Welcome to Christmas City!"

"Looks like that's crossed out," the director says.

Rajula Magbi, in a blue suit powerful enough to weaken the kidneys of kings and diplomats, steps closer to the wooden sign's big letters: DYSON. Pop. 2,334.

Cars zip past, ignoring the thirty-five mile-per-hour speed limit. Between bursts of motors, endless golden fields of wheat sway with papery dry applause.

"Okay. I'll just welcome everyone to the Saint Patrick's Central, then." Rajula's hair whips across her face.

"That's even more scratched out than the other."

"I know, I know." She shrugs off his inability to get the joke. The guy never laughs unless someone is getting injured, she swears. "God, what's that one near the bottom? It's all faded."

"Beats me," one crewman says.

"Lin . . . Linc . . . oh, forget it."

"Lincoln Crapped Here," the director's words are slow.

"Ew." She stares for another moment.

"That seems a little off-color," the soundman says in his thick Brooklyn accent.

"I bet it's one of those words that meant something different back then," the director says.

"You're an optimist, Clark," the soundman says. "Either way I kind of like it. It sticks with you."

Rajula waves her hand for attention. "Let's just drop the tag lines. We don't need them. I think Dyson is going to be our best show yet. There's a wave of positive energy flowing through here. Do you feel it?"

"It's electric. Ouch." The director takes a bored step back.

"Bet you ten-to-one her pacemaker's on the fritz again," the sound guy mumbles.

"I heard that, Skinny." Rajula's face gets stiff, but melts into on-air pleasantness. "The doctor said I don't *need* a pacemaker. Everything's perfectly normal." Rajula pats her chest.

"Whatever you say, boss," he calls, adjusting the boom mic.

Her shoulders drop, wishing someone, anyone, shared her enthusiasm for this show. She is going to convert it from bottom-feeding, late-night garbage with an awkward title into a rich program full of hope and patriotism with an awkward title. She finds strength in this and decides to carry the load alone, like always.

"Let's take it from the top," she tells the cameraman.

She centers herself in front of the city's welcome sign and tries a few greetings.

"Welcome to Dyson, a small town in the middle of nowhere, where Pearl Krupp promises, *nothing* ever happens. Is it the Boringest City in America? Let's take a tour and find out!"

FRIDAY, 11:32 AM

Several vases of fresh cut flowers give Donna's office that funeral home smell.

"Garrett, turn off that stupid radio," she commands from the other side of the room, sitting with Wendell Dixon. "I can't stand Cody Kellogg's voice."

Garrett's footsteps echo across cold marble. He clicks the stereo, situated atop an antique table that cost the same as his first car. Even if their attorney wasn't in the room, Garrett still would have done it. After all, she is CEO, president, and God around the Queen household.

Donna does a magnificent job on her husband's nerves, constantly convincing Garrett he is one slip-up away from sleeping in a shipping crate by the railroad tracks. This is impossible, though, because some days her heart still jumps with adrenaline just looking at him.

Dixon's hair is in a permanent, spray-hardened brush across his forehead. His shirt and tie are pressed stiff. His chin is held deep, cocky. He runs marathons and it shows. "Okay, well, normally, Mr. and Mrs. Queen, I would say you should pay for the new hood yourselves and save some embarrassment." Dixon scurries through his briefcase. A vein creeps to the surface of his forehead. It always does when he grows annoyed.

Wendell Dixon, Esq. likes the Queen family just fine and loves the steady stream of income their various holdings and financial endeavors provide, but he hates making house calls. Working outside the office is torture.

Dixon's workplace is a two-room storefront on Main Street, surrounded by condemned buildings. That office is like a child's messy room: an outsider may get lost, but Wendell knows which scrap of paper is tacked to which corkboard, what drawer every memo is crammed into, and which case law book holds up what table leg. He says people aren't smart enough to understand his filing system, or anything he does for that matter.

Wendell Dixon considers himself Dyson's smartest man. He self-awarded this honor after realizing he is the only person in town with a graduate degree. Well, except for a handful of elementary school teachers, but he doesn't count them.

Deep inside the Queen Compound, with all his necessary papers clipped in neat briefcase piles, he has the attention span of a whirling slot machine. Neatness brings wicked anxiety. The spinning sensation reminds Dixon of times when his wife, Stephanie, threatens to leave.

"I sense a *but* in your voice, Wendell," Donna says, kicking her head back and admiring the exotic taxidermy. The lion, the leopard, that scaly grey one with the big horn on its nose. Dead animals make her feel powerful, and when Donna Queen feels powerful, people lose their mortgage, their pride, or even a limb. "Honey, did you pick up a *but* in our lovely lawyer's voice?"

"You'd say, 'save the embarrassment, *but?*'" Garrett scoots his chair close.

Dixon's Adam's apple tenses while looking at Donna. Even from across that massive marble desk—which Donna never hesitates to mention was carved by some Italian hillbillies in the Pyrenees—she isn't so perfect. She is, he reminds himself, after all, a high-school dropout. "But . . . people have been talking about this *thing*. My guess is some prankster's running around in a costume."

"A menace." Donna smacks her hand on the desk. "Who dresses like a mummy?"

"A nutjob, sweetheart. A nutjob," Garrett says.

"I agree," Dixon says. "Now, the police aren't releasing anything, but I've heard rumors accusing this *person* of giving pornography to Mrs. Summers at the volunteer firehouse. There was that whole weird angel dust story floating around town. Father Donnigan from Holy Mary's claimed a guy wrapped in bandages handed him a movie by a fella named . . ." Dixon slips on reading glasses. "Jean Luc Godard?" His voice drops to something low and private. "My wife has even alluded to a grown man in a mummy outfit giving her a painting."

Wendell's sharp mind wanders into hazy territory for a moment. His palms grease with sweat when he combines Stephanie's recent mummified claims with her likewise recent threats of divorce.

"Come again?" Garrett is out of breath from the angry yellow blaze coming to life in his chest.

The lawyer shoos off those hazy thoughts of infidelity. His confident eyes return. "An actual *painting*. I researched it. Some blurry yellow and orange squares by a joker named Mark Rothko. It's clearly a print. Practically worthless, but still." The haze returns as he asks: *Why would she cheat on me? I'm the smartest man in town. She knows that, right?*

"Wendell, I have an interview at noon. Where is this going?" Donna says.

"We worked hard for that car, and I demand a new hood," Garrett says.

"I don't know if I'd call it *working hard*," the attorney mutters.

Donna's eyes shoot bright and annoyed. "Wendell, just finish up please . . ."

"Just look at the evidence. Dealing drugs, distributing bootleg videos, art forgery. This guy is shaking the morals that make our small town special. If we caught and exposed him, this could be big."

Instantly, Wendell thinks of his wife again. *I need to impress her. Win Stephanie back. She's probably cheating on me with this lunatic. Though, a mummy doesn't seem her type. I thought she had a thing for younger men.*

A look beams from client to attorney and it bulks his forehead vein. Dixon knows what Donna wants to hear. The lawyer understands the real reason she pays so well. Just this once he holds back before it kicks down the door and runs amok through vague memories of ethics classes. "I'm sure there is a certain amount of justice this hooligan could be brought to for both your *injuries* suffered during the automobile accident."

Garrett cocks his head.

Donna isn't so slow.

"You mean my *neck*? And poor Garrett's ribs? That seatbelt must have broken at least six. Not to mention the mental trauma of some delinquent dressed as a mummy charging at us while we peacefully drove to church."

"Wait a minute, you two. I don't agree with this idea."

"*Garrett!* Don't forget the dented hood."

"We'll never feel safe on the road again." He winces and wraps arms around his ribcage.

"Fantastic," Dixon says. "I'll file the appropriate paperwork. In the meantime let's lean on Chief Grover a little, get him to keep an eye peeled for this wacko."

The dull flame in Donna's husband must have ran across some fireworks or tanks of propane, because that anger now spreads at a scientifically impossible rate. Garrett slaps his hands together. "And I'll start hunting it. Citizen's arrest, am I right?"

"Well, now." Dixon's voice slows.

"Oh, Garrett, you are so brave." Donna's eyes are in heat. She snatches his hand from across the desk, rubbing erotic strokes.

Their lawyer focuses on an empty corner in the room. "Do what you think is right."

"Delicious." She winks at Garrett. "Now that that's solved, let's move on to more important business. I have to be out of here in a few minutes."

"Yeah. People keep asking what we're up to," Garrett says. "You can't start construction on a four-story log cabin with beds for a hundred and fifty without drawing some attention. I can't keep our little business venture a secret much longer, Wendell."

"Listen . . . speaking as a friend and not your lawyer, I think you should reconsider this investment," Dixon says.

"You're an accountant now?" Donna snaps.

"No."

"Good. Then don't worry about *how* we spend our money, just make sure it's legal."

"Of course. It's just . . . " He holds his gaze waiting for Donna to speak, but she doesn't. "Just answer me one question."

Donna, bored, says: "What?"

"You have more money than a small country."

"So what?"

"Why are you still here?"

"You mean at this meeting? I'm beginning to wonder myself."

"I mean here, in Dyson."

"Don't worry about it," Donna says, growing stiff in her posture. She fidgets a little.

"You and Garrett could travel the globe. You could have a house in

Hawaii, a penthouse in New York City, a condo in Paris . . . probably all the above. But you are here. After all these years. I've never been able to figure that out."

"Dyson is home. You can't buy home with a credit card."

"Okay, sure. But—"

"Alright, that's enough. Let's change the subject," Garrett interrupts with a sharp voice.

"No. It's okay, sweetie. But *what*, Wendell?"

"It just doesn't make sense on paper, Donna."

"Hmmm," she says and folds her hands, thinking. Her voice goes a little emotional, a little soft and unsure. "I see your point. Well, about twelve years ago we had a problem—"

"Donna, no," her husband says, stern. "That is our business. Nobody else's. Nobody needs to hear about our problems."

Donna nods slowly.

Dixon coughs. "Sorry. That was uncalled for. Well, on to other business, then." He opens the briefcase and removes more paper. "I have a researcher putting the final touches on everything, but it sure looks like your bloodlines check out. Congratulations. There's no reason why you cannot move forward with opening day ceremonies. Although, I advise you to legally add your ancestral name. Plus, it'll provide an air of legitimacy."

"Donna *Urinating Bear*-Queen?"

"Or Donna Queen-Urinating Bear, whichever you prefer."

Garrett groans, "Ugghhh—"

"Sweetie, I don't care if my great-great-great grandfather was named Chief *Monkey Blowjob*, this is the sacrifice I have to make to become a hero." She stands. "Now, if you'll excuse me, I have to go on the radio and announce our plans to pull this ungrateful shithole out of the mud."

FRIDAY, NOON

"They were just saying on the news an impact was highly unlikely. When did it jump to ninety-five percent?" The mayor massages his hands with sanitizer.

"We're pretty accurate. I mean, we are NASA." Eggleston is as cold and constant as a Mission Control recording. He wears last night's black suit, but doesn't look tired. His hair is in place, his mustache neatly trimmed and his eyes bright.

The mayor keeps the air conditioning cranked in his office because neckties make him sweaty.

"But television said you guys couldn't calculate that stuff." Bo's hands scurry with confusion. "Dyson was just mentioned as a *possibility*."

Eggleston's voice thaws. "I know what you're thinking: it's a like being a little kid all over again. You suddenly have to know the difference between Wyoming and Colorado just by their shapes. It's confusing."

"Huh? No. That's not what I'm saying."

"Oh, really? Sorry, my kid is failing geography. We've been working to help him. Seemed like a good metaphor." He gently brushes breakfast crumbs from his lips. "Look, NASA just tells reporters we can't be certain. It's a fib. A white lie. Come on, we built a satellite that peeks a few million light years into space, you think the dog ate our calculus homework?" He slouches in the chair. "The satellite, Orion 2781233, is gonna hit Dyson. It's a done deal."

"How much time do we have before it . . . *lands*?" Bo pauses. "Wait, hold up. Nobody's even told me what exactly is going to happen."

"Hard to say." Eggleston shrugs. "We've lost a few satellites over the ocean before. Once over the outback of Australia. Usually, they break apart upon reentry and you'll have a few nickels of shrapnel rain down. Window and roof damage at the worst. But keep in mind, those others were Serbian-made. Your satellite is American-made. This puppy heading for Dyson is the CIA's, and the CIA doesn't build Wal-Mart crap like the other guys."

"What other guys?"

"I don't know. China and India, probably?" He leans forward with a smile. "Oddly enough, this particular model was built down the road, in Findlay, at the McMahon Satellite Works. Funny, huh?"

"That sounds about right."

"Since it's built so solid, this sucker might stay in one piece. Top of the line, a modern marvel. We're very proud."

Bo goes silent in the cold office. He rubs his eyes hoping it will soften those anxieties. Boots leaps onto his lap.

"Cute cat," Eggleston says.

"Thanks." The grey fur warms him. That warmth moves from his lap up to his entire body.

"Does it live in your office?"

"No. I'm taking care of it for my grandma. I brought it from home. I didn't want it to be left alone."

"I think cats like to be left alone," Eggleston says.

"Not this one," Bo says, but realizes that maybe it's him that isn't so fond of flying solo.

"Fair enough. Where were we? Ah, yes. The Orion satellite is built like a tank. It's really a sight to see. A modern marvel."

"So we'd have a modern marvel hitting town like a rocket?"

"Less of a rocket," he chuckles. "More like a comet. Estimates suggest a crater about a block wide. Probably only flattening a few square miles."

"But Dyson's only a few square miles total."

"Well, then . . ." Agent Eggleston clicks his tongue several times. "Orion 2781233 could very well destroy this city."

"We're a village, not a city." Bo realizes he is shivering. He cradles Boots. "What can we do to stop it?"

Eggleston shifts his lower jaw far to the side with a cockeyed glance. "I like you. You have a dry sense of humor."

Bo chooses his next words carefully. "Can't the government, you know, shoot it down?" Bo demonstrates with his hands.

"Probably. But look, that stuff costs a *ton* of money. We're in a recession. Everybody needs to make sacrifices. Plus, those missiles are reserved for killing people on the other side of the planet. Uncle Sam's not lifting a finger."

"How do you know this? Can't NASA and the Army, or whoever, work out a deal?"

"Don't worry. You can easily evacuate the area and nobody will get hurt. If this bastard were headed for New York City, then maybe we'd see some missile action. But, well, let me put this delicately . . . Dyson hasn't earned a missile."

Bo massages a temple. "What's our next step?"

"Well, this is uncharted territory. Common sense says to get everyone out of town as soon as possible. Shut off the utilities. Empty your gas stations' reserves . . ."

"Thank God we only have one." Bo sees Eggleston isn't amused.

"Shut off the electricity, too. That should help keep things from catching fire."

"There is so much to do. How much time do we have?"

"I don't know. A week, maybe two." The agent's voice goes flat again.

"I thought you guys were math wizards?"

"That was a joke." A keyboard of white teeth spreads a smile. "Seventy-eight hours."

"So?"

"Three days and about five hours, give or take a few minutes."

FRIDAY, 12:15 PM

"Donna." Cody flips through his address book for old contacts at bigger radio and television stations. "Buzz off, will ya? Your silly little announcement can wait. Did you hear my broadcast?"

"No, sorry. My car has satellite radio for *real* DJs."

The booth is so tight Donna hardly has room to cross her legs. Just two chairs, the controls, and enough wood paneling to give her flashbacks of working at the bowling alley. WDSR is headquartered in the trailer she and Garrett once called home.

"Donna, I just informed the listeners a satellite is headed straight for Dyson." Cody is overcome with a fear of the unknown. It reminds him of first radio jobs and the hissing mysteries of places like Reno and Dubuque. "The *Gazette* quoted some NASA guy named Eggleston. It's legit."

"Yes, the world is ending. Cute." She gives the DJ her foreclosure stare. "Now, which buttons do I need to press? And play some Elton John when we're through." Her sparkly finger hangs over the controls.

That board is the simplest Cody has ever worked. Only a series of yellow buttons and faders, some glowing red lights, and a few needles bouncing with the song's beat. The microphone was built during the Second World War.

"There won't be any more music." He pinches her finger and removes it from the board like a dead rodent. "I'm talking all day. The biggest story in town history won't be preempted by some British asshole with a piano. Get out of my way."

"You leave Elton John out of this. He was knighted, you know. Plus, I have bigger news than a stupid satellite." She looks around the DJ and her hand goes for the volume fader. "So, I'm guessing this one lets me talk and that one lets me play 'Goodbye Yellow Brick Road.'"

"Donna, I'm a professional journalist. You're a walking Botox advertisement. Please let me do my job, the commercial is almost over."

"Get up." She rolls her chair into his. "I'll figure all this out."

Cody is pinned against the paneling. The heads of tacks dig into his skin. They are holding up an aged poster of Chief Bert Grover in a tuxedo and his ex-wife Joyce standing before an audience of a thousand, an orchestra at his feet.

"Funny." He squirms. "Aren't there kittens that need running over or orphans you could evict?"

"No, but there are has-been disc jockeys that I could fire. Don't forget who signs your paychecks." She lowers her face so all Cody sees are dark, mean eyes. "Right, Mr. Razzle-Dazzle?"

Cody knows he is pinned against more than paneling. He begins biting his lip until his mouth is filled with the coppery flavor of blood. "Oh now, come on. Don't. Please. Not *now*." Cody's throat gets sawdusted. "This is big news. I have a journalistic responsibility. Who's going to cover it, the *Gazette*?"

Cody's sad face looks familiar.

Donna didn't know about such looks back when she still waxed bowling lanes and rented shoes by the hour. But these days Dyson's wealthiest resident knows when a person loses their home or their job, their eyes go shiny and their mouth unhinges. When people underestimate Donna and she sneaks up, this ruined face is all that's left. Donna never gave birth, but imagines that glowing helium balloon of pride in her chest that comes with crushing someone's hopes feels about the same as squeezing out a brat.

"Clearly you don't know what counts as news in this city. I'm *giving* you the story of the year." She makes the announcement like it is lit in neon: "*Donna Queen comes to the rescue during Dyson's . . .*" The Human Thesaurus returns. "Whatsit . . . you know, its . . . financial bad times!"

Donna is filled with the same electricity as when she foreclosed on Old Man Packwicz. She simply lifts the DJ by his scrawny arm. Kellogg is smaller than her—smaller than a boy scout. She scuffles him beyond the stunned receptionist, out the door, and onto the blacktop. The pork pie hat hits the ground with Frisbee accuracy.

Donna heads back inside and parks behind the microphone. She clears her throat and somehow manages to push the correct button. "Hello Dyson, this is Donna Queen, and I have some very special news." A pinch of magic twirls through her throat, watching little red needles bounce with each syllable. Her voice spreads across the town as she prepares to shock listeners.

"Identity matters, don't you think? I do. Knowing who you are . . . I mean deep down where nobody else can see. That kind of deep. That kind of identity. We all need to know who we are, am I right? Well, that's why I am here today. On behalf of myself, my husband Garrett, and Queen Enterprises Unlimited, I'd like to tell you that, from this point forward, I will be taking my ancestral name, Donna Urinating Bear-Queen."

Her jaw tightens with pride. She hopes her husband is listening. This plan is partially Garrett's and will make him so proud. Too bad he had other business and can't be in the studio, admiring a display of spectacle and bravery that makes the Olympic opening ceremonies come off more like a cheap Christmas Pageant.

"Now, dear listeners, you are probably saying, 'Gee Donna, how did you get such a regal, proud name? And why are you changing it now?'

"Well, ladies and gentlemen, I have never been one to brag, but the time has come to explain that I am one twenty-fourth Huron Indian. My great-great-great-grandfather was the chief of his tribe before being brutally forced off his land.

"Well, as reparations, I have worked out an agreement with the government. One square mile of land off West Lambers Road is now officially American Indian property. My first decision as governor of this reservation is to unveil something that will certainly pull our beautiful community out of its slump by creating jobs, bringing publicity, and bolstering the local economy.

"All by myself. Absolutely no help from our baby-faced mayor. Please come to our property tomorrow afternoon, because we are hiring hundreds of employees for the new Urinating Bear Casino and Resort.

"I'm certain you've all wondered what Garrett and I have been up to, but now the secret is out. Please remember it was me, and not our runny-nosed mayor, who has fixed Dyson's problems. I look forward to seeing you, dear listener, at the interviews. Until then, I am Donna Urinating Bear-Queen, and this is the incomparable Elton John on WDSR, Dyson."

America's newest Native American princess puts her feet on the control board and lets the soaring harmonies of Sir Elton's journey into Oz act as the soundtrack for thousands of people at home dropping to their knees, thanking God for delivering them an angel like Donna.

Sadly, Donna ignored those bouncing red needles when they went dead following her introduction. Immediately after she told the public of her new name, an ex-employee razzle-dazzled over to the pesky black cable he'd battled earlier, unplugged it, and let it dangle impotently against the grain elevator.

FRIDAY, 2:08 PM

Rajula Magbi fishes clothes from her suitcase and organizes them in the dresser. She is looking for her best on-air suit. This is the first time she's stayed in one place long enough to unpack since Baghdad. With an ear on the phone, she pauses to pound a fist on the shaky dresser.

"Wendy, come on," she begs. "This is a huge story."

Her former producer is skeptical. Wendy's been skeptical since her prodigy's star dropped from orbit so quickly in Iraq. But if Rajula's pitch works she'll be back on at the Network, doing real journalism again.

There is a hungry tear dividing the reporter. On one side, *America's Boringest City* was ready to live up to its potential. But this starving other side of her brain says only the big stage will satisfy.

"Look, I'm working up a hell of a story. Especially when this satellite hits." Rajula pauses to let Wendy interrupt. A purple hanky silently runs under her nose. "I don't think anyone will die, Wendy. Satellites break apart, right? This is a great story; a small town dying from natural causes isn't news? I don't think most people here have caught on yet. I mean, some have, walking around like there's a serial killer on the loose. I mean, the *dread* in people's eyes. They're numb; they're lost. It sends a shiver up your back. You ask me, this is what's happening to America right this minute. Not just here, but in small towns everywhere. Believe me, I came from a small town. Think about it. Not just satellites."

Rajula finds Bo's undershirt, forgotten beneath the bed. She holds it up and breathes its smell before throwing it in her suitcase, running the zipper tight.

"I know people need to die for it to be *real news*. But trust me, even if that doesn't happen, people here are interesting. I could spend an hour just telling you about the mayor."

She hesitates, then unzips the bag and pulls out the shirt to admire it one more time.

"Alright!" she says with joy. "You're the best. You won't regret this. I have to do some shots for *Boringest City* and after that I'm going to deliver you the finest profile on America you've ever seen. I owe you."

FRIDAY, 3:00 PM

The priest and the mortician shift in their chairs, sweating a little. Garrett Queen, P.I., knows they are playing dumb. There is a powerful focus in his eyes. Garrett's pale mustache seems pure as snow. His head reflects the lights. There's a bigness to him, of bygone muscle gnow softer.

"Father Donnigan, I've heard the stories about your visitor." Garrett paces his office using a low, sharp voice.

"Son, I appreciate the coffee. But I don't have a clue what you're talking about."

Garrett's office is much smaller than Donna's: a simple white room with a window overlooking the trout pond and a few rows of swaying trees. Those young pines block the endless flat acres of corn, soybeans, and tomatoes surrounding the Queen compound. The water ripples with light summer rain.

"Garrett, I really have to get going. In the future, only contact me when it's an emergency." The mortician nods to the priest and stands.

"Not so fast." Garrett raises a long finger. "Tell me everything you know about mummies."

The mortician stands for a moment and slides a hand across his lips. "Most movies about them suck."

"But their brains are pulled out their noses, right? Presumably by morticians?"

"Maybe? But nobody does that anymore. The deceased are embalmed or cremated, *not* mummified."

"I'll cut the crap. I think we all know what's going on here." Garrett's eyes slit with suspicion, his smooth head shines under white lamp light. "How many mummifications have you performed?"

The mortician opens his mouth to say something quick, but pauses and frowns. "I'll see you at Mrs. Rutili's funeral, Garrett. Hopefully, by then, you'll be rid of this *disgusting* fascination."

The mortician leaves the door open. The priest shifts and looks hard at the exit.

"You know why you're here, don't you?" Garrett snaps a pencil, hoping to scare the clergyman.

He is all wrinkles and pale grey hair. The priest seems behind schedule. "I turned the movie off. I had a difficult time following the subtitles. *Week End*, good gosh, it looked like a miserable way to spend a weekend to me. This Jean-Luc Godard has *problems*. Now, I must be going."

"Not the movie." Garrett drops the pencil chunks.

"I'm not following." The priest is old enough to be Garrett's father. His face is pink like most people in confession.

"You're a holy man. I've done some research. Only *you* can tell me how to kill it and send it back to Hell. Or better yet, just capture it and keep it caged." Queen's face is stern and confident. In his mind, Donna watches with pride as her man beats the crap out of something long dead.

"A mummy?"

"*The* mummy."

"I'm a Catholic, not a voodoo whatchamacallit."

Garrett draws near, holds eye contact for more than is comfortable. "Let me guess, this is the part where I give the church a donation for your services?"

"Goodbye."

FRIDAY, 3:30 PM

"Shouldn't we get out of the street?" Rajula says to Pearl.

Rajula lifts her chin and ignores the weeds creeping through sidewalk cracks, the boarded windows, and crumbling brick lining downtown's two blocks. She particularly loves old buildings and the trim around the top. They aren't that unlike the ones in her hometown in Missouri. Some have swirls carved from concrete, some are etched with Latin, others feature faded busts of notable historic figures—she's seen a million different architectural flourishes like this. To Rajula, it's a building's fingerprint.

Rajula also has a firm belief that towns have fingerprints, too. They just take more work to understand. Detailing that rich history of America, town-by-town, has been on her mind since returning from her last assignment in the Middle East. When she lost her job interviewing jihadists, sweating through a black burqa, and riding in some near-dead Jeep across the sand, she joined *America's Boringest City*. It's a shock how much the show has come to mean to her. How one little misguided turn has defined her. Even if ratings stink.

The ratings will come once she uncovers Dyson's charm and history and importance. Once she puts this small town on the map, and then another, and another. She loves Ken Burns documentaries and pictures herself like that someday, but with a better haircut.

She's a detective dusting for fingerprints. Those unnoticed whorls that made this country.

"No. We can totally hang out in the street. There usually aren't more than a few cars all *day*. I mean, Dyson is so boring, Rajula." Pearl's Tinkerbelle cut is wavy and spiky in all the right places. The bruised knot on her skull is spackled to invisibility with makeup. Her black skirt is slimming, and she wears a tasteful blouse to hide bony arms. She needs to squint without her big sunglasses. "I bet you really miss Hollywood and all your friends and parties. I mean this is just so . . ." Pearl sticks a pink tongue out and chokes herself.

An uneven, drunken breeze blows a large soda cup along the gutter. Rajula hates litter in charming places like Dyson, but blocks it from her thoughts. Speaking on camera and listening to the director's cues require full concentration.

"No, I love my job. All this. I like this better than covering war." Rajula waves her manicured fingers. "This show is what I live for now. There isn't enough attention on small towns. These little communities are wonderful, they're so important to America. They're a vital chromosome in our DNA . . . or something. Sorry. I ramble." Her eyes roll. "It took me a long time to finally appreciate that." She crinkles her nose with joy. "My goal is to show that even the most boring places on Earth are special."

"Really?"

"You want to know a secret? There is no boringest city. Every place is unique. It's just a stupid title our producer cooked up."

That dual ripping takes hold of Rajula's heart. Maybe, she thinks, there's a way to help these towns *and* be a major reporter again. This story she just sold to Wendy is a start.

Pearl's face tightens, reminding her to think cool thoughts. It's been a while since she's had makeup professionally applied. She forgot how they put a little clear antiperspirant on your upper lip and hairline so you don't sweat all the foundation off. "So, wait . . . you're not making fun of small towns and rednecks and uneducated—"

"God," she jumps in, "it really does come off that way, doesn't it? I used to think it was in my head. Starting with this episode I have final say on edits. These jerks back at the studio, give them a heartwarming piece about grandmothers baking pies for charity and they turn it into kiddie-porn. There's a hell of a lot I don't miss about Hollywood."

"Oh." Pearl goes numb. Her boring plan to tour the plastic fruit factory, the nursing home, and the grain elevator won't work now. The crushing weight of Dyson finds Pearl again and the young waitress knows Rajula is the only way out. She takes comfort knowing Los Angeles' heat is dry and her makeup won't run there.

"But, you know, we still need to keep things mellow. The show's laid-back, countrified tone serves a bigger purpose. Don't think I'm weird telling you this, but we keep it calm on set because I have heart problems. I don't normally tell people that, but I feel really comfortable with you." Rajula lays a gentle hand on Pearl's, like old friends. They share a knowing smile.

Handheld light meters are checked, long boom microphones moved into place, and an assistant adjusts shirt collars and hair.

The village pushes down like dirt shoveled atop a casket, and Pearl needs to unearth herself. Slowly, *tastefully*, working into Rajula Magbi's heart is the answer.

Unfortunately, Pearl rarely listens to her own advice. "Rajula, thank you, that's so sweet." She gives a camera-ready giggle. "Can I come back with you and be famous, too?"

The soil of dread and guilt are bulldozed over Pearl. She is sweating, the back of her blouse clings.

"Uhm," Rajula inspects a set of note cards.

Pearl's chest fills with needles. She knows just how to sabotage herself at the right time. A wicked ice cream craving scratches at her stomach, promising to settle these nerves.

The hollow rattle of another paper cup is the only sound for a long while.

"I wouldn't call myself *famous*." Rajula looks up and Pearl stiffens. "God, what's gotten into me today?" She smiles, which jolts Pearl a bit. "You know, it's totally not my style, but yes, you can come with me. I have a good feeling about you."

Feet start tapping, arms shaking, tongues stuttering—an earthquake of relief shakes all the sod and worms off her grave and delivers a dream on a chrome platter. "Thank you," is the most Pearl can manage, but even that comes out whittled and quiet.

"Great. We'll talk about it later. I know some people who can help you get a foot in the door." Rajula smiles again. "But now, let's nail this shot."

"Thank you."

The director counts down and calls action.

"Okay, Pearl, now we've had your tour of Dyson. Can you tell us what makes this place special?"

Pearl feels a surge of inspiration wedge into her spine and sends self-doubt packing. "Well, Jules, *nothing* happens here. People farm, they have kids, and they die. But, you know, under the surface, there are some really great folks who make this whole beautiful place work. It's not easy to survive with only two stoplights, a gas station, and a bar."

"But what about the yummy wine and coffee shop?"

"Oh, yeah, that too."

"I also heard one of your most popular businesses just closed?"

"Yes." Pearl pouts out a lip. "Unfortunately, our Civil War reenactment store went out of business."

"That doesn't sound boring. Do a lot of people play war?"

"No, oddly." The two share a laugh and sense an on-screen chemistry blooming. "I guess that explains a few things."

Pearl continues to outline the many ways this small town's fabric is cut from the cloth of the bigger picture. The country as a whole, ups and downs, pulling itself by its bootstraps. But on their third take, just as the pair really hits some dynamic question and answer badminton, an odd noise fills the soundman's earphones.

Pearl has never been to a marathon, a decathlon or even a dance-a-thon, but if she had, her skin might not have grown so cold. Because if she'd ever spent time near the sound of hundreds of stampeding feet—that infinite *smack-slap* of rubber soles attacking hard ground—she would have at least a clue.

The *smack-slap* grows bold and more colorful. A vibration shakes across the crew. The cameraman twists his neck, the microphone operator curses at someone ruining the sound, but Rajula continues. This disruption is nothing compared to her former life.

Who knows? If Pearl wasn't talking about Dyson, she may have been home. And she could be one of the thousand-or-so people going from door to door, passing the news of the spy satellite. She might've abandoned her car, too. Dozens deserted their autos at the mention of Cody's shocking news. It's a stretch, but she may have flooded the street with the mob of *smack-slapping* feet, crazed, scared, and defiant to the news of Dyson's interstellar Hiroshima.

The crowd aims straight for the Mayor's office, only a few blocks away from the *America's Boringest City* crew.

Most people in the center of any riot say there's a black patch of memory. Instinct is known to hop in the driver's seat and bring down its lead foot. So it's not surprising that half the city's population, on its way to interrogate the mayor, flies right through this interview without hesitation.

Pearl saw Pamplona's Running of the Bulls on cable once. And like guys dressed in white with red sashes, she and the crew sprint ahead of the mob, dive for cover, or find higher ground atop the truck.

A flood of bodies rushes through the streets and makes scraps of the paper cup. Nearly a minute goes by before the street is clear.

The crew stumbles back to their shooting locale and finds Pearl leaning over the host, screaming.

"Rajula. Rajula." Tears drip onto the host's chest. "Please . . . say something."

Between shouts, there is a heavy silence. Something depressingly quiet. Something queasy.

"No. No."

Pearl puts her ear to Rajula's chest and waits for something. She raises her head after a minute, sobbing.

"We had plans. We were going to date drummers." Pearl's voice shatters into a thousand jagged chunks the way spy satellites are supposed to when they enter Earth's atmosphere. She hugs Rajula's lifeless body. "We were going to snort free *blow*."

FRIDAY, 7:00 PM

Ashes are laid to ashes and dust does its usual thing.

Coincidentally, ashes and dust are all that's left of Bo's nerves when Grandma's body lowers into the ground. Fear of satellites and sorrow over two recent deaths combine with humid July heat to form a punishing mix.

Clusters of nervously shifting bodies surround the fresh grave. Hearts say to pay respect, but common sense says to get the hell out of town before a satellite crushes them.

The sun sinks into the horizon and humidity wraps everyone in sweaty summer moisture.

Grandma's death is in such a distant orbit compared to the swirl of Bo's duties that, until he places a rose on her casket, the boy mayor remembers he had promised to check on her. They'd had lunch last week and he said he would drop by and change Boots' litter. The bag was still in his trunk.

He feels oddly responsible, even though she died peacefully and naturally. In unspoken terms, he has been responsible for the last ten years or so, since he graduated high school and she broke her hip in a month's span of time.

He had a scholarship to Stanford, a long plane ride away. He knew he'd only be back to Dyson a few times a year at best and that his brother was God-knows-where. He applied and got a scholarship to the state school in Findlay, just in case. Grandma said, "Go. I'll be fine. Your mom and dad always wanted to live in California. They were saving and planning. They were always saving and planning and dreaming. But, God love them, they were not doers. They died with those dreams in their heads, wishing they could, when all it really ever takes to make a change is to just go and *do it*. Everything comes to an end, and if you don't shake a leg, you won't have done anything. Like me—I always wanted to see the Northern Lights. Well, when your grandfather passed and your dad and uncles were about yay-high, I went. I left those boys with my sister and boarded a boat for a month, headed straight for the North Pole. I bet you didn't know that. It was the dumbest thing I could have done at the time—me, thirty years old, widowed, mother of three—but I did it. It was beautiful. When I die, those shimmering skies will be on my mind. So, go. Don't wait to live."

Bo had a plane ticket and had talked to his new roommates on the phone. Then Grandma fell doing yardwork. The pain in her face, her eyes sealed tight and tears crawling down as they waited for an ambulance, made him woozy. Her grunts of agony, lying in the grass, were permanently sculpted into his memory that afternoon.

They inserted a steel rod where her hip had shattered. Grandma needed constant help. Medicare would not cover the type of nursing and attention she required.

He talked to the admissions people in Findlay and worked out a deal for him to retain his scholarship and only go part-time. Even then, his political savvy for negotiation was shining. He called Stanford and told them. The dean of the political science department gave Bo some advice he never forgot. "I like this plan, Mr. Rutili. We are sad not to have you here, but you will learn more by doing the right thing in life than any classroom can teach you."

For a decade Bo carried those words and that responsibility to his grandmother. He didn't have a chance to miss her until just now. He knows the tears are there as he waits in the darkness of shut eyes, but nothing comes. His throat goes dry and painful.

One responsibility is over and another is just starting to boil. So he opens his eyes, but his throat still aches like sobbing. Bo determines not to speak. Making his way to the car, dodging countless mourners, the funeral reminds the mayor of a Town Hall meeting.

"*We're going to handle this in a swift, professional manner.*" Blubber-jawed bartender Murray Kreskin does his Rutili impression, shaking the mayor's hand. A certain agony overcomes Bo's eyes, listening to his own voice fed back to him. "Just like you said, me and the rest of the volunteer firefighters are here to evacuate folks before it lands."

"I know you told everyone, *only take what you need to live for a few days,*" Joyce Camden says a few minutes later, quietly, as if this helps respect the dead. "But I think I'll take my birds. Haley loves them so much."

The mayor nods, grief tightening its chokehold.

"It was a brave speech you gave this afternoon, Bo," Chief Grover says a little further down the line, giving his belt a jingle. "It'll be hard, abandoning ship in three days, but I'll do what I can. And it sounds like the National Guard will be a big help. I know you're going through tough times, but just know I'll make this transition as simple as possible. Also, I'll start looking into this Rajula Magbi thing. God that's weird."

Bo nods and senses those tears plumping his eyes again. He stares off, like trying to map the clouds at sunset.

The Chief doesn't see this going anywhere and steps back into the crowd without a goodbye.

"That idiot." Bo hears a dagger-sharp whisper from the crowd while he walks toward his car. "Who does he think he is, shutting the whole town down? I have orders to fill. I hope this stupid satellite destroys Dyson. Wait, better yet," Troy Gomez chuckles, "I hope *nothing* happens. That would teach him for overreacting. Nobody'd trust Bo again."

Marci walks with the mass of mourners. She speeds and slows her pace, eying Bo. He looks so ragged, his eyes have gone completely sour.

"Hey Marci, wow, you look great." Troy Gomez adjusts a black necktie. "I had a moment of inspiration back there. Maybe it was all Father Donnigan's religion talk, but this satellite has me thinking."

Troy slides in close. Technically, Marci is an employee of his father's company—FruitCo owns the museum—so he wonders if there is a line. Is it an HR violation to wipe a tear from her eye or, say, go ahead with his original evacuation plan and invite her to Acapulco?

Marci's voice is distant. She runs her naked fingers over the cool tombstone tops. "Thinking about how short it all is and how we shouldn't waste time? How we shouldn't wait for life to find us? Like maybe it's time to move on to something better?"

Gomez's face evolves to a wrinkled pucker. "Well . . . sure, yeah. Since you bring it up, taking charge of life sounds good. I'm all for it." *She's sending you a sign*, he thinks and determines to wrap a loving arm around her shoulder. He makes a few false starts, but gives up. "Actually, I'm thinking about the Rosinski Festival."

Maybe it's the funeral, maybe it's the impending doom, but something has turned this normally sunny girl darker than normal. "Who cares about the festival?"

"Oh, now, you're too pretty to frown like that."

That frown bends deeper.

"Hold on. Just one second. Hear me out here." Troy gives her body a quick scan. He doesn't agree with all the drunks at the bar, saying Marci has a big ass and a bad complexion. "What if we really worked hard on the Festival and rescheduled it for," his throat clears, "next week?"

"Next week?"

"Next week."

"The festival is scheduled in six months, to encourage Christmas shopping from tourists, remember?"

"Right, right. That's what Mayor *Dipshit* said." That makes Marci laugh. Her cheeks go red and the chuckle vanishes, but Troy heard it. It was encouraging. "I mean, I feel for the guy losing his grandma. But stand back and ask, what Christmas shopping was Bo referring to? His hoity-toity liquor store? Stick with me here: when this satellite hits there'll be newspapers and television from around the world." Troy grows boyish. "What better time to show off our town spirit and its leading export than by having the festival *then?*"

This, Marci realizes, could make the mayor *ache,* seeing her and Troy accomplish the impossible without him. It's a guilty feeling, conspiring against a guy at a funeral for the woman who raised him, but Marci realizes it's time she thought about herself for once and not him. "You're nuts, Troy. But I'm in."

Cody Kellogg turns the ignition and waits for the procession to leave the cemetery. He checks a phone message that vibrated during the funeral.

"If this is Donna begging me back to the station, I have demands." He enjoys hearing himself broadcast from the mouthpiece and into his ear while voicemail picks up. Like a private radio show.

"Cody, Mark Grauman here. Boy, was I surprised to get your phone call. Heard about this satellite business. Well, long story short, I'm sorry, but we just don't see much of a story in it. If someone gets flattened by a solar panel or something, call me. But right now nobody cares about some patch of corn out in B.F.E. Best of luck. Next time you're in Manhattan, swing by and say hi."

Kellogg lets the phone rest against his ear for a moment. The heat from rolled-up windows is thick as sand.

"Oh, the humanity," Cody says, head resting against the steering wheel, quoting his favorite radio broadcast: the Hindenburg Disaster. "Oh, the humanity," he repeats a handful of times.

Thinking about whether or not he has enough gas money to even get out of town ignites the tiny spark inside that nitrogen-filled zeppelin. But the prospect of finding a new job amongst all the computerized playlists and wacky drive time DJs turns his little blimp into a bomb. His thumping heart crashes to the ground as onlookers flee for their lives.

Mark Grauman was the last name in Cody's black book.

Packwicz pulls the Chief close and tells him about meeting the mummy. Foie gras looks horrible, but tastes delicious, he says. He leaves out the part about swan diving off Dyson's tallest building.

Shaky and licking lips, maybe looking for a morsel of delicious goose guts for strength, Packy waits for the police officer's reply.

There isn't one.

"I've been thinking, you know, about fate." Packy wipes sweat from his head, because the idea of fate—of some special message airmailed directly to him—makes Dyson's former mayor equal parts nervous and excited. "There's a satellite crashing down, and there's a mummy on the loose. It seems like maybe someone upstairs is telling us something."

"Packy." The jangle of a hundred keys fills the air. "Sometimes a mummy is just a mummy." Grover removes his sunglasses and leans in to whisper close. "But there is no mummy."

A mummy isn't *just* a mummy, but Chief Grover's mind is preoccupied. He weaves in and out of funeral goers, stalking Joyce Camden.

She wipes tears and slips a cigarette lighter from her purse. The flint wheel spins with a constant click. Joyce is lovely in black with her full cheeks and hair twisted up ballerina-style.

"Joyce, hey, I was hoping to catch you." The Chief stands very close, blocking her path. "What time do you want me to come over and help you and Haley pack?"

"Help? I don't think that's a good idea." She moves to break eye contact. "Plus, who knows, maybe we'll stay put. I mean, what are the odds something would hit our house?"

Grover's normally sleepy eyes grow large and round. "You have to. It's an order from the mayor."

"Eh, we'll just get a hotel somewhere," she says, looking beyond the Chief and clicking the lighter.

"Well, now, you know you can always go stay at my mom's house in Findlay. She loves you and hardly gets to see Haley."

"Oh, God, we'll never get any sleep, Bert." She sighs, fishing a cigarette from her purse and lighting it. "All that *singing*. I do not want my daughter picking up Italian. I thought we'd hit rock bottom with Haley's drug fiasco. Opera trumps angel dust in my book."

"*Our* daughter, and you used to love singing. And Italian. Both together, remember?" He searches her familiar eyes for that long-forgotten look. The look of happiness after a performing *The Barber of Seville*, Strauss' *Elektra*, Wagner's *Siegfried*. But those high notes are replaced by a world where falling satellites and destroyed hometowns can't even bring back their love.

"I think the police chief has a full enough plate without trying to wine and dine me, thanks."

Eugene Rutili steps around a puddle, keeping his feet dry and marveling at the crowd. "I didn't realize this many people still lived here," he says, low and casual. "I just pictured the streets empty and the houses vacant. Nothing."

He pauses a moment, looking over a grave he hasn't seen in years. He removes his glasses, fogs the lenses, and wipes them.

"Is this a relative?" Sloan asks, hovering above a tombstone, massaging her belly.

"My mother and father."

"I'm sorry, sweetheart." She rests a hand on his back.

"Bo and I never quite understood one another after that."

"Well, like I said." Sloan smiles and pinches his arm. "It's time for a new start. I don't want this baby growing up without an Uncle Bo. And I don't want you growing up without a brother. It's not healthy."

Wendell Dixon finds his car and hops on the bumper so his head is above the crowd.

His afternoon has been full of unpleasant meetings—mostly about his responsibility to hang around this deathtrap longer than everyone else since he is a volunteer fireman—but that isn't what pretzels his intestines. Frankly, the lawyer was relaxed until he pulled out a will from a disjointed file cabinet before the funeral.

"Where is the mayor?" he says under his breath. "Come on, come on, come on."

He's worried about evacuating his wife before things fall from the sky. And he's worried about Stephanie's infidelities. Probably leaving him for someone more successful, or worse, less successful and mummified. But that isn't exactly what makes Dixon want to vomit.

Dixon begins to gasp, practically jogging across the cemetery toward the Mayor's brother. He tugs his necktie loose, anticipating cool air hitting a red throbbing neck.

"Eugene, right?" Wendell says smooth enough for late night commercials. He latches the tall man's arm. A sharp face and oversized glasses look down on the lawyer. "You don't remember me do you?"

"I'm sorry," his voice is deep. His limbs are long and beveled with muscle. He wears one of those intentional five o'clock shadows.

"Wendell Dixon. *Coach* Dixon." They shake hands.

"Oh, sure. Good to see you. This is Sloan."

Dixon shakes the woman's surprisingly strong hand. She is pretty in a softball-player sort of way, muscled and short, except with an obvious bump. "You haven't grown much since junior high, Gene. Thank God." He shifts his attention. "Your husband was about two feet taller than the other kids. His basketball scoring record still stands for eighth graders."

"We're not married," she says.

The giant nods. "It was nice talking. Thanks for coming." Eugene turns around.

A stressed purple vein reappears near Wendell's temple.

How am I going to explain this to the Rutilis? he thought earlier, looking over this shocking paperwork on his cluttered desk before the funeral.

"Eugene, quick question. Will you be in town long?"

A few feet ahead, he turns. "In *Dyson?* No, I have work to get back to."

"Well, I need to meet with you and your brother soon. Hopefully tomorrow? Edna left a very interesting will and we'd all better review it together. You, Bo, and myself."

Wendell's neck feels like a pitcher of cold water has rushed down his shirt collar. It is the fresh air. *There, that wasn't so hard.*

Donna is not amused by being ambushed beside her car like this. Packwicz dragging along the mayor is never a good sign. She doesn't look, just flips through her phone, even though she has no messages.

If there are two people on this planet she doesn't care to see, it's this pair.

"I'm glad I caught you both," Packy says, forcing a grin. "I have something important to say."

Bo stands silent, glaring at Queen.

"I told myself not to do this, and it was very hard for me," says Packy.

"Yippee," says Donna.

"Listen. I love this town more than anything, so I want you both to shake hands. I always say a funeral isn't about an end, it's about new beginnings."

"You used that line at every funeral you ever spoke at when you were mayor," Donna says. "Gag."

"I did say it a bunch. That's because it's just about the most honest thing I ever heard."

"Begin what, exactly?" Donna says. She checks her phone and taps a few keys.

"I want you two to shake hands. Are you blind? You two are the most powerful people in Dyson. It doesn't take a genius to see what good could come of you putting your heads together."

"Good thing there are no geniuses here." She gives them both a half glance before returning to her phone.

Bo remains silent, looking very uncomfortable.

"I know nobody believes a word I say these days and for good reason. It's just, I want what's best for everyone. In order to do that, you both need to work together. It hit me the other day, *crash*, like a boulder."

"Cute. I'm honored," Donna says. "I'll try and say something as charming at both of your funerals." She turns to walk away and glares at Bo. "Hopefully yours first, you little brat."

Garrett Queen peels away from the crowd. He weaves between head-stones toward the mausoleum. His bald head is dotted with sweat, and his white mustache is matted wet. Garrett leans into the rusty gate covering the door. Iron bars squeal as he steps through the dark entrance. "I bet I know where you are, bastard. Just call my insurance agent and nobody gets hurt."

"Oh, hey, Bo. I wanted to tell you something," Pearl says.

He is climbing into his car, silent, still dazed. He looks up at her, cool shades and tight black dress.

"Thanks," she says. Her lips begin to shake.

Bo coughs and debates whether to speak. He stands and knows he can't resist helping someone in need. "Is everything okay?"

"Yeah. Sure. I just wanted to say thank you for . . . helping me write that letter way back when to *America's Boringest City*. Nobody else cared. You did. That was . . . " Waterlogged mascara begins running down her cheek from behind sunglasses. She sniffles. "It was really cool meeting Rajula Magbi and . . . "

Pearl begins to heave with tears. Her shoulders bending hard and awkward.

Bo steps near and hugs her.

"I'm sure you heard about her . . . her accident." Pearl's voice is torn apart.

"Yeah." It's all he can manage, picturing the lovely reporter.

"She was good. She was nice. She was . . . damn this stupid town."

They stand by Bo's dented, discolored Taurus.

Pearl is moaning with tears. It spreads to Bo slowly, starting with a sting in his eyes.

"She didn't deserve to die. She . . . she . . . she had a heart problem."

"I didn't know that," said Bo, trying for anything to take his mind away from this heartbroken place. He didn't realize how badly he missed Rajula, after only knowing her this long. "I did know—" He snuffs back the wetness in his nose. "I knew she was a vegetarian."

"Really?" Pearl says with wonder.

"Hadn't had a bite of meat since her last boyfriend was in the picture."

"How did you know that?" Pearl asked.

Together, they cry under the brutal summer sun as other cars start and drive off. There is movement in the sky, a clutch of dark birds briefly overhead.

They share tears for another few seconds, both struggling to stop and to say something to end this back and forth, each unaware of the other's sadness.

"This stupid town," says Pearl. She pulls back and lowers her glasses to reveal bloodshot eyes and the muck of wet makeup. "I hate it. Tell me you don't. Tell me you don't hate this stupid, awful place."

He stands for a moment, unable to move from her accusation. "I don't think it's that simple."

PART TWO

That speck of pepper has done it.

Where once it was a nameless black dot along a state highway, Dyson is now getting noticed. Sneezes are happening because of this pepper. Policymakers and average people from around the country are *just* starting to know the name.

Not yet are they finding a faint pulse hiding beneath Main Street and its crumbling brick storefronts. Not yet have millions come to see Christmas Park as a symbol of much more than tacky holiday tourism gone wrong. Not yet has something as simple as a plastic collection of apples and bananas become the subject of a national controversy.

Right now, the only people who care about little Dyson are those in uniforms in charge of turning it into a ghost town.

In two days, Dyson's pulse is scheduled to freeze. No residents. No traffic. No electricity. A lot more nothing than usual.

The National Guard quickly covers the town and begins a job they consider easier than scooping beans at Fort Johnson's mess hall. Keeping people from Dyson requires fewer GIs than it takes to pilot an Abrams Tank. Satellite duty is a vacation compared to the endless marches and drills back at base.

They stand at the city limits with long dark guns at their hips, holding stop signs and redirecting cars. From these posts, the town is nothing but a tight cluster of trees surrounded by endless fields of crops.

A mild level of chaos hums through Dyson's streets. "Code Beige," the military jokes. There is a run on fuel and some people want to stay home, but mostly the National Guard's mumbled bullhorn orders from atop camouflaged trucks do the trick.

The previous day's breeze has disappeared and a heavy, wet humidity blankets everything. Clothes weigh more, air breathes thicker, muscles move slower.

Army electricians storm the small brick building that controls Dyson's power. They spend ten minutes looking at the grid and the rest of the afternoon napping in trucks. Dyson's system is about as electrically complicated as a Ferris wheel. Soldiers have two more days to wander the streets and ask themselves, "Why do small towns even exist when you could move somewhere good?"

The civil engineer corps has an equally simple time determining how to cut the natural gas from the city and, like their camouflage comrades, soon discover what Dyson does for fun.

They discover the Kreskin Inn.

SATURDAY, 10:00 AM

Everything in that dusty museum reminds Marci of her boyfriend. *Ex-boyfriend*, she corrects herself confidently, but still with a fringe of sadness to it all. Losing something always does this to her, even if it's time to go. She tries pulling out of this catatonic state to work on parade floats and costumes, but some sinking magnetism escorts her around the haunting exhibits.

I've been here every weekday for five years and never actually saw what kind of museum it is, she thinks.

Outside, the streets are jammed with cars. The air is choppy with an endless blast of bullhorns. There is disorientation on so many levels.

Before this moment, Gerald Rosinski's first pear mold was just some hollow metal shell on display. Prior to this afternoon, that bizarre page from Rosinski's diary was just a scribble. During sleepy-headed days when nobody visited, the "Imitation Fruit in the Twenty-First Century" exhibit was just some relic of what the Gomez family thought 2015 would really look like when they opened this museum years ago.

But since deciding she doesn't need Bo treating her like trash, Marci's life is colored with fresh paint. Where previously she would have collapsed with self-doubt, she has found strength. She is punching with muscles she never even knew she owned.

Marci remembers Bo walking into the Destination: Dyson meeting with that woman from *America's Boringest City*, her dark skin and large eyes.

Without even noticing, the idea of marriage has been scrubbed with steel wool until it is nothing but a collection of dents and scratches and ugliness. A relic from her past. "God, the rest of your life would be spent listening to Bo rattle on and on about sewer problems," she tells herself. She pounds the counter and a wire postcard rack shakes. "Meanwhile, he wouldn't hear a single word you ever said. No thanks. Do you think he'd ever encourage you? Compliment you? Love you?"

As long as she can remember, Marci has been clapping her hands and whistling, waiting for life to hop into her lap. But life, she realizes, is a selfish puppy and not willing to share.

Everything comes to an end.

It didn't feel so cold and lonely five years ago. A pre-mayoral Bo had walked in rubbing his hands together that drafty January afternoon, watching Marci's breath fog around the postcard rack. They didn't recognize one another, and he kept browsing the museum.

"What the heck is this?" he asked, over one of the glass cases.

"Oddly enough, that's Mister Rosinski's diary." Instantly she liked Bo's scent—faded shaving cream and fruity shampoo.

Her vision didn't automatically turn to white weddings when they met. Frankly, Marci was more annoyed than anything.

"Is that in Spanish?"

"I wish," she grumbled. "It's some code. Letters, numbers, pictures of fruit, all jumbled up. The guy was not born to be a rocket scientist." She looked at Bo and released one of her signature laughs: a warm, contagious bubble of happiness.

That's all it took for Bo. "Hey, Marci, right? Wow, I didn't recognize you. You look great. Holy cow, how long has it been?"

"Wow, I don't know." Flirting eyes instantly lit up. "Years."

He noticed a tag and tucked it back into her shirt.

They began dating soon after. One night, Bo helped clean up after a pack of school children left the exhibits for dead. They placed the antique pear mold back into position. Their hands brushed together and Bo grabbed tight. "I love you," he said.

They spent hours talking. Bo asked questions about what she wanted to do in life. Where her dream vacation was. Her favorite meals. Her fears. She never had a boyfriend dig like that, and she loved it. They didn't agree on everything, but they understood one another. Neither had ever felt that kind of understanding before.

A few weeks later, Marci and Bo stumbled over from the Kreskin Inn and kept the lights off. The first time they slept together, Marci's jeans hung over the twenty-first century mannequin's space suit. Her famous giggle burst to life each time Bo pushed harder and the spaceship walls shook. One-by-one, like an orchard in a hurricane, plastic fruit snapped from fishing lines and dropped across his damp, bare back.

A few years later, he won the election and things changed.

A National Guard siren shakes Marci's focus, and she flicks a dangling peach. She dabs her eyes. That famous giggle comes back, low and weak, at the thought: *If nobody's around when a town falls, does it make a sound?*

She looks out the window; cars are lined around the gas station for three blocks. The convenience store ran out of supplies hours earlier. Men in green military uniforms direct traffic under the blazing heat.

"Will I miss you if you go?" she asks the streets, the boarded up buildings, and the nuggets of memory buried around town. "Will anyone miss you?"

"You'll miss me. No doubt about it," a strong voice says from the back of the museum.

Marci doesn't turn because the voice doesn't exist. It comes from a man who died in 1933 and whisks her away to Tahiti whenever life gets tough or boring.

"You can save Dyson, darling," her imaginary boyfriend, Gerald Rosinski, says. He is dapper in a tailored, three-piece herringbone suit, a brushy mustache, and eyes that explode with confidence. Historically dashing. "Bo would be so jealous. It'd burn him alive when you said you wanted to break up."

"So?"

"Maybe then you'd get what you really want."

SATURDAY, 10:30 AM

Hours of free jazz didn't make it go away. The one thing that kept her sane—her tuneless but heartfelt dancing to Ornette Coleman's quacking saxophone—helped, but didn't soften the pain. So she turned to her other vice.

Now she can't stop.

A sugar rush whisks Pearl Krupp through the streets. She considers driving, but knows traveling by foot will be faster. She's taken in maybe a gallon of ice cream since her hero died.

The pretty Krupp sister's bare feet burn across scalding summer sidewalk. A Jackson Pollack of Mint Chocolate Chip, Rocky Road, and Cherry Cordial splatter her shirt. A pint of chocolate pumps in her fist.

Cars hum past the girl as honks and the buzz of locusts mix together amidst Dyson's humid skies. Clouds of summer bugs prey on her flesh and her sugar.

A gooey choco-smeared smile grows when she reaches the gas station. At the head of the line is the *America's Boringest City* van. Pearl's brain plunges into another worried gulch. Why does something always get in the way of leaving Dyson?

Once again, a spoonful of ice cream freezes that quitter mentality along with its yucky emotions. Inhibitions go blank as vanilla.

"Excuse me, Mr. Director." She sneaks up on the middle-aged man pumping gas. Krupp's big sunglasses reflect his image as she latches his arm. "It's me, Pearl. Hi."

His face jerks into tragic territory upon receiving a mint chocolate handprint on his shirt. "Jesus, did a Baskin Robbins explode?"

Her mind is a vibrating pair of bee wings and this doesn't even penetrate the wall of sugary denial. "Take me with you. I can fill in for Rajula. I'm up to it. Take me to Hollywood, please."

The director looks around, embarrassed for her. Pearl's hands are shaking, clumps of something delicious harden in her hair and he counts stray rainbow sprinkles in her teeth. How can this be the sexy woman he met yesterday, the one he couldn't stop staring at?

"Listen, the crew's had a rough one. We have to sign some papers at the mortician's and hit the road. This town is dangerous. Rumor is that satellite could land any minute. You should evacuate, too." He stammers for a bit. "But not with us."

"No." The urge to spoon more ice cream and close off doubt calls, but she can't move.

"Maybe shower first. You know, get some of that . . . " He plucks a hardened maraschino from her shoulder. "*Off.*"

"*No,*" she says louder.

"Best of luck." The director pulls out the squeegee and cleans the windshield for a few minutes, ignoring the tears slipping down her cheeks.

A waiting car honks wildly.

"Hey, Bruce." The cameraman exits the store holding a phone to his ear. "We aren't going anywhere."

"Bullshit. Get in the van, Skinny."

"No, it's Network. They've got an assignment." He passes the phone. The director nods and says very little as the entire line of cars lay on their horns. He hangs up and consults Skinny, but speaks loud enough for Pearl to hear.

"The National Guard isn't letting any media into Dyson. We're the only people on Earth able to get first-hand footage."

"So what are you saying, Bruce?" the cameraman says.

"I'm saying we're staying put and calling in a favor from the boss's old friend." Turning, facing Pearl, he pinches the bridge of his nose and snaps both eyes shut. "Alright. You want to help?"

Her back straightens, and she flattens wrecked hair. "I'm ready to go on the air right now," she declares, rubbing goo from her lips. "The light looks good over there."

"Not so fast. My producer wants us to find a guy named Cody Kellogg. You familiar?"

SATURDAY, 1:00 PM

Most people would be a little nervous, arguing with a linebacker holding an assault rifle. The average citizen would simply turn her car around after disagreeing with a trained killer. Sadly, there is no amount of military preparation and target practice to match one particular temper nearing nuclear meltdown levels.

Most people aren't Donna Queen with a chip on her shoulder.

"Listen, weekend warrior." A long red fingernail dives into the soldier's nametag. "I am a business owner in Dyson and *you* and your little buddy over there cannot stop me. There are looters. Thanks for stopping them. Good job out here sticking your thumb where it don't belong."

The city limit is dead space. Grain fields the color of pyramids and honey and pineapple rustle in the tight breeze. Dyson's boondocks offer nothing but humidity and asphalt. Worms of heat wiggle above the road, turning the nearby village into a desert mirage.

"Ma'am, we have instructions from the mayor. Nobody enters the city."

Her lips fart: "*The mayor?* Get serious."

"Please turn your automobile around or we will arrest you." Beyond all his impenetrable muscle, the man's nose wrinkles a few times, catching Donna's bold perfume.

"I'm sorry, what did you say?" She steps closer with such force the soldier's innards tighten the way only rabid drill sergeants have made them.

His sneering, clean-shaven oval face stays frozen. Mr. Weekend Warrior repeats the words his supervising officer instructed him to use at the morning briefing. "*Nobody* is allowed beyond his checkpoint. Not the president, not God, or even the Easter Bunny."

Donna's voice grows airy and her finger pulls back. "That was pretty firm."

The soldier's heart slows, appreciating the victory. Flies and gnats land on his sunburnt neck.

Donna removes mirrored shades and nibbles on the end. "What do you do when you aren't playing dress-up and keeping everyone from their homes?"

The soldier recalls psychological training. The woman's voice shifted tone, something is up but he doesn't know what. The man reminds himself to keep quiet. If interrogated by the enemy, only give your name, rank, and serial number. His innards remain coiled.

"Ma'am?" He wants to crush the fly biting his salty neck, but holds still.

"Your job." She eyes the soldier from toes to eyes. "How do you earn a living?"

His nose twitches. He doesn't see any harm. "Tow truck driver, ma'am." He adjusts his stance.

"Gawd, I bet that pays like shit." She opens her purse and hands him a fresh Donna Urinating Bear-Queen business card. "I'm opening a casino down the road. I need someone to run security. Muscles, I think you're the man for the job. We're a little short staffed. My husband and I waited around for interviews today, but nobody showed. Apparently, my radio broadcast didn't beam out or . . . whatever radios do . . . you know. Not your problem. Point is, my husband, Garrett, and I are starting some grassroots hiring." She gets a little flirty. "Give me a call when you're off duty."

"I'll consider it, ma'am." Muscles doesn't notice the gnawing fly anymore.

"Great. I'll be waiting. Now, please, let me properly lock my bank, radio station, and pizza parlor so I can save enough money to pay your salary."

"Thank you, Donna," he says outside of his tough soldier character. Her stomach wobbles with pleasant electric waves, seeing what happens when she is nice to people. It isn't something she's used to.

"We open in three days, I'll see you soon."

"Ma'am, that's when the satellite is supposed to . . ." He clears his throat. "You know."

"One little disaster won't stop us. Will it, Muscles?"

SATURDAY, 1:45 PM

"It's fate, that's what it is. You can't stop it," Packy says to himself, whittling a stick. He wears a rumpled denim shirt and jeans. "Fate's fatal."

Christmas Park is the centerpiece of Dyson. A greenspace taking up an entire city block with fat green pines and leggy oaks. Thousands of branches dance overhead, swarming with birds. The breeze and pine needles mix into a smell of clean hardwood floors.

"Everything comes to an end, Packwicz. Even you. That's fate."

Christmas Park's focal point is an enormous plastic snowman. With that awkward frozen smile, the jolly snowstack watches the panic around the park. On the bordering streets, heavy traffic zips around bullhorn squawk, and car horns marry into a single, wild static. This anxiety floods Dyson's citizens and hangs off their limbs and urges them to curl into fetal safety tucks. It's armageddon ringing the doorbell.

Whittling always helps Packy focus. Shaving away bark is better than a morning cup of coffee. As mayor, his drawer held an assortment of pocketknives, a bundle of sticks always stashed under the desk.

Packy finds the core, finishing the fine blonde point with a few light strokes, and sets it next to the bench. A stack of sharp, crooked branches piles just a little taller. Either he is doing some serious thinking or building a fort.

He looks up and a thin white cloud stretches across the sky. The jetliner making the trail is a dark speck inching across his vision until it goes behind a tree. That delicate rope of exhaust captures his attention for a much longer time than most people.

Packy convinces himself fate is kind of like that plane flight. Your little 757 is going to slowly get from Point A to Point B and there is no exit between. Whatever is bound to happen is inevitable. Whether it is God, some tiny angel in his head, or even a mummy, Packy doesn't much care. He will be a mummy himself someday, and even he can't predict when.

He looks back up and tries imaging the few hundred people on that plane, trying to get comfortable in their unsavory surroundings, watching some film they'd never pay money to see anywhere else.

"In-flight movie," he mutters, shucking another virgin stick with the silver blade, sawdusting the air. In-flight movies distract people on their way from Point A to Point B. In the real world, things like gossip and being mayor and winning lotteries and foie gras create pointless filler until the mortician throws a sheet over your head. Life, he thinks, is an in-flight movie.

The reason he has spent most of the night and morning carving sticks is simple. Packy needs to know which way fate is pointing: is it inevitable that Donna Queen and the biggest distraction of his life are pushing him to suicide? Or is he supposed to wait around for this satellite and let gravity finish the job?

One last time he looks up at the fading white cloud. Next, he imagines a satellite crossing that path, leaving its own smoke trail. X marks the spot.

Packwicz continues grinding away with that pocketknife, building the stack taller, until the answer becomes clear.

SATURDAY 4:00 PM

Skeet owns an industrial-sized truck with tall sidewalls along the bed. When he finishes loads of corn or soybeans, he fills the truck to the spilling point and drives to the grain elevator. With shocks pressed tight against the frame, he can haul several tons.

This yellow behemoth, now chipping and fading back to its original green, is the perfect tool for his treasure hunt. The rebuilt engine runs like new and, beyond the paint, the only blemish is a crumpled right front—bashed like a broken cheekbone.

"Skeet, don't you think maybe you should be packing a suitcase and finding a hotel somewhere?" Dyson's lone sanitation worker says, planning to snag a favorite hat from his office. He's in a hurry, but can't just walk past the town's finest basketball player taking a ratchet to a bronze statue on Town Hall's front steps.

A flag snaps above them. The sun is blocked by a tight flock of dirty clouds. Skeet smells like he just played four quarters at point guard.

"I'm not Skeet today, Chris. I'm *Deputy* Brown," he says filling with accomplishment as the first fat nut pops loose under the ratchet. "And I order you to wait a sec and help me get ol' Hans into the back of my truck."

Hans Dyson founded the town in 1872. Not much is known about the German immigrant other than his love of the accordion and farming. During America's 1976 Bicentennial Celebration, the town commissioned this statue of its founder. It's a plain man with a large beard, holding an acordian and a shovel.

"I don't think that's how deputizing works. Shouldn't you be out, you know, upholding the law?" Chris is thin and quizzical. A family man.

"Grover deputized me to help make sure folks evacuate." Skeet wipes sweat with a rag and points toward a trail of Humvees loaded with bullhorn barking soldiers. "Right now, the National Guard is covering everything. So I'm out of work. Heck, Chief Grover's off investigating stuff right now that has absolutely *zip* to do with satellites."

"So you're stealing the statue?" He looks into Skeet's face—all those hard lines of pink, flaky skin.

"*Preserving*, Chris, preserving." The second and third bolt around Hans Dyson's feet twist off easily. "I was really disappointed after my proposal got shot down at Town Hall. It's like nobody cares about the past. Then it hits me—if this place gets bombed, what'll happen to our history? Nobody's thinking about preserving our legacy, they're just thinking about themselves. Imagine all those cities in Germany and Japan after World War II. Do you know anything about Dresden or Nagasaki? I sure as hell don't. I can't let that happen to us. I've got the vision to save our memories."

"Well, *Deputy*, what good are memories and legacies and all that horseshit if Dyson's a square mile of nothin'?" Chris slips his weight on one leg and chaws some tobacco. "Besides, what about the bad memories? Those are here too. You of all people should know this town ain't all rose petals, Skeet. You'd be faking history." He is silent for moment. "God rest her soul."

Chris is referring to what happened to Skeet's wife fifteen years ago. Skeet ignores those emotions, longing for the past so hard. Back when she was still alive.

"I've been doing some thinking." Skeet grunts and the fourth bolt pops free. A rush of pride fills him. This is the right thing to do.

"All a town is is memories. It's like a giant catalog of the stuff. I remember watching the mayor dedicate this statue in seventy-six. I was in high school, dressed like Abe Lincoln, drunk off my ass that Independence Day. Gave Tammy Richter a sip from my flask, and she returned the favor with a hand job later that night."

"*Tammy?* She was smokin' hot. You should put up a plaque commemorating *that*."

Skeet stands and lets go of the statue, rubbing a forearm across his hot brow.

Hans Dyson is poorly crafted and unbalanced. The statue topples in a flash of tarnished copper lightning. A deep metallic clatter echoes down Main Street.

"Sorry, Hans. I'll do better with the rest of my list," Skeet says. "Come on, Chris. Help me load him into the truck."

SATURDAY, 4:02 PM

Confusion is a thief. It robs the mayor's face of color. It snatches his concentration. It leaves Bo's vaults empty, except for a burning urge to take responsibility for saving this dying town.

The thick metallic explosion of Hans Dyson striking the cement makes Wendell Dixon jump and sprout a pair of eyes three-times larger. "What was that?" he yelps to his guests across the wrecked office. An oscillating fan flutters papers. A silver framed picture of his wife, Stephanie, glints in the light. The room smells old and moist.

Dixon's nerves are frayed beyond repair. Since reading the headline of yesterday's *Gazette*, the drinks all but pour themselves. His normally perfect hair resembles an unweeded garden, and a new crop of purple veins crisscross his face. Dixon's oxford shirt is mustard-stained and crusty.

"It's nothing." Bo, dressed in a golf shirt, looks like he has better things to do. He just doesn't know what. "Probably a manhole cover." He leans toward the floor. "Come here. Come here, sweetie."

Boots recovers from the statue's crash and leaps back onto Bo's lap.

"Look, Coach Dixon," Eugene says. His collar is open, displaying a silver crucifix. His face is babyish like his brother's, though with a better haircut. "I know people are worried, but nothing's going to happen. My guess is this satellite business will fizzle out and things'll be normal. Comets and space shit probably drop through the atmosphere all the time. They all burn up."

"Easy for you." Dixon pinches and focuses bloodshot eyes. "I just found out my homeowner's insurance doesn't cover satellites. Stephanie and I are three payments away from owning it outright. Twenty-some odd years of scrimping and saving." His nervous little voice syncs with jittery fingers. "She's been looking for a reason to leave me. You watch, it'll be my fault when something happens to the house."

Dixon's hand creeps toward the top desk drawer, but shakes itself free and flips open Edna's will instead.

"Wendell, I'm a little strapped for time here," Bo says. "Can we please just read this and move on?" He nuzzles the cat's fur. Boots has

Grandma's smell. The cat hasn't been out of Bo's sight since the funeral. He only speaks to it in sweet voices.

"Move on?" Dixon snorts. "That's what you think."

"Listen." Eugene smacks his hands on the table and a stack of court files topple like a bronze statue.

"Ahem . . . " Dixon shakes on reading glasses. "'I, Edna Rutili, being of sound mind and body . . . '" He pauses and breathes heavy.

"Wendell?" the mayor says.

"This section is standard," Dixon's unsteady voice replies. "Basically, she has nothing in the bank. You get the house," he points to the mayor, "but *you* get all her possessions," he points to Eugene.

"Seriously?" Bo says and looks to his brother.

Gene stares forward, blinking.

"*Seriously?*" Agony fills Bo's blank face. "Can you imagine selling a house in this economy? Not to mention the real estate market after this satellite business."

"The cross stitch? The porcelain cats? The cuckoo clock?" Gene rubs hands over his face and comes out smiling. "That stuff's mine?"

"Ah, yes, congratulations," Dixon says, distracted, running a finger, line-by-line, across the will.

"So, that's the big news? I think this could have waited." The mayor's normally cool tone grows irritated. He pets the cat with force.

"I wish it was all." Dixon dabs forehead sweat with a sleeve. He opens the desk drawer a touch and a gin bottle winks back.

"All those crock pots, the mismatched salt and pepper shakers. Hell, there has to be a couple dozen cookbooks." Eugene is nostalgic, already redecorating his and Sloan's apartment into a replica of Grandma's house. A living museum to his childhood, to happy times. "How do you think a house gets that worn-in grandma smell? Does Glade make a plug-in?"

"There is a small addition here at the bottom." The lawyer clears his throat and pats the desk drawer, telling it, *not yet, my little friend.* "This part doesn't necessarily leave you boys anything tangible. And, frankly, I debated whether to include this in the proceedings. But I had a quick look at your grandmother's health history and it seems like she was, surprisingly, of sound mind . . ."

"What? Speak up, coach."

"I'm just doubting what she wrote."

"Which is?"

"You'll think I'm nuts."

"Mr. Dixon," Bo says, half standing. "If we're playing games, I ought to go."

"She claims," his voice raises to stop Bo, "to have had an affair with Gerald Rosinski in 1933, before he was married. She goes on to call his wedding a 'sham' and the fact that Rosinski's honeymoon yacht sank near Tahiti to be, 'just what that plastic fruit-loving bastard deserved.'"

"That's screwed up," Eugene says, daydreaming about spreading his grandmother's afghans and quilts around the baby's room.

"She claims your father is the product of this affair. Basically saying you two are heirs to the FruitCo Factory."

This news doesn't sink in right away. Eugene and Bo sort through the lawyer's words, wondering whether they heard things out of order. On a surface level, the two seem deep in focus. But beneath the skin is a fireworks display of confusion.

"Now, Edna says she knows the factory was legally sold to the Gomez family, so she's not suggesting you two take control or anything ridiculous, but she claims there is other compensation."

A passing bullhorn's distortion fills the room, adding a fresh coat of paint upon the stacks of bewilderment, clutter, and tangled final testaments.

"Your grandmother says, and maybe you've heard this one before, Mr. Rosinski converted his assets into a bowl of golden fruit. An apple, a banana, an orange, two bunches of grapes, and a cherry."

"Excuse me?"

"She claims this gold is your birthright. Frankly, I don't think it exists. But, just to get my mind off the satellite, I ran some figures last night. For curiosity's sake. I couldn't sleep—something about satellites crashing from the sky kept me up. Funny, huh?" His throat clears and cheeks go red. "Rosinski's assets at the time of death were supposedly about four hundred thousand dollars. So if that was converted to gold, in today's numbers we're talking—"

Dixon shuffles through paper scraps spread across the desk.

"Fourteen-point-three million."

"Fellas, I'm sorry, I know this is probably confusing and strange. But there's one more piece. And I think that this seals the deal as far as your grandmother's mental health, in all due respect."

More racket echoes from the street. The lawyer's head moves in erratic sync with the cat. Eyes both huge. Dixon shakes off the sound and shows the brothers the bottom of the will.

There is a heading: KEY.

Under the key is a series of numbers, letters, and pictures of fruit.

SATURDAY, 4:22 PM

Projecting this voice comes naturally to Chief Bert Grover. His legendary vocal range allows for the gruff bad cop, the reassuring good cop, and a Broadway cast of others.

Leaning into a grease-faced teenager, Dyson's top law enforcer slips fingers under his belt but freezes. Good cop wouldn't jingle his keys.

"Come on, son, we'll all be better off if you just confess." The Kryk's house smells like breakfast, but nothing is cooking. The family's furnishings seem brittle, so perfectly orchestrated that a stray touch would collapse them. That's nothing new. Almost every day Grover and his hulking frame feel like they'll ruin anything they touch.

"I dressed like a burrito for Halloween, not—" The skinny Kryk boy's total confusion tells Grover everything he needs. "Not a mummy."

The Chief crosses another name off the suspect list—his fifth today. But the grilling continues, because Mr. and Mrs. Kryk are watching. It is important to let the taxpayers know they are being protected by a tough cookie. Grover's never been one to shy away from a little dramatic flair.

After a few minutes of sparring, he holds a conference with the parents on the front steps. "Normally, I tell suspects not to leave town." He looks up the trees, through the dancing leaves, to the painful blue sky. "But under the circumstances, I'll trust you to notify me if anything suspicious happens."

"Suspicious?"

"Pick up the phone if you find your son in possession of anything out of the ordinary . . . narcotics, bandages, a sarcophagus."

The street is fairly quiet when the Kryks go back inside. Most families have evacuated by noon. One man, a few doors down, anchors a piece of plywood over his windows like it's hurricane season. Traveling that fast, a stray satellite chunk would make toothpicks of it, but Bert doesn't blame the guy. Nobody really prepares for threats of extinction, no matter how much church they've been to. The townspeople have done all sorts of strange stuff lately. Some move valuables into the basement. One man hung an enormous crucifix from his chimney. Most just load cars with photo albums and jewelry.

Joyce's house is only a few blocks away, and Bert gets sweaty picturing his ex-wife and daughter trapped in a hail of shrapnel. He pulls up, and that sweat turns cold. The driveway is empty.

"Joyce," he says into a phone moments later. "You're not home."

"There's a detective joke in all this somewhere. I'm too tired to make it, though."

"Don't you need to pack?"

"It's done, Bert. Haley and I are in a motel."

"I was going to help . . ."

"We're fine. We don't need a police escort. We haven't needed your help for about five years."

"But you need my alimony?"

"Don't start. You know how our fights always end."

"You could still earn a living if you wanted. Your voice is beautiful. People want to hear it. New York threw roses at your feet. God, I could hardly focus on my lines."

"*That's plenty.* Walk down memory lane after you get people evacuated, okay?"

"National Guard's doing most of it," he says, helpless. "Hey, don't forget to stop into Mom's. She'll make you a hot meal."

"They sell hot meals at restaurants. They're everywhere outside of Dyson. Maybe you remember that from when we were famous?"

"Mom will be disappointed. She's still Haley's grandma."

"Enjoy the evacuation." The phone clicks.

Joyce's street is filled with stillness like that graveyard. These moments lift the opera elevator up Bert's gut. *Pling-Pling-Pling*, it creeps past lungs and he sucks in a breath. *Pling-Pling-Pling*, his posture straightens. *Pling-Pling-Pling*, his jaw drops and his eyes warm with tears. The funeral march from *Siegfried* begins, and his heart starts to mangle.

SATURDAY, 4:45 PM

"When did you and I . . ." Eugene touches the tips of his index fingers and moves them apart. "Split?"

His brother watches clouds curl against the blue above, wishing a satellite would smash down and save him from resurrecting the past. "I guess when Mom and Pop died."

"I don't remember us stopping being friends. Is that wrong? I remember things being good when we were kids." The brothers stand with driver's doors open, each holding a copy of Grandma's will. The sun stings the backs of their necks.

Bo has the cat curled in one arm.

"Most of it, yeah."

"And then I just remember things being awkward. Just boom, it happened one day."

"It wasn't that smooth a transition for everyone else," Bo says.

"It wasn't *that* bad after I ran away, right?"

"Listen, I'm not getting into this now. You might have noticed I have some things to worry about around here." Bo's eyebrows soak with sweat.

"I was seventeen, you know. It's not like I couldn't take care of myself."

"She missed you. You were Grandma's favorite. So, yeah, things were that bad. You disappeared for a couple years only to turn up in a Cambodian jail." Bo's mind is elsewhere, avoiding Gene's eyes. "Meanwhile, I went to college and became deputy mayor by twenty-four. But you were all Grandma ever talked about. I always thought she loved you more. She kept this little sort-of shrine to you by the bed." Bo shakes his head.

He rubs Boots; it's relaxing.

"That has nothing to do with this, and it shouldn't keep us from getting closer," Gene says. "I want to be brothers again, Bo. Please. I need a family. It took a long time to realize that."

Moments pass. Twice in less than a minute, Wendell Dixon's venetian blinds split and his nervous eyes appear.

"Look, Grandma wasn't all there anymore. I thought so the last few years, but this settles it." Bo flaps the will over his car roof.

Eugene nods stiffly. "Absolutely. I don't know if she was ever all that mentally-stable. I mean, do you remember us hunting through abandoned buildings and the woods when we were kids? Grandma talked about treasure a lot. We went on all those hunts."

"That's all the Rosinski Treasure is. Something to entertain children. Keep them busy on summer break."

"Yeah. Tough to forget," Eugene says. "Hey, before I go, just know I'm sorry for everything. I never meant to put you in that position. Let me know when you leave town you can crash at my place and catch up. I teach Tae Kwon Do every day, but I can cut out early for you. I want to talk," he says. "I guess I can't get anything now with the evacuation. I'll grab it after everything dies down."

"Poor choice of words. But, yeah, that sounds like a great idea." Bo knew from the moment he saw the will's KEY he probably wouldn't leave town. Fourteen million will more than fix the city's economic crisis. That money will bring Dyson roaring back to life. "Tell you what, get a spare bed ready for me and Boots. I'll see you tonight. I have a few loose ends to tie up. There's no doubt I'll be the last person out of town."

"Man, that just made my day. Thank you, Bo."

Troy Gomez shivers. Hammer strikes reverberate through the empty warehouse. *God,* his hand grows weak driving nails, *I'm actually going to miss this town.*

Recently—like very, very recently—Troy's sour heart was sprinkled with sugar. He drops his head and tries crying without any success.

His father's company, Gomez Plastics, owns several operations around the country. When time came for the youngest Gomez to begin running part of the family business, his father conveniently overlooked the milk jug plant in sunny Miami and the rubber hose factory in posh San Diego. Even though Troy threatened to quit, his dad decided the boy should move back where he grew up

Troy resented the offer, but relished the power. His childhood was so chaotic with moves and new stepmothers that he always needed to fill the hungry part of his gut with control. Dyson was his fondest stopover as a kid. He took the job.

That power and comforting control mutated, quickly creating an angry, bitter young man. However—very, very, very recently—golden veins of Christmas City goodwill wrapped around Troy's thorned ticker.

Before the satellite made itself known, young Gomez considered Dyson's citizens lacking the sophistication, diversity, and straight teeth he demanded since graduating from the University of Chicago. But the threat of an entire town being demolished stirred up memories. Memories whipped up worries. Worries converted Troy's anger into some unique inspiration.

Though he's been denying the facts since returning to Dyson, his childhood was a good one—riding bikes, playing shortstop, wandering through the woods, even winning a blue ribbon at the art show.

But Dyson has changed since then. It has lost its self-sufficiency, its survival skills. *If Dyson evacuates,* he thinks, while taking a weak hammer swing, *who's coming back?*

Gomez's mouth drags open another notch, deciding the answer is probably "nobody." Some people will shuffle back, but this satellite will be the end. Dyson will simply wind down and disappear with the momentum of a dying heart rate.

He sighs. *Everything comes to an end.*

Troy holds his face in both hands. Hot, worried breath steams over his eyes, and his goatee grows moist with humidity. For the last few years as manager of FruitCo, Troy has done nothing but kick this place in the mouth.

The Rosinski Festival is more than a way to get Marci in bed. The festival has the power to save Dyson and possibly this factory, too. That would give Dad something to chew on. But, hey, if sweaty hero-worshipping sex with his dream girl is included, Troy decides he'll roll with the punches.

"Coffee. A man needs coffee." His voice echoes through the warehouse.

Decades earlier, this airplane hangar was necessary for stocking eighteen-wheel trucks with an orchard of plastic produce. But lately, shifts have been drastically cut back and distribution mostly erased. Now only a few trucks from the Dollar Bomb and Deal-a-Buck stores load up each week.

In the dead space of the warehouse, Troy determines to reverse FruitCo's fortunes. A lovely pride is uncovered. Dyson and plastic fruit should survive. He is the one to do it. Staying up all night is the only solution.

Troy runs across the concrete and up the green spiral stairs to his office. He looks down across the floor, lit by a crown of dirty windows passing light like dozens of squinting eyes. This motivation to do well, or any motivation for that matter, has avoided him for most of adulthood. *It's thrilling,* he thinks, *to have a purpose.*

Troy freshens up the caffeine supply and, with steam rolling from the mug, inspiration races through him. The highlight of the parade needs to be something unforgettable. A climax capable of breathing life back into Dyson. Something that'll put smiles on faces.

To pull off this dream, he needs to make a weapon of the stone that has long been in his shoe.

The production line practically runs itself, so why not crank it up full blast?

The factory hasn't run at maximum capacity for ten years. At its peak, the production line could fill the entire warehouse with plastic fruit in twenty-four hours, floor-to-rafters.

Troy pops in *Sticky Fingers*. He cranks up the intercom. There's a humming flow of adrenaline, waiting for "Brown Sugar" to load. *Here is the moment you'll look back on after you fix everyone's problems.* He stands with alarming confidence as his favorite album nears liftoff.

A door slams just before the song rackets to life. Troy looks down and sees Marci caressing his lone parade float the way he wants to be loved.

Keith Richards strums those big famous chords, and Troy's enthusiasm bursts larger.

An enormous, papier-mâché Gerald Rosinski head, the approximate bulk of a water tower tank, rests atop wheels. Its mustache matches the wingspan of small airplanes. A bowler the dark color of dead leaves sits atop the head. Troy spent almost an entire day constructing this awkward first draft.

Marci runs her hands over every inch and nuzzles its nose.

Ten years ago, as a budding Stones fan, Troy wanted to study sculpture at art school, but Dad demanded a mechanical engineering degree. How else could he mind the factories? Grudgingly, Troy earned the Bachelor's but filled his electives with sculpture classes. This parade is shaping up to be the perfect marriage of both worlds.

"Do you want to see the finale?" he calls over the music as he descends the iron stairs.

"There can't be more!" A massive giggle plucks each word and overpowers the Rolling Stones. Marci has never seen something as beautiful as her imaginary boyfriend's head blown cartoonishly out of proportion. How could it get better?

"Stand back, I haven't tested it yet," Troy says, holding a toy car remote.

He presses a button. An airy hiss erupts into a bazooka-load of plastic fruit rainbowing from Rosinski's head. Apples, oranges, bananas, grapes, and pineapples rain down in the vivid colors of fresh tulips and sugary sodas.

Troy sees love in Marci's eyes. If Troy knew who that look was actually for, he wouldn't follow through with his vision. He wouldn't turn the antique brass key and start the factory production lines.

SATURDAY 6:30 PM

Cody Kellogg tapes another flyer to another door of another deserted house. The dull breeze flaps the orange papers across dozens of porches. His heart kicks when someone is finally home.

"Hello, ma'am." He removes the pork pie hat, bald spot moist with sweat. "My name is Cody Kellogg."

"Oh, the radio man?" a gentle elderly woman says with amazement.

"That's right—Mr. Razzle-Dazzle," he says, summoning a little on-air gusto. "I have some important information to share." Eventually she takes a fluorescent sheet.

"I thought you'd be bigger, stocky." She lifts bifocals from a neck chain. "What's this?"

"Ma'am, you're not planning on *evacuating* are you?"

"Of course. My son and his family are picking me up. My suitcase is packed." She points into her living room. "The cats are in the crates. I even took my birth control."

"I wouldn't, if I were you, " Cody stammers. "Evacuate the cats, that is." Some alarm buried under all that radio swagger blinks to life, telling Cody to shut up. Whenever these alarms sound, he reminds himself that the civilized world's laws and regulations don't apply. He has been backed into this corner by the Fart Box, and he must come out on top.

"Stay put? That sounds dangerous. The mayor and the Chief and the National Guard . . . "

He raises both hands. "Ma'am, I'm a journalist and you can trust me. You're being lied to." He lets it hang for a moment. "Why, I overheard

Mayor Rutili and Chief Grover talking the other night, in some dark alley behind the Kreskin Inn, smoking funny cigarettes—"

Cody actually cooked this plan up in the bathtub after Edna Rutili's funeral.

"They were whispering about some *hoax*. Something about robbing Dyson blind. The gist I got . . ." Cody leans close, " . . . was that we'd all return after this *evacuation* and find our valuables missing. These two bureaucrats are staging an emergency to fleece us and line City Hall's coffers."

"No?"

"Modern day Trojan Horse."

"Awful."

"The only option we good citizens have is to stay put. Fight these greed-mongers and protect Dyson. Please, urge your son and his family to stay. This pamphlet will tell you everything."

Printed in large font across orange card stock: *The Truth About Fake Satellites. Plus! NineteenElectricity-Free Dinner Recipes for a Can of Beans.*

"I don't know . . ." She lowers the spectacles and focuses on Cody.

He gulps.

Birds and locust weave each other's calls together.

" . . . are there really *nineteen* recipes?"

"Straight from my mother's heart. Those'll come in handy with no electricity or gas." That hidden alarm sounds again within him. "Ma'am, we need all the help we can get. Dyson is under attack from the inside out. We're not going to take this." He steps off the porch and gives a sweeping, political campaign wave.

Following the trail of orange flyers, the crew from *America's Boringest City* finds Cody razzle-dazzling a cigarette on an abandoned doorstep, staring at a bean can, imagining recipe number twenty.

"Mr. Kellogg, what is all this?" Pearl asks, having cleaned up her ice cream-bombed appearance. The forehead gash from nailing the countertop has scabbed pink.

"Well, it's kind of a long story." Cody continues to explain.

"Okay, okay, I get it. You can do a lot with a can of beans." The director pulls on a tuft of hair. "We're here for a reason. You know a gal named Nancy O'Doyle?"

"Used to work with her in Memphis. She produced my show. Had this peach cobbler she'd bring in on hot days, whooooo." Kellogg's hands rub fast. "But we both quit over a minor controversy. I'm sure you've all heard about the Fart Box."

"Great, sure, whatever. Well, Nancy just called. She works at our network now. The National Guard ain't letting anyone in, so we're the only media outlet for fifty miles. Our on-air talent . . . passed away," he pauses, "so Nancy suggested tracking you down."

Cody fans himself with the hat. "I never knew Nancy liked beans that much."

"No. The network needs a report from the front lines if this satellite thing happens."

Cody tosses the director a calm, uninterested look. Not breaking down with joy and screaming is is the most difficult thing he's done in years. A vision of a black and white newsreel spins in Kellogg's head—a zeppelin hemorrhaging flames. "You guys know much about Herbert Morrison?"

All say no.

"He was the guy reporting on the Hindenburg crash. The only radioman on the spot. If you remember, the broadcast starts off quiet and boring. But then everything turns into the seventh circle of hell."

"Then they all cooked beans over the flames. Happily ever after. The end. Do you want this job or should we give it to Thirty-one Flavors over here?"

"There are two reasons people remember that broadcast today." Cody stands and flicks his smoke. "One: because in the face of danger, Morrison stood strong and reported this catastrophe like a journalist should. Even with tears running down his face and humanity burning before his eyes. Two: because people died. If that blimp crashed and everyone walked away, or everyone found a life raft before the Titanic sunk, do you think that'd be more than a footnote?"

The director pops his knuckles with a neck twitch. "The job. Do-you-want-it?"

Cody points. "I'll take this work under two conditions."

"Fine."

"You guys help me pass these out." Cody flutters a sheath of orange pamphlets.

"Are you kidding? You *know* the satellite is real."

"Come on, what are you, an amateur?" Cody says. "Nobody dies if the town is empty . . . and if nobody dies, the world doesn't care about Dyson. And if nobody cares about Dyson, I'm screwed." He has a hungry, lost look in his eyes. "But if we get a few casualties . . ."

The group looks seasick. "God, alright. What's the second thing?"

"You guys don't use a Fart Box, right?"

SATURDAY, 10:37 PM

Nighttime is usually slow in Dyson, but after the evacuation, things are arctically silent.

Garrett Queen takes nervous steps down the hall above the Dyson Drop. His heart beats wild. "Wait, what if she's in there?" he whispers.

"Good. We'll all just have a *talk.*" Donna recalls those lock picking skills from the bowling alley. Often, her manager, Packwicz, wouldn't show up to open and she'd be forced to break-in simply to work.

Garrett's nose discovers a wet, musty *something.* "Then why don't we knock?"

Garrett and Donna haven't been in the gossip loop lately and missed the tragic recent death of Rajula Magbi.

"Because . . ." He can't see his wife's eyes in the darkness, which is fortunate. They are filled with a dangerous determination usually saved for the IRS. "She's probably out interviewing some idiots at the bar. I just wanted you to shut up, now shut up."

"Well then, what are we looking for?" Garrett doesn't really need to know. It just felt like the appropriate thing. He's no dummy. He realizes there is an eerie parallel between the rise of mummy sightings and this new woman in town. He isn't positive, but she looks sort of Egyptian.

A sharp metal clink fills the silence. The door swings open. Suddenly, the source of the musty old stink isn't a mystery.

"We're looking for proof," Donna says, turning on a flashlight and opening drawers. "Proof this Magbi woman has been sabotaging us. Have you noticed something strange since she arrived?"

"Yes!"

"My attempts to save Dyson are just about all but forgotten," Donna says.

"Oh, right. I did, yes." With that mummy running loose, it hadn't actually occurred to Garrett.

"Turn this room inside-out."

The pair flips the mattress, empties the dresser, and even takes framed pictures from the walls.

"I've been thinking," Garrett says, on his knees, looking under the bedframe.

"About?" Donna says, pulling apart the toilet tank.

"Maybe Dixon was right."

"Honey, I don't know what you're saying, but I can promise you Dixon is wrong, whatever it is."

"We could move anywhere. Retire. Live on our savings. I liked Paris that one time we went. I could live there. Eat that fresh bread all the time. Or the beach. You love the beach."

"Where is this coming from?"

"I just . . . look at us. This isn't who I thought we would be when we got married. We're set for life, but here we are wasting our free time going through some stranger's bedroom?"

"You can go. I can handle this if you're not up for it. Go back home and play that video game you like. The one where you shoot zombies."

"Hey." He moves to the bathroom doorway, dimly lit with a thirty-watt bulb. "I married you through thick and thin, through good times and, hell, whatever all this is, I suppose it's under that umbrella, too."

"That's sweet, but you married me because you thought you

knocked me up." She gives him a kiss and moves into the main room, scanning everything, wondering what she missed. "Now, we need to find *something*."

"I'm serious."

"Scraps of paper. Maps. Something . . . you know . . . *sinister*."

"Donna, hey. Listen to me, please. I hate when you do this. I can't even tell if you hear the words I say."

"What's to talk about?"

"We have to live our own lives. Ever since your dad's stroke, your confidence has been shot. I know you don't want to hear that, but it's true. It's been almost twelve years." Garrett sees his wife cringe at the mention of her father. "I understand. Big fish in a small pond. You're comfortable here. But I'm starting to think all this familiarity is what's holding you back."

"You are speaking a foreign language to me, bub." She tries to keep it light, but Garrett senses the dark clouds brewing inside her.

"Let's get away. Start over. I think it'd be healthy for you."

For the first time, she stops hunting. She turns shyly to Garrett in the near-dark. Her blonde hair, glimmering strings in the light. Garrett knows this look, it's rare, but he's seen it. When he swirls the tea leaves of emotion just right, they form something in Donna. These little nuggets of truth and history get her to open up and actually think about herself for once, instead of distracting herself with little jobs and chores and plans for domination.

"I was hurting for a long time," she says.

"And you thought bringing pain to everyone would make you feel better."

"Yeah," she says softly.

Garrett breathes deeply, teasing these bits from Donna carefully, so as not to scare them away. " . . . And now . . . "

"Now . . . I see helping people might be the only way to fix what's broken." A small grin forms. "It'll make Daddy proud."

"Honey, he can come with us. We'll just pay his nurse extra. Wherever we go, your dad can come."

"I am not taking him from his home. Just because he doesn't talk, doesn't mean he doesn't have feelings. It doesn't mean he's not important."

"I never said that. I love your dad. Everyone in this town loves Big Dan Wilson. It makes me very proud that we are able to take care of him. It's just . . . we need to start living for ourselves, too. This casino, running for mayor, foreclose on everyone like that. It's like you think if you do something big enough your dad will snap out of it."

"Daddy *will* snap out of it. I can see it in his eyes. The man who took me fishing and taught me to change the oil in my car is still in there. That's still the man who walked me down the aisle."

Garrett takes a long breath and rubs the flesh on his head. "Okay. You're right. Let's just try and make things good in town. We'll stay."

Donna spends a long moment looking at her husband. Her lips curl into a kind grin. "Tell you what, stick with me for a while. Let's really take a shot at making Dyson a decent place. If we can't fix the town . . . if we can't make life better for some of these schlubs, we'll move. Anywhere you want. The whole family. Me, you, and Daddy."

"Honest?"

They step close and touch. She is warm and comforting. She still gives Garrett a dizzy spell sometimes.

"I love you. We'll get through this and end up better, hell or high water. I promise."

They don't kiss, even though that was Donna's first move. Garrett glides past her lips and wraps his arms around her. A long hug, because he knows how impatient she gets. She fidgets for the first minute and finally slows her breathing and is there, in the moment with him. It's rare he can get her mind out of planning mode, and he savors it.

A wooden *crack* stops the burgling. A collapsing sound that turns the worry switches in Donna's mind. If she is caught breaking and entering, will her Dyson rescue project come to an end?

The *crack* grows louder and rattles down through her skull to her feet.

For the past few weeks one thing burns inside the Chief's stomach hotter than even an opera composed by Satan himself.

This simple question robs him of sleep.

Standing over a stack of whittled sticks in the middle of Christmas Park, Chief Bert Grover finally asks that question.

Thanks to a soft blue security light, the bandages or rags or toilet paper covering this hooligan glow at ghostly levels. The chief is too shocked to think about tugging his belt. Grover licks his top lip and finally says what has been gnawing inside. "Who are you?"

Grover exhales a long breath of built-up anxiety.

The mummy goes deep in thought, scratching the side of its head. Its foot nudges the pile of sharpened sticks until some roll to the ground. A leaping squirrel shakes tree limbs overhead.

"Okay, we'll start with an easy one. Did you whittle all these?"

The mummy looks at the Chief with black pit eyes. It shakes an ancient skull and holds up both hands, as if saying, "No way, Jose."

"Must've been Packy. Jeez, you should have seen the pile behind Town Hall back when he was calling the shots." Grover laughs. "That guy's got an obsessive personality. He's a tiger cub with a T-bone. He ain't letting go of nothing." His chuckle winds down. "Sorry. I probably shouldn't be socializing with Public Enemy Number One."

Dyson is as dark and eerie as the park. No cars, no people, no life. Just bold white moonlight covering everything.

Focus, Bert, he chastises himself. *Solve this case so you can win back your wife.*

"I'd like to take you down to the station for questioning."

The mummy's movements are gentle and friendly. It shakes its head, sort of implying: "No, thank you. I'm fine where I am."

"Now, look. I know you're just some joker playing dress-up. And I know you know there's nothing I can really take you in for. There were no fingerprints with the angel dust, and frankly, none of the other stories I've heard are illegal."

The mummy flashes a thumbs-up. A breeze buzzes between trees and converts loose wrappings to flapping banners.

"But you're scaring everyone and that's something to consider. I'm responsible for these people. It just ain't normal to be given French movies, drugs, dirty magazines, art." Bert rubs his neck. "I promised I wouldn't mention this, but Packwicz told me about that little snack behind the grain elevator. There wasn't any poison in those bird guts?"

The mummy crosses its arms the way most people would, before saying: "Just what are you implying, sir?"

"The part that has me confused is all that stuff—you can't get it in Dyson. You must've brought it in from the city. Seems to me you aren't going to rest until everyone in town has some exotic trinket they don't know what to do with. If I hear of someone going to the doctor with a case of shawarma or the babaganoush or whatever, it's your ass."

The mummy's head twitches and tilts to the side.

"Now, I got too much going on thanks to this satellite. So you and I should be friends, okay? Let's call a truce. And maybe you can at least tell me whether you're a man or a woman under all that."

The mummy strokes its chin for a long moment. Grover waits for a muffled voice to rise from the wraps. A soft, juvenile voice, probably. Grover is proud—good cop was the right character to go with tonight.

Tires squeal around the corner and a husky engine rips the quiet evening into nerve-jangling bits. A fading yellow farm truck, the kind used to haul grain, roars down the street. Powerful headlamps chew up the darkness. The truck's front corner is smashed.

Grover follows its trajectory like a shooting star.

Something falls from the back with a dense metallic clunk. It is a body. It rolls, spitting sparks as the truck speeds away. Grover runs to the street and finds the bronze statue of Hans Dyson, hot to the touch and scuffed from asphalt.

The Chief looks back but the mummy has vanished.

With a great deal of strain and cursing, he eeks Hans to the curb, out of the way of traffic. Grover wanders to the wooden bench. In front of the pile of sticks, a CD case is tied with a bow. A place card rests on top with flowery cursive writing:

To Chief Grover.
From Mummy.

SATURDAY, 10:37 PM

Slipping the rope past his ears and around his neck, Packy thinks of the last thing—the only thing—that brought true joy.

Standing on a chair, he tightens the knot so every surge of blood is a wave of pain. He gives the other end a solid tug to make sure it is securely around his apartment's ceiling beam.

Some stained, third-hand bed sits in the center of the room. Piles of clothes stew on the floor. Empty tuna cans line the kitchenette countertop.

A foggy memory of sautéed bird intestines fills Packy with warmth. That was one of the few truly surprising moments of his life. He doesn't even picture the mummified waiter anymore, just the silver tray surrounded by darkness. Never in a million years would he have ordered foie gras from a menu, which makes the overwhelming pleasure of surprise that much stronger.

An innocent part of Old Man Packwicz says there are millions of other happy surprises waiting if he'd just forgive Donna Queen. But he wants to get as far away from Donna as possible, which means death. Just the thought of Dyson's richest woman makes his teeth grit until the fillings burn.

Packwicz gives fate a final salute and kicks the chair from beneath him.

SATURDAY, 10:38 PM

Wendell Dixon's wife needs a snow shovel to get him off the Kreskin Inn's floor. Nobody offers a hand when her desperate eyes search the neon haze, not even the soldiers packing the cramped room. Stephanie Dixon grabs her husband's wrists and pulls the lawyer through the door—grunting and cursing—and into the calm Dyson darkness.

No help was offered for two reasons.

First, the National Guardsmen drank so much of Murray's beer they can barely count their fingers.

The second reason Stephanie Dixon didn't get any help is because Murray is too dazed by what Dyson's Smartest Man said before he fossilized on the barroom floor.

Murray never turns away a paying customer, but this shocking news can't wait. "Okay, ladies and gentlemen, we really appreciate your help around town," he announces, reaching behind the jukebox until it goes dark and silent. "But I have to close up and you have to get started on the evacuations early tomorrow."

Pale yellow house lights come to life. A deep groan floods the bar.

"We'll still have electricity tomorrow. Feel free to stop back for cocktails. But after that, you're on your own." Under his breath: "Crazy drunk sons-of-bitches." Murray's joyful eyes tighten until his face seems happy. It's a lot of work. They broke the pinball machine and a urinal. The soldiers got into no less than six fights tonight. Plus, they are lousy tippers. "Have a great night, drive safe. Now beat it."

"I think I'll be moving on as well," Ed Lee says, still dressed for the Battle of Antietam. He leaves Murray a generous tip and wobbles toward the door.

Murray swabs the bar with a towel, but stops, glimpsing the back of his hand. "Oh, damn, right," he mutters, snatching a felt pen. He lays that left hand flat on the bar and carefully writes a name between tattooed lines.

"I forgot to get a receipt." Ed Lee says with a slur, standing before him. "Oooh. Hey, Murray, I've always wondered what that is."

He caps the pen. "Beat it, Stonewall."

"You wrote what's-his-face's name, that lawyer."

"Ed, you know Wendell."

"That's it, Wendell Dixon. Class president, Rotarian, and amateur pilot."

Years of experience tell Murray the fastest way to get rid of a drunk is to simply answer the question. "Wendell Dixon, esquire, is now *officially* on my Shit List." He holds up the left hand.

Ed twists his neck to read upside down. "Who are the other names?"

"Nobody."

"Why are they on your Shit List?"

"Trust me, you don't want to be on my List. And if you don't and go home, you'll get there fast."

Ed covers his mouth to beat a hiccup and scoots toward the exit.

When the final guardsman leaves, Murray snaps the deadbolt tight. Kreskin hasn't sipped alcohol since taking over the Inn fifteen years ago. But tonight he plucks a bourbon bottle from the shelf and fills a shot. It burns.

He fills the glass again.

A second drink doesn't peel away the tension. He tries hard to remember the "Birth Control to Major Tom" joke, but the old adage proves wrong. Laughter isn't the best medicine. It isn't even a Band-Aid.

The front door bangs twice; someone trying to enter. They try again and the door goes silent.

"Use your head, Murray," he says to the emptiness. "Dixon was drunk. Drunks never tell the truth. But still . . . "

Spending over half his life around booze and all the tall tales that go with it, Murray can't escape stories about the Rosinski Fortune.

Normally, he laughs it off with the rest of the drinkers. But tonight, after Dixon rambled on and on about gold and all the weird details in Edna Rutili's will, Murray's famous temper shows its disfigured face.

Maybe it's the fact that he's been tricked his whole life into thinking there is no golden fruit. Maybe it's simply the idea that these riches are out there for the taking and someone else could get it first. Maybe he is going to teach them all a lesson for disrespecting him. Either way, Murray Kreskin takes an educated guess as to the treasure's whereabouts and shatters the bourbon bottle against the wall. He pulls the pistol from beneath the register and stuffs it into his pocket.

"Meant to ask you, you know Wendell Dixon? The, you know, whatever it's called, the lawyer guy." Ed Lee hiccups, stumbling through the employee entrance in the back. "He was saying something totally crazy earlier that got me thinking—"

"Beat it!"

SATURDAY, 10:40 PM

Old Man Packwicz wakes, gasping for air and swallowing floating dry-wall grains. Flat, white chunks of ceiling lie atop him. Splintered beams and other remnants of a second failed suicide ruin the apartment. Everything smells like a hardware store. The room is dark except for the orange glow from a lamp upstairs.

White soot shakes from his short push broom hair when his head kicks back. "Satellite it is," Packy hollers up to whoever pilots the airplane of fate. "I'll let the satellite finish the job. I'm through killing myself. Suicide is for the birds."

"*What* is around your neck?" The voice makes his spinal column chatter. Donna Queen rises from beneath tumbling sheetrock and wiring. Her feather boa is clotted with debris. "Packwicz, what have you done to me? I nearly broke my leg. This mess has your idiot name written all over it."

Another rattle unveils Garrett Queen. His bald head and face glow white in the dimness.

Normally, Packy does everything to avoid Dyson's power couple. But Packy knows fate has its claws wrapped tight. He is firmly planted among this disastrous suicide attempt. Here is another of life's unexpected moments. It tastes chalky, unlike delicious foie gras bliss, but Packwicz is ready to swallow.

"What have I done to you?" He rises and the frayed rope dangles from around his shoulders. "This is because of you." He swings the noose in her direction. "Because of those stupid tickets."

Donna wipes powder from her clothes and spits little dough balls. She is a ghost, covered from hair to feet. "You called in sick. How many times do we have to go over this?" Even with all the strangeness and wreckage, her voice is still bored by this familiar topic.

"It was personal."

"When coworkers chip in on Powerball tickets, you need to actually give money or you don't win. It's like . . . the . . . you know, law or something."

"I put my five dollars into the bowling alley lotto fund every week for ten years. I get the flu *one day* and you think I don't want in? I would have paid you the next day."

"But we won that night, Packy. It was too late."

"Where does that leave me?"

"With *that thing* around your neck, I guess."

"Forget suicide. I should kill *you*."

"Packy," Garrett says, stepping through the rubble with peacemaking hands raised. "You're a good guy. You were a great mayor until you let this get under your skin."

"It's not fair. I would have cut Donna in if it were her."

"Bullshit," Donna says. "I'm not the one slipping a worm into your apple, Packy. After I've seen how big of a baby you can be these last few years? Look at you—you're practically homeless. You lost your job at the bowling alley. Lost your job as mayor, too. The fact is, you don't *want* to move on, because then you'd have nobody to blame for the failure you've become. Who'd be Dyson's sympathy magnet if you actually moved on?"

"I don't have to take this."

"Go." She shoos him with both hands. "Kill yourself somewhere else. See if I care." Donna stows that sharp tone and returns with something sweeter: "But if you really wanted to find out what it's like being rich, I could help."

Packy freezes.

A cloud settles between them.

"We need someone very discreet and professional for a job. When you were mayor, you were very professional when your head was out of your ass, Packy."

"Donna?" her husband says.

"I was?" His jaw unclenches.

"But I can't stress enough, *when your head was out of your ass*."

"How much money?"

"Where's your head going to be?"

"Donna," Garrett mutters.

"I'm okay now." Packy's eyes bloom with happiness. A plank of timber crashes from the hole in the ceiling.

"Fifty-grand," she says.

"That's not rich."

"That's a *down payment*. You'll get a few million when the job is done."

"DONNA?" Garrett gestures for a private conference.

She doesn't flinch, except to mount both hands on her hips. "You do a small job for me and I'll help you. Then you can stop being a baby and learn what a pain in the ass all this money actually is. Walk a mile in my . . . you know . . . whatever."

SUNDAY, 2:00 AM

"Oh, good, you're still awake," Bo says into the phone. Downtown at this hour is dead, dark, and cool enough for a jacket. It is unlike any July he remembers. "Marci, I need a big favor. It's urgent."

"Really?" She isn't nearly as enthusiastic as Bo predicted, stretching the word into several syllables. In the year since he's taken the city's top role, she's always been there to help. He assumes one tiny late-night request won't even faze his girlfriend.

"I have Dyson's future in the palm of my hand. We're talking miracle proportions—water into wine, that kind of stuff." He uses a soothing voice that always earns some leverage with the town budget committee. "First, I pretty-pretty-please need you to open the museum."

"It's two in the morning. Relax. I'll probably be there tomorrow."

"This is a mayoral emergency. A miracle emergency." He rubs tired eyes, sensing a shift in Marci's tone. Does she know this isn't really *mayoral* business? Did she get wind of his pelvis-shattering night with Rajula Magbi? Maybe she is just paranoid about the satellite? Too bad the Kreskin Inn closed early, because he needs a drink.

Downtown's holiday lights are off, but their silhouettes swing from one side of Main Street to the other. The gentle Christmas City setting is a frigid winter blast that reminds Bo that only Marci knows his sacrifice. Only she understands he has to do everything to rescue the town. And suddenly, she seems pissed.

Bo takes no pleasure from his night in the reporter's bed. It was fun and liberating, but he realizes, once liberated, the world is lonely. There's been too much death lately, first with Grandma and then the bizarre news of Rajula Magbi. There's a bottomless well inside him that goes cold when he thinks about his own death. It's what has drawn him to Boots. It's what has made him realize he needs to focus on Marci more. *I have been selfish*, he thinks.

Old habits don't break so easy.

Her voice is dull, like a gentle palm covering the phone. "Yeah, I'll have another. Two sugars and a cream." Her famous giggle reports through the line.

"Marci, are you ordering coffee?"

"Troy and I are working super hard on the Fruit Festival. He's such a genius. His ideas are finally going to save this city."

"*His* ideas?" Bo leans against the brick wall of the Imitation Fruit Museum. His balance melts and he slides down. There is a roaring wind bellowing down that bottomless well inside him now.

Something else sneaks through the phone—Troy's voice. "Oh, hey, your tag is sticking out. Allow me."

"Listen, we need to keep working. Another load of bananas has to be started at the factory. Not to mention building floats, sewing costumes, getting fireworks . . ." A rustling fills the phone. "Troy, we're going to have to come up with some way to stay awake *all* night." Marci's giggle hits like a broken rib.

Bo wonders why Marci would want a new Dyson-saver when a perfectly fantastic mayor is right under her nose? Why buy plastic fruit when she has fresh apples at home?

He hangs up. He is once again liberated and alone.

Bo decides to just stay here.

He closes his eyes, convinced a nap isn't a horrible idea. Even in an alley of his ghost town.

He drifts and his breathing slows just before springing up in a moment of inspiration. "Grover's keys!"

Inside Town Hall, Bo makes an extra stop. He creeps into his own office and clicks on the lamp. He runs his fingertips across the notepad next to his phone. All day, promises of help poured in from other communities, none bigger than his enemy. Findlay's mayor offered the unlimited assistance of civil engineers, road crews, ambulances, fire departments and, of course, a financial stipend. "Solidarity among mayors," he said several times. This reminder fills Bo with hope. Maybe liberation isn't so bad. Liberation matched with responsibility feels like something worth fighting for.

Next, he swings by Chief Grover's office, searching the desk for his spare set of keys. Minutes later, the mayor plays cat burglar with the enormous key ring back at the museum. He realizes under most circumstances this constitutes breaking and entering, but everything is legal when you're saving the city you love.

After tripping over a few buckets and weaving from the back exit to the museum floor, a howl fills downtown Dyson: "Son of a bitch!"

The spot where he and Marci first connected, the glass case with Rosinski's squiggly diary with the funny code of numbers and pictures of fruit, is empty except for a dusty outline.

SUNDAY, 2:15 AM

Just as the city touches its peak of quiet—when it seems even the crackling, screaming summer insects have evacuated—joy finds the former owner of the Blue and Grey for All Occasions. "All that money, fourteen million, hooo-weee," Ed Lee whispers in the darkness. His train of thought much clearer after a few cups of coffee and an egg sandwich. "Wouldn't need a bank loan with fourteen million. Keep the store open until kingdom come with fourteen mil."

Ed has a key to the house. He and his wife were in charge of feeding Boots the cat when Edna was out of town.

"So, Dix, your drunk ass thinks the treasure's hidden here at Edna's," he whispers, recalling their slurred conversation at the Kreskin Inn urinal stalls. The attorney was pretty convinced. So convinced he got worked up and soaked his expensive loafers. "Well, buddy, I've been checking under all the couch cushions and in the attic. Nada." He catches sight of the shed through a window. The orange security light hums above it, showcasing scars and sag and the missing planks of time. "Maybe it's not in the house. Maybe you were a hair off."

By dim light, he finds the tool shed full of junk. Lawnmowers, weed trimmers, plastic bottled chemicals, faded boxes from decades ago. At least a dozen hammers—ball peen all the way up to a two-handed sledge—hang on the wall from back when Edna's husband was alive.

"*Hello*," Lee says, unbuttoning the heavy wool general's coat, sweat making things damp along his body. "What's this?" He uses a stool to peek into a storage loft.

"Tell you what, Dix. I find a few million bucks worth of gold, I'm hiring a maid for that office of yours. Fix that leak in your ceiling." He is on boot-toes, stool wobbling. He reaches into the mysterious space, fingers in something crunchy and guano-smelling. "Heck, I'll buy you a new *building* if all this crap is worth it." The loft is dim black, odd shapes everywhere. Any of it could be treasure. "Maybe buy something nice for Donna, too. If she never closed me down, I wouldn't have been drinking at the Kreskin, never would have heard Dixon and his theory on Edna's will. I never would have—"

The stool leg splinters.

Crusty, guano-smelling things aren't enough to grip. Fingernails scratch as Lee's body swings backward. His shoulder crashes into the tool bench. His bones reverberate as he thumps the dirt floor.

He moans, hoping nothing is broken.

His collision with the tool bench jarred something loose—a thin metal snapping. In the darkness, Lee never sees the two-handed sledge fall from the wall. It gives little warning as it barrels into his forehead.

SUNDAY, 9:14 AM

The cameraman's camera is empty. There is no film. It isn't beaming directly up to a successfully orbiting satellite. It may as well be a block of wood. The camera is just a prop while Cody rehearses.

"Cut—cut!" The director walks toward Kellogg, yanking that tuft of hair. "What is this stuttering?"

The pre-noon sunrays turn the earthy rug of grass below their feet into something Crayola couldn't dream up. It smells freshly cut. Cody is wearing the kind of deep blue suit that comes free with a casket purchase.

"Sorry, sorry." Cody runs a greasy palm over his face. "I'm a radio guy, this is a little new. I'll get everything straight by tomorrow. When that satellite drops, I'm your man."

"You're a regular Herbert Morrison."

"Thanks." Sincerity glimmers in the DJ's eyes. The director doesn't have the stomach to explain.

If the camera were actually taping, viewers would see a modest group holding picket signs in a baseball field over Kellogg's shoulder. Cody and the crew managed to convince about thirty people to stick around.

"Take it from the top."

"The citizens of Dyson have revolted in suspicion of the local government's motives. You can see behind me a small militia has formed with the intent to patrol the streets. In their words, 'We barely get satellite TV out here, there is no way we're getting a spy satellite. We're not dumb enough to r-r-run while we are robbed b-b-b-b-blind.'"

"Cut!" The director's deep, doubting eyes meet the crew.

Cody smacks his hands together. "Damn, okay. I'm better at improvising. When the chaos arrives, I'll be cooler than a deli case. You'll see. Don't worry. *Don't worry.*"

"I'm a little worried, honestly," the director says. "*This* is how worried I am." He calls to the daydreamer lying in the grass, staring at the sun. "Pearl. You want to give it a shot?"

Her eyes locked upward, she imagines fire. Little comets crashing. A mushroom cloud of dirt, trees, and houses. "You think this thing will really hit?"

"God, I hope." Cody dabs his head with a towel.

"Who cares? Do you want to get in front of the camera? I think . . ." the director gulps, "you'd be a natural."

"Now, hold it. I'll be ready." Cody wobbles, thinking of dropping to his knees and begging.

Pearl's pixie haircut swirls around her head as yellow as her sundress. Her voice still sounds far off. "You know, my sister used to say tying me to a train couldn't get me to leave Dyson." She is motionless, wondering if bombing pieces of satellite will drop straight down or come at an angle, like a landing airplane. "But I think all it takes is this." She points up. "I have too much to live for. Forget this satellite."

"Shush." Cody runs to her. "Someone will hear you. Pearl, how hard did we work to convince them there was no satellite? Don't blow it now."

"No. I won't." She is calm when her bare feet sink into the healthy grass. The lemon-colored dress snaps in the wind and lifts slightly above her knees. "I'm leaving. There's too much to do. Rajula Magbi didn't sacrifice her life so I could cross my fingers, hoping people die."

She walks into the scorching air and blue sky without even glancing back.

SUNDAY, 11:45 AM

"Old boy, maybe that ceiling collapsed for a reason." Packwicz even wears a smile shooing away a rat. "Your lotto number has finally come in." The excitement in his voice is a wonderful, foreign feeling.

The former FruitCo headquarters is a three-story building overlooking Main Street, a few doors away from the Kreskin Inn and the Imitation Fruit Museum. Of all the abandoned buildings in Dyson, this is the most ruinous. Haunted houses and the paths of tornadoes look like the Windsor Castle. Thirty years earlier, FruitCo moved its operations next to the factory. In the following decades, the building's floor planks warped, gallons of water drained through the ceiling, and the entire office succumbed to rust and rot and reek.

After secretly witnessing the mayor enter Town Hall, Packy broke down the old headquarters' back door. Now, he works past collapsed beams and raccoon nests. Up the stairs as quickly as possible—catching unknown quantities of tetanus from stray nails—Packy finds the top floor.

He trailed Bo Rutili across town all morning. He watched through binoculars as the mayor got into an argument with his girlfriend, Marci, in front of the fruit factory. The rejuvenated Packwicz actually came close to doing the deed last night when he witnessed Bo break into the museum. Packy had held his trigger finger because it was too dark for a clear shot.

The top floor's windows project a raw, brownish light. The musty stink reminds Packy of how long it has been since since anyone walked in here. He inches through the corner office and pigeons buzz his shoulder. Packwicz has no clue this was once Gerald Rosinski's office.

But he will.

He tugs on leather driving gloves, lays an orthopedic foam pad below a windowsill, and loads a hunting rifle. The only thing standing in the way of a few million bucks is a grimy yellow pane of glass that won't budge.

Packy jiggles the window with no luck.

The room is stuffy and sweat pinches his eyes. "Damn," he whispers. He lines the butt of his rifle up to the window and swings back, worrying briefly about some innocent person taking a glass shower.

He needs to act quickly. He licks saltwater from his lip and pauses to steady his shaky hands.

There is a gentle knock at the door. Packy turns and prepares to shoot whatever unfortunate soul is standing. He knows it's impossible, but hopes it is his new employer, Donna Queen.

"You? Aren't you scared of satellites?"

It isn't Donna, but his foie gras dealer, holding a metal can in its fist. The mummy shuffles toward Packwicz. It points at the rifle, then at the scummy window. It wags a finger as if Old Man Packwicz had tried stealing a candy bar.

"It's not what you think."

The mummy sprays something oily into the cracks and crannies where the window meets the sill. It presents the window like another entree.

"Well, I'll be damned." The glass slides easily up, offering a shot only Lee Harvey Oswald could love. "You got a bad reputation around town, but I say you're alright. We should get a beer later. I'm a little short on friends lately."

The mummy drags toward the door.

"I'm good at buddying up with misfits. I was in Vietnam, did you know that? A lot of the guys'd paint nudie girls on airplane noses. One fella, Howard Castrucci, wouldn't. Howard was pre-med at the University of Alabama-Birmingham before he enlisted. He only painted four-color models of the circulatory system or the digestive tract. Right up under the cockpit. Every pilot hated him, they all said he was an idiot. Everyone wanted something sexy." Packy's voice fades. "He was my best friend."

The mummy stops at the door and brushes a few pieces of wood from a massive metal box sagging into the floor. It knocks, "Shave-and-a-haircut," and spins a silver knob. The steel safe grinds opens.

"How do you like this?" Packy says, blowing dust off a stack of papers signed by Gerald Rosinski. Behind that, he finds a map of Dyson and the remains of a ham sandwich that could collect Social Security. There are circles, Xs, and multi-colored lines running all over the map.

Packwicz stuffs the document into his pocket at the sound of voices, three stories below.

"I'm sorry, Bo. You're the only one who's ever been nice to me. I hate myself. I really do." He kneels into the foam pad, flipping off the gun's safety, and peeks through the scope. "I have to do this. I have to. I have to."

SUNDAY, 1:00 PM

Skeet is a little puzzled as to why Chief Grover brings the police flashers to life behind him. The truck's bed is so full of history he fears the axle might shatter. Skeet really had to punch the accelerator to even think about breaking the speed limit. So getting pulled over is a mystery.

He leans out the window, watching the cop lumber toward him. Phone lines sway overhead. "Bert, damn it, there's no time to chat. This town'll be gone in another day. There's work to do."

Skeet hops from the truck, his weathered leather boots cloud the dirt. He sees the Chief's eyes, red and puffy the way his wife's got after watching black and white movies. Grover gives a half-hearted belt tug, barely making a jingle. For a moment they stand with only the papery sounds of corn stalks blowing next to the country road.

"Gimme it," Grover says behind heavy stubble.

"Later. Later. Hell . . . I don't even know what you want."

"Your badge, Skeet. Deputies can't steal. Damn it." Bert lifts his weak body up the truck's side. "Why are you doing this? You never took anything that wasn't yours. You're an honest man. A little weird, but *honest*."

From atop the truck tire, the Chief sees a green pile of street signs, Christmas decorations, a rusty Civil War cannon, and other bits of Dyson.

"This has nothing to do with the badge. You give me the sign and I'll start evacuating folks. Until then," Skeet says, sounding desperate, "I have to do this, Bert. Nobody else seems to give a damn. If this town blew away in a storm there wouldn't be fifteen people that'd notice. History's important."

"Law's important, too."

"What I'm doing is above the law. I'm preserving memories."

"That a basketball hoop?"

"Went into the old grade school and tore it down. I scored forty points in the league championship on that rim. It's just been sitting there, rusting."

"And, uh . . ." The Chief shifts metal signage around. "The old 'Welcome to Dyson' sign? I thought we just nailed a new one over it."

"I wasn't gonna spoil the surprise, but that one's for you. Remember the cover of the *Gazette* with you and Joyce standing in front of *this very* sign before you went on that world tour?"

"Don't care to, no."

"You guys are the biggest stars Dyson ever had. Still are. How two kids like you who learned to sing so pretty . . ."

"I see what you're doing and it's dangerous, Skeet." Grover's face lifts, eyes still swollen.

By this point, Skeet has hauled himself up to the other side and admires the cargo with big wild eyes of love. "This is my second truckload. People will thank me."

"You're living in the past. C'mon, this hoop? Is that the street sign you bent driving a tractor through town?"

"With Janet sitting on my lap. 1988, one of the happiest days of my life. That was right after I proposed. God knows why the city never bought a new sign, but every time I drive past I can't help but get a little drop or two of that juice. That happiness. I ain't had happiness like that for a long while."

Mosquitoes of pride buzz to life again.

"Memories are not happiness. Trust me, I have more than my share. Do I look happy?"

"Memories are only sad if you make 'em sad. That's the beautiful part. Memories change in your mind. They grow and they shrink. They always get better."

"Give me your badge, nutjob." The cop's hand digs deeper into the truck. "I need to make sure everyone is out of town tomorrow. The National Guard shuts off the utilities bright and early. Then they're gone, too. That is, if they roll out of bed on time." He stops the interrogation and locks eyes with his friend. It's like they are sitting by a pond fishing. "Is it just me, or are those soldiers not taking this seriously?"

"The thought has crossed my mind."

"Forget it." The Chief lifts a hand. "Anyway, the NASA wizards say this thing should land around one in the afternoon. You can bet your ass I'll be disappeared by then. You better, too."

"So, you're telling me the chief of police has the night off?"

"Skeet, I have a thermos of coffee in the squad car. It'll sober you up good."

"Just give me a hand and I'll help you. I need help like crazy out at the factory."

SUNDAY, 2:30 PM

Garrett hasn't talked much since last night. When he finally asks what she was thinking, plotting a murder, Donna is more prepared than for any business meeting.

She speaks, but is interrupted by the hammering and sawing of construction. The racket silences and she opens her mouth, touching tongue to teeth, when a power drill cuts in. Hot sawdust smell fills the temporary business office as workers finish the Urinating Bear Casino. "Name two bigger thorns in my . . . in our side?"

"You can't just kill your problems, Donna." She sees a sickness in his eyes.

"What about that rat in the attic? We killed that problem."

"Donna."

Her head shakes, blonde hair shimmering, and smiles like the answer is obvious. "Come on, this is jittery old Packwicz we're talking about. The guy can't hold steady enough to pump gas. You think he has the stones to shoot the mayor?"

Garrett doesn't look impressed or any less nauseous.

Donna's hands mimic wobbling scales of justice. "But maybe he tries, gets arrested, maybe he goes to jail." Her brow arches: "Worst case scenario he does kill Bo and *still* goes to jail."

"And then Packy tells the cops it was your idea."

Donna doesn't recognize this Garrett. This man who is so disappointed in her. It is unsettling.

Donna moves over and delivers a backrub. "Like anyone in their right mind would believe Packy wasn't setting me up."

"This won't help you become mayor." Garrett tries to stand. Donna forces him back into the seat and clears her throat.

"Honey, I don't want to be mayor anymore."

"Donna, that's all you've talked about for years. Are you worried about this satellite?"

"Are people still talking about that flying garbage can? No, I've been thinking mayor is too temporary."

"What's less temporary?"

"I'm shooting for *hero*. Someone remembered for performing the Heimlich on this choked town. We're the only ones who can, Garrett."

"Once that satellite falls, there won't be anything left to save. Hell, maybe we won't be here. Maybe the casino won't be here."

The Queens have a simple setup on the casino's main floor. Decorated like a hunting lodge with an enormous synthetic grizzly head over the entrance, there are five poker tables, five blackjack tables, two roulette wheels, a few hundred slot machines, and a heavily diversified liquor selection. The Urinating Bear Inn offers fifty rooms. It is the only place to legally gamble in the state. This is something even big cities can't compete with, and Donna knows it.

The idea of pushing her own boundaries to help Dyson brings amazing gusts of pride to her sails. Heroic accolades line up in Donna's mind. Dysonian of the Year. Picture on the Rotary Club Wall of Fame. A speech at the high school graduation. Grand Marshall of the Fourth of July Parade. Full, one-page interview in the Dyson *Gazette*. With each step, the Donna Queen legend stretches toward infinity.

"Some local who got lucky on the lottery will be remembered for, what, a generation, max? But a hero will be an inspiration. A beacon of light so bright the name Donna Queen lives forever. Garrett, we never had kids. I want this to be our legacy."

"Donna, you're not making sense."

"Think about Daddy. That man built half this town with his bare hands."

"He ran a construction company. I don't think they were bare."

"Point is, he had some results from his hard work, you know? All he ever wanted was for me to do something to make him proud. Instead, what have I done?"

"You've done a lot."

"I need to do something to make him happy before he . . . before he's gone. So, that means I am very busy right now."

"That's all fine, Donna. But you've got to stop and think about this satellite."

"Oh sweetie, don't be dumb. Nothing is going to happen tomorrow."

She gulps. Making Garrett proud means being strong. And being strong means doing things she doesn't like. "The big, bad whatever-it-is will burn up. Drunk teenagers with BB guns make a bigger mess. Remember the front window at the pizza parlor? I . . . for one . . . uh . . . you know . . . it's nothing to worry about."

Garrett picks a stack of poker chips off the desk. "I just can't help but shake this feeling. I want to call my mom and say I love her, you know, *just in case*. Life feels so short, so haunted. There are so many things I want to do before I die." He stacks and unstacks the chips with dozens of nervous *clicks*. "But killing innocent people isn't one of them."

"Hush. Honey, I love you, and I won't let anything horrible happen."

"Hey, here's an idea. Let's just focus all this energy on killing that stupid mummy."

Donna's whistle cuts across the room like an arrow. There's a new angle in her face—a look of cracking this case wide open. "So now we know what's eating you."

SUNDAY, 5:31 PM

Marci catches herself looking.

For God's sake, she thinks. *Our senior class voted him Most Likely to Torture a House Cat.* But as the hours pile up, her opinions change. Marci spends more time than necessary fixing messy hair and praying the sleepless purple half-moons under her eyes will disappear.

Did Troy and I just share a moment?

Marci, of course, has no idea of the X-rated moments Troy imagines them sharing.

Once that little germ was loose—the possibility of a *connection*—it grew deep fangs that slowly dug in. Her heart bursts with brightness whenever Troy fetches her a cup of coffee. She grows breathless each time he says what a great job she is doing. She notices Troy has adorable dimples. The biggest shock: Troy is a good listener. Marci forgot what it was like to be heard. The comfort and closeness of being listened to is wonderful.

She considers, for only a flash, what baby names sound good with Gomez. Admiring all they've accomplished in one evening and his contagious, positive attitude, a red blush infects her cheeks, thinking, *What do Troy's lips taste like?*

"It's gotta be about dinnertime," she says, marveling at the sea of fruit quilting across the warehouse floor. A swirl of yellow, red, orange, and green. "If they shut off the power tomorrow, I don't think we can do it." Her pouty face goes to work.

Behind them massive machinery pours hot liquid goo into metal molds, making the entire place smell like rubber utensils French kissing hot stovetops.

"It's okay." Troy blows across a coffee and passes it. "I have a secret weapon."

"I'm not making fruit by hand." There's a dash of sass in her voice.

"I would never make you do something like that . . ." he says. "Oh, that was a joke. I get it."

His total lack of humor is suddenly kind of . . . adorable. It catches Marci off-guard.

"My secret is a pair of three hundred horsepower generators," he says.

Her famous giggle fills the warehouse. "Well still, I have about a dozen costumes to sew. You still have a few more floats to build and about a million more pieces of fruit to crank out."

"Nah, don't sweat it. Our plan is going to be awesome. We're really going to make a difference. You know, even if there is no media swarm, even if there is no satellite, I think the festival will put a smile on people's faces. It's going to bring hope. It's Christmas morning, 1987, all over again."

"Huh?"

"Nothing. Just the happiest Christmas *ever*. That's the year I got my first Erector Set. I never stopped building stuff after that."

"Cute," she says, not certain whether she means the story or the storyteller.

"You and me," he says, head lifted high and proud. "We're like the Glimmer Twins of Dyson."

Marci looks embarrassed, like she doesn't want to repeat "huh?" again.

"The Glimmer Twins. Keith Richards and Mick Jagger."

"I didn't know they were brothers."

"They aren't twins. One writes the songs and the other sings. Just like you and me. One of us is the technical wiz, the other the creative powerhouse. One of us has the brains, the other the looks."

"Which one does that make me?"

"I'll give you the brains and the looks. Maybe I'm just Charlie, the drummer, keeping the beat."

"You think they'd come up with a cooler nickname." Her giggle fires a soft, loving bullet into Troy.

He steps close, lowers to her level, wets his lips, and says a quick prayer that his breath isn't toxic. "What would you call them?"

The screech and pound of the factory dies away. The hazardous plastic stink turns suddenly sweet. His mouth hums with the prospect of a kiss.

"I'm not . . ." She closes her eyes and leans forward, " . . . sure."

Troy has been picturing this moment since high school. His fists bunch.

He leans in with moist lips.

His sizzles. This is it. This is the moment he's been waiting for since—

"Shut it down, Troy," a voice growls. A set of keys jingle in the distance.

A split moment away from scratching the number one item off his *Things to do Before I Die* list, Gomez turns and realizes they've been snuck up on. He shakes the Chief's hand. "I'm sorry?" he yells over the factory noise.

Grover flips off a pair of sunglasses. "Shut it down!"

"Chief, this is my livelihood. We need all this fruit."

"Troy, I worked here one summer when I was a kid. And I don't want to tell you how to run the business, but your old man never kept the product on the warehouse floor. Look at that mess. You're waist-high in oranges and bananas."

"And pears and apples," Marci giggles. "And grapes and lemons."

"I am not my father, Chief." His chin lifts high and proud.

"Troy, put yourself in my shoes," Grover says.

"This project is bigger than Oscar Gomez and it needs to be finished. Marci and I are saving this town."

"There's no saving anything."

"Have you heard about the Rosinski Fake Fruit Festival?"

Grover's stomach groans for dinner; he doesn't want to sit through this. He wants one of those microwave burritos from the gas station. "Make my job easy. I have a signed order from the *mayor*. After some nut took that shot at him today, everyone needs to be out by midnight."

"A shot?" Marci's foot knocks over a coffee. A muddy pool spreads around three pairs of shoes. "Like with a gun?"

"Damnedest thing. Two bullets, right on Main Street. Poor Wendell Dixon took one in the shoulder."

"What about Bo?" Her voice snaps to life and makes Troy wonder why he even tried in the first place.

"Mayor's fine, not a scratch. He's rightly spooked. So now I gotta bail everyone out and find some jester taking target practice on Main Street." The mummy and its musical taste also jump into the Chief's mind. His lip shakes with operatic urges. Grover wisely bottles it.

"I'm sorry to hear that." Troy leans forward. "But we have a job to do—"

"Okay, where were you a few hours ago?" Grover flips open a notepad, scratching in pen.

"Are you serious? We've been here. Look around." He motions to the giant head on wheels, the huge bowl of fruit float, the enormous "I Love Dyson" float.

"Look. Cut the power and evacuate, okay? You two don't want to find out what happens to people who ignore the rules."

The Chief disappears and Troy stands, nervously groping the back of his neck.

"I'll only be gone a little bit, I promise," she says, putting a set of fingers to Troy's cheek. A sickness overtakes his belly, realizing he'll never share another of those famous giggles.

Marci walks out the front door, and Troy sulks for a few minutes.

Shockingly, she returns. "Hey. What happened to the wreath?"

FruitCo's corporate symbol is a wreath with each of its famed plastic treats placed in a circle. A granite likeness of this image stands as large as a tractor tire by the parking lot.

Exiting the warehouse, into the dampening dusk, Troy finds a rocky white stump in the grass, like a grave marker snapped in half.

"Who steals a two-ton wreath?" Troy says.

SUNDAY, 11:45 PM

"Joyce, I miss you," the Chief whispers into the phone.

His headlights are off, the car is practically invisible in the silent night. The moon has vanished. The Small Town Songbirds' CD roars over the squad car speakers. Joyce's vocals cut Beethoven's uplifting *Fidelio* to bits before Bert's heavily charged tenor—the voice a reporter for the *Opera Times* said "Demands you hide the good crystal. Grover's vibrato is enough to shatter hearts and ear drums alike." This album was their best-selling.

The stereo is almost as powerful as the spicy beef burrito torching Grover's belly.

"Joyce, I need you. A friend gave me a copy of our first record." The mummy's gift ribbon weaves between his fingers. "We were so good together."

Grover accidentally clicks on the windshield wipers. He doesn't seem to notice the squeak of dry rubber skidding across glass.

The orchestra hits a crescendo of soaring violins and pounding timpani. Joyce and Bert's harmonies melt into a singular beam of light. The recording engineer was stricken with goose pimples the entire time he mixed the album. "When you get this message, call me. Call me, please. I'm not too proud to beg."

Bert and Joyce Grover were known as the Small Town Songbirds. Sold-out crowds in New York and London. Appearances on Johnny Carson. The Adam and Eve of booming vocals were even nominated for a Best Opera Album Grammy.

It seemed, for a brief window in the early 1990s, everyone on Earth was charmed by the story of a police officer and a recent high school graduate who discovered a talent for opera the way most people stumble across a nickel on the sidewalk. No two tryouts in the history of community theater were ever so fruitful. Within a few years of meeting, they were married and filling auditoriums.

Everything went well until their career ended up like one of the Italian tragedies they so famously nailed.

Grover's mind is so deeply wedged into the music, even recalling what color bowtie he wore during the recording, he doesn't notice the mayor hop into the passenger seat.

"Salsa in your eyes again, Bert?"

Grover rubs away redness and tears. "Damn jalapeños, Bo. They'll kill me yet."

"I'm going to buy you a pair of goggles."

"Burrito goggles. Funny." His throat excavates a chuckle. Grover returns to Earth. He flips off the wipers and lowers the stereo. "What's with the cat?"

"This is Boots."

"I wasn't exactly asking for an introduction. What's with the cat?" Grover's voice is suspicious.

"She was Grandma's. I think it's a girl, anyway. Somebody has to feed her and love her, you know? She's my responsibility."

"But what's with the cat? Why are you carrying it around in the middle of the night?"

He rubs Boots' back fur. The cat stretches and cuddles. She brings Bo a level of peace he never knew possible. "It's complicated."

"Seems like everything is these days."

The mayor looks at his only policeman. "How is it going? I'm worried sick about getting folks out of town."

"Good as could be expected, I suppose. You could hear a mouse fart out there."

"What about those *protestors*?"

"Haven't seen a one. Maybe they gave up."

"This satellite is spooking people, Bert. Multiply a full moon by ten. Frankly, it creeps me out, too." Bo clutches the cat tighter. "You know, we're here one minute and then next, bang, nothing." He sniffs Boots' head and scratches an ear.

"Who's we?"

"Me. You. I don't know. Dyson, I suppose. Everything comes to an end, but the world keeps spinning. Who really notices if we die? Do you think anyone's life is different if one town disappears? It's making me wonder: what's the point? Dyson's not worth getting shot over."

"You realize you're talking to someone carrying a gun in order to defend the town you just pissed all over?"

Bo laughs a little. "You got me there."

"I'll take care of things, boss. You just focus on schmoozing the government and FEMA, whoever is supposed to help us get back on track after . . ." He blinks dry eyes. "Whatever happens tomorrow."

They look into the empty ruins of their dark community. Dots of streetlights shine like a glimpse of the lonely future. A Dyson without people.

"Oh, Bert, one more small problem."

"Don't joke. I can't take any more problems."

"I'm serious. There's been a robbery."

Grover laughs. "I'll add that to my honey-do list. Right behind the evacuation, finding a sniper, and dealing with our bandage-loving friend."

"Him?" Bo waits a moment. "I thought I saw him last night."

"The mummy?"

"I don't know. I think it's just stress. My mind playing tricks. I'm on the edge, Bert. I'm about ready to drop to the floor and start crying. I don't know what's right or wrong, real or not. I used to think I had a responsibility to everyone. Used to."

Bo's face is thin and veined and pale. The worry has worn him down quickly. That vim and verve that impressed voters is entirely gone. Grover takes notice.

"By the way." Grover's voice lowers. "Should've said this sooner, but you're doing a good job. None of us were sure how you'd handle things. And man, what a bitch of a test. But you're doing fine. Folks notice, Bo. People appreciate you—"

"Thanks. That means a lot. You're a good guy, Bert."

"Well, you know." A long wait. Grover's face clenches. "So, a robbery?"

"The museum. Have you seen anybody around there? Marci's over in my car right now and she said the whole place was looted. Even Rosinski's diary."

"What's that now?"

"You know, Gerald Rosinski's diary. It was behind glass at the museum."

"Can't say I've ever set foot in that museum."

"The one with all the crazy writing."

"Ah, okay. I've heard about that thing," Grover says.

"I know. Who'd want *that?*"

"I'll try and dust for prints or something." Grover frowns until he gnaws off another burrito bite.

"Keep your eyes open. That stuff is important. It's our legacy. Proof Dyson had a past, even if it might not have a future."

"God, is Skeet writing your speeches now?"

"I'm sorry?"

"Look," he speaks through a mouthful of meat and beans. "Know that I'm handling the evacuation completely. But, if you are worried about stuff missing—street signs, the FruitCo Wreath, and probably even that stupid little diary—I know where they are."

The mayor slowly turns toward Grover. He is a ghost of himself. He brings the cat to his chest.

"It's Skeet. He's been throwing shit in his truck. Go out to his farm and see for yourself. The barn is turned into some bizarre museum or junkyard. Take your pick. But hey, don't get mad at him. He's not handling the stress well, either. You know how sensitive he can be. Skeet's scared the satellite will wipe our past off the map. I'm making him return everything later, but he's my only deputy, and I need him."

The mayor pats Chief Grover's leg and exits the car, hauling the cat under his arm. Bo is so stunned, so secretly thrilled to be within arm's reach of that diary, he doesn't even notice the poison-tipped arrow zing by his nose and plunge into a nearby telephone pole.

MONDAY, MIDNIGHT

That fistful of aspirin eases gunshot pain about as well as flyswatters stop rhinos. Writhing on the couch, Wendell Dixon learns the agonizingly hard way that his shoulder needs medical attention. His hair is a tangle, his clothes are sticky red with drying blood, and his flesh has lost color.

Dixon kicks and cries against the pain for an hour after waking. But when the front door slams open, that shoulder sting disappears. Fear, it turns out, is nature's anesthetic.

Under the soft lights, potpourri smell, and pastel décor Stephanie chose, Wendell's anesthesiologist comes in the form of Murray Kreskin. The anesthetic courtesy of a pistol barrel rubbing between the lawyer's tonsils and tongue.

"Where—is—it?" Murray slides the gun deeper into Dixon's throat with each pressurized word. It tastes of black oil.

Wendell's reply is a wet, gummy question mark. He suddenly doesn't feel like Dyson's smartest man.

Kreskin's eyes are as twisted and unnatural as his crooked teeth. He's wearing a faded red shirt and black jeans. "After you told that little story at the bar Saturday night I've been wandering around town for two days, thinking. And I think I'm tired of being the guy everyone jokes about." Each word Kreskin speaks has the finality of a tombstone inscription. "I'm tired of breathing all that smoke and cancer night-after-night. I'm sick of watching my friends slug a few back and leave the bar for home. That stupid bar is my home and it turns my guts green."

The gun has been wedged between Dixon's lips so long it isn't cold anymore.

"My old man used to say, just because you're talking don't mean folks are listening. So just so we're clear, *I'm* talking and *you're* listening." Edgy metallic nubs slice Dixon's mouth flesh. "You better not have been bullshitting me with that story about Edna Rutili's will. Tell me where that treasure is. It's out there and nobody's claimed it. That means it's *mine.* So if someone else gets it, like one of your *clients,* I will be angry and irrational." Murray's voice is as smooth and quiet as the gun in his hand. But like that pistol, it holds a power aching for exposure. "Bad things happen when I'm angry and irrational."

The gun knocks past Wendell's teeth as Murray steps back. He lifts a mantle photo of the Dixons wearing swimsuits and sunburns.

"How did you get in my house?" Wendell feels his crotch and frowns.

"The door. I rang a few times, but it wasn't locked." Murray's eyes show someone suddenly cool and rational. He makes a face at the wet spot on Dixon's trousers.

"You rang the doorbell before you tried to kill me?"

"Ma and Pa Kreskin raised their kids on diet of matzo and manners." His cherub face burns with memory. "More important, they taught us the value of a buck."

"Look, I was drunk." He covers his lap with a throw pillow. "It was a mistake. I was just upset that Stephanie was leaving town without me."

"She carried you out of the bar last night."

"And then promptly left me." He leans over his knees, breathing. "I have to get her back."

Dixon recalls a tense conversation with the mayor earlier. Stephanie wouldn't be so mad, he realized, if she knew there was a good reason for his fear—a good reason for him to fall off the wagon after almost seven years.

"Bo, let me explain this to you. I have a new contract drawn up. Legally speaking, I recommend signing it because your attorney deserves *compensation.*" He tugged the mayor's arm as a camouflage Humvee passed, leaving strong diesel fumes down Main Street.

"Wendell," Bo said. The brutal sun worked hard into his skin outside of Town Hall. "There is no Rosinski treasure."

"Even better. I wholeheartedly agree. So, if there is no treasure, sign-ing this contract isn't a big deal. It just says *if* there *is* a treasure, I get twenty-five percent. *If.*"

The pair spun when a Hummer wrecked into a metal litter can on the sidewalk. A block away, the vehicle's nose was pressed against the side of an abandoned building, smoke slithering skyward. A pack of uniformed men and woman rolled out, howling with spring break joy. They inspected the damage, passing a tequila bottle.

Bo ran shaky hands through his hair. "I have a bad feeling about those guys. The National Guard hasn't actually done anything for a couple days. Not to mention, I'm pretty sure I saw some looting houses earlier."

"I saw them try and pick a fight with Ned Granger when he wouldn't sell them any more beer at that gas station." Dixon grabbed Bo's shirt and brought him close. "Now, what about my finder's fee?" He was frustrated by the stubborn mayor and wasn't thinking much like the town genius.

"You should evacuate. It's not safe in Dyson."

"Bo, you're being irrational. There is absolutely no harm. I'm your attorney."

"You're Grandma's attorney, not mine."

"Where is your brother? He needs to sign as well." Dixon tried forc-ing a pen into the mayor's hand.

Bo backed up and, for a split second, Dixon stood in the exact place the mayor had, on Main Street, outside the mayor's office, three stories below Gerald Rosinski's old window. "He went back to Findlay. He has to work."

And then someone lit fireworks. Or at least that's what Wendell thought when two hearty cracks echoed. Suddenly, his shoulder burst with pain and blood, and the world turned black.

"Tell me where it is, Dixon. Man, I need a break. I deserve a break. Look at you. Fancy law school. Live in a nice house. Great family. My education was a thousand one-liners, a bed in the back of a bar, and nobody to share that piece-of-shit business with."

Dixon's fancy law school education comes back. He remembers the basics of contract negotiation.

"Murray, you have a lot to be thankful for. You are a successful businessman. You've got the highest batting average on the softball team. You're funny." Dixon eases his posture. "Let's just say if I do know something, we have to make a deal."

"This baby doesn't make deals." Kreskin shakes the gun.

"If I'm dead, I can't help."

Murray's cheek sucks in, biting it. "Go on."

Dixon stands and drops the pillow. "Let's get in your car. I have a hunch. But you have to share whatever we find down the middle."

Kreskin nods. "Nice pants."

MONDAY, 12:01 AM

Skeet almost doesn't need this beer—he is plenty light-headed without help. Moving every combine, tractor, and wagon from his enormous barn was complicated, but the curator knows his new museum is worth the trouble.

His chest buzzes with the excitement of another completed job. Almost complete, at least.

Dyson's distant church bells chime twelve across the calm midnight air. They are some sort of warning alarm in Skeet's mind. Ringing a dozen times, informing him life is turning a corner. The bells are the start of a newfound confidence. He has been so unpredictable since his wife died. Janet's funeral was held at noon about fifteen years ago—twelve bells signaling the start of Skeet's depression. Now, twelve more chimes help him become someone new, someone proud, someone with purpose.

The barn's soft dirt floor holds almost every scrap of Dyson Skeet determined worth saving. Artifacts like statues, plaques, even the City Hall photo of Bo Rutili's inauguration. Personal memories like the public pool diving board that he met Janet on when they were kids; things he knows are important to others, like WDSR's archive of recordings, especially the Small Town Songbirds' Radio Hour, and the FruitCo Wreath that David Rutili carved by hand—the last work of masonry he finished before he and his wife died in that car wreck, leaving behind two young boys.

Pride brings a smile to Skeet, watching sparrows flapping and nesting in the rafters. Hay stalks of bedding float down.

Mementos hang on the walls from rusty nails or propped against posts, soaking up the barn smells of motor oil and freshly turned dirt. He uses every bed sheet in the house to protect some undersides. Skeet doesn't need the blankets, he will not sleep tonight.

Street signs reflect dull and green, each sealing in meaning and memory. He gets an impossible chest tug passing them, thinking they could've been forgotten. Or worse, not hold a future memory for someone else. He now realizes it's his responsibility to do something with all this. That brings the first love chest patters back.

"Skeet?" someone calls from the gravel driveway.

He recognizes the mayor's voice and takes a gulp of warm beer. *The museum's first customer*, he thinks. *Someone to recognize my sacrifice.* With that, the loneliness of being the only person who gives a damn disappears.

"Mister Brown?" a woman's voice cuts through the statues and trophies.

"Come in, come in." He steps outside, into the dark, backlit by barn light. His large head and shoulders atop a filthy checked shirt with sleeves rolled to the elbows and jeans. His warmth is a shock to Bo and Marci. They didn't expect to find *anything* out here except some farmer foaming at the lips. Instead, here's a fairly impressive shrine. Cluttered, but impressive. Like Dyson had a going-out-of-business sale, so many random scraps of municipal property packed tight under the roof.

"Chief said you'd be here, Skeet. So, what're you up to?" Bo says curiously.

"Doing a job a man like you can appreciate, Bo. Preserving our past," he says, straightening a YIELD sign with a million shotgun pellet holes. "There won't be a Dyson once that satellite hits. It breaks my heart."

"So you made your own Dyson?" that Krupp girl says.

A desperate ache, like waking up thirsty, fills Bo. The giant leprechaun the decorating committee dressed up like Santa leans against a hayloft, its shaggy white beard hanging by a strand. It reminds Bo of his village tour with Rajula. Sad, guilty sweat appears.

She is dead and Bo has barely given it a moment's thought. *What is wrong with you? Stop waffling. Dedicate yourself to Marci. You don't want to end up alone like Packwicz. Get Marci to love you again.*

Then, genius strikes Bo. A genius Wendell Dixon only dreams about at his most delusional. The mayor stumbles, spinning propeller arms. His body crashes to the floor with a plume of dust.

"Bo, sweetie," Marci cries and scoops him into warm arms. He knows this cake must be thicker if she is going to eat it.

"Whoa. You alright?" Skeet asks.

"It must be the stress. I've been working too hard," Bo's voice is weak. "Trying to save Dyson is just . . ."

"Oh, honey." She smoothes his hair.

"Listen," he whispers. "Grover says he okayed this, Skeet." He staggers to his feet and knocks dirt off his khaki slacks. "Frankly, I have too much to worry about, evacuating the rest of the town. Just make sure you put everything back after tomorrow, okay?"

"If there's any town left to put it back in, you have my word." Skeet toasts the idea with a beer slurp.

"Thank you." Bo leans on Marci, though he has all the balance of a ballet company. "Now, we need a favor." The mayor pulls out a tiny bottle of sanitizer and rubs some between dirty palms, a move he hasn't done in several days. He feels the backslide starting.

"I'll try. I'm going to be pretty busy tomorrow getting people out of town and then filling the last two holes in my collection." Skeet points to the far end where a large circle and a small one are scratched into powdery dirt.

"What goes there?" Marci says.

"I lost the statue of Hans Dyson. That's the small one. And the big one, well, I wouldn't want to worry anyone." His laugh fills the barn.

"Fine, fine," Bo says. Magically, he is cured of whatever made him faint. "Look, we know you cleaned out the Fruit Museum."

"*Preserved.*"

Bo shakes his head. His girl and his city are nearly back to normal. Backsliding to him. That diary is the key. "Right. There was a diary. It had a bunch of gibberish written in it. Belonged to Gerald Rosinski. We need it immediately."

Marci shoots a sharp glance. "You didn't tell me that."

MONDAY, 12:30 AM

A funny thing happens on the way to the city limit. Troy Gomez's sunny outlook on life crashes, burns, turns to ash, somehow catches fire *again*, hardens to a crispy black lump of coal, and still finds the energy to torch itself once more to be sure.

Reason being: before this, at the factory, among the floats and boxes of freshly delivered fireworks, a National Guardsman with a large gun entered the warehouse and directed him to evacuate.

By the time the fruit production lines were switched off and cooling, Troy linked the parade floats in a daisy chain to his bumper. "If I get one scratch on this truck," he told the soldier Donna Queen had nicknamed *Muscles*, "a crashing satellite will look like a bird crapping on your windshield."

Troy isn't really all that mad. In fact, he half expected the visit. But since Marci disappeared, life's irritations have taken a more severe tone—a cold cup of coffee makes him punch the wall, a skipping Stones CD makes him clank a hammer across the warehouse. He leaves her costumes—yards and yards of herringbone-patterned cloth and a long strip of fake mustache fur—spread across the table with secret hopes the satellite will drop directly on her hours of patient work.

Troy's glacial parade to the Dyson city limit makes the soldier wonder if this is somewhere he could actually live. Muscles admires the moonlit fields and lonesome farmhouses. He is sick of being the only responsible soldier on duty. The other members of his squad are goofing off, drinking, screwing, and generally abandoning their responsibilities. As a man who loves responsibility, their lack of discipline is a disappointment.

Working at a casino sounds pretty terrific right now. But if people around here spend the hours before certain catastrophe building parade floats, he wonders how many crazies he'll have to kick out every day.

Just beyond the town limits, Troy Gomez parks the truck, clicks on a flashlight, and resumes work on the giant papier-mâché fruit bowl.

Muscles kind of admires his work ethic. *Here's a guy with discipline,* he thinks.

MONDAY, 6:00 AM

The porcelain kitties are the worst.

Dixon looks sick as their shells burst on the floor.

"What now?" Kreskin says, shaking glassy shards from the bottom of his shoe.

"Nothing, nothing." He gathers breath. "My mom had glass cats like that. It just gives me one of those bellyaches, you know? Thinking about better times, I guess."

"Tough," Kreskin says, launching another against the wall. "Pussy tummy aches don't find the gold, do they?"

All around Edna Rutili's house, chaos roams without consideration for anyone's nostalgia. Cross-stitches are ripped from frames. The cuckoo clock is a cluster of splinters and springs. The rubble of porcelain figurines is all around. Wendell Dixon and Murray Kreskin are ruthless in their search.

"What are you doing? We have work," Dixon says at one dark point, hours later.

"Getting a can of pop. I'm exhausted."

"No, I mean, why are you tapping it?" he says, finding a touch of his smartest-man-in-town voice again.

"You tap the top so it doesn't spray everywhere."

"There is no proof that works."

Kreskin cracks open a cola. "See, no spray. I win."

"That doesn't mean anything. Jesus, you're getting on my nerves."

"Ooh, somebody's over their bellyache."

"Don't worry about how I feel. Just shut your mouth and work."

The destructive duo moves to another room. "It has to be around here. That crazy old broad had to be hiding gold, right?" Murray says. Dixon watches him slug soda and chew a cigar until it's a brown stump. Murray sets a glass elephant on the floor. *It's a Boy!* inscribed into blue porcelain. It was a gift to Edna when Bo's father was born. A black boot slowly crackles the trunk like the surface of an icy pond.

"You ever wonder why they don't make grey neon?"

Prying wall paneling with a crowbar, Dixon looks back. "What are you talking about? That is the stupidest thing I've ever—"

"It's not stupid. It's a business decision. I was looking through neon sign catalogs for the bar and . . ." He pauses. "Good God, Dix." Kreskin's eyes pinch together at the rising sun beaming through the windows. They've been hunting and destroying all night. Murray notices a beefy, sour fragrance spoiling the air. "Have you done anything with that shoulder?"

A moist red patch of business shirt clings over Dixon's bullet wound. The blood is nearly purple at the center.

"Neosporin and aspirin, why?" Glassy crackles follow his words.

"Nothing." Kreskin pulls apart a bookshelf. "Just saying, they make blue, red, green, all that shit. But no grey neon. Guy who makes grey neon, that son-of-a-bitch won't need to dig through some dead lady's house for money."

"Brilliant. I'm sure that'll be a big hit in Vegas. Nothing says good times like grey neon."

"Forget I said anything. Man, you're grumpy." Kreskin breathes heavy, resting a crowbar over his shoulder. "I guess it's true what everyone says."

"What?"

"Nothing."

"Quit playing games and say it," Dixon says.

"They say you are a kind of an arrogant jerk."

Dixon shakes the eggshell porcelain off a shoe. "Bite me, Murray."

"Bite you?" Kreskin mumbles from behind a cigar, ramming a hammer into a family portrait. A shower spray of glass tinkles. Under his breath: "Didn't know I was partnered with a guy like *that*."

"Something to say?"

"Forget it."

"Come on, Barkeep. Let's hear it."

"Yeah, okay. *Bite you?* What does that even mean? Am I supposed to bite you like I'm your boyfriend?" He points to Dixon's stained lap. "Har, no thanks, bub."

"It's an expression. Too bad you're too dumb to know that. It's not gay, it's not anything."

Murray holds a hand to Dixon's face. "See this tattoo. It's my Shit List and your name is on the top." He pulls out a pen and starts writing.

"You want help spelling it?" He reads the tattoo. "My name's already on there, moron."

"Yeah, you get on twice. Double shit list."

"Now I'm worried." Dixon sighs and drags his feet down the hall, fatigued. "On to the bedrooms."

Edna Rutili's house is bathed in the egg yolk yellow of morning sun.

"One step ahead of you," Murray says, holding a shiny pink pig from the bedroom. Coins bang against its stomach. The bank splits apart on the floor and nickels roll everywhere. Kreskin bends to sift through the remains. "Well what do we have here?" he says, unfolding a piece of paper covered in glass sparkles.

MONDAY, 8:09 AM

"I should have guessed." Chief Grover spits the words like cheekfuls of tobacco.

Skeet's enormous flatbed truck is backed up to the city's largest symbol of holiday spirit. A gurgling tailpipe breathes steam into the heart of Christmas Park. The moist morning haze is flavored with the smell of pine needles.

Under Mayor Packwicz's regime—way back when Dyson's tourism hopes depended on three hundred and sixty-five Christmases a year—the highlight was weekly carol singing. Volunteers sang "Jingle Bells" around the enormous snowman no matter if April's rain and mud were in full force, if August heat forced holiday revelers into tank-tops, or January blizzard warnings were in effect.

The three-story Frosty, with a carrot nose the size of a road cone, is crafted from fiberglass wrapped around a steel frame. Thousands of bulbs are wired inside the skeleton, giving the bundle of snow a pleasant, white glow.

At least it was once white.

A decade of dirt buildup gives the snowman a roasted brown glow more befitting pork tenderloin.

"Just forget the badge bullshit, Skeet." The Chief runs to the ladder and looks up, keys banging like a fistful of dog tags. "Just get out of town. For a long time. I don't want to see you. I don't want your *help*. And I certainly don't want you stealing any more city property."

"This is it, Bert. I'm all yours after this. I'll evacuate the entire state if I have to." Skeet never looks down while working.

Pinecones rain on the Chief's hat brim. "Nobody's left, Skeet. No thanks to you, everyone's safely out of town."

He calls down: "That's good. What I'm doing is more important anyways. You'll thank me. This is the last piece for my collection. Well, sort of. I lost Hans Dyson the other night."

"I'm aware."

"Oh, good."

"What are you doing?" A pinecone bombs Grover's shoulder.

Skeet climbs down the metal ladder, shaking a ratchet. His ragged face is bright. "Unhooking the guy wires. Old Snowball is strapped down so he won't blow away. I'll get him, though."

Grover rubs his temples and flips off his hat. He wets his lips for a minute, picking his next words. The Chief sees more than a little of himself in Skeet's idiotic quest. Wrestling a snowman into the back of a truck isn't that different from wrestling Joyce back into love. "Quick."

The Chief sounds weak. "I don't want to see you or the snowman today. If I do, I'll cuff you to a park bench. Let you get a faceful of satellite."

"No problem." Skeet pats his buddy's cheek. "This baby probably weighs nothing. It's all fiberglass. Man, is it sturdy. I'll have Frosty loaded in the back of the truck and strapped down in a jiff."

"Just go. I'm responsible for everyone, even crackpots like you."

"I'll be out of your hair in two minutes."

"Where'd you get a tow truck wench anyway?" the Chief calls, noticing a thick tow wire running from the snowman's top hat to the back of Skeet's yellow truck.

"Had it for years. Tractor's always getting stuck out in the soybean field by Ben McGregor's place. I own about five hundred acres of swamp, I swear." A motor winds wire into a spindle. Motorized grinding fills the silent park. Clouds of birds flap off. Slowly, the snowman bows downward. According to Skeet's math, its back should land in the truck bed like naptime.

The wench struggles and the snowman won't move.

The Chief covers an inner-elbow over his nose to escape the burning smell. It's now that he realizes the tree before them. That specific spruce, the fourth-largest in the state, the one prominently featured on Dyson's tourism brochure.

"Whoa!" Grover waves his hat for attention. "You stubborn bastard. Stop. Stop!"

Skeet lets out a wildman yelp and presses the truck's accelerator. The wheels jerk forward an inch and then nothing happens. Grover watches the wire pull tight. Fierce wooden crackles fill the air with a hail of errant pine needles.

The Snowman's steel joints groan. The truck engine roars louder. The tension between the wire, the tree, and the snowman sucks Chief Grover into some immovable calm. Something deep within knows he can only be a witness to the chaos.

Grover is delivered from that calm and into panic as the pine uproots itself with a snapping trunk and a massive rooster tail of soil.

The truck catches traction and sprints across the park, dragging the snowman along with the state's fourth-largest pine.

An apocalyptic cloud of dust and green needles swallow the Chief. He blindly finds the car. Sitting in the cab, Bert coughs lumps of mud while the dusty veil filters away and Skeet's V-shaped silhouette walks through a haze of dirt and July sunshine. "This is the last straw. Kick that idiot out of town. Hell, get a restraining order against Skeet. He's lost his mind."

The dust has left a skin across everything as they stand on the edge of a crater where the tree once grew.

"Damn it, Skeet. How am I gonna explain this?"

Darkness swirls thinner and thinner.

"Skeet? You gonna pay for a new Fourth Largest Pine Tree?"

The dirty cloud lightens until it's just disgusting smog like the kind above Findlay.

"Skeet?" the Chief pauses to spit out another wad of mud. "You have never listened to anyone but yourself, and I'm getting tired of it. I've been holding that one in for a long time."

Skeet kneels closer to the earthy cavity. "How long do you think it takes a tree to grow that big?"

"Hundred years? Eighty years I heard once."

"Son of a bitch," Skeet says, looking across the dismembered root system. Naked, fleshy tentacles wrap themselves over a wooden box the size of a beer cooler.

It isn't until the pair snips the thin vines from around the chest and wipe the dirt off the top that they read the brass inlay:

–ROSINSKI–

MONDAY, 8:59 AM

"Cody *Razzle-Dazzle* Kellogg here on the scene . . ." The DJ gargles saltwater and lemon again. He is standing in boxers and an undershirt. The white fabric gone to a shade of parchment from years of sweat and washing. "More serious. You're on the air and something tragic just happened." His throat clears, a hand covers the imaginary earpiece, and his faded eyes lock onto a mirror. "Thank you, Keenan. The scene here is panic. Fire trucks have been dispatched, but the citizens of Dyson don't know how much longer they can hold out. Rumors of cannibalism are everywhere . . ."

The town is so quiet this evacuated morning that Cody marvels at the pure silence between words. The room is humid with the greasy scent of chorizo and eggs.

Cody crosses the tiny apartment to begin ironing his only suit. "Keenan, the people I spoke with today are relieved that casualties have been minimal. Looks like, sadly, Chicken Little was right. The sky has fallen. I'm Cody Kellogg, reporting live . . ."

The phone's lonely bell interrupts rehearsal. He lifts the cordless landline model he's owned for years from the nightstand, watching the morning sun beam through tree branches. "Kellogg here."

It's the elderly woman from his pamphleteering. She is leading the protestors. The group wants to stand in the center of the baseball field, waving signs and banners, waiting for a great big nothing to happen.

"Yep, the satellite is scheduled to drop in four hours. You guys just camp out. The news crew will get some shots and expose the fraud. No prob." He swallows a mouthful of sausage. "Oh, and all of your valuables will be safe." He pictures solar panels and space-aged circuitry diced into a bloody heap of bodies. A dashing Cody Kellogg in a camera shot, reporting the carnage. He is suddenly not hungry when the phone goes blank. "Hello? Hello?" Cody says as his alarm clock numbers flicker to black. "Shit."

All utilities shut off at nine.

The pants get finished with a cold iron. "Cody Razzle-Dazzle Kellogg," he says in a deep, serious voice, but doesn't like the result. "Cody Kellogg, live in Dyson," he says with the same eulogy tone.

He presses the iron firmly down. Each pass reminds him how important today is. If he ever wants to get back to a decent paying drive time slot again, this is his last chance. There have been so many missed opportunities before. He loses himself, thinking about Kalamazoo, Olympia, Santa Rosa. They all ended so poorly.

A tight crease forms along the navy blue pants when a knock rattles the door. The television director stubs out a cigarette as Cody opens up. The man's face is sagging.

"Hey, you're early. I thought we were starting in a few hours?"

A grimy window welcomes a pale haze into the hallway and throws a mask of hideous black shadows across the director.

"The game's changed." He moves like he doesn't know what to do with his hands.

"I'll say," says Cody. "You should see my suit. I just talked to the protestors . . ."

The director holds a hand up between them. "We have an inside guy at NASA. Gave the network anchor an exclusive. Said the calculations are off. Nothing's landing in Dyson. Satellite is actually bound for Findlay. Bigger city, unsuspecting citizenry, massive casualty rate. Story of the year material."

Each consecutive word from the director turns a shinier shade of gold. Cody's face grows assured and confident. His future burns with potential. "Great! I'll get dressed. We're only about thirty minutes away. That's a sure thing. Findlay's a homerun. I am back in the game, baby."

"Cody!" he calls through the entry as Cody darts toward the ironing board. The director tries not to stare at the thin, veiny legs poking through boxer shorts. "Keenan Eubanks, the network *anchor*, he's handling this. Live remote."

"Whoa, wait," Cody says, watching each of the director's words turn a darker, wetter shade of brown.

"Keenan'll be doing all the on-screen work. We don't need you." The director's face molds into something close to apologetic. "But on the bright side, your little town isn't going to get destroyed or anything." The director turns toward the door. "Try not to look so upset. That's good news, trust me. Anyhow, best of luck."

Cody, half-dressed, scrambles to the door. "The stutter, I *lost* the stutter for you," he echoes through the hall as the director disappears down the stairs.

His hands hum.

His eyes tingle.

That chin bobs, silently reciting a dizzy spin of letters, numbers, and fruit pulled from the diary. The weight of Rosinski's puzzle dominates Bo's attention.

He stopped counting the hours spent decoding the diary after morning sunlight branded a migraine behind his eyebrows. "If apples are Ws, and fours are Rs, then banana twenty-one must be a silent K," he mutters. This muttering began after he'd filled up the first notebook with possible answers to Rosinski's diary code. "No, no, you idiot, silent P. It's a silent P, like . . . like pneumonia."

Marci's house is cute and hip and simple in a way that suggests most of the furniture came cheaply unassembled from boxes. Her walls are bold shades of yellow and green. Photos of family everywhere.

"Or psychotic," Marci says with a yawn. Bo had focused on this treasure all night while she focused on getting some sleep. Neither was successful. Scenarios of torched buildings, of nuclear flashes and feverish decay, filled Marci's brief dreams. "You do remember someone firing bullets at you? You are still aware of this satellite, yes? Bo, you can read that diary anywhere. Let's get in the car."

A frightened tick has developed in her face. An itch that won't go away. A nervous crawling sensation against her temple as she anticipates the wasteland. She slowly opens the curtain, half-expecting a satellite in the yard. She chides herself for being so scared of nothing, but doesn't really stop it.

The mayor keeps scribbling and debating the value of grapes and double Ls. His sleepless body smells of long missed showers. Marci leaves the room and sizzles enough eggs for two, hoping hunger will bring Bo back to life.

"No, no, no," he says, frustrated. "There are two pages missing. Two pages are missing."

Bo doesn't respond when breakfast is announced. She eats the entire meal in the kitchen, alone.

"Two pages missing."

After dishes are cleaned, she stands in the living room doorway. "I have a bag packed. Do you want me to throw some of your stuff in?" Her eyes grow desperate for a response. She debates calling him "honey" but skips it.

He reminds Marci that two pages are missing from the diary.

"Bo, I'll be honest." She pulls her hair back into a nut brown doorknob and sits among his pencil scratchings. "This thing scares the hell out of me. I want to save Dyson as much as you, but unless this diary can reverse gravity . . . "

She snaps the thick leather covers together and carts the diary to the bedroom, into the luggage. Bo doesn't move, cycling through notes, still scribbling.

Since the moment she heard of the attempted shooting she's been ignoring the obvious. Marci gets that now. She shakes her head and feels like crying. She isn't sure whether it's from loss or embarrassment. This morning has been just like the last five years—a one-sided conversation.

"Phone," she yells from the bedroom. Bo's distinct ring repeats and repeats and repeats. "Mr. *mayor*, your phone is ringing." She clasps her suitcase tight. "Forget it."

When she finds the phone sitting right beside Bo, it's his brother.

"So where is the boy wonder?" says Eugene. "I've been trying to call him since I left."

"Don't ask. Your brother is . . . God, let's just say busy."

"Shouldn't you guys be, you know, leaving? I thought that thing was supposed to land soon."

"Oh, it is, but he has . . . " she looks at trance-state Bo, " . . . mayor stuff to do right now. You want me to take a message?"

"Just have him call me. I wanted to talk about getting my stuff from

Grandma's. I have a big plan for it all, actually. Just call me whenever you guys get out of Dyson. I have Tae Kwon Do later, but should be free all evening. Actually, scratch that."

"Okay."

"Just tell him I miss him. Tell him I think he's going to be a great uncle and that I want to have dinner together tonight. You're welcome to come, too."

"Thanks. I'll pass the message."

"Be safe."

MONDAY, 12:52 PM

Troy Gomez is snoring, feet sticking from under a float resembling Carmen Miranda's hat. Sometime before dawn Troy ran out of coffee and crashed quickly while doctoring a weak axle.

A sharp kick opens his eyes. The cool morning air smacks with aftershave zap. He skids from beneath the chassis.

"Now *that's* a piñata." Pearl Krupp smiles. She is washed and beautiful again, but still with a purple bruised forehead. She wears beige shorts and a black tank, exposing those slim arms.

"Keep your opinions to yourself," he snaps. "If you weren't an idiot, you'd know it's just about the best float ever." A massive push of nausea arrives whenever his art is open to criticism. In college, he never went to any of his gallery openings because of the crushing anxiety. It's a big reason why he never pursued art as a career—too many idiot critics. "I worked very hard here. What've you ever done with your life? That one stupid commercial?"

"No, it looks very *fruity*." She has a deeper giggle than Marci, with a rasp as untamed as her rutty blonde hair. The breeze twists a green soybean field near their feet. Hollow pods rubbing like maracas.

"Thanks?" Troy tastes a need for toothpaste in his mouth.

"What are *you* doing out here, Troy?" She waves a weak hand across the landscape. They are miles from town. Pearl always has a sharp look in her eye—Troy knows exactly why Pearl doesn't like him.

"What are you doing out here?" He waits for Pearl, The Kreskin Inn's only waitress, to mention it. He knows she can't hold back.

"Well, for starters, your little parade is blocking the road. I'd have to drive through a bean field to get around. Second . . ." She looks up and lets the sun spotlight her cheeks. Troy sees why she is called the pretty one. "I told myself to bail out all night. But I just sat around eating ice cream and listening to records. I'd like to get a motel room in Findlay, but I can't afford it."

"That sucks, I'm sorry—"

"Maybe if someone was a better tipper . . ."

There it is. She always complains about his ten percent gratuity. He resists Pearl's bait. "Oh, well, that beats my night. I was out here in the dark, working my ass off, fixing floats. Hey, wait, I thought I'd heard you were helping Cody Kellogg with something."

"Don't even get me started."

"Okay, I won't."

"Cody Kellogg is evil. Take my word for it. I wanted to get as far away as possible, but since you've blocked the road, I guess," she begins staring at the hypnotic sway of the fields, "I'm here to see what happens. Get a good view of *whatever*."

Dyson is a few miles away; a tight centerpiece of green trees forms a nub above the surrounding farmland. The grain elevator's cement tubes punch through the leafy ceiling and hang a halo over the entire mess.

"Look. Sorry, I'm grumpy in the morning." He rubs his eyes. He looks down at his khaki pants and white oxford shirt, spackled with coffee and glue and paint. "I think it's great you're staying."

"When did you get so upbeat?"

"If Dyson is going to survive, we need young, vibrant people like you to help."

"Vibrant?" She gives a hammy whistle. "Don't teach that one to the Kreskin drunks, I'll never stop hearing it." She rubs the float's red paper tassels between her fingers. Everything flutters with the breeze. "Besides, I'm not in the habit of helping people who are such . . . what's the word?"

"Artists?"

"No."

"Dreamers?"

"No."

A sheepish pride arrives. "Geniuses?"

"Creeps."

He jabs a finger her way. "Right there. That's what's ruining Dyson. You're all such quitters. You're all only looking out for yourselves. If people would work together they'd realize how great this place is."

"Me? You're the one who never stops calling it a hellhole."

"I changed my mind. It's a free country." His voice slows and saddens. "That hellhole talk was just me hiding from the truth. I regret it."

The soybeans play their song for nearly a minute.

"I wish you had ice cream." Pearl climbs the float that gives her the best view. "This seat is the worst."

MONDAY, 12:55 PM

Rubbing sleepless tension from her shoulder, Marci pictures sharing the Rosinski festival with Troy. Their focus was so tight while getting the parade ready she didn't even make time for imaginary adventures with dead Fake Fruit barons.

Marci surprises herself, realizing Troy—the current Fake Fruit baron—was so natural and open with her, sharing feelings and dreams. Something Bo would never do. Bo is so private and guarded with his emotions. He never even cried about his grandmother dying.

It seemed like second nature for Troy to give some of himself to Marci. They were so close to that kiss. It was exactly what she needed, except they were interrupted by—

"Chief Grover." Bo's voice is crackled. "Come in." He coughs and dislodges something gooey. Boots snuggles on the mayor's lap as he scratches her ears.

"Thanks, but no thanks. Gotta be on the move. Pulled in a million different directions this morning, Mayor. Oh, by the way, you find what you were looking for at Skeet's?"

"Thanks for that," Marci snaps.

Bo looks back at her with confusion. The cat leaps onto his thighs and he cheek-nuzzles its back. "Yeah. What can I do for you, Chief?"

"Just wanted to alert you to two things. One, seems like the city is evacuated. I'd get out of here as soon as possible."

"I'm working on it. You're not the only one with responsibilities." Bo's voice is back to normal. He is no longer the mumbling mess that sat here all night. Marci's chest pierces with fire, realizing anyone involved with running Dyson can walk in and gain the mayor's attention, but his girlfriend is little more than a watery shade of invisible. It's the moment she makes a vow to her future and her happiness.

"Second . . . " Bert smiles uncomfortably. "I don't know how to put this, but there was an accident at the park. A pine tree, *the* Pine Tree, got uprooted."

"Bert, if that's the most damage we suffer—"

The chief imitates Mayor Rutili, " . . . *it'll be a good day.* I know. I'm on your side here, but, well . . . "

Bo unlocks some political charisma and pats the cop's shoulder, ignoring the impression.

Marci bites her lip and twists hair around a finger until the tip turns purple. That nervous itch is back and she's trying to ignore it.

"Well, that's not all. Now, this sounds kooky, I get it. But stick with me."

"Bert?"

"How do I say this? There was a box buried beneath the tree." Grover straightens his brass badge with shattered movements. "So, that's weird enough, right? But this wooden chest didn't have much inside except some paper scraps. This is going to sound nuts, and remember I don't believe in fairy tales or ghost stories or any of that garbage, but . . . have you ever heard about the Rosinski Fortune?"

Strange cartoon noises ring from the mayor's lips before he stumbles backward and trips into white carpet. The cat screeches and runs to another room.

"Mayor?" Grover crouches.

Marci is slow to check his vitals.

"The diary?" Bo's birthday-jubilant voice says.

Grover locks onto the mayor's arm and hoists him up. "Did you hit your head?"

"We should be so lucky," Marci says, gnawing a hangnail. She goes to fetch her suitcase.

"Tell me it's two pages. Two pages, right?"

"It's a bunch of gibberish, Bo." Grover stops and squints. "Yeah, two pages. Wait, how'd you know—?"

MONDAY, 12:59 PM

"Hope it lands right on Keenan Eubanks' head. I hope it blows all of Findlay off the map. I hope . . ." Wearing his blue suit and black hat, walking the down middle of empty streets, Cody Kellogg hates the sound of his voice.

"The folks at home want to know, where am I going to get work?" he says, throat stiff with tension. He can't stop himself.

The satellite will be dropping on Findlay any moment. Cody walks toward the baseball diamond to spoil the news to the protestors.

Stupid Findlay robs Dyson again.

Cody's opportunities to stay on the air look grim. "Oh, the humanity."

The snowman settles with a hollow thump.

"Easy, big fella." Skeet pushes the frame into position among his barn's other treasures. "We're almost finished."

He steps back to admire the snowman stretching up to the thick rafter beams. Skeet circles around and hums for the emptiness of all his memories. His ratty jeans and boots have a cocoa dusting of filth.

At this moment, he understands Alzheimer's. Here, among his collection of memories, is a dark gap. Something familiar but empty. Something he used to possess, but is now little more than a circle in the dirt. "Just got to find old Hans and we'll be set." He gives the snowman another long glance. A wide rip in its white plastic flesh is large enough to walk through.

Skeet steps into the crowning mid-day sunshine. He huffs in a breath of fresh air and shakes his head at the snowman. "You're disgusting. Let me get a brush and clean all that scum." Mosquitoes of pride never buzzed harder than this moment.

"Packy? What are you doing behind the bushes?" Bo calls as Marci locks the front door.

The jittery man stands and pushes aside the neighbor's shrubbery, holding some small box. His scabby hand touches a red knob on the box, then backs off, then inches closer. "N-nothing, just some gardening." Those fingers shake closer to the button and pull back.

"At Greg Tompkins' house?" Marci calls. "I didn't even know you two were friends."

Packy's hand graces the little knob, which Bo realizes is attached to a wire, and that wire slithers beneath the car.

"Packy, buddy, something you want to tell me?" His eyes blink from the light.

"*Packy*," Packy's Rutili imitation is squeaky and childish. "*Buddy, something you . . .* eh, hooey." The former mayor drops the box and backs away. Smiling. "I gotta go. Evacuation and all."

"Mr. Packwicz, wait," Marci says.

"We'll give you a ride, no problem." Bo steps toward the ex-mayor, extending a friendly hand. His other arm locking the cat against his chest. "Let me help you."

Bo's warm touch drops Packwicz to the ground. Tasting grass, Packy's lungs hiccup with sobs. His fist uproots dandelions.

"Packy?"

Bo looks back at Marci as if he doesn't recognize her. That look is a reminder of where they stand right now.

"I'm sorry," Packwicz sobs. "I'm sorry. I shouldn't have tried."

"Packy, stand up. Tell me what's wrong."

"I can't kill *myself*. I can't kill *you*. Fate is sending a satellite with my name on it. That's that."

"Kill?"

"I can't even blow up your car. I tried. I screwed up, like everything else."

"Easy. Let's start from the beginning, Packy."

He stops whining. "What's with the cat?"

"Folks, you have to leave. It's not safe. Mayor's orders."

The protestors won't listen to Chief Grover. One woman says the cop only wants her lawnmower. An elderly gentleman gets foamy in the mouth explaining how Grover would love to take his Mazda Miata for a spin, wouldn't he? A sweetie in pigtails claims Bert probably can't wait to wrap his arms around her teddy bear collection.

"Now, hold on. You're losing me here. Everybody's losing me today. Let's back up to the beginning. Can someone explain, please?"

"Everything we want is right here, Chief," one says, holding a picket sign. "There's nothing out there for us. We're just keeping you honest." The small mob, maybe fifty people, begins a chant.

Grover goes to the car to think quietly. Sticky hot vinyl seats leave that smell. *The satellite is due any minute, and if people die it's on your conscience.*

The phone rings.

"Hello?"

"I just wanted to let you know we're not coming back," Joyce says.

"Wait. Slow down." He turns the ignition and cranks the air conditioning.

"Haley and I are staying in Findlay. End of story. We're looking at houses to rent. I thought you should know." She hangs up.

The Chief squeezes the dead phone until it is greasy with sweat. Slowly, both eyes drop, drop below the steering wheel, below the dash, and onto his jangly belt. Most times he forgets that gun is even there, he's never once fired it during duty. But at this moment, with the cold air and the thick heat meeting, that dull black pistol is inviting. He's blown life in so many different ways, who'll miss him?

His hand rubs the gun butt, fingers the crease where the clip shucks into the handgrip. His tongue runs over teeth, imagining a steel barrel snuggling in. He senses the blackness to follow. He pictures his young daughter.

"That's not for you, old man," he says, and promptly removes his hand from the dash.

A moment later Bert walks back to the protestors, slings up his belt once, and realizes what they are actually talking about. "So, do you guys have one of these signs for me?"

Until this moment, Murray Kreskin couldn't stop thinking about that message he found earlier, inside that shattered piggy bank at Edna Rutili's house. But that stops in a hurry. "Dixon," he cries, digging through Edna's tool shed.

"What?" Dixon is violently rearranging the garage, making a ton of noise.

"Come here, please," Murray's voice wobbles. He looks at the blank line on his Shit List and decides there is room to add the Rutili brothers after what he just found.

"We're wasting our time out here." The lawyer walks through the perfectly cut grass to a shed with a rotting paintjob. "Can't you read? Is that it?" Dyson's smartest man climbs up some arrogant mountain. "Are you too stupid to know what that riddle you found said? That paper says we're wasting our time out in the tool shed." His bandaged shoulder is stained a hundred shades of ugly.

The bartender motions toward the shed and Dixon gets a gold-plated charge.

"You're kidding? Tell me you found the treasure, or at least another riddle." He shoots a whistle. "I guess even illiterates can find clues."

The charge fizzles into nausea. The corpse of a well-known Civil War reenactor lies on the dirt floor.

"Man, he was a good tipper," Kreskin says. "I'll miss Ed."

"Shut up, Murray. That's my best friend." Dixon's voice is quiet and shivering. "My only friend."

"Shit. I'm sorry. You're right," he says, stepping back, averting his eyes.

"Is it just me or are there a lot of people dying lately?"

"You aren't wrong there."

"God, this town's going to hell."

"I just had another bad thought. I don't think we know who we're dealing with." Kreskin holds a handkerchief over his mouth.

"What do you mean?"

"I'm saying, obviously, Bo and Gene Rutili are murderers."

The visions are gone.

Where he once pictured a mushroom cloud of black vapor and orange flame spinning cartwheels of fate—where he imagined himself melting at the base of that mess—he now embraces the helium sensation of relief.

"I'm free," Packwicz says.

"What?" Bo drives through empty streets, unsure about what to do with the assassin in the rearview mirror. The cat sounds antsy, sending long, strained meows like a violinist tuning up. It rests on Bo's lap, but sways when the car turns.

"Jesus. Quit stopping at the stop signs. We're the only ones in town. Just go." Marci digs her fingernails into the armrest.

"I've been punching myself to death for years and all it took was admitting I was wrong," Packy says. "Like confession at church or something. I've been blaming the whole world and it's been me all along."

"Churches use holy water, not dynamite, Packy," Bo says and gives a comforting laugh.

"Not funny. What Bo means . . ." she says as she turns and smiles, "is thanks for not blowing us up. That was very generous of you, Mr. Packwicz. You, *unlike some people around here*, are selfless."

"Oh, that." Pack gets bashful. "It was just road flares and and the controls to my old model train. It wasn't dynamite. I don't really know what I was trying to do."

It's clear the mayor doesn't hear. His fingers scratch the cat's ear. "We're okay, sweetie. Everything is fine. Shhhhhhh, we're okay," he says in a lover's voice.

"This reminds me of that time before you throw a party at your house."
Troy tries to be friendly, sitting atop the fruit bowl float with Pearl. A
rapidly heating summer breeze ribbons through their bare toes. A few
miles of soybean fields shiver between them and Dyson.

"Do you have enough friends to actually *throw* a party?"

"I'm serious." He sounds warm and smooth. "You know, when the
house is all clean and the decorations are hung and everything is just
silent and packed with anticipation. All the prep work is done, so you
don't know what to do with yourself but wait and wonder who'll arrive
first. I always crack a beer and watch the clock tick. Feels like forever."

"God." She chuckles. "I just always worry nobody is going to come."

He gives Pearl a long, solemn smile, not wanting to spoil that heavy
anticipation with chatter.

He doesn't have to worry long.

"Son of a bitch," Troy says, whipping off sunglasses and staring into
the sky.

A black Jetstream tail grows against the white and blue over Dyson.
It stretches closer and closer, like a crashing plane.

Pearl holds a hand over her brow. "I didn't think it would actually . . ."

Before Troy can respond, a sonic wallop finds their ears.

PART THREE

Our speck of pepper is no longer a speck.

Our speck of pepper has grabbed all the attention of all the other dots on the map—large, small, and in-between.

That spot of spice has finally done its job and caused a national sneeze. American's *gesundheit* quickly follows. This little black dot called Dyson has not grown in size, but it has most certainly blimped in reputation.

It is the site of a catastrophe. A million-to-one shot. A ghost of a chance.

Now, Dyson is getting its wish. Visitors are aiming for the village in great numbers. And that is trouble.

Cody Kellogg doesn't know what has begun until it has ended. By the time he catches on to what that noise was, the smoke of burning metal and clouds of soil have worked throughout town like humidity.

There is no fear at the sight of this display. "Eat your heart out, Herbert Morrison," he says. He doesn't hate the sound of his voice anymore.

The backs of Cody's legs burn, sprinting through the street, across yards, and around parked cars. Kellogg aims straight for WDSR's broadcast center.

Dark haze blocks the mid-summer sun, turning Dyson into some sweltering blackened hothouse. Cody can't breathe right. At the studio trailer door, in the shadow of the grain elevator, blood surges through his body with scalding intensity.

"This whole mess is my fault." The baseball field horror he witnessed stays sharply focused in his mind. Gasping, coughing, choking, he fights back a little longer. For a flicker, he thinks maybe he should have stuck around to help people. "Beat yourself up about it later; this is your shot."

Kellogg places the crown of his hat over the front door window and punches. The glass takes a bite from his knuckles. Grinding teeth, Cody reaches through and unlocks the studio door.

Exiting the outside chaos, he takes a moment for himself—just a breath of congratulations. This is a special moment. Those NASA creeps were wrong. The television crew was wrong. This is *news*. Nothing's going to stand in the way of Cody Kellogg's massive comeback.

He flips yellow switches, turns silver dials, and sits behind the control board. A river of black smoke gropes past the window. A terrifying campfire smell filters into the room. It bubbles a nervous energy to the surface that Kellogg kind of likes.

"C-C-Cody Kellogg." He breathes and pictures the Hindenburg. "Cody Kellogg, here in Dyson. If anyone is listening, the time is," he flashes to his watch, "one-fourteen p.m. and a satellite has crashed. The television reports, which claimed it was heading for nearby Findlay, were incorrect." Sweat beads on his face. "Dyson's satellite has nearly killed a few . . . dozen . . . people . . ."

Cody taps the board's dead needles, which normally bounce with his voice.

"What happened to the electricity?" he curses, licking his wet, red knuckles.

MONDAY, 1:16 PM

"Is that all?" Her bored sigh is as subtle as the rattling soybean field.

"What do you mean?" Troy says, muscles stiff with confusion.

Afraid any movement will offset some higher balance and drop more satellites toward his beloved town.

It seems so strange, to see the blue sky and to feel the sun's heat. So normal and pleasant, except for what just happened.

"I was expecting a fireball. An earthquake. *Something.*" Pearl hops from the float and squints toward the distant town. The deep black smell of burning finds them.

"God, that sounded like a pretty big explosion." Troy's ears squeal.

"A couple, I thought. I hope everyone is alright."

She removes her sunglasses and shakes them toward the skyline. "But it wasn't *huge.* Where was the atomic whoosh? I can still see the grain elevator and that ridiculous halo. All the stupid trees are standing. I mean, there's really not even that much smoke."

"Don't you dare sound disappointed." He reaches for her shoulder, but pulls back. "I used to think that way. It's dangerous."

"Good for you."

"Dyson's got something."

She crosses her arms. "Well, I want explosions. It doesn't have that."

"What is wrong with you?"

"I just lost a very close friend, okay? I'm emotionally damaged. Plus, every time I try and make life better, something blocks my path." She kicks the float.

"Pearl Krupp, the human tragedy," he says, cooling down.

Troy remembers the secret weapon back at the factory. Dyson isn't destroyed, so work can resume. He begins swallowing pride for the first time in his life and realizes the flavor isn't so bad. Humility actually feels nice. It feels comfortable in a midwestern sort of way. "Look, I've been an asshole to you for a long time. You're really smart and a hard worker. Everyone says so. If you want, I could use some help with the parade. We can do something terrific. But you've got to lighten up . . ."

He pictures it: the parade, the fireworks, face-painting Rosinski mustaches on kids, plastic fruit juggling contests.

"Me lighten up? Maybe if I had a career like you. Maybe if the *one* person on Earth who understood me wasn't dead. Maybe if you pay me all those tips you stiffed me from the last few years."

He closes his eyes, feeling the tug of drama. Knowing the rabid pleasures of argument. But Troy smiles, and it feels so unlike him. "I'm sorry. You deserve better."

"Well." Pearl runs a nervous finger up and down her arm. A tic from childhood. She is knocked off balance by Troy and this vulnerability. "I don't know, I mean, I might have a few extra minutes . . . maybe."

"Cool," he says and pauses, wondering what next.

Pearl, tall and soft, points into the distance. "Hey, more smoke!"

A drizzle of blackness leaks toward the sky from a distant horizon point.

"That's over by Skeet's."

MONDAY, 1:35 PM

"Listen, I'm a lawyer. You're a bartender. If we were debating the best sawdust to use on vomit, okay. But you need to trust me on this. First, we find Chief Grover, *then* we follow this note. Otherwise we could be in hot water not reporting Ed's murder." Jamming a finger toward the windshield, Dixon's voice raises. "Drive faster. What are you scared of?"

Smoke ghosts hang from treetops and give the town a claustrophobic density.

Those familiar threads of barroom happiness are stripped from Kreskin's voice. In its place, something childish and jumpy. "I'm scared I don't know what's out here. I can't see shit. We could drive right into a crater or something—"

Across Dyson, flags snap, bushes are still rounded and manicured, rainbows of aluminum sided houses sit neatly. Nothing terrifying, nothing out of the norm except the complete lack of traffic. And, really, Dyson was never exactly the downtown Chicago commute.

Dixon's voice is calming. Dyson's resident genius is back in his element. His shoulder wound is dry and scabbing. Things could be worse.

"Let's find Bert Grover; he can handle this murder mess and move on to phase two. Then, *boom*, we're rich."

"Wrong." Murray nervously sucks his upper lip until half the mustache disappears. "We should find this treasure like this baby says." Murray passes the folded sheet of paper found in the piggy bank. "*Then* find Chief Grover."

"Are you questioning me? I have doctorate in law. You have a doctorate in daiquiris. Not reporting this is a criminal offense, Murray. Something strange is happening in town. Three dead now. We have murderers out there. These Rutili kids, I never trusted them. Not even when Eugene was on my basketball team," Dixon says. "We need to talk to the Chief. I don't want these maniacs on my conscience. What if they kill again?"

Finally, the peaceful summer sun wedges through clouds and blesses healthy green lawns and FOR SALE signs.

"Oh, then Grover starts asking why we were over at Edna's house. Why were we poking through the garden shed? Who ransacked her place?" Kreskin stops the car in the middle of a street. Dixon notes clear eggs of sweat bunching around the bartender's sideburns. "Wait. You hear that?"

"I think it's your mustache talking," he says. Dixon unfolds the note again. The paper is weathered and brittle. Rosinski's autograph is at the bottom. The faded ink is hard to read in spots. Dixon has a hunch what Rosinski's little poem is talking about:

> *Under fifteen feet*
> *of solid concrete*
> *the golden fruit*
> *Doesn't fall far*
> *from the plastic tree*

Dyson's smartest man knows it is best to keep quiet. "It's your imagination. Hey, have you heard the one about a priest, a rabbi, and Chuck Yeager? They're all in a hot air balloon—"

For once, jokes don't interest Murray. "I don't know, man. What if something just drops out of the sky. Think about it, we could just die at any moment."

"Then I'll be pissed." *Fifteen feet of concrete* whirls through Dixon's mind. His fingers begin to pick at his pantleg lint, to adjust the air vent repeatedly. Whenever he has a good idea or a secret, nothing can hold it inside.

This quirk has made him a courthouse joke. He hasn't won a case in years. Dixon prefers wills and jobs that keep him away from court because of an embarrassing tendency to blurt out confidential secrets. One recent divorce client learned this lesson the hard way when Dixon began a long-winded speech about the husband's stag film collection. Not old-fashioned bachelor party pornos, but actual deer in heat. Close-up penetration shots, the whole nine. Judge Amos was not amused.

"Fruit. Concrete. It's got to be at the factory." Wendell slumps, feeling helpless to stop this cycle.

"That's not a horrible thought." Murray is silent for a minute. "Yeah, I think I have a hunch where to look. I worked there one summer. There's this giant X painted on the factory floor, like X marks the spot. I always heard it had something to do with where the delivery trucks were supposed to park. But *this* makes so much more sense. So we'll check there first, then tell Grover about the Rutilis murdering poor Ed Lee." Life flushes back into Murray's face. "You know, I used to think you were some silver spooned bastard. Some dipshit with a degree. I might have had you wrong, buddy. We're actually a lot alike."

"Touching. Just keep driving. Take a left here." Dixon doesn't understand why he is arguing. He does the same thing with his wife, which accounts for much of the last decade's tension. There's an instinct to play devil's advocate and prove his smarts. Whether it is arguing about building a new porch or seeking out the Rosinski fortune, Dixon inherently takes the opposite stance, even if he doesn't believe it. "Alright, in court we do something called a *settlement.*"

"A settlement? Like a camp? Like Plymouth Rock?"

"A settlement is kind of like a *compromise.*"

"Plymouth Rock was a settlement, too. Look it up."

Dixon's stray fingers touch his raw shoulder wound. "Here's the deal: if we see Grover, we'll talk. If we don't, we'll go right to the factory."

"Alright, fine. I'll take the settlement." Murray turns down by the baseball diamond. "But if you think you can outfox me, I'll use your spine for a golf club—"

The thin squeal of truck brakes slashes through silent Dyson. The ballpark's smell reminds Dixon of a tire fire. "Holy shit."

"Look at that hole."

"Are those bodies?"

"I'm going to be sick."

MONDAY, 2:05 PM

Donna moves in jerks and sighs, listening to Old Man Packwicz. She is half-relieved, but nauseous. Her plan worked, but it worked too well.

Queen's casino office is less impressive than her home office. Construction is still underway. The space is all drywall and exposed ceiling wires. The coffee pot in the corner brews something robust. A muted television flickers with helicopter views of a smoky ribbon rising from a Midwestern town, but it may as well not be on since Donna is so focused.

Packy's voice is the voice of a man who could kill again. "So when it was over I took our friend out to the woods. Deep into the woods, you know?"

"No, I don't know." Donna sounds dumb and gullible—two things she's never been mistaken for. "Like where nobody will find him?"

"Not unless they have a backhoe." Old jittery Packwicz relaxes and casually crosses a leg. His jeans are frayed at the hem, his shoe has a hole. This killing seems to have brought him back to reality, back into confidence. "Let's just say Bo put a down payment on a dirt condo."

Packy seems human again, which scares Donna. She fully understands her responsibility in that young man's death, and it makes her mouth fill hot with saliva. It makes her stomach collapse with pain.

She undoes the top button of her black blouse, aching for something to cool her down.

Judging from that story, Packy might never get caught. This scrawny, pale excuse for an ex-mayor actually did the job like a professional. Bo Rutili is out of her hair, but wasn't removed in the reckless fashion she predicted. This spins her head with dizziness. The Queen fortune is currently wrapped up in the casino and there is no cash for a hit man. Not even that fifty grand down payment she promised. If Packy handled one murder so capably, what would stop him if Donna doesn't deliver?

I've created a monster, she thinks.

"Well," she swallows dry. "Thank you. Now I think you should go home and relax."

Packwicz lifts his chin. "Don't have a home. Ceiling collapsed, remember?" His grey flattop turns to translucent pins in the light. His eyes burn with something unfamiliar to Donna, something brooding.

Packy is planning to kill me, she thinks.

"No, no," Garrett says, surprising her. Out of nowhere, he's chummy with Packwicz. "Packy should get a tour of the casino. Hey, have you ever thought about being a pit boss?"

"What's a pit boss?" The murderer grins, and Donna clenches to stop her bowels. "Nah. I'll just take my money and move on. You guys promised a *few* million. How many is a few million, exactly? We never drew up a contract or anything."

"Plenty of time for that. You should see our buffet. First class. Donna planned the menu herself." Garrett smacks Packwicz's arm. "Tater tots far as the eye can see."

The pair walks out and leaves Donna's office door cracked.

Something is crushing Dyson's richest woman. Foggy memories of panic attacks return. The last time the walls closed in this tight and the skin around her neck choked like angry hands was after that lotto business.

She honestly wanted to give Packy a cut of the money, but the other winners didn't. All together, the group won one hundred eighty million, what was the harm? When they voted, she was the only one to raise her hand in Packwicz's favor. The seven other bowling alley employees moved to the Caribbean or Spain—anywhere guilt couldn't find them—leaving Donna to answer this sad man's claim.

She and Garrett planned on moving far away, too. First, the French Riviera and then to Mexico, but she got cold feet both times. The answer is so clear to her.

Donna digs fingernails into her temples, groping for a pressure valve. *I am as good as dead. Or at least I'll go to jail*, she thinks. She stops rubbing and looks up. *It's time to do what you do best. It's time to convert this negative into a positive.*

"Heroes don't cry."

MONDAY, 2:10 PM

"Go now. Go!" Chief Grover swats them both with a police hat. "You're the only able-bodied men I've seen all afternoon."

Murray Kreskin and Wendell Dixon walk off slowly, arguing something about a *settlement*. The baseball diamond smells burnt, but there isn't any fire. The heart of the mess is a jagged, earthy divot he could drop a car into. Smoke disintegrates upward into a wavy cobra charmed from a basket.

Bodies are spread around the grass. The Chief tries remembering what happened. One second he was holding some sign, protesting with the group, and then Cody Kellogg stormed up, whining about how there was no satellite. Everyone scurried to home plate, asking what Kellogg was talking about. Jesus, that guy loves hearing himself talk.

Among the confusion, something sudden and violent shoved Grover into the grass. Shirts and hair flapping. A hurricane of dirt and rocks and death-like darkness. Then, an amazing sound—like holding a stethoscope to a blasting shotgun—ripped across them.

Remembering it all, self-hatred begins to jab a pitchfork into Bert's back.

Whatever fell from the sky would have reduced this entire crowd to meat scraps and bone dust if they hadn't moved a few hundred yards and gathered around home plate.

It's a policeman's job to keep people safe, he thinks.

"You're weak," Grover says under his breath. "Why didn't you know this was happening? If the protestors would have stayed put, they would have died. It would have been your fault. You have a responsibility."

A bonfire builds in Bert's shoulders from the stress. There is something even worse than causing those deaths—someone else preventing them. Worst of all, some beatnik like Kellogg.

The injured lay across the grass. Many have red, swollen eyes. Lots have scrapes and bruises. A white, irregular bone actually pops through one man's arm.

Thankfully, nobody died.

"Are you sure there were forty-six people here?" he asks the elderly woman in charge.

"Yes, I phoned everyone myself and reminded them. Well, forty-six not counting you and Mr. Kellogg."

He thanks her and stumbles to the police cruiser. "You're a piece of work, Bert. You're a horrible father, a shitty cop, and . . . a waste of talent."

That does it.

Bert knows rolling around in sentimental pig shit ends this way every time. There is only one cure for his pain. He begs Mahler to ease his wounded conscience.

Out around the ball field something dull cuts the air. Muffled opera, the huge, desperate voice of a man falling off a cliff mingles with the blistering crackles of a disintegrating satellite.

His mouth opens wider than an expectant catcher's mitt. That baritone pushes beyond the windows and welds. Few things are as heartbreaking and powerful as Bert Grover in full force.

Someone knocks on his window. "Hey, Pavarotti." A man in an orange hazmat suit stands by the car. "You Chief Grover?"

Grover is out of breath and his throat stings.

"Do you know a man named Skeet Brown? We need help looking for survivors."

MONDAY, 2:45 PM

"Is this your sister's sixth zither, sir?" Cody's mouth tastes like it's been on a hot date with a gas pump.

A small generator behind the radio station purrs with siphoned gasoline. His lips are raw and another swish of water doesn't help. Mr. Razzle-Dazzle could have just pulled the WDSR van alongside the generator and run the tube from one tank to the other, but that would sabotage everything. Cody needs the van. He had to suck fuel from some other car down the block.

"Lesser leather never weathered wetter weather better." He coughs and gags. Fuel sting lava trickles down his throat. "Sam's shop stocks short spotted socks."

The remote switches are turned and the feed is ready. WDSR has a portable transmitter in the van so they can broadcast from high school basketball games. Cody doesn't know if anyone is listening, but the studio tape is rolling and the Internet audio is streaming.

Cody's vocal chords finally feel loose. His Hindenburg has finally landed.

MONDAY, 3:00 PM

The only other business with enough foresight to purchase a generator actually owns two. Troy has FruitCo running at full speed within an hour of the satellite blitz.

Great, noisy industrial machines smash hot goo into molds. The hardened results drop from a chute and stack across the warehouse floor, still warm to the touch.

"What is all this?" Pearl says, running a finger down the window of Troy's office, daydreaming how all the jumbled colors across the warehouse resemble a bowl of jellybeans.

"Can you believe we didn't come across any of those Army idiots? What luck!"

Pearl shuffles through Troy's desk, spotting a stack of CD cases. "Don't you have anything but the Rolling Stones?"

"Why would I?"

"Seriously, this is a little O.C.D. I count, what, ten albums. All the same band."

"I was in a Stones mood. I have other stuff. Just not here."

"You should get some jazz."

"Yeah, sure. That schizophrenic crap I hear coming out of your car half the time?"

"Ornette Coleman is not crap."

"That's the name." He laughs. "You're just as bad as me."

"What?"

"I have the Stones, you have Oliver Coltrane or whatever. We're creatures of habit," Gomez says.

"You're hopeless."

Troy switches the coffee maker on. His mind is stalled without stiff, black French roast.

Had Pearl not also been a witness, he still wouldn't believe the satellite. "God, I honestly never thought anything would happen."

"Troy?" She wears an impressed grin. "Seriously, what have you been doing here?"

"Those soldiers were probably raiding the bar. Probably drunk again. *Idiots.*"

"They drank everything but the toilet cleaner during my last shift." Pearl's movements are delicate, almost nervous—the way she acts as a stranger in someone's house. "But, hey, what is all this down there?"

Troy blinks burning red eyes and watches her. This Krupp is more timid, less confident than Marci. Troy isn't sure if he likes that better. Pearl is very pretty, but lacks Marci's spark. Spark is important to him.

"The fruit, the floats, the costumes—it's all part of my plan. Well, Marci's plan, too." He waits for her reaction, but none comes. Pearl holds a plastic pear up to the light and lets it glow green. "We're celebrating Gerald Rosinski Day a little earlier than planned. Like now. Tomorrow."

"Why?"

"Do you want to be from the town Lincoln shit all over?"

"I don't really care what Dyson's known for. I'm leaving." She flips on her sunglasses and looks the part of a jet setting television cohost.

"Like I said, I used to agree with you. Thought this town was a waste. But something changed. You can see your whole life here. Building blocks, foundations, the things that really make a life worth living."

"Hollywood has building blocks, I'm sure."

"Not the same. I mean, okay, so Dyson isn't perfect. But some stuff is really great. If you lived in any city, your memories would be vague and scattered across miles, changing every year. Trust me. I went to school in Chicago."

"Good for you." Arms fold across her chest. "What about bad memories?" Her eyebrows raise. "Lots of shitty stuff happens here. Stuff that wouldn't in a city. My friend Rajula Magbi, you know, the TV star? She died because of Dyson."

"Okay, that's fair. It's not all good. But think about it, every three steps around town, some memory makes you laugh or breaks your heart all over again. This town is like a concentrated, pure point of our lives. There aren't many places that can offer that."

Pearl's mind drifts. She replays Rajula's last moments. That flicker when her weak heart stopped, lying in Pearl's arms. Pearl's face goes limp, her jaw hangs open in a daydream.

"Look, you can pitch in if you want . . ." Troy goes to the door and slips on a hard hat. "Or you can bail. I stand for something and that makes me feel good. If you want to wallow, knock yourself out."

Gomez pauses in the doorway, adjusting the hat, waiting for something.

"Sorry." She watches Troy turn and leave. The office is empty and suddenly endless.

She remembers Rajula's philosophy about small towns. Rajula's honesty and positivity shiver down Pearl's back. *Is that what's missing from my life?*

A few minutes later, down on the floor, Troy is inspecting Marci's patchy costumes. That familiar stomach cramp of heartbreak is building. He cannot stop thinking about her laugh. Troy's mind drifts. It imagines a Christmas card with their picture on it—him, Marci, and a couple kids.

"Hey." Pearl taps his shoulder and speaks over the hammering factory. She has a real smile, not the usual condescending smirk. "I think Rajula would have wanted me to help. Besides, maybe some TV camera will catch me at the parade."

"Sounds good. Thank you."

"So what are you doing with a million pieces of fruit?" She points to the growing plastic pile, now taking on a pyramid shape.

Troy doesn't hesitate, doesn't spend a second wondering if she is serious. Like Mick and Keith catching a good riff, he runs with it. "Come on, I'll show you. I drew a diagram!" He grabs her wrist. The soft skin is just like Marci's. "For starters, there's not a million. Only about three hundred thousand pieces, actually."

MONDAY, 3:28 PM

An open window is the only light in the mayor's office. A brass-colored beam fills the room. Hot breaths of wind lift the paperwork. Bo runs a sleeve across his wet forehead. The room smells like attic boxes of musty books.

"What?" he says to the man. This is the twelfth time Bo asks him to speak up during the meeting. The mayor wipes his face again, panting, very desperate for news.

"This is only tem-PO-rary. The quarantine." The orange hazmat suit crinkles and squeaks each time his posture changes.

"Why is there a quarantine at all?"

"Consider yourself lucky the satellite wasn't nuclear. Those bastards take forever to clean up."

"Does this happen a lot?"

"More than you want to know. This Orion model satellite isn't anything special, so it won't take long. We're just being careful. Nobody gets in or out of a five-mile radius. Period."

The man phoned Bo's cell a few moments after impact—a few minutes after the mayor told Packwicz he had a plan to keep Donna Queen off his back. The man in the plastic suit is from some branch of the government that apparently handles such disasters. He is in the habit of speaking with jabbing hands.

"Be honest, sir, what's the damage? I drove around a bit, things don't seem too bad." Bo wipes his forehead. "Ugh, I can live without lights, but no air conditioner—"

"Try walking around in Saran Wrap." The man chuckles and fogs the clear plastic face shield. "According to some initial findings, the satellite stayed together remarkably well. Two smaller chunks broke off, but the bulk held tight before impact."

"The damage? I haven't heard from my chief of police. I don't have any idea of damage. I'm very concerned for my citizens. We're like a family here."

"We're not one hundred percent sure ourselves. My men are looking into it. One piece fell near a crowd of protestors at the baseball field."

"Shit. Grover was supposed to handle them." Bo fans himself with a report. He begins to consider his role in this. His responsibility to get everyone out of town, even those unwilling to leave. The feeling makes him want to find somewhere to hide. He wishes Boots was here to pet, to calm his nerves. He left the cat in the basement where the temperature was still cool.

"Another made impact near the intersection of Maplewood Drive and Main Street. It may have destroyed an automobile."

"Was anyone hurt?" Bo leans forward. The hazmat man looks familiar.

"Hard to say right now. We're sifting through remains. It's just a burnt hole with some suspension springs lying around. I should know more within the hour. We're pretty perfect at our job."

Bo slugs back a large gulp of water and undoes another shirt button, exposing chest hair.

The hazmat man speaks again.

"What?" the mayor asks. His mind drifts toward the Rosinski

Diary. Tucked in his back pocket, it hums for this meeting to conclude. Grover's two missing pages bring all the squiggles and gibberish into focus. Dyson's Rosetta Stone. The diary alone is useless, but combined with the map Packy found in the old Rosinski Headquarters, a lot of possibilities unlock. Dyson needs this gold, he reminds himself. He tells himself to think of those electric paddle things EMTs use.

"I said, the main satellite portion touched down beyond the city limits. NASA's calculations were slightly skewed. We know very little about this rogue section. We didn't find it right away."

"Is it bad?" Bo catches something familiar in the man's face.

"Can't say. However, we can confirm this is the majority of the satellite. So if these little scraps around town wiped a car from the road, imagine something ten times its size. We're talking solid."

"I was told by this NASA guy, Agent Eggleston, that the satellite would wipe out a couple square miles. That doesn't seem to have happened, so how can you be sure?"

"Trust me. We're pretty accurate. I mean, we are NASA."

Bo squints, but can't see much through the suit's glass. The man seems familiar. "Agent Eggleston, is that you?"

"I'm not at liberty to answer that," he snaps and looks away.

The pair speak until Bo's face is red and wet. According to the man, the President of the United States is debating whether to call this a disaster area. He hasn't pulled the trigger yet and if he doesn't, clean up might be Dyson's responsibility and not the government's.

"Keep me informed," Bo says and shakes hands. "Agent Eggleston, that is you, isn't it?"

The man in orange plastic leaves without reply.

Bo tidies up his office and finds the copy of his grandmother's will. A tickle of guilt forms in his chest. His big brother is probably worried.

Bo's cell phone is cued up to call. He makes mental notes to ask about Gene's new house, his Tae Kwon Do studio . . . do they call it a dojo? That might be a good question. How did he meet his girlfriend, where—

This reminds the mayor to call someone else in Findlay first. He shuts the window with the intention of heading to the cooler climate of the basement, dials the new number, and waits.

Findlay's mayor picks up after six rings.

"Mr. Mayor, it's Bo Rutili. We're in a real pickle here. I think Dyson can certainly use that aid you offered. The emergency medical workers, the road repair crews, the mobile soup kitchen, I'll take the works."

No response.

"Hello? Hello?"

"About that," Findlay's mayor stammers. "We're going to pass."

There's a childish slant to Bo's voice. "But you promised. What happened to solidarity among—"

"*Solidarity among mayors?*" he impersonates. "Look son, satellites are so boring. Here in the city, we're already over them. They're yesterday's news."

"But Dyson needs help . . . today."

"I wish I could. But I'm a public servant and the public, frankly, isn't interested in your problems. There was a tornado in Nebraska yesterday. Terrible stuff. A lot of people without power. These poor bastards have to drink warm Coke. All the meat in their freezer has turned . . . I don't even want to say it. My constituents think we should focus on helping tornado victims in Nebraska get back on the grid."

"But we don't have any electricity, either."

"Yeah, I mentioned that at a meeting. But the others were sort of . . . what's the word?"

"You're saying you don't care?"

"I'm saying . . . yeah. Sort of. I think you're the only one who really does."

Something scratchy in the back of Bo's throat wants to fight more, but he just pulls the diary from a pocket and hangs up.

MONDAY, 3:45 PM

"I know it's wrong, I was just *saying*," Murray Kreskin says in the firehouse darkness. The entire place still smells like charcoal after last week's fundraiser rib cook-off. Kreskin and one-armed Dixon struggle to lift the dead garage door. It raises a crack, sending whiteness and shadow across the room. "Just that I wish I never had all this medical training right now. Part of me realizes that's a pretty cruel thing to say. But the other part, well, you know what he thinks. I just don't know which is the angel on my shoulder and which one's the devil."

The door rolls up its tracks and they squint toward the sunlight.

"We signed up to be volunteer firefighters for a reason, Murray."

"Yeah. So I could ride in a firetruck whenever I wanted."

"We have a responsibility to help people. It was one thing with poor Ed Lee's dead body. But there are dozens who need us at the ball park." Dixon buckles into the passenger seat of the fire department Jeep as Kreskin backs out. The Jeep is loaded with medical supplies. "We took an oath."

"I never took an oath."

"Really? You should have. Let's talk to Donnie Grimes as soon as we can and get your hand on a Bible."

"Listen, my pop used to say you can't help others 'til you get your own shit square. And man, that gold is just sitting there. Didn't you hear me? It's nobody's, so it might as well be ours." Kreskin's voice growls low, aiming to hurt. "I hope *nobody* takes it."

"Grow a backbone."

"Easy for you to say, moneybags lawyer," he mutters under his breath. Murray runs the sirens and aims for the ball field. "Hey. That shoulder looks terrible. You want me to dress it? God knows we have the training."

"No."

"Plus, we don't want people asking questions, offering to take you to the hospital."

"I'm fine."

They drive in silence for a few minutes. Halfway across town, Murray stops the Jeep. He stares straight ahead.

"Last chance to skip this shit and get rich."

"Damn it," he hits Murray. "Look at my hand shake. You think that's because I'm *nervous* about these idiots at the ball field? Or do you think it's because I want that stupid gold more than anything?" Dixon drops the hand to his lap. "We'll get it, but we have a responsibility. You might not believe it, but I have a few principles left."

"Fooled me."

"If you don't think this is tearing me up, you're wrong. And, while we're at it, drop that moneybags shit. A lawyer in Dyson doesn't make much more than a bartender. And that lawyer has a job he hates and a wife who hates him and an uninsured house that is probably a pile of sticks right now!" He pounds a weak fist into the seat. "So let's hustle up, bandage some heads, and get that stupid gold and go our separate ways."

"You're right. I'm sorry." Murray nods with stiff lips and gasses the motor.

Dixon gets hot and uncomfortable in the silence. He needs to settle down. "So, I've always wanted to ask something."

"You're looking at an open book."

"It's personal. Well, maybe not. It's actually very public."

"Go on."

"The hand; the tattoo. What's with it?"

Murray lifts his left hand—Eugene, Bo, and Dixon are scribbled on it. Dixon twice. "It's a Shit List."

"I see that. But, why keep a shit list on your hand?"

"Forget it. It's stupid."

"Come on."

"I guess so people know where they stand. My dad had one. That's where the idea came from. Remember? I got the tattoo after he died."

"No, I don't."

"He was a Ranger in the War. Crazy bunch of SOBs, according to Pop. Each got a tat just like this. Theirs had Hitler and Mussolini and sometimes their commanding officer listed."

"But why you?"

"I don't know. I miss Dad. He was my best friend. We kept each other company. Now this keeps me company."

Dixon grunts a small understanding.

"It makes me feel less alone. I guess that's kind of screwed up, right?"

"I think any decision to be less alone in this world is a good one."

"Thanks, Dix. You're alright, man."

"When all this is over," he says, "we should go fishing or something. Hang out more."

"Who couldn't use more friends?"

"Murray, whoa." Dixon points. A cluster of people in orange jump-suits hold stop signs in front of the abandoned school. The blue sky above is hazy with the now familiar incense of fire.

"Jesus, what the hell is this?"

A plastic orange man approaches, holding a badge. Murray rolls down the window.

"You're the EMTs?"

"Look at the side of the Jeep and let me know."

"Sir, are you familiar with the Baseline Road area?"

"Nice to see you, too." Kreskin slides a hand toward his pistol.

"Sir, this is government business."

"Yeah. Baseline's out by Skeet Brown's place."

A pause. The man behind the mask flaps some clipboarded papers. "We need medical assistance out there immediately."

"We were going to the baseball field."

"We know about the field. The General has designated this as a higher priority."

MONDAY, 4:00 PM

"But Donna," Garrett says, trailing her through corridors. Past fresh-cut flowers, past Italian marble sculptures by some guy they can't re-member, under the dangling, glittering chandeliers, and all the way to their restaurant-quality kitchen. The chef is bubbling up a fragrant pot of Donna's favorite vegetable soup, but she doesn't even pause. "Wait, Donna, wait."

She doesn't.

The CEO of the Urinating Bear Casino loads her husband's nervous arms with gallons of bottled water. Cans of chili and carrots and creamed corn are slid into a sack.

"Take this out to the van, sweetheart." Her bright green eyes land daggers into Garrett's resistance. "We don't have any time to waste. That new maid, what's-her-name, is rounding up all the clothes we were saving for the Salvation Army."

Garret watches Donna hustle. It isn't that he's never seen his wife rush. Frankly, she always moves at maximum pace. But this facial expression, this stoniness, is a force that cannot be stopped. It's a jolt.

A minute later, on the driveway—with distant sirens and helicopter blades breaking the country peace—Garrett sees their old white van from before Donna had money. "Hero Mobile" is hastily painted in large, dripping red letters along the side. The back end is packed with gauze, insulin, antibacterial soap. "Four cases of bandages . . ." He swallows tough, reminded of that evil, bandaged *thing* strutting around town ruining car hoods at will, mocking him.

Donna brings more supplies, but has a new look. Garrett recognizes this face. She is mad at herself. "If you wouldn't be such a poor planner, you'd already be in town, saving lives. You don't have much time," she says to herself.

"Where did all this come from, Donna?"

She makes her way back to the house.

"Donna?" He looks over his shoulder, toward the stack of bandages.

Her legs charge forward, mumbling about going to jail. About being as good as dead.

"Donna, damn it, stop!" Garrett spins her until a high-heeled ankle wobbles.

"Garrett, *what*? I need to help."

"Where did this come from?" What is happening with the woman he loves? It is like she has a secret life. Jealousy becomes a factor. "I thought we got rid of that van years ago." He recalls the old, analog stereo and its comforting orange tuner. "Does it still have that JVC?"

"I did something terrible. I never should have hired Packwicz to . . . you know." Her eyes go fragile. She takes a reassuring breath.

"But I decided to turn this negative into a positive before that madman kills me . . . us. It's time someone stepped forward and . . . you know . . . *something-something-something.*"

"The van, the supplies. I counted twelve pairs of crutches . . ."

"Twelve?" Her lips pinch. "I bought twenty. I bet that new housekeeper stole them. We need to hire Sylvia back." She kisses Garrett's cheek. "Never mind. I decided to honor Bo's life by being the greatest hero this town's ever seen."

"Just slow down. Don't you think Packy would have taken care of us by now if he were going to? I mean, he wants that money pretty bad. That's as good of leverage as we can hope for."

Donna returns to the house without a sound, and he is alone, watching something blackly mysterious rise across the fields. It's Dyson. He hasn't even had time to pay attention. The smoke captures his gaze. Tragedies always happen in far off places, isolated by television screens. But this is real. This awfulness paws at the front door. He hopes none of his friends are hurt.

A stranger with a crew cut walks up their long driveway. Stiff posture and military fatigues. "Sergeant Robert Mosley, sir." He gives a stiff salute. "I'm looking for Mrs. Donna Queen."

Garrett once looked at Donna's unpredictability with a smile. He loved the way she'd buy a bank or a radio station on a whim. Even before being rich, he frequently came home and discovered a small suitcase packed for a surprise romantic getaway. He misses those days, because lately her impromptu ideas are alien and uncomfortable. Hero Mobiles and stacks of bandages and soldiers showing up a day before the casino opens.

"Huh?"

"I spoke with Mrs. Queen about a job. Head of security. Sir, if I may be frank, the rest of my battalion was being irresponsible. Drinking and fornicating while they should have been carrying out our mission. It's only fair you know I am AWOL from the Guard."

Garrett's blinking eyes come down with the force of rusty shutters. "Right . . ."

The soldier stands patiently. Chopper blades and sirens dance around their silence.

"Oh, *goodie*," Donna squeals from the doorway, zipped into a full-body jumpsuit the color of plastic apples. "Muscles, you're just in time. Garrett will fill you in on Casino goings-on. Me, I'm off." She arches her back so the patch below her shoulder sticks out. It reads: DONNA QUEEN—HERO.

"When did you have time to make a patch?" Garrett says.

She doesn't even turn to say goodbye. The van's engine comes to life and she disappears.

Garrett dissects the strange shifting in his guts. He's never been disappointed by his wife, not even when she decided to cover for the other lotto winners and exclude Packwicz. This sticky gross feeling tells him what disappointment is like. He wants to forget it immediately. Garrett nervously grins at the soldier, "Uh, hi . . . "

"Sir."

"So . . . "

"Sir, I am patiently awaiting orders." Muscles salutes again.

"You know, if Donna can cover up her pain and worry with distractions, so can I."

"I . . . sir . . . I came about the security job."

"Oh," Garrett says. He notices the car's crumpled hood, and the image of fistfighting the mummy flickers through his mind. The bandage pile is sluggish and Garrett's punches are wrecking balls. It makes Donna proud. It makes Donna hot. "Right. Well, people cheat and . . . ah . . . your job is to toss them out. Plain and simple."

"Affirmative, sir."

"Now if you'll excuse me, my car needs a new hood."

MONDAY, 4:30 PM

"I am never dating a politician again," Marci says to nobody, stepping from the car.

Thin, grey clouds climb from FruitCo's lone smokestack and fan into invisibility. Troy told her the smoke isn't smoke, but steam from the plastic molding process. "My biggest goal with this stupid factory," he said, "has been to remove all the toxins in the process. That way the only thing this crap pollutes is good taste."

Bo would never be so thoughtful.

Late afternoon sunshine burns across her freckles. Marci walks past the granite stump where FruitCo's logo once stood. She admires it, breathing fresh air laced with strains of molten plastic. Before that satellite dropped she thought this rocky chunk made the building vulnerable and sad. But now, the bare podium looks proud—it says, *everything comes to an end, but strong people deal with it.*

"I am one of those people," she declares. She's waited nearly thirty years for life to find her, now it is time to hunt down happiness and pin it to the ground. It's time to make the Rosinski Festival something memorable. It's time to grab Troy by the neck and give him the kiss of their "lifetimes."

"Four, five, six . . ." Walking down the hallway, head high, she tries remembering how many costumes need to be sewn. "What time should we start the parade? How will we promote it? Troy and I should probably recruit volunteers. So much to do."

Briefly, she thinks about baby names again. Kyle Gomez rings strong and proud. Laura isn't bad either. They were so close to that kiss before. It warms her throughout, determined to tell Troy how she feels—no distractions.

Marci plucks a hardhat from the wall and presses through the swinging doors. Her eyes adjust to the dull warehouse light, her ears wince at the brutal factory racket, and a blotch of vomit creeps into her mouth after laying eyes on her.

"Hey!" Marci's sister says. "What do you think?" Troy holds Pearl's face, gluing on a mustache. The prettier Krupp wears one of the dozen Gerald Rosinski costumes. The herringbone suit wraps her curves like a glove.

Her kid sister begins marching around the room with her straight white teeth below the mustache. "I like fruit, I like fruit, I like fruit," Pearl chants in a deep, masculine voice.

Marci swallows the acid and her mouth tastes about as pleasant as her heart feels.

MONDAY, 4:49 PM

Above the dark crater, tree leaves whisper into the mic the way Cody Kellogg hopes listeners are whispering. Discussing his fearless reportage in the face of doom, and maybe his gorgeous voice—wondering why he hasn't yet cut an album.

"Folks, I've never quite seen anything like it. I'm standing beside a hole in the ground, about as round and deep as a backyard swimming pool. But where you'd expect glassy blue stillness, there is nothing but char. The smell, the smell is burning fuel, along with something stiffer. Singed hair, but more nauseating. There is a man in an orange plastic suit collecting scraps. At my feet lie a suspension spring, some bolts, a twisted metal rod, all ashy and dark. Torched husks of beer cans and whiskey bottles spread around the perimeter." The airwaves fill with the rustling of Cody's footsteps. "Sir, excuse me, sir."

It is fortunate the man can't smell anything from behind a few millimeters of plastic mask. He doesn't give Cody the same disgusted look every other interview subject has. It is hard for Mr. Razzle-Dazzle to make a lot of friends with breath reeking of premium octane gasoline. The generator is a guzzler, which makes Cody one, too.

"What happened here?"

Cody places the microphone to a small white ventilation opening in the hazmat suit. "We are about ninety-nine percent certain this was a military vehicle."

"One of the National Guard patrols, perhaps?" Some hidden mechanism spins within Cody upon discovering this crater. During rehearsal, he spoke with swagger and personality, spewing catch phrases and name-dropping himself. But in the real world—with humanity's mangled ugliness reaching out for his hastily bandaged hand—Cody simply reports. He is more Herbert Morrison than he realizes.

The hazmat man's voice is stiff. "Unfortunately, that looks to be the case."

"Terrible, sir. A tragedy. Can you tell the folks at home how many casualties we're dealing with?"

"We don't have an exact number. We'll have to check with the Guard. A Humvee can hold . . . gee, I don't know. About eight passengers."

"Thank you. Ladies and gentlemen, the scene is absolute silence. Another man, also in an orange suit, has collected a clutch of dog tags with a pencil. The tags are deformed and still smoking. It does, in fact, seem the satellite has claimed brave volunteer soldiers among its victims."

"Tragic."

MONDAY, 5:02 PM

"Bo, thank God," his brother says. Bo holds the phone with his shoulder and neck, while rifling through his office desk drawers. "We've been glued to the television. Tell me you got out alright. Come on over to my house. You remember the address? We'll get you a meal. Plus, I've been wanting to talk about Grandma's stuff. How cool would it be to buy a place here and decorate it just like hers? Sort of a memorial. It'd be like our childhood never went away—"

"Look, I'm still in Dyson."

"What?"

"Everything's fine." Bo searches for hand sanitizer. Germophobia has returned with vicious clarity. "But I need to hang around town. I really do want to get together and talk and, you know, reconnect. But right now—"

His phone makes cricket clicks.

"Bo?"

"Look, I'm sorry, Gene. I'll get back to you later. I just have another call. Bye." He sighs and watches dabs of sweat drop to the table. "Rutili here," he says, expecting maybe an apology from Findlay's mayor.

"Please hold for the First Lady," says a man sounding stiffer than Bo's neck.

Bo wipes his forehead and deposits the leftovers on his shirtfront. "I'm sorry, what?"

The phone hums.

He squints into a shadow of bookshelves. Silhouettes resemble sanitizer but prove to be honorary statues, Dyson salt shakers, and even a small bottle of rum from a sister city in Trinidad. While the rum might kill germs in a pinch, his anxiety craves the genocidal sting of sanitizer.

"Bo Rutili?" A thin, feminine voice comes across the phone.

The shock of words catches the mayor off-guard. "Hello?"

"*The* Bo Rutili. The fourth-youngest mayor in America. Correct?"

"Yes, ma'am. How can I help you?"

"This is the First Lady of the United States." Bo tenses with disbelief and quickly softens with pride. It's an amazing feeling that makes it hard to listen. "I have heard about the terrible, terrible," she spreads the word *terrible* into a long, hushed whisper, "news about the satellite."

"It's terrible."

"*Terrible.*"

He stops searching. "Well, thank you for your concern. It's an honor, ma'am. I voted for your husband in the last—"

"Bo, I'm thinking we should help your recovery. The President decided this wasn't *technically* a disaster. Well, that broke my heart. I have a lot of friends who could raise some money. Really help those families affected."

The idea of money, acquiring large sums of it, springs a bear trap in Bo's mind.

"Ma'am, how do you know all this?"

"My husband *is* the leader of the free world." She sighs. "But seriously, Cody Kellogg, that brave reporter. Everyone here in the White House has been listening to his broadcasts online. A true patriot."

"Yes, we're all very proud of Cody." Bo sticks his head out the window and fresh air splashes like cold water. "We would be honored by any assistance."

"Don't think of it. Just try not to focus on the *grief.*" She says grief like she said terrible.

"Grief? Ma'am, I don't follow."

"Oh, I can't even *say* it. Don't make me start crying again. It's so sad."

"Sad?"

"Just keep a brave chin up. The world is watching, Mr. Mayor. I'll make some phone calls, get the wheels rolling. I'll be in Dyson by tonight, tomorrow morning at the latest."

"That's wonderful. I have a few questions."

The phone is as dead as the air circulation in his office.

"Hello? Hello?"

MONDAY, 5:22 PM

Chief Grover uses incredible restraint to keep from unholstering his gun. "Cody, I'm telling you for the last time, turn that garbage off. Show some respect."

"I will not lie, ladies and gentlemen." The DJ speaks into a microphone under the shade of Skeet's oak tree. His once-blue suit is filthy and his tie has long since vanished. "This is difficult for everyone involved, myself included. This man, Rufus 'Skeet' Brown was my best friend. When I moved to Dyson years ago, Skeet was the first to shake my hand. Asked me to join his softball team. Shared a beer with me." Grief clogs Cody's delivery. "He treated everyone like a best friend."

About a dozen people in hazmat plastic stand around the wreckage. Cody chokes. "I'm staring at the remains of a barn. This structure, once at least forty feet tall and about one hundred feet long, belonged to Skeet Brown. Now, it's a scatter of wooden planks. A small fire in the center crackles. Nobody extinguishes the flames; they don't see any point. A popular member of the community, Brown was a farmer and captain of the 1980 runner-up state championship basketball team."

"Best jump shot I ever saw," Wendell Dixon says, his knees in the grass, tears forming bullets. His shoulder doesn't look so good.

"Pull it together," the Chief says numbly, biting his lip, eyes glossy. He finishes wrapping yellow plastic POLICE LINE tape around the property. "There's too much work to be done."

"First, Ed Lee. Now this." Dixon snorts and sniffles every few words.

"Ed? What about Ed?"

"Oh, it was horrible, Bert. We found him in Edna Rutili's shed. Eugene and Bo Rutili, or maybe just one, killed him." Dixon rubs a red nose. "Gene couldn't rebound for shit."

"Kid was a horrible center, but murder? Wendell, come on. I don't need this. You can't accuse the mayor of . . . forget it. He's working his butt off right now. Not to mention, I got some nut shooting at you and him, remember? Plus, this satellite mess and . . ." He pictures the mummy. "Well, you get the point."

"It's true, it's true," Kreskin snarls.

All the Chief can think about is his dead deputy, Skeet. He wants to cry and sing and loathe every breath he takes.

"I was there, Chief," Kreskin says. "We saw poor, poor Ed Lee. His skin had turned blue. Made me puke."

"You aren't serious."

"We should have told you sooner."

"What is going on in this town? I don't think I ever heard of anyone—*anyone*—dying of anything other than natural causes. And in the last week—"

One of the hazmat men interrupts: "We swept it with our equipment. There's no one alive under that pile."

"How can you be sure?"

"We're scientists."

"Should have *made* Skeet help with evacuations. Should have been tougher. He'd still be here if—"

Cody continues: "Stay tuned, ladies and gentlemen. WDSR will be broadcasting and bringing you further coverage of this tragedy. After a small break we will return to share more memories of Skeet Brown."

"Turn it off," Chief says. "Act like a human being."

Cody's back is to the wreckage, smoking a cigarette. His are the only pair of eyes not fixed on the tragic lumber. He can't look again.

Opera bangs at Chief Grover's door, but the situation is too serious for self-inflicted singing. "Wendell. Murray." He speaks quietly, finding them by the fire department Jeep. "Let's go into town. Show me what happened to Ed Lee. I need to get my mind off Skeet. Let's pray he's the last of the bad news. I can't take anything else."

Kreskin turns pale. Dixon sinks his head and says, "Hey, what about those people at the ballpark?"

"They're fine. Army's got them covered. Now do you want to show me to Ed or not?"

"Is that really an option?" Kreskin says.

"No."

"If we do," Dixon says. "Promise not to ask why we were there?"

They walk straight back to Edna Rutili's shed. "Can't believe I voted for a psychopath mayor," Dixon says.

"Now, hold on. Where's your proof? You see one of the Rutili boys here?"

"No. But who else could have known?"

"Known what?"

"Nothing."

"I admit, it's a little odd, Ed being out here and all." Keys jangle. "There something you're not telling me?"

"Never mind. You have too much to worry about, Chief."

Sparrows feast on a spilled birdfeeder. That cluster smacks wings when Kreskin opens the shed door. All around the backside of the house, birdhouses and plastic feeding cylinders lie cracked and shattered. Freshly dug holes, hunting for treasure, spread over the lush green yard.

"Last I saw Ed was Saturday night. Had a few too many at the bar," Kreskin says. "Left a real nice tip."

The Chief eases the door open a slat further.

"I think we have a dangerous man on our hands, Chief." Dixon sighs, almost embarrassed.

The shed is full of tools and garden hose and a thick layer of dust. A pale, soft, lifeless thing in Union blue lies there.

"Sick, sick, sick," Dixon says.

"This is not what I wanted to see, fellas." Chief Grover's throat tenses. "I wanted you two to be wrong in the worst way."

"Sorry."

"Sorry."

"This town is falling apart. Just about makes me want to turn in my badge, all these good people gone. You guys better tell me what's going on here. How'd you find him?"

There is a long wait filled with bird chatter.

"Legal business. Executing a will," Dixon says.

Kreskin bumps the lawyer with a hip.

Grover looks with suspicious eyes. His body slumps tired. "Whatever you say. I give up. This is all too much."

"Chief, we gotta go. Wendell promised to help me get the bar in shape in case it's damaged."

Dixon takes small steps toward the car. "Yeah, I'd love to stay, but . . ."

MONDAY, 5:30 PM

Emotional rewards. Donna recalls helping Muscles find a job and the selfless satisfaction embedded within. She's sure she's done other good deeds, it's just that nothing comes to mind right now. She sets out to fix that.

"Donna, please, no." A man lying in the grass locks fingers over his mouth. His tight grey curls shiver in the wind. "I don't need more antibiotics, put that spoon away."

"Artie, do you see this badge?" She points to her HERO patch with the spoonful of orange medicine. "I'm here to help. Here to nurse you back to health, lift your spirits, and make this town better."

The man shakes from behind the finger cage. "With antibiotics?"

"With *heroism*, dummy. Now, open your stupid trap." That *pop*— the rapid discharge not unlike a string of firecrackers—fills Donna with energy. She always grows hyper whenever someone needs to be convinced she is right. "Don't you *want* a hero? Don't you people want a . . . you know . . . *whatchamacallit?*"

Most of the baseball field crowd has disappeared. Their wounds were dressed and, besides, all the men in radiation suits were creepy. Everyone who narrowly avoided wearing a satellite for a hat simply went home to inspect for damages.

A tail of yellow CAUTION tape flaps in the breeze a dozen feet from the world's newest hero.

Artie shrugs. "I'm just glad I didn't die."

Artie actually went home already, but since the cable was out and his house was intact, he decided to lie in the grass and guess cloud shapes. He did not register for the gift of heroism.

"Well, I'm glad you're alive, too." Her hyperactivity slows. "God, what would Dyson do without a guy . . . " her voice gets feeble. "Who does . . . whatever it is you . . . do." She moves the spoon toward his mouth to avoid looking stupid.

"Jesus, Donna, I work at the bowling alley! We had the same shift for five years." Artie the cloud-watcher pops to his feet and storms off. "Some hero."

"But the antibiotics." Donna's firecrackers get dunked in a pail of water. That *pop* never ruptures like promised. *Stay positive*, she thinks. *Heroes aren't frowny.*

Donna watches a paper cup tumble across the outfield. It's from a gourmet coffee shop in Findlay. She guesses a hazmat fella forgot it. Either that or Findlay's trash is spilling over into Dyson.

Her phone rings and she removes it from the Hero utility pocket. "Donna, we need you back at the casino," Garrett says.

"Sweetie . . . " She lugs an unopened case of rubbing alcohol back to the Hero Mobile. "You'll have to handle this. We've talked about it. I'm Dyson's hero. They need me for *inspiration*."

Out of breath, he pants, "I was going to hunt that bastard mummy down, but then, all the sudden, every hotel room booked up. Just like that."

"Wow." Donna stops and inhales a fresh breath of success. "Good job, babe."

"I got a call from some government official. All fifty rooms. We don't have a staff. How can we accommodate?"

"Garrett . . . " Over the years Donna has become excellent at motivation. She knows when the situation calls for a positive swat in the ass. And there is nobody she swats better than her husband. "I'm going to be the hero in town, but I need you to be the hero of the casino. Can you handle that? Being the hero of *my* life?"

There is a rare confidence in his voice. "You bet."

New firecrackers ignite around Donna's heart. Lifting Garrett's spirits never fails to pickle her brain in happiness. Maybe even more than heroism.

"What about that mummy? Bastard owes us a hood. I was gonna—"

"Just do it in your spare time. Bye-bye."

As she drives through the streets, looking for heroic deeds, she slouches low because Packwicz, the brutal murderer, is still loose. She doesn't want death spoiling heroism.

The Hero spots a middle-aged woman in shorts going into cardiac arrest. Donna runs to her rescue and begins administering her miracle cure. After being force-fed an aspirin the dying woman kicks Donna's thigh and squeals. "What is wrong with you?"

"Just relax, Trish. They say the first minutes are the most important during a heart attack."

"Heart attack? Do I look like I'm having a heart attack? I was *jogging*. I stopped to catch my breath."

"So, you don't need a hero?"

"Donna, get out of here!"

The streets are empty of people and heroic deeds to perform. "This world's not the same as it used to be. Everything comes to an end."

A camouflage truck with a red cross on the door roars. Donna realizes this is all their fault.

MONDAY, 10:00 PM

"I apologize, ladies and gentlemen." Cody Kellogg swallows another gulp of whiskey, trying to erase the taste of gasoline. "We were supposed to have Mayor Bo Rutili in the studio for a little interview. Unfortunately, he could not be located."

By moonlight, he siphoned two more tanks to keep the studio's generator purring. Cody leaves all but the console lights off to conserve fuel.

He slices more chorizo. The spicy sausage tastes like a gallon of unleaded.

"We were going to discuss the rumor that approximately seven National Guard soldiers are feared dead."

He commits the biggest radio sin in the book and lets silence fill the airwaves as he eats. The bouncy red needles lie flat and rest, much like Cody wishes he could do after countless hours on-air.

That moment of quiet reminds him of Memphis and his last decent job. Drive time DJ, his picture on a billboard, and a condo in the suburbs.

"Ladies and gentlemen, I apologize for that. I'm still with you." Needles spring back to life with his tired but charming voice. "Here in this town without power and hope, everything's quiet. As quiet as dead air on the radio. What you just heard is what we hear now. No advertisements, no televisions, no cars, just peace and silence. It ain't too bad." His throat clears and something sticky dislodges. "Let's talk honest, folks. I used to think I was being punished by working in Dyson. Punished for a stretch of silence like you just heard. But I'm starting to think maybe fate did me a solid."

Those staff meetings, held so many years ago in Memphis, zip through his mind. "Cody, you have to use it. Your little *dead air* protest was not acceptable," his boss said. "This is what the drive time jocks at the other stations use. Guaranteed three percent boost. You want higher Q rating, right?"

That meeting room in Memphis was larger than the entire WDSR trailer. Real wood floors, and it smelled like clean hotels.

"Come on, Mark," Cody fought back. "This isn't me. I have a master's in English Literature, for God's sake."

"Cody, you push that button on the air or face the consequences." His boss' face was red and webbed in veins. "Ask Shakespeare what he'd do."

"You see folks . . ." Back on Dyson's airwaves, Cody swishes a mouthful of booze. The gasoline's bite still wins. "Not all radio stations are like this one. Sure, we're a bit smaller. Sure we play too much Elton John. But there's one thing we don't have, and it's a blessing."

Cody slips in another bite from his uncle's factory. The bitter nausea in his mouth is much like being out on his ass after that meeting in Memphis. "It's one button, Cody," his sidekick and producer Nancy O'Doyle said. "It's not that big a compromise."

"I'm not touching anything called the *Fart Box* on my show. I'm not sinking that deep. If every other DJ in town wants to turn this into a junior high locker room, be my guest. The Mr. Razzle-Dazzle Show will keep its chin high. We make jokes about the president and fast food and the way white people dance. I draw the line at *that*."

Occasionally, when remembering that day, the same pride he walked out of that Memphis station with returns. Other times, a painful stomach cramp tells him there's nothing wrong with flatulent buttons. He is undecided about the matter. Either way, his broadcasting career needs this curveball.

"There's one thing we don't have here." He thinks of that nasty Fart Box. "But in its place, WDSR has a little bit of dignity. And for that, I'm grateful."

He leans back and that hot red pride fills him.

"Dignity reminds me of something Keats once wrote—" Metal banging interrupts. Cody squints out the window, but only sees the reflection of a middle-aged DJ with a small glimmer of happiness in the corner of his exhausted eyes.

"We'll be back in a moment, folks. But here's 'Bennie and the Jets.'"

Cody presses PLAY and covers the console light. The world outside comes into clear focus. Parked cars, trees, and houses sit blue and silver under the moon. A truck's hood slams closed. Cody's face presses tight against the glass, his jaw dropping open.

Someone wrapped in bandages staggers around the truck and crawls into the cab. It leaves the door open, and the dome light shows clumsy hands touching two wires together beneath the steering wheel.

The engine coughs to life and the mummy swerves off like a drunk National Guardsman.

MONDAY, 10:45 PM

"Ed, I'm sorry," Murray Kreskin says, standing behind the Civil War re-enactment shop with a sledgehammer. A flashlight helps him aim. The thirteen-pound mallet turns the door into an explosion of splinters, dust, and brassy hinge fragments.

Wendell Dixon, holding the light, watches the door disintegrate. Particles float through the beam.

"Thank God nobody bought any of this stuff," Dixon says, briefly touching his bullet wound and crushing more sour aspirin between his teeth. He doesn't feel nearly as upset about breaking and entering as his partner.

"This is stupid," Kreskin says, flipping his flashlight on and pushing the lawyer aside. "These Rutili boys are dangerous. You think Civil War stuff will keep us safe? What, are we going to stampede them?"

"I don't care about that goody-two-shoes mayor or his brother. I only care about the gold."

Yellow light scans across a showroom, highlighting racks of Civil War uniforms—spotlessly pressed indigo wools for generals, all the way down to tattered rags for bullet-catching infantrymen. The Ladies' section is a bright pop of pinks and ginghams, all for the wives of Civil War reenactors getting into the spirit. The lights send back silver sparks from the knives and swords displayed behind a counter.

CLEARANCE signs taped to everything.

Dixon speaks up: "Bingo."

He begins swinging a long musket in all directions.

"These are toys. You know that, right? Why are we wasting our time here when we should be hunting down those murderers or busting that stupid factory apart?"

Dixon's hairspray helmet sparkles in the light. His voice goes strict and professor-like. "We'll need guns to protect our treasure. Tell me something, smart guy, do *you* own a gun?"

"Yeah, this one." Kreskin presents his pistol. "Maybe you remember it from between your lips?" He squeals a laugh much like after Birth Control to Major Tom. Kreskin flicks the light at his partner and sees *the look*. That look Murray gets so rarely, but loves so tenderly. When someone takes Murray seriously, all his years of cleaning pukey bathrooms and serving drinks aren't regrettable. Usually, he is only taken seriously when his temper cracks some guy with a bat or scratches a new name onto the Shit List. Customers don't laugh then. They tip big. That thrill always eases his loneliness.

"Jesus, Murray, relax." Dixon's hand shields the flashlight shine. "Well, I *don't* own a gun. In fact, the only gun I ever fired was one of these." He shakes a musket.

"Calm down, buddy. I could teach you how to fire a pistol in about three seconds."

"Something about this old technology, it makes me feel—" He wants to say, "like my wife doesn't hate me, like I'm not a horrible lawyer, like my hair isn't disappearing by the fistful." Instead Dixon settles for, "like a man, Murray."

"Real healthy, Sigmund Freud." Helicopter blades pad the silence. Kreskin smiles: *That would have killed at the bar.*

"Muskets have been around for centuries. If we're going to do what we're going to do, this is how I plan to do it."

"Don't these pea-shooters only get, like, one shot?" A lighter glows under Kreskin's face until orange cigar embers appear.

"Hopefully I won't even need one shot. I'm not a violent person. I just want what is ours. Look at this thing." He raises the long black barrel and stained oak stock. "This is *intimidation*."

"Yeah, I'm sure whoever's guarding the treasure at the factory will piss themselves." A wicked smirk is outlined by cigar light in the darkness. "You wearing one of these costumes, too?"

"Of course not." Out of Kreskin's sight, Dixon sets a blue infantry hat on the counter.

"Good," Kreskin says. "Anyway, I thought they just fired blanks."

"What? No, it's Stephanie, her fallopian tubes are all messed up."

"The guns . . . I thought they just shot blanks."

Dixon coughs. "At the reenactments, like the one Ed Lee took me to, yes. But Ed said he keeps real musket balls for target practice."

"Well, when we're millionaires, you'll have to take me to one of these fake battles. You got me curious, Custer."

"Custer didn't fight in the Civil War . . . forget it." Dixon feels around the darkness collecting wadding, gunpowder, blasting caps, ammunition, and a ramrod.

"What are you doing with all that shit?"

"God, I have to explain everything? When you load muskets properly, they're deadly from a hundred yards. Like a hunting rifle."

"Honestly, it takes a few minutes to learn to shoot a pistol. Shit, just hold it. You don't have to fire it. It's like a movie, snap this back to load a bullet into the chamber . . ."

Not listening, Dixon grabs a second musket. He has a secret plan, and in the dark, with that idiotic bartender egging him on, Dyson's Smartest Man knows that secret plan has to work. Stephanie won't accept second place.

TUESDAY, MIDNIGHT

"If fate wants me to fall, I'll fall," Packy whispers, several stories above the ground once again. "If fate wants me discover the treasure, maybe become famous, maybe become mayor again—well then, fate, do your thing."

Bo gave Old Man Packwicz a key to the town ladder shed a few hours earlier. "Packy," Bo said, rubbing a scatter of growing whiskers, "with that map you found in Rosinski's old safe and my research last night, I think we're on to something."

"The fruit doesn't fall far from the tree?"

"That's what it says. If it wasn't for the Chief's missing pages we wouldn't even have that much."

"Doesn't that seem . . . a little vague?"

"No. I think I know where the tree is."

Packwicz inched away in his seat—the mayor's focused eyes were something terrorizing. He wanted to pour water over this human bomb. "Don't you wonder, *why us?*" Packy's eyes got big, full of curiosity. They sat in Bo's car behind the City Works building—a blocky brick garage with an American flag snapping over the door. "You mean, something about being mayors?"

"No. No. *Fate*, Bo. Why did fate give us these hints?" He raised Bo's pencil scribbles and the Rosinski map. "Why was this hiding for so many years? How come we get to be the heroes?"

"Well, Packy." The mayor's face was tight and unpleasant when he lied. "I'd say it's because we dedicated our lives to this town, and now it's giving us a chance to really leave our mark."

"You think? What if it's all a load of bologna? How is it possible that I didn't kill you?"

"You're a lousy shot, for starters."

Packwicz's cheeks filled pink.

"Look, I'm sorry." The mayor didn't make eye contact as Packy stepped out of the car. "That was dumb."

"No. You're right."

"I think it's time some chips fell your way, Packy. That's what I think."

"But, why me? This entire town has given up on me except you. Why?"

"You're a good guy. That's all it takes."

"I can tell when you're hiding something. I always knew when folks were not giving me the full story when I was mayor. It's all in what they do with their hands. Calm hands are the sign of a calm mind. Itchy hands mean something else."

Bo laughed soft and short. "Guilty."

"Okay."

"I always thought you got a raw deal between the lottery business and the way you were forced out of office. I always said if I could help right some of those wrongs I would." He tried to steady his hands, not wanting to go into the real reason. "All I did was give you a place to sleep. It's not like I performed CPR or anything."

"Eh, call it what you want. I appreciate it." There was a certain glimmer in Packy's eyes. A hopefulness that had been elusive since losing his old job. "You're a good egg."

"Just follow that map. Be careful and let me know what you find. I've got to track down some antibacterial soap. Oh, and if you see Donna again, don't forget, you killed me. So, pretend to be a good shot, I guess."

The mayor had translated the map, written in some code Packy couldn't read. The big X, the one they decided represented the treasure, was scratched into the most obvious place imaginable.

After choosing a tall ladder and driving across town, Packy decided not to go through FruitCo's doors. He knew something was up, thanks to the locomotive reverberations from the building.

The former mayor now finds a thin ledge circling the top of the factory's warehouse. Stepping across this brick tightrope, Packy wipes away window grime.

Interior lights glow through. Wind whistles around his ears and his fingers lose color from gripping the building so tight. "*Huh,*" he says, noticing his fingers aren't so jittery any more, even in this chill. "How am I supposed to see the warehouse floor when it's all covered in fruit?"

Directly below Packwicz, Troy Gomez applies a screwdriver to some strange papier-mâché thing on wheels. It says "I LOVE DYSON" in tall rainbow letters. Two girls Packy only partially recognizes walk past one another. Their shoulders collide violently. They exchange a quick glance and keep walking in opposite directions.

Packy notes the army of men waiting. Polite, well-postured, and quiet—some private death squad hired to protect the Rosinski Treasure. Most likely mummies. "Those guys are everywhere now."

One of the girls begins fiddling with a soldier, and Packy realizes they are plastic men dressed in herringbone jackets, stiff black bowlers, chocolate brown pants, and wide, swooping mustaches.

"This is going to be easy. The only thing between you and saving Dyson are three kids, a dozen mannequins, and a floor full of plastic fruit."

He steadies his foot to descend the ladder and repeats the situation, it sounds so good. "The only thing standing between you and saving Dyson . . ." A car door slams. He turns toward the noise and, under the security lamp, sees someone step out of the Volunteer Fire Department medical Jeep." . . . Shit. Murray Kreskin and Wendell Dixon."

TUESDAY, 5:45 AM

At dawn, Bert Grover rubs a towel over his forehead, its fibers crusty with dried sweat. He blindly reaches across the grass for a water bottle, but it is empty. The Chief hurts. Crumpled into a ball in his ex-wife's backyard, he is thankful the wind is knocking over lawn statues and peeling off aluminum siding. *At least no one can hear you,* he thinks.

All night he sang with an unknown violence—sweat poured, muscles burned, and the backs of his eyes fried eggs. He hasn't worked like that since singing professionally. Sadly, his vocal chords aren't near their old standards. Every devil-dealing line from *Faust* crushed Bert's throat into bloody threads. He was filled with so many rippling, black thoughts: snipers, satellites, and Ed Lee's puffed skin. But the clincher was Skeet buried dead under that rubble. So much death out of his control.

"I could have prevented it," he said over and over.

He fed *Faust's* beautiful lyrics through the meat grinder again. Thoughts again went evil. This time, Haley and Joyce abandoning him. Bert clenched his abdomen and shifted gears to the sugary sweet lines of *Nessun Dorma.*

He sang until sunrise, imagining how far the glacier had split between him and his ex-wife. *Turandot* was the last production they performed together, at the Ghent Opera House many years ago.

Gentle notes wilted the second they swam from chapped lips. Bert remembered the awful cracking, the hellish sound of bending steel, and the disgusting silence as the opera house's balcony ripped from its girders.

Joyce and Bert were celebrated as heroes in the Belgian papers and television. Ghent's opera house had never seen a crowd so large. Too many fans had packed the upper levels.

When the crash stopped echoing and the cloud of debris settled, there was nothing but a series of arms and legs poking from the rubble at odd angles.

"A medic, we need a medic," a man screamed in Flemish, then French, and finally English.

"Bert," Joyce's stunned voice barely broke the oxygen between them. "Help them."

"Please, someone," the man begged in three languages. "I see survivors."

The two hundred fifty-eight injured and fourteen dead, the newspapers later reported, had all come for Bert and Joyce.

His wife's plea didn't compute until hours later. Grover just stood clutching his abdomen onstage. A crushing stomachache of guilt poisoned him. He couldn't move. Couldn't use the first aid he'd learned at the police academy.

"Bert," she snapped. "Bert, help them, *please*." Joyce, in a full-length green gown, ran to the mess of humanity bleeding under balcony shards.

For the next twelve years, as Bert recalled that day and sang those lines, he never knew why he froze. It was impossible to explain after Joyce grew so ashamed and resentful. "You were given the gift to save a life, and you wasted it. You stood onstage with your mouth hanging open." She divorced Bert soon after. He tried to carry on solo, but the crowds faded.

A man like Bert Grover has never heard of self-flagellation or any type of self-mutilation. Nevertheless, the Chief rips himself to shreds from the inside out, thinking about lost opportunities for good deeds. He works twenty-four-hour days because he never wants to be responsible for another death or injury.

All that work and Skeet is still dead. All that work and Ed is still dead. All that work and . . . God, if the reports are true, so many more are dead.

The worst moments of his life seemed to always involve piles of rubble.

TUESDAY, 6:30 AM

For the first time in days, the factory is silent. Last night, Troy determined there was enough product for the festival. He shut down the presses and fell immediately asleep.

A mound of fruit, like a rainbow ski slope, now dominates the warehouse.

Marci is the only one awake. She pricks her finger with a sewing needle. She's too wired for shuteye and too upset to do a decent job on the costumes.

"I know what I saw." She takes a break from hemming the last vest. "Troy and my sister went up there about the same time, said they were 'tired' and 'calling it a night.' I know what that means."

"Oh, now, darling, you need to stop worrying. Those two are not *intimate*. They've been working hard on these floats and helping with your costumes, planning this beautiful celebration. They're the closest friends you have. It's foolish to get angry. Don't be so dumb." Marci is surprised by Gerald Rosinski's ghost.

"Jesus, even you're against me."

"Never, my sweet. Blunt honesty is the universal language. We thought for a while there it was going to be Esperanto, but—"

"I know what I saw."

"Troy and your sister don't have anything in common. Not like you and Troy with this *beautiful* festival."

"You don't have to have anything in common to screw each other, ask my parents."

"Marcella." The ghost inspects a row of mannequins dressed exactly like him. "What are you really angry about?"

She shoves one and watches the fake Rosinski crash to the floor. "I just wish you could take me to Tahiti. What if I wasn't working on this parade for Bo or Troy? What if it was for you?"

"I would say you are out of your pretty little mind. I've been dead for decades." Rosinski places his hat over his heart. "I might not even be a real ghost. This could just be your imagination." His face grows puzzled. "Oh my, how sad."

The ghost floats between likenesses, and Marci feels hollow. She's done it again. First Bo, then Troy, now her imaginary friend. She pushes away every man who comes near. "Is it the marriage thing? Should I just give up on finding a husband?"

"I think you should worry less about love and more about finishing costumes for this *beautiful* festival."

"Quit saying that."

"See how big your ego gets when someone plans a parade in *your* honor." Rosinski peeks playfully around a mannequin. "Incidentally, how are you going to find enough people to dress like me, drive these floats, and do heaven-knows-what with all that plastic fruit?"

"Forget Tahiti," she says with a wicked, annoyed sigh. "I don't even know why I'm bothering to sew this, and you're giving me shit? Why don't you go nail my sister, too?"

The ghost shakes his head and disappears into the silence. Marci kneels before a tattered pantleg.

The howling wind outside nearly, but not completely, finds a rhythm. She listens to this orchestration while working. Long breaths, short breaths, vacant space—she waits for a pattern in the breeze, but nothing makes sense.

"Marci?" Pearl's sleepy voice calls from across the building. "Who were you talking to?"

She swallows quickly, dry. "Just, rehearsing my lines."

"*The Music Man* doesn't start for a few months."

"Practice makes perfect."

"You're so weird."

Marci turns, hair wild and unbrushed. "Why are you down here? Shouldn't you two be upstairs?"

Pearl, with punching bag eyes, sassy Tinkerbelle cut flattened, and no makeup, doesn't look like the pretty one. And that makes Marci sort of sad for her.

"Troy was asleep under the desk when I went up there. That stupid wind is keeping me up, so I thought I'd help. I'm sorry. I never meant to piss you off. I just wanted to be useful."

TUESDAY, 7:30 AM

Was it the wind?

Was it the relentless morning heat?

Or was it the noise—the clatter of wood being pulled apart plank-by-plank—that sparked his brain into motion?

Skeet doesn't know, but something rattled him hard and rattled him fast. His muscles now burn and smoke with painful fire.

The racket of wood and metal fills his little globe of darkness. He tries to move, but feels the iron bars all around. The cage smells melty, like FruitCo in high gear.

The shaking and noise continue until a crack of dull yellow light filters through. The fresh, clean smell of oxygen is invigorating.

"Hello? Hello. I'm alive. Help," Skeet cries. His surroundings come into focus. The white plastic skin has melted away, and its steel skeleton has mashed into an odd womb. "I think I'm inside the snowman," he says. "One minute I was cleaning all the brown muck from its body and the next—"

The shuffling wreckage goes silent. Skeet tries without luck to move the weight surrounding him. He sweats and grunts. Using his arms and feet and back, anything for leverage, the rubble begins to shift in his favor. Skeet manages to work between the bars and planks to stand on a pile that used to be his barn. Purple daybreaking clouds swirl overhead. Dark lines of filth fill his face.

"Hello? Hello?"

He catches a glimpse, like grainy Sasquatch films, of someone dressed head-to-foot in bandages staggering behind his garage. It spins around and points over Skeet's shoulder and gives a *howdy* wave.

Skeet turns and finds the bronze statue of Hans Dyson in the grass. Hans' face is scarred and rubbed down from its recent truck fall. It's a reunion, and a funeral. Skeet will miss his museum.

"Thank you?" he yells into a balmy wind.

FAKE
FRUIT
FACTORY

TUESDAY, 9:00 AM

"So *what* if Murray and Wendell are at the factory?" Bo says through gritted teeth.

"I'm just saying, this complicates things." Packwicz is panting.

"It'll be fine. We are on mayoral business."

"Sitting mayor goes first, then."

The jackhammer weighs them down like a dead man. Bo's hands are sweaty, and the urge to rub sanitizer into his palms is unbearable. *If Packy would only carry his half,* he thinks. Small, exhausted grunts spit from the mayor. "Little further, little further."

"What?" Packy says.

Power lines take violent, hurricane swings. The parking lot outside the City Works building—where the construction crew locks its bulldozers, cement mixers, and jackhammers—is empty. Leaves and newspaper scraps shoots past them.

Morning is fully upon Dyson. Humidity and sunlight fills every inch of space.

"Up, up, up," the mayor says as they drop the jackhammer into Bo's trunk. The car squeaks and lowers until the tailpipe kisses the ground. Both men shake the blood back into their throbbing arms. Boots climbs into the back window, meowing for her life.

"What now?"

"Halfway home, Packy." Bo, out of breath, wipes his forehead. "You did good. You did really good. Couldn't have done it without you."

"Bo." He tugs the mayor in close to avoid screaming over the wind. "I'm worried about the factory. I'm the wrong guy for the job. You need someone more . . . *something* . . . anything."

"Don't worry you make up for it in other ways."

"How?"

"In heart and stuff." Bo's eyes are level and sober. "You inspire me."

Bo can't bear to explain why Packwicz really inspires him. The complexities of the situation turn Bo's mind off whenever he really digs into it. Packy is—above all—a cautionary tale. Bo looks at him and asks how Packy handled things when he was mayor in order to do things the opposite way. It's rotten and Bo knows it. But it's also true, and those moments when he is honest with himself are rare. It gets complicated when Bo realizes Packwicz is far and away his best friend, too. There's nobody on earth Bo talks to more—about everyday things and about issues buried deep within a man. Only Packy had the kindness to listen when Bo debated whether he should break up with Marci, realizing she would be so much better off without him. Only Packy listens to the mayor—everyone else in town complains to him or wants something from him.

He wants to take care of Packy. He wants to take care of Boots. He wants to take care of Dyson. Bo realizes he only feels satisfied in this life when he's denying his own happiness to care for others. He thinks maybe it's time for that to change.

Standing above the jackhammer, Bo smiles. "Nobody else cares about this town like you, Packy. That's a fact."

"That's the nicest thing anyone's said to me in years. Thank you."

The wind masks the sound of the white WDSR van. By the time Bo notices, Cody Kellogg has one hand clamping down his hat and the other pointing a microphone in their direction.

"What? Cody, I can't hear you." He points to his ears.

Cody stuffs the microphone closer.

They move inside the van, which the wind rocks with honeymoon suite force. He speaks as if this awkward meeting is as natural as breathing. "Thanks for finally sitting down with me, Bo. I don't hold it against you for standing me up last night."

"You don't happen to have any hand sanitizer, do you?" He looks at his grimy palms. The mayor's hair points in a hundred confused directions. "Wait, what?"

"Man, I saw the damnedest thing while I was waiting for you like a girl on prom night. Have you heard about some dude dressed like a mummy going around stealing cars?"

"God, what happened to your hand?"

"Oh, this?" Cody raises a collection of gauze, stained dried blood brown. "Had to use the *master key* on the station door."

"Cody, I'm a little busy right now. Can we talk later?"

"Boss, I think people are listening. This is news. *We* are news. Just make a statement. *Please.*" Cody's face wrinkles until he is nothing but a pair of desperate eyes.

Cody clearly shares a morsel of that love he and Packy own. Bo sighs, realizing he is a sucker for Dyson disciples.

"I don't know all that much." The mayor seems distracted. "A good reporter like you probably knows more than me."

"Okay, here's a softball." Wind forces through gaps in doorframe and vents with impatient teakettle hisses. "Tell the folks at home why Donna Queen says you're dead."

"Dead?"

"She went on at length recently about how you are missing, presumed dead, and that she was here to help lead the city. The word *hero* came up an awful lot."

"Oh, well that's sweet of her to say." Bo shrugs.

"She meant herself."

"Oh."

"Why would someone say that?"

"Look, Cody, this has been a traumatic event. A carload of drunken soldiers died, not to mention Skeet."

Cody tenses. "Herb Morrison wouldn't cry, Herb Morrison wouldn't cry," he mutters.

"I couldn't hear you."

"Nothing."

The mayor's eyes turn to dashes. "Here's a statement. Things are looking good. The Army found no radioactivity and Dyson will be opened to the public soon. We'll all get to pitch in and begin the rebuilding process."

The mic inches closer to Bo's face. "Is that why you and former mayor Packwicz were carrying a jackhammer?"

"That . . ." Bo battles an urge to rip plugs and boxes along the van's circuitry panel. "Yes. Absolutely. We were getting everything shipshape for our excellent road crew."

Cody leans in. "Seems like there's already enough holes in Dyson. What gives with the jackhammer?"

His lips tighten, thinking maybe Cody doesn't love the town after all. The mayor sniffs several times. "Do you smell gasoline?"

Cody pops in a mint.

"Look, I really appreciate everything you're doing." Bo takes a long tug at his hair. "But I am terribly busy."

"Sure, sure. Just one last thing: is it true the First Lady is coming? Donna Queen told our listeners that she'd heard—"

"No." The mayor's voice is as sharp and twisty as the wind outside. "I mean, I haven't heard any such rumor. Enjoy the weather and not being dead."

"Donna also said she expects thousands of people to visit. Curious folks from all over. Her hotel is booked solid. What are people doing here?"

The mayor opens the door to wide-open howls. He wraps his arms around his torso and walks across the lot.

"What was that all about?" Packwicz says, getting into the passenger side as Bo slides into the driver's seat.

"Just a friendly chat."

"Buckle up, Bo." Packy does the same, loving the way the belt clicks. There is no middle ground. No room for confusion. He wants his world to be more like a seatbelt. He figures fate is kind of like that: it's with you or it isn't. "Should we wait for Cody to leave?"

"Cody? Forget you ever saw him. You're going to do a great job. I really believe in you." He gives the ex-mayor a leg slap. "Now, we'd better head out to the factory before the National Guard opens the barricades. I'll have to go back to being the mayor then."

"Then? Who are you now?"

"Don't ask."

TUESDAY, 9:12 AM

They wait all night outside the factory for the right moment, and when the time finally arrives, Dixon wastes another twenty minutes wrestling his musket with that bad shoulder.

"Not so smart, are you?" With a smoldering cigar between his lips, Kreskin keeps the handgun close, safety off. Dixon waddles through the building with both long rifles under his arm, even clumsier than in a courtroom.

"God, something stinks," Kreskin says when they push through the swinging doors.

"What?"

"It's that shoulder. It's disgusting. Does it hurt?"

"Aspirin helps." He crunches down on more tablets. "I can't smell anything."

"Rotten meat. Like in the trash can."

"Oh, go easy," he says as Kreskin handles the door.

The warehouse is silent except for the *shoosh* of a sparrow whirli-gigging between the rafters. A light creeps through the windows, giving the gentle glow of preheating ovens.

"Rise and shine," Kreskin hollers on the warehouse floor before pulling a trigger.

Two shots echo. Bits of ceiling drop.

He loves the gun's kickback. That pulsating hand tells Murray he is someone to be taken seriously. Kreskin glances at his stupid partner fumbling with that enormous musket. Dixon takes him seriously; the lawyer's eyes are full of fear.

"Hey, Murray," Dixon says. "Why are you shooting? There's nobody here."

"Quit being so antsy."

"Okay, smart guy," Dixon says, resting one musket on a table. "What is this crap?"

They stand before an enormous papier-mâché head. Mannequins in business suits clustered shoulder-to-shoulder around the floats and costumes are brightly packaged fireworks. Not the big, fancy Fourth of July ones, but the backyard kind—pagodas, roman candles, M-80s.

Dixon's head twists and arcs. "What in the hell is going on?"

"I don't know, but it makes me nervous." It doesn't make him nervous. Kreskin just wants them to hurry up. Kreskin has a busy day planned:

1. Collect treasure.
2. Shoot Dixon.
3. Move to Aruba.

"Don't worry. I've got your back." Dixon grins.

Kreskin smiles. Dyson's smartest man is so dumb he can't read the writing on the wall.

The pair moves toward the base of the mound of fruit, twice as tall as either of them. "I remember it being *here*," Kreskin says with a sad drawl. "Back when I worked at the factory, there was a big, fat X on the floor."

"If it's not one thing, it's another. God, I need to find this treasure. Stephanie will never take me back. I need to do something right, or else." He leans on the musket like a cane. "Okay, I haven't been honest."

"Dix, don't start like this."

"I have been lying to you. You need to know why I'm here." He gathers steam. "We can't have kids. It's my fault. Things don't work right with me *down there*. It makes our marriage tense—"

"Whoa, easy. More than I care to hear."

"I'm just saying, I'm not doing this because I'm greedy. I need this treasure for, you know, medical reasons."

"I get it." Kreskin sizes up his partner. He can't wait to find that gold and shut this guy up permanently. "Just relax."

Kreskin kicks a stray apple back into the pile. He wonders how many pieces they are looking at—a thousand, a million?

"Mr. Dixon?" an echo-heavy voice calls. "Mr. Kreskin? What are you doing here?"

Kreskin turns and sees that little shithead factory manager, Troy Gomez, inching down a metal staircase, the Krupp sisters in tow. Adrenaline surges through Kreskin's body. He assumes it is destiny, the moment where his plan folds together perfectly like one of those paper swans.

"Boss, did you guys come to help with the parade?" Pearl Krupp says. The huge smile on her face is almost strong enough to make Murray forget why they walked through the doors.

"Sis," Marci says from the top of the stairs, sharp and scolding. "The guns."

"Oh."

By this point Kreskin has a pistol digging into Troy's ear. "What's the bright idea? Did you know we were coming? You trying to ambush us?"

"Murray, how would I know that?"

"This sure looks like an ambush. What's with this mess on the warehouse floor? You little prick, you think you got it so rough? Always talking shit, laughing at me behind my back. You think your balls are brass enough to stand in Murray Kreskin Jr.'s way?"

"Murray, calm down." The gun leaves a circular purple dent on Troy's face. "I like you. Everyone likes you. You tell the best jokes."

"Give me one reason not to pull this trigger."

"Because I don't hate this town. I love Dyson. And I never laughed at you behind your back." Troy's last word weeps out. "I—I—I like you. You t—t—tell the best jokes."

Something softens inside Murray. He fights to ignore it. In a rush, Kreskin and Dixon tie the group's wrists instead of opening fire. "Where is it, kid?" Murray gets pushy with the gun.

Troy's Adam's apple blooms with a nervous gulp. "What?"

"Back in my day, there was a big X on the floor. I have a hunch, but I want you to tell me where it is."

"The X? The one that tells the trucks where to park for loading?"

"You think you're so smart." Murray shakes his head. "Yes. That one."

"The X, it's painted on the cement under all the fruit. I mean, that's where everything comes off the conveyor belt. See for yourself."

Murray looks at the massive pile of crap with a little conveyor slide hanging overhead.

"Good boy." The gun's hammer clicks back. He looks at the girls. His finger makes invisible tick marks. "You're lucky I wasted two shots." He stuffs the gun into his belt. "Let me borrow your pen, kid."

Kreskin snatches a red marker from his shirt pocket and writes *TROY GOMEZ* on the Shit List.

Fruit is everywhere at that end of the warehouse. Each time he lifts a foot, the imprint fills with bananas. Kreskin finds himself knee-deep in apples and oranges when the answer hits. *It's so obvious.* A grey neon light zaps to life in his head. *Show them who's a joke in this town.* With his back to the group he speaks: "Dixon, let's make a chain gang. Those three can clean up this mess so we can find the X." Under his breath: "I gotta catch a plane."

He pulls out his cigar, lights it, and bitter smoke rolls between his cheeks. A victory puff.

Before the smoke exits, a blown stick of dynamite erupts behind him. *CRACK-crack-crack* echoes around the walls.

There's Dixon, a few dozen feet away with that ridiculous musket, pointed right at Kreskin. A cloud of grey fog billowing around his head.

"Oh, damn," Dixon says, and drops the rifle. "I think I missed."

TUESDAY, 9:12 AM

A few soldiers eat sandwiches outside a big green tent on Maple Street. They are battling a monstrous wind, ensuring the tent doesn't lift off like an AWOL balloon. "Hello. Donna Urinating Bear-Queen, town hero." She extends a delicate hand. "Who's in charge?"

The canvas beats like a gang of helicopters. The dry dirt scent rolls in from surrounding farmland. "Ma'am, I'm sorry, but you'll have to step back."

"What's going on in there?" Donna bobs her head to peek through the tent flap.

"We're searching for remains."

"Remains of *what?*"

"Ma'am."

"Remains of what?"

"The guardsmen."

"Who?"

"The National Guardsmen killed by the satellite."

"Really? I hadn't heard." Donna steps forward with the grace of a stealthy jungle animal prowling tall grass. "Me, I've been trying to help people around town, but it looks like you guys are cornering the market. Me, I'm sort of in charge. Our poor mayor's missing." She checks over her shoulder for Packwicz. "I'm looking for your boss so I can tell everyone to go home. I'll handle the hero business. You're wasting tax dollars."

Her foreclosure stare goes to work.

"Ma'am, I will not repeat myself." The soldier looks down.

Donna frowns. This guy just doesn't have the same spark as Muscles. "My, my, aren't you the sober one?"

"Excuse me?"

"Nothing. Just that those other soldiers were a lot more fun to be around. Anyhow, back to my point: go home. Mama's here now."

"We will stay until it is time. Until then, please vacate the area so we can conduct this sensitive business or you will be placed under arrest."

"How many soldiers died?"

"Ma'am, please."

"How many? I need to know."

The man rolls his eyes, annoyed. "Seven, ma'am."

"That's a shame." Donna's surgically enlarged lower lip slides out with the drama of a cash register making change.

"Ma'am." The soldier shifts gears, placing a soft hand on her shoulder. "Please, it's time to go."

Donna backs up a little. "Listen, pal, Donna Urinating Bear-Queen doesn't take no for an answer."

A tent flap rips open and a man with a wash of white hair and dangling neck skin pokes out. He seems slightly spooked. "Say your name again, miss." His hands rub together like they are cold.

"Donna Queen, sir." She salutes.

The man's face grows deep red and agitated. "Again?"

"Donna Queen, Urinating Bear-Queen. Town . . . uh, you know . . . hero." She blushes. The plan suddenly isn't working so hot, and she grows embarrassed.

"That's what I thought." He steps from the tent. He is small and square, with tan and green camouflage fatigues. Several golden stars line his shoulder. "Young lady, you need to sit tight for a few minutes."

She pulls a small date book from a jumpsuit pocket and consults it. "Well, I have a lot of heroic deeds on the agenda."

"Johnson."

"Sir." The soldier stiffens.

"Don't let this woman out of your sight."

"Yes, sir."

"Wait just a minute," Donna says.

"There's an important phone call waiting for her." The man disappears back into the tent.

TUESDAY, 9:15 AM

Still buried in a haze, Skeet almost doesn't stop the truck in time. There is a set of roadblocks at the edge of town where tilled farmland dovetails with manicured green lawns. Two soldiers tip a blown-over orange barricade back upright.

"Sir, we haven't received permission to allow people into town. You'll have to wait like the others," a sergeant says through Skeet's open window.

"Others?" He blinks and shakes his head.

The soldier points behind the truck, to the side of the road. A scatter of cars, only a few, sit parked.

One soldier drags a new sandbag and lays it over the roadblock's base. He wipes a moist forehead. A green canvas hat lifts off his head and enters orbit.

Skeet has never been ranked high in the handsomeness scale. However, right now, with a thin layer of soot covering his face and clothes and a set of disturbed, red eyes peering from behind the muck, he is borderline frightening.

He reverses his truck to the end of the line. As he steps out, both legs still weaker than wet towels, Chris yells, "Skeet? I'm not trying to start nothing, but Cody Kellogg's on the radio telling everyone you're dead."

"I feel like it." Creased cheeks puff and ease out a breath.

"Sure look it."

"Thanks, Chris."

"So, you're bringing Hans back, huh?" says Chris, the sanitation worker who helped Skeet make off with the statue. Hans' feet currently poke from the back of Skeet's pickup.

"You were right," Skeet says, his voice dense and small. He's overcome with exhaustion and sadness like he never knew possible.

"What do you mean?"

"It was a mistake. This statue is all that's left. Dyson's history is in a million pieces thanks to me. If I'd just of stopped hoarding and left well enough alone . . ."

Skeet can't make eye contact.

"That's too bad, pal. But think about the bright side, it looked like you had a blast doing it. That's got to count for something, right? Another of those *memories* you were so hot and bothered about."

"I hope so. I can't fight the present, can't live in the past. Stuff ends, stuff begins. Whatever." He smiles and pats Chris' back. "Hey . . ." Skeet counts a dozen carloads waiting. "There's Irv Tucker and his family and Betsy Montgomery. But I don't recognize all these other people."

Skeet watches one strange car extend some fiberglass rod up from a truck bed. A man wearing a denim jacket with motorcycle patch starts pulling a thin rope. An American flag shimmies to the top and catches the wind like a sail.

"Oh boy, you haven't heard? Skeet, you'll never guess why all these folks are here."

TUESDAY, 9:18 AM

"Seventeen black!" Garrett hollers. "Paying three hundred to the lucky lady."

A skeleton crew spins roulette wheels and deals clumsy blackjack.

Garrett recruited a neighbor girl to run the bar; she's maybe eighteen at best. He needs all the help he can get. The Urinating Bear Casino is bursting with business.

The lights are dim and the walls are stained to an espresso dark finish. Garrett and the staff wear green shirts with Donna's logo on them. The squall of karaoke bleeds in from the nightclub.

"Madame First Lady, I'd say you're on a roll today." Garrett passes a stack of chips to the woman in a powerfully conservative canary yellow suit. She runs red fingertips over chip ridges, smiling. She looks so much older in person than Garrett figured. The First Lady's hair is tightly bunned and that face makes it seem like they're old friends.

"Well, let's keep it going. Split the zeros, handsome." She tosses a hundred dollar chip toward the top of the board. A sunglasses-wearing man in black delivers a mudslide, speaks into his cuff, and whisks away empty glasses.

The previous night, a line of stretch limousines snaked into the parking lot. The First Lady didn't make an appearance until a dozen men in those same sharp black suits checked under every bed and waved some wand over every electric device.

Garrett was surprised to find the entourage has a pretty decent gambling habit. The First Lady's tastes lie with the random chance of roulette. "I like how the odds are always the same every time you spin that cute little ball. There isn't much in this world that's as fair as a game of roulette," she tells Garrett, slightly drunk. "Rich, poor, black, white, dumb, smart, from New York or, heck, *Dyson*—everyone's equal. I wish life were as fair as roulette."

"Sounds like you believe in fate."

"Amen, Junior."

"You should meet my friend Packy."

"I'd be happy to." That famous voice is wispy, slurred. "Where is the little fella?"

"Wish I knew. He was supposed to be the pit boss, but my wife owes him money . . . long story." His face drifts from the wheel's spin. "Anyway, we were talking fairness. I couldn't agree more." Garrett begins explaining how his wife could use a fair chance once in a while. He recounts Ms. Urinating Bear-Queen's unsuccessful efforts to spin her fiscal good fortune to improve Dyson.

"That's horseshit," the First Lady snaps, shaking an empty glass in her security detail's face. A new mudslide arrives, fresh, cold, and chocolaty. Her eyes are cracked with blood vessels, her words eighty-proof. "I could use a good woman like that on my staff. Where is Donna? I wanna meet her, too."

Garrett describes his wife's latest heroic deed, and the First Lady dashes off a quick call to have the Army find this wonderful savior.

"Oh, Garrett." The First Lady's smeared makeup and bloated face goes sad. "I hate to leave you while I'm riding such a streak, but I'll be spending most of tomorrow on television. This old catcher's mit needs some beauty rest." She waves a hand around her face.

"You look lovely, ma'am."

She wags a finger. "Nice try. Off to bed for all good girls."

"It is nearly ten in the morning."

She looks at her wrist; there is no watch. "Right on schedule."

Garrett gives the nation's wife a great smile. His bald skull has grown a ring of stubble around the sides. "What was this about television?"

"Oh, the *tragedy*." She wobbles until a Secret Service agent locks her elbow. "Thank you, Julio."

"Ma'am, my name is Douglas," the agent says.

"I'm sure it is, sweetie."

Garrett stands in her path. "Television. Wow! Folks around here really appreciate your effort." She returns a twisted, confused stare. Twelve straight hours of mudslides will do that to a person, he decides.

She walks away and Garrett mutters. He calculates all the hours wasted at the casino instead of mummy hunting. He decides to bring the video camera along on his quest so he'll have proof and Donna can be proud.

This is all Packy's fault. If that murderer would have accepted Garrett's invitation to become the casino's pit boss, there'd be more mummy time. That Army guy, Muscles, isn't bad, but he's a little light on conversation.

With rapid fingers, Garrett cleans up the chips and restacks everything.

He is ready to burn that walking stack of bandages to the ground. Garret loves little obsessive chores like this now that his life has gotten so streamlined with money. He can't wait to play detective.

The First Lady makes a gangly return, slapping palms atop the green felt. "One last thing, darling." She burps with sealed lips. "If you see that Cody Kellogg, let him know yours truly loves his work. What a brave American. I'm his biggest fan."

TUESDAY, 9:22 AM

Packy's feet don't want to move. Bo promised the factory would be empty, and it's anything but. The mayoral duo peeks through the entrance after a gunshot rippled their ears.

"Bo, we should call the Chief," Packy says with firm conviction, something that still feels funny. "Bo?" He rattles the mayor's elbow.

"We're close, Packy. Just let this play out." Bo's voice is pressed thin and angry.

Through the door they see Kreskin and Dixon weaving between floats, around mannequins and other obstacles. Dixon hangs onto an enormous black musket with one hand. Kreskin huffs and puffs and shakes a handgun. A cigar sprouts into a beautiful flower of sparks when it falls from Kreskin's mouth and strikes the cement near a bunch of brightly-colored boxes covered in Chinese writing.

"This is too dangerous. Let's go, Bo. Our purpose in life isn't to die here. Fate wouldn't do that to me."

Bo turns with huge blue eyes twitching. Your purpose is to wait for our chance to save Dyson. Got it?" The black, dead pits of his pupils remind Packy of the mummy. Except that guy was friendly. Bo is on the edge of something dangerous and mean. He waits for Packy to nod. "Don't forget the wagon."

They found an abandoned red wagon in someone's backyard and used it for lugging around the jackhammer.

The wagon reminded Bo of childhood. Guilt bled under the mayor's skin. Eugene has left three messages on Bo's phone. Dinner would be hot and on the table. He was teaching Tae Kwon Do later. Would afghans and cross-stitch be too much for his house?

"Bo, this might sound odd, but are you feeling alright?"

The mayor's eyelids squirm a bit while nodding.

An explosion rips through the building. A full-throated pop that causes both to lie flat on icy concrete.

A burning smell finds them. Dozens of sharp whistles and *rat-a-tat* pops go for a solid minute.

Fireworks.

The silence that follows, that dense nothing, reminds Packy of being told by town council he should resign. He was "unreliable" since Donna and his coworkers hit the jackpot. The council waited for his response in awful silence. Standing there, before his friends and advisers, the hurt and sorrow and paranoia set in, stinging deeper than Donna's stupid lotto tickets. Packwicz walked away from Dyson. After that lonely meeting, his fingers inherited a jitteriness not unlike Bo's new eye twerks.

Bo is his only real friend not wrapped in bandages, and Packy is starting to consider ending it.

Packy stands to peek into the door window. Bo joins him. The I LOVE DYSON float is prickly with flames. Some strange smoke breathes from the fruit bowl float. One Rosinski mannequin has a shoulder on fire—he is the best of the bunch. Fireworks lay black along the floor, burst like spent shotgun casings.

"C'mon, let's go," Bo whispers. "Be sensible."

"No way."

"You're coming with me."

"No, I'm not."

"Do it for Dyson."

Bo's eyes grow larger.

"You're making a mistake," Packy says. The pair push open the doors, towing the jackhammer. "It's not worth the risk."

"Hi, Dix," Bo calls, stern but friendly at the sight of Dyson's only lawyer. He laughs uneasily. "Got any hand sanitizer?"

"You psychopath. Stay away from me." Dixon sits on a table among bolts of fabric and bowler hats. His pink, worried head lifts from his hands. He grabs the rifle.

"Hey, now, settle down. Let's not go calling each other names."

Dixon tenses. "Well, let's not go murdering Ed Lee."

"Okay, I think that's a great idea. Let's not do that."

"Who asked you? Get out before I blow your brains out, too."

"Wendell, what's going on? Tell me everything."

"Nothing, nothing's happening." He pulls the hammer back on his musket and bobs the barrel toward the mayor. "I have a doctorate degree. I'm smarter than you."

Bo's filthy hands spring up, but his feet measure slow steps. "Easy, easy. We know why you're here. We know about the treasure. Look at this jackhammer. We want to help. Now put the gun down and let's discuss. A smart guy like you understands that."

"I'd rather turn your head into a birdfeeder." Spit and gummy mucus leak from lips as Dixon aims.

"Oh, can it." Packy stands in front of Bo. "I went to just as many reenactments as you, Dixon. And we both know it takes a few minutes to reload. I heard the shots . . . both of them."

The light crackle of flaming papier-mâché sounds epic with warehouse echoes.

Dixon pulls the trigger. A soft *snap* joins those echoes.

Bo jerks slightly and opens his eyes. "Thanks, Packy." Their eyes lock, sanity filling both. Each grateful for the other.

"Go on," Packy says at an encouraging whisper.

"Now, Wendell . . . " The mayor moves forward. "You know where the gold is, and we have a jackhammer. Don't you think we could cooperate? For Dyson's sake?"

Dixon drops the gun. His fingers tense. His eyes seal shut. "Maybe, Bo, if you would have included me in Edna's will, we could have a deal." Dixon's lungs work harder. "Maybe if you would have cooperated earlier. But this is my treasure. I think I've earned it." His eyes open and he finds the mayor gone. "Hey, what are you doing? We are in the negotiation stage. You can't leave."

Bo is halfway across the warehouse. He heads toward the three people tied up with plastic apples between their teeth. "Marci?" The mayor bends to her level. "Oh, I'm so glad it's you." Bo's face fills excitement.

Marci's head tilts to the side. She lets out a relieved sigh.

Bo says, "Do you have any of that hand cleaner in your purse?"

Her relief doesn't last.

Murray Kreskin's lifeless body appears in the corner of Bo's eye. Spread facedown across the cement, a red pool surrounds him like a stomped ketchup packet.

TUESDAY, 11:00 AM

"It's quickly approaching lunchtime here in Dyson," Cody says, wiping his forehead with a rag, looking out at the edge of town. The wind has tamed to something cool and comforting. "And I'm looking at a beautiful sight, ladies and gentlemen."

"It's happening," Donna says, quiet and humble, like a little girl rubbing sleep from Christmas morning eyes.

WDSR's van is parked a few hundred feet from a series of tangerine-colored barricades and road cones.

"I'm joined by Donna Queen, proprietor of this radio station." He passes the microphone.

"All these people." Her voice slowly takes back its regular glass shardness. "They're here to help Dyson. To support us."

Cody wraps his arm around his boss, overcome with amazement. "Donna is referring to this amazing crowd before our eyes. A line of cars stretching into the horizon. I am reminded of gatherings like Woodstock. Some are Dyson residents, but many are not. Visitors, here to help rebuild Dyson, and maybe discover some of the magic that makes our community so special. Donna, any thoughts?"

"I spoke with the First Lady herself earlier this morning on the phone," she says, holding back tears. "She's here to honor the sacrifices and hard work she's heard about through your wonderful broadcasts, Cody. She asked me to help lead, and I said I'd be honored. I predict that once these blockades are opened tomorrow, we're going to see a rejuvenated town."

"Tomorrow? Can you confirm that with our listeners?"

"Oh, yes. The First Lady told me our utilities would be restored tonight and that the blockades would be opened so people can deal with the tragedy."

The DJ smacks his lips, knowing gasoline is finally off the menu. "Amazing. Simply incredible. If you are at home and you want to show your support and love for small town America, here is your opportunity. Come to Dyson. We welcome everyone with open arms. For Donna Queen, I'm Cody Kellogg. Please enjoy Elton John while we take a break."

Admiring the crowd, Cody feels life finally finding momentum.

"Cody," Donna says in a voice that has always made him suspicious. Usually it precedes requests for unpaid overtime or giving her a ride to Findlay for a doctor's appointment. "Are you feeling generous?"

"Pardon?"

"How'd you like to help me with a little problem? I need an interview, of sorts. It'd make the First Lady of the United States happy. She's a big fan of yours."

TUESDAY, 11:10 AM

Embarrassment hasn't hit Pearl this badly since watching her commercial two years earlier. This type of embarrassment, she knows, is suffocating.

A star in school plays and community theater, Pearl once dreamed of movie roles. Not superstar famous, but recognizable-at-the-mall-famous. Her parents, seeing this surprisingly passionate spark, took her to the city, snapped some headshots, and found an agent.

The young blonde was quickly cast in non-speaking commercial roles for shoes and teenage makeup, earning a meager income from them. At eighteen, she moved to Findlay and sharpened those acting skills in small plays.

She had a nice boyfriend named Wes. He was into far-out jazz, which is where her devotion to Ornette Coleman came from. Wes eventually moved on, but his record collection stayed with Pearl.

Pearl's agent finally landed her a speaking commercial and felt the concrete of a career being poured. Hollywood had never seemed so close.

Pearl rolled her eyes after reading the script: Showcase the product, taste the product, smile, and say how great the product is. It was only ice cream.

But still, a speaking part. A step forward!

Pearl told everyone about this television premiere. Everyone—family, friends, ex-boyfriends, ministers, teachers, dogs, cats, toddlers, senior citizens, the Kreskin barflies. Everyone.

It would be the biggest regret of her life for decades.

Pearl's lines were cut from the commercial in favor of voice over. In fact, all her acting got axed. Instead, the director used an outtake of Pearl—hair glowing under bright studio lights, seductive eyes made-up perfect—slurping melted ice cream from the bowl. The lights had turned the ice cream to swamp and left her face covered in wet strawberry goo. "Pinkley's Ice Cream," the voiceover said. "You don't *have* to act like a pig, but you'll want to."

Pearl's self confidence and dreams were slipped into a bag and beaten with hammers. She retired from acting and returned home, vowing to bottle up that disgusting embarrassment until she died.

She did a fine job of that until a plastic apple is pulled from her mouth on the warehouse floor, surrounded by flaming parade floats and a dead bartender.

"Oh, Marci," she says, stretching her fingers, sore from being bound. "All your hard work." Pearl doesn't know where the embarrassment comes from. It isn't like the entire city saw her sister in some awful commercial. But still, that horror is molten within her gut. "You stupid animal!" she yells at Wendell Dixon.

Pearl and Marci quickly fetch extinguishers and douse the flames.

Floats sit charred. Scorches run like black ivy across the mannequins, all melted mustaches and destroyed dreams. This depressing sight makes Pearl want to hide in a closet with a pint of Vanilla Toffee Crunch.

"What is the matter with you?" She shoves Dixon and he stumbles. "They worked so hard and you ruined everything."

"Hold on."

"Hold on nothing. What's wrong with you?"

Bo opens his hands in peacekeeping mission formation. "Pearl, please, this is more important than the parade."

"More important? *More* important?"

"You know," Dixon mutters, "I liked her better tied up."

"Oh, no you don't." She knocks Dixon to the ground with one shove.

Without much effort, the mayor and Packwicz retie Pearl, stuffing the apple back between her teeth and sitting her next to Troy. Her embarrassment doubles.

Lying there, kicking and crying, the men ignore her and argue. "Look," Bo says. "We brought a jackhammer. Unless you plan on digging up this treasure with a spoon, Packy and I are in charge. Where's the X, Wendell?"

"Well, now," his voice sags. "I didn't think of that."

Pearl bucks at her bonds. She stops when a soft hand wraps around her shoulder. "Relax, I'll get you out of this," Marci says.

Pearl watches her sister stride confidently across the floor and raise an arm. "Hey," she calls. "I know where the X is."

They pause and look. The mayor blooms with a tooth-hearty grin. "Oh, you're the best. Where is it, sweetheart?"

She stops and rests a hand on her hip. "Don't *sweetheart* me." Marci's voice booms with power. "I have a few demands before I tell you a thing."

TUESDAY, 11:28 AM

Donna prowls the streets, talking on the phone while cruising through stop signs. Dyson's emptiness is a bell sounding for a hero. No children playing in yards, no dogs being walked, no one changing the car's oil in the driveway. Dyson is empty and Dyson is hers. Donna is the owner, the boss, the chief.

"I don't know," she tells Garrett. He sounds tired from the First Lady's late night roulette redux. "For a guy who won't stop talking, Cody sure shut his mouth when I asked for help."

Donna wishes she had an extra hand, the radio sucks and she wants to change the station. She briefly steers with her leg.

"So, does that mean *he's out?*" Mechanical skittering fills the line's background. Garrett is calculating receipts.

"Sweetie, I don't know. I gave Cody some time. He'll tell me soon if he'll do the interview. It's not, you know, what's the word? *Important.*"

"If you say so. Look, I took a quick tally and we made about fifteen grand last night. Just with a few tables open. Isn't that incredible? Alright, to be honest I was a little skeptical—"

"Honey, that's great, but we have bigger . . . ummm? I'm so close. Herodom is sitting in my hands, but I don't want to make a sudden move. I'm scared it'll run away."

"You don't think this deal with Cody is a sudden move?" He yawns.

"Garrett, please." She spies down alleys and wide-open streets for a sign of life—one sign of life in particular. The air is peaceful and warm and perfect for heroism. "Do me a favor. Get my suit. The dark blue one and a top to go with it, those blue pumps and a set of panty hose. Check for runs this time."

A jerk of fear fills Donna. For a moment she thought she saw a man in the shadows behind a tree. *Was that Packy?* She has to find someone desperately. A bullet or a knife or whatever from that dummy Packwicz will spoil her plan. She slouches low.

She feels awful, having hired such a cunning hit man. Who knew?

"Isn't it a little hot to be so dressed up?" The calculator noise stops. "Besides, I finally have a free moment. I'm out the door looking for our bandaged buddy. Maybe beating it to death, too. You know, no big deal. Unless, of course, you want to watch."

"And my makeup. All of it. Sweetie, the First Lady will be dressed up, why wouldn't I? If I'm going to rescue Dyson and be remembered for generations, I have to look the part."

"Blue suit and stuff. Got it." Garrett sighs. "Please sneak back tonight. I could really use the help. It's not like there's anything to do in town right now."

There's a shocked little gasp intended to pluck the guilty string running from Garrett's heart. "The power will be back on soon. There's a *ton* to do." Donna slows down and peeks into Main Street's vacant storefronts. "This is only about the most important moment in Dyson history. If you think I'm sitting on my hands tonight, you're crazy."

"You're right. Sorry."

Donna jams the brakes hard. "*There he is.* Sitting on his bumper, staring into a brick wall, for God's sake. Like some kind of mental patient."

"Who?"

"Chief Grover." Her voice picks up a hint of girlish delight.

He is so stiff and silent Donna thinks an aneurysm might have killed him sitting upright. The strong wind hurls dust into Grover's glacial face.

"You're doing a great job, sweetie. We're going to make a difference. You just keep your end of the empire running and I'll tell Grover our plan, okay?"

"I'm not even sure I know our plan." His voice is dragging, needing sleep. "Either way, I'm killing a mummy."

"Garrett Norman Queen." She opens the door and cuts through the thick, humid afternoon, orange with sun. "Stop wasting time with that. I'll buy you a dozen hoods. Love you. Bye!"

The Chief twitches, but doesn't look. His car bursts with radio chatter and static, someone calls his name through the distortion. The Small Town Songbird doesn't budge.

She leans down with hands on knees. "Bert, everything okay?"

His lips are the color of bruises. They move slowly. "Does this happen to you?" His head gently lifts. "Every time something good happens, something shitty happens. I swear I never get to appreciate the positive news, because the bad is always kicking me in the stomach, harder."

She sits beside him. "You're asking the woman who won thirty million only to have Packwicz claim she ruined his life?"

"I did everything I could for the evacuation, and Skeet still died. Dyson is finally reopening, but Joyce isn't coming back. I stopped to think about it. The good comes down like rain, but the bad rushes in like a flood."

"Sounds familiar."

"If this is life, I don't think it's worth living."

"I'm so . . . you know . . . sorry."

Bert breathes a light chuckle. "Looks like things are turning around, though. Seems like half the planet came to help. Who'd have guessed so many people listen to Cody?"

"It's pretty amazing." She takes in the silence for the first time. A purity and clarity she hasn't felt in years. Not unlike opening the bowling alley alone. She loved those hours of calm reflection. "Don't put anything past my disc jockey. He's good."

"No offense." Grover's motions grow more fluid and alive.

"Chief, you look like you need a distraction."

"Dying for one, Donna."

"Good. I need your help tomorrow." That far-off pleasure of helping someone fills her rosy cheeks, giving Grover the gift of Heroism.

"I'll be a little busy." He stands and tugs at his belt.

"It'll be worth your time. Plus, I'll make it so Joyce *can't* ignore you. Heck, the entire country won't be able to ignore you." She cocks her neck and gives a warm smile. "How're your pipes these days? Do you still sing much?"

TUESDAY, 12:15 PM

"You're doing this for Dyson. You're doing this for Dyson," Bo says so nobody can hear. His passion for saving this town nosedives, fighting Marci's demands. *"You're doing this for Dyson,"* Bo imitates himself, kicking away some plastic fruit. He, Packy, and Dixon have spent a solid hour sweeping up apples and bananas until finding a faded black X on the concrete floor. "You're doing this for Dyson."

He repeats that little chant, but doesn't believe it. "Your town's ruined. Marci won't speak to you. You are ignoring a dead body in the corner and you're doing it for Dyson?"

All Bo can think about is an apartment. One he's never lived in before. A simple place with a big, bright window. A place he can take Boots and bunker down. Start a new life.

"Alright, boss." Packy tugs the heavy wagon through a parting sea of fruit. Wheels squeak and grind. "Jackhammer's ready to go. Just hold it to the X and squeeze that big button on the handle. Next thing you know, we're rolling in money."

The jackhammer is dark grey and battered like some antique machine gun. The smell of ancient grease is heavy. Don't think about sanitizer. *Don't think about those filthy, disgusting, germ-infested handles.*

"Ah Bo, legally speaking, I'd still like to recommend you sign my paperwork," Dixon says. "If it wasn't for me, you wouldn't be standing here. Clearly, that warrants *something*."

Ignoring the attorney, Bo looks back and studies the burnt scraps of floats among a sea of loose plastic fruit. Troy and Pearl are still bound and gagged. Marci is on her knees patching a blackened pair of Rosinski pants.

Marci, Bo suspects, will never speak to him again. He promised her he'd agree to her demands if she showed them where the X was. All she asked was that they untie Pearl and Troy and help repair all the damage to the floats. Simple requests. But as soon as Marci said the X was under the plastic fruit, his vision of that gold forced him to ignore her demands.

Bo asks himself what kind of man behaves like this?

"We'll discuss my commission later," Dixon says, kicking a free circle of cement until no plastic fruit touches him. "How deep do you think it is? Really fifteen feet like that riddle?"

"Who knows? Maybe six, like a corpse," Packy says.

Bo squeezes the trigger. The motor roars with jostling fury. The noise of several jet engines echoing against one another fills the room. Sharp flecks of concrete dig into his knuckles and face. He can't stop thinking about the awful creature he's become as he begins to bleed.

The sting is a trip to church and confessing sins.

The jackhammer punches the rock and wins. Now this sound rips apart some unwritten list of rules deep within Bo's conscience.

With about six inches of concrete carved out, Bo drops the hammer. "I can't do this. You know what? If saving Dyson means being greedy and mean and negligent, then forget it." His voice crashes into something desperate. Tears seem close behind. "Maybe this town doesn't deserve to be saved."

"Bo?" Dixon says, trudging forward through fruit.

"Wait, we're so close," Packy whispers through the puffing cloud of concrete dust.

By the time their words register, the mayor is untying Pearl's ropes and pulling her gag. "I'm sorry."

Bo does the same with Troy. "I'm sorry. Please. I'm sorry—"

"Idiot," Troy snaps. "I'm sorry. Please. *I'm sorry I'm such a careless, dumb shit who makes everything that he touches worse—*"

Bo raises a hand. "You know what, shut your mouth."

Troy's eyebrows lift, his lips pucker.

"I'm sick of everyone treating me like this. And I'm sure as hell sick of everyone trying to talk like me. I have busted my ass for this town, for ungrateful, self-centered assholes like you, and where does it get me? Just deeper into the doghouse."

"Deeper into the doghouse?" says Troy. "What does that even mean?"

"Don't worry about it. Just know . . ." Bo's words hang for a second, he's never spoken so openly before. He looks back at Packy, who gives him an encouraging nod. "Just know I'm not anyone's punching bag. I don't deserve to be treated like this. Maybe this town should just fall apart. See if I care."

"Oh, okay." Troy recovers from being so stunned. "I was just saying . . . you know . . . if you'd have just mentioned you were looking for that stupid Rosinski fruit, I could have told you."

"What?"

"It's not buried under the floor." He cups his hands to yell across the warehouse: "*Idiots.*"

"What do you mean?" says Packwicz.

A crowd gathers around Gomez. His fists are only a few millimeters from jackhammering the mayor's face.

"There was a riddle . . . and a map," Packy says.

"Yeah, this dopey little poem. Not even in iambic pentameter. I took a few semesters of Shakespeare," Dixon says.

"Sit still. I'm going to enjoy this." Troy runs up the metal stairs to his office.

The small cluster stands silent for a minute. The wind rushes with whitewater force. The thin aluminum warehouse walls spasm like a set of nervous hands.

Troy thumps down the stairs. "Here. Here's your treasure, idiots." In a simple wooden bowl, he holds a collection of fruit with the shine and luster of expensive jewelry. "Congratulations." He launches the bowl through the air. It lands with tin can *clonks* across the cement. The golden apples and bananas spin to a stop among bright plastic ones.

Packwicz chases one and returns hurt. "Wait, gold's supposed to be heavy." He weighs it with dramatic arm lifts.

"Let me see." Dixon snatches the golden fruit.

"It's *brass.*" Troy's face is sour. "*Idiots.* There never was any gold fruit. This crap has been around since Rosinski ran the place. My old man told me the story years ago. I can't believe you all didn't know."

"The story?" Marci says with hope, picturing her imaginary husband.

A strange blend of contempt and pleasure fills Troy. "The story is, there is no story." He watches each blank face, waiting for reactions. He spins the wooden bowl between his hands. "Rosinski was broke when he died. The guy was delusional. He told women this shit was made of gold so they'd think he was rich and sleep with him."

"But imitation fruit was so popular." Marci can't help sliding into her work speech—but now with wounded speed. "The 1949 smash hit

South Pacific was our biggest single sale ever. So, to answer your question . . . everybody loves . . . plastic fruit."

Troy stutters a bit, wanting to console Marci. He doesn't, and his voice plunges to a remorseful register. "Nobody's ever bought this crap. It's a miracle we're still in business. I'm shocked people thought Rosinski was so rich. He was a terrible businessman and a terrible person."

Dixon's voice squeaks. "Stephanie's going to be so upset with me."

"Don't you wish you'd let me explain before all this?" Troy points at each tragic corner of the warehouse. Kreskin's body and the ruined floats and the hole in his floor.

The group goes silent again, the aluminum siding chattering its teeth. After a minute or two of resentful silence, Packy expects Bo to say something. He twists his head back and forth. "Hey, where's the mayor?"

TUESDAY, 8:15 PM

"It's absolutely amazing." Cody wants to blow warmth onto his freezing fingers, but knows Herbert Morrison wouldn't break focus like that. "I'm atop the Dyson Grain Elevator, seventy feet in the air, the highest spot in town." His voice is slow and perfect. "The sun is setting into a pale orange and the air is fresh. I guarantee nobody's ever seen a sight so beautiful, ladies and gentlemen. I have a panoramic view of eager people in every direction. A few thousand cars are parked along the city limits. Dyson has suffered through a mighty downturn and this satellite crash, but now, looking out onto the—by my estimate—five to ten thousand volunteers waiting to help, I realize humanity will always persevere.

"To anyone listening, the people of Dyson thank you in advance for your help. I hope you extend a hand with cleanup. And if you love what you see, make an investment—buy a house, and if you can't do that, simply buy a pizza, and if you can't do that, just come back again. Someone smarter than me once called America's small towns *the lost continent.* Don't let them stay lost.

"I'll be back on the air early tomorrow morning with full coverage of this amazing day. This is Cody Kellogg, signing off."

He lays down the microphone and blows into his hands. The tingling heat spreads. Pride doesn't begin to explain the emotion running through Cody. He is a hero.

His hands warm and his limbs vibrate with satisfaction. It's a powerful force painting his life—scraping away the weathered coat and applying something fresher.

That emotional color dulls quickly, though, considering Donna's request.

"I'm a journalist, not a jingle writer, not some commercial pitch man," he said earlier.

"You've interviewed me before. Just read the questions I whipped up, that's all I want," Donna told him. "And then I write you a check and make a call to my friends in the radio business. Memphis is nice this time of year, don't you think?"

Holding a scrap of paper to the light the way counterfeit bills are checked, he said, "These questions, they're lies, Donna. There's no way you inoculated a bus of school children. I seriously doubt you have any clue of how to fill a pothole. And no church in its right mind would sculpt the Virgin Mary in your image. The silicone budget alone would be through the roof."

"Is that what it says? Sorry, it should say I *declined* to pose for that statue."

"This is ridiculous. I'm a journalist." He crumpled the questions.

"Since when? So I'm getting loose with history. I'm doing it for . . . you know, what's-it? . . . Dyson. It's a little shot in the arm. Some needed publicity. It'll give your career a shot in the arm, too."

The wind speeds as the sun crashes into the horizon, melting into the lines of cars. A shiver works deep into Cody's bones. Above him, an electric hum sounds. It grows bigger and buzzier every few seconds.

"I'm a journalist," he says, looking above, wondering what the hell that noise is. "You're being backed into a corner. It's like the Fart Box all over again."

The buzzing continues as Cody winds up the microphone cable. It would be nice to knock the dust off Mr. Razzle-Dazzle and get back to Memphis. There's an ex-girlfriend there, maybe she's still single.

A heavy click sounds, like someone flipping a tilt-a-whirl into action. The enormous neon halo lights and a yellow glow fill the rooftop. Everything is sunrise up there as Cody makes his way down the ladder. "Let Donna know you're a journalist."

WEDNESDAY, MIDNIGHT

"There it is," Gene sighs after endless laps around Dyson looking for his brother's green car. "What are you doing here?"

FruitCo's parking lot lights illuminate Bo Rutili's battered Toyota.

Gene's chest tightens like a fist, letting anxiety grab hold. "Hope he's not mad for some reason. Why couldn't he just pick up the phone and return a call?"

"Sweetie," Sloan said earlier. "What are you doing? Bo's probably overwhelmed right now. Why are you in such a hurry to find him?"

"It's a brother thing. I've been neglecting it for way too long," he told her.

"Come on, you can tell me." She grabbed his arm.

"Just what it looks like. I'm pathetic. I'm a terrible big brother. Grandma would be ashamed."

"Gene," she said, back at their place, rubbing hands across her bulging belly. "You're a good guy. Live your own life. You're a successful business owner. You do tons of charity. Plus, you have a hot girlfriend."

"Good point," Gene said, kissing her cheek and grabbing his keys. "But I have to go. I'm sorry." He knelt down and kissed her stomach. "Take care of this dude for me."

"Knock it off, you know it's a girl."

Inside the factory, blindly looking for anyone to ask, he rounds a corner and pushes through two swinging black doors into a warehouse alive with color. He is immediately spotted by a group surrounding burnt paper tatters on wheels and weird, melty mannequins.

"Hey, Coach Dixon! I'm so glad to see you."

Coach Dixon isn't excited to see his old player. "Murderer!"

"Whoa. What?"

"You murdered Ed."

"Ed who? I'm just looking for my brother." Words dissolve as he stares at the fat guy anchoring a pool of blood in the corner. "What is going on here?"

"I . . ." soft groans puff from Dixon's lips. "I guess that makes both of us murderers."

"I didn't kill anyone."

"It's alright, son, denial is the first step to recovery. I know."

Everyone else carries on like they have better things to do. Dixon explains about the treasure being brass, and how the floats were ruined, but he avoids explaining whatever happened to the dead man. When Dixon says that Bo disappeared, Gene's shoulders stoop with disappointment.

"Wow, okay, that's really messed up, and I'd love to stick around and help . . ." His focus returns to the motionless legs and fingers in the corner. "But I gotta run and find Bo."

Gene walks back toward the door.

"Dyson is depending on us," Troy Gomez says. Marci Krupp nods. Gene finds himself suddenly surrounded. "I know this sounds corny, but the Destination: Dyson Committee put their faith in us, and we can't let them down. We can't let the town down. I bet your grandma liked parades."

Gene stops walking backward, away from them.

"Maybe this could be a tribute to her?" Troy says.

"Hey, how'd you even get into town?" Pearl asks.

Gene shrugs. "Give one of these soldiers a hundred bucks and they'll sell you a kidney."

The warehouse is steamy in the July heat. His normally stuffy sinuses pick up the aroma of sweaty bodies pressing themselves to the limit. He rubs a shirtsleeve over his forehead and cheeks. There's an incalculable passion in their eyes. It's something Gene hasn't seen in himself for years.

Gene begins helping repair costumes without a word. Yeah, he thinks, Bo is probably too busy right now.

Night closes over FruitCo, and the women he is supposed to be working with stitch together scraps of costumes from burnt fabric. The other men duct tape papier-mâché fruits and letters and crispy bits of the Gerald Rosinski float.

And still there is a bloating body in the corner.

This small army works until near dawn—until the parade has been rebuilt with less-than-stellar results. All the time, with the flair of a circus master, Troy explains this plan to turn Main Street into something visitors will never forget.

"Fruit-tastic" is a word he throws around often.

WEDNESDAY, 8:00 AM

Fingers of morning daylight run through Dyson's treetops as soldiers open the barricades. A landslide of cars bungle the community's streets. Front doors of homes are flung open in relief. Ladders are applied to roofs and inspected for damages. The crucifix on Mr. Riley's chimney is even removed.

A firm pack of new visitors stand around Christmas Park, looking puzzled at the plastic Santas affixed to phone poles, the thousands of wooden snowflakes dangling from power lines, but especially the giant dirt crater.

When Chief Grover arrives, his feet stumble. His hands don't have the energy to chuck up a belt. Absolutely nothing will help this funk he's in. Grover's body is a tangle of nervous energy after Donna's strange request. This, on top of the dread of his wife and daughter being gone forever.

He wanders through the crowd. Thousands sip free coffee provided by who-knows-who and watch a stage being erected. Most speak in whispers. The somber tone of the crowd, thousands of people, makes Grover paranoid there is some tragedy he is unaware of.

"I just got a call from a guy named Spiegel," Grover mumbles to a tall man in a black suit and tinted glasses. "Said to talk with him."

The man speaks code to a cufflink. The agent holds still for a moment and then nods. "Colonel Spiegel is behind the nativity scene in the south quadrant."

"The south quadrant?"

The agent points nonchalant.

"I didn't know we had quadrants," Grover says, weaving through the crowd.

Spiegel is a lean cut of leather who would prefer to evaporate entirely into an invisible cloud, but instead hangs around the manger and speaks into a cuff. Grover finds him crouching behind the wise men. "Colonel Spiegel?" The Chief lowers himself and calls into the manger. The plastic light-up nativity figures are the size of kindergarteners.

"Shhhh," hisses from the blackness. "Get behind the wise men before you blow my cover." The inner manger is humid and smells of moldy hay.

"Hello, I'm the Chief of police. You phoned me earlier . . . "

"What part of *get out of sight* did I say in Latin? Down, down." Grover crawls toward the voice. "Of course I know who you are."

"I see you're enjoying our manger. Little known fact about Dyson . . . " His eyes adjust and see the man has features and a black hat to match a black suit.

"Known as the Christmas City from 1998 to 2005," Spiegel says with the gusto of a telephone operator.

"Oh, well. Yes. But did you—"

"Regional Pork Chop Capital from ninety-three 1993 to 1997 and . . . " He drops an embarrassed cough. "Known as the place where President Lincoln once defecated from *date unknown* to 1992."

Grover settles on the ground with arms resting on knees. "Looks like you did your homework." He pauses and squints. "Agent Eggleston? Is that you?"

"It's Spiegel."

"You're not Agent Eggleston?"

"Spiegel."

"Because this fella who came and talked to me out by the graveyard from NASA looked an awful lot like you. Why is NASA here?"

"I never said I was from NASA. Just that I was a representative of NASA."

"There's a difference?"

"I work for the government. Let's say I solve problems." He peeks over the baby in swaddling clothes at a suspicious group of teens. "I do whatever it takes to solve problems. We need you to make sure there are none. The First Lady hates being embarrassed. I assume you've heard about the Clearwater, Florida situation last year?"

Thirteen months prior, the President's wife went to the Gulf Coast to cut a ribbon on a slavery and environmental awareness museum. In a rush, she didn't have a chance for a tour before the ceremony, and was as shocked as the camera crews were delighted to discover the museum was funded by the Ku Klux Klan. This museum explained the environmental benefits of slavery—such as a dramatic decrease in tractors and combines. This used fewer fossil fuels, which, the museum argued, would save the environment. "Slavery!" declared one banner hanging above the First Lady in a photo that stayed atop the newscycle for weeks.

"We make it our mission to ruin anyone who embarrasses her." Spiegel sounds sharp.

"I kind of remember reading something about that museum mysteriously burning down."

"What a coincidence."

"So first you're here to warn me about the satellite, now you're protecting the First Lady? I don't understand."

"Excellent."

"Excellent?"

"You're not supposed to understand what I do. If you understand, then the terrorists understand."

"There are terrorists?"

"Not on my watch."

Grover waits a beat or two until politeness kicks in and changes subjects. "Well, I think this will be a pretty great celebration today."

"Celebration?" Eggleston's dark eyes look sore. "Get your head out of your ass, Grover. This is a solemn moment, and I don't want any flubs."

"Solemn? These people are here to repair the roads and help the injured. You know, disaster relief. Aren't these FEMA volunteers?"

"Again . . ." He pauses and puts a hand over his ear, receiving a tiny message through an earpiece. "Remove your head from your ass, Grover. Now get out there and maintain law and order. And remember . . ." Eggleston pokes his nose around the manger like a spooked owl and quickly jabbers code into his wrist. "I'll be watching you for flubs."

Working through the hushed crowd, the Chief doesn't make eye contact. He presses all that recent disappointment to the bottom of his body. "What counts as a *flub*, exactly?" he mutters. "Even if I knew, a big dummy like me couldn't prevent one if my life depended—"

One stranger from the floating, moving pack of onlookers grabs Grover. The Chief jerks his head and comes out of the trance. "Skeet!"

The word bursts through the somber crowd at a sprint. Grover lifts his buddy and spins him like World War II just ended and they are in Times Square.

"Easy, easy." Skeet slaps Grover's back, both feet dangling over the grass. "I'm a little dinged up."

An elderly couple press fingers to lips. "Don't you have any *dignity?*"

Grover and Skeet shush with confusion and walk off. Skeet is a little unclear how he ended up under all that rubble. Grover explains the satellite's trajectory.

"Skeet, I can't tell you how glad I am you're alive. We saw the barn. I thought the worst." For the first time today, Grover notices the sun and the smell of grass and his spine stops shooting with violent pain. "Maybe the world isn't so awful."

"Don't get me wrong, I'm happy as hell to be standing here. Oddest damn thing, though. You'll never believe how I got loose."

They duck into a neglected playground and take shelter from the powerful sun under a metal slide.

"Skeet, buddy, I could talk for hours, but I need to ask something. I'm going nuts and I need a hand. Something weird's happening."

"Don't tell me twice."

"Can I re-deputize you while I do Donna Queen a favor?"

"A favor?"

"This is the weirdest part of all."

WEDNESDAY, 8:45 AM

"Do you really need a suitcase? Just toss it all in garbage bags. Two or three sacks in the back seat and step on the gas," Bo says. He is driving around town, chewing on a pen. "No, no. Get a suitcase, act like an adult. There's that nice big one at Grandma's."

Boots is on his lap, tail swaying happily. Bo cradles the cat with one arm and steers with the other. He has decided not to go anywhere without Boots.

He turns the wheel, dodging people. The streets are jammed with parked cars and people and life. It's the scene he's waited so long for. But after everything at the factory this sight twists his stomach to nasty colors.

Bo pulls into his grandmother's driveway and stares at the flapping yellow police tape X-ing the doorframe.

He pulls the pen from between his lips and begins writing a letter:

> Dear Dyson,
>
> After the last few days, I have come to realize the role of major is above my abilities. In my quest to improve this town I have become someone who is holding it back. I have become a person I am not proud of. Perhaps Dyson just isn't for me anymore?
>
> Please consider this my official resignation letter, effective immediately. By the time you find this I will

*be gone. I do not plan to return for fear of losing a
grasp on who I am.*
Thank you for the opportunity.
Sincerely,
Bo Rutili

He signs the letter and slides it into an envelope. "Get a suitcase, toss your stuff inside, leave this note on your office desk, and run. Oh, and cat food. See if Grandma left any cat food." He opens the door and is pelted by stuffy, musty air. "Get one of her cuckoo clocks. That'll make Gene happy. Bury the hatchet a little."

The soon-to-be former mayor runs his fingers along the thick plastic ribbon crisscrossing the door. He inspects closely, as if maybe this is a joke. Poor taste, but maybe just a joke.

Inside, he finds glass kitties in shards, wall hangings crumpled, afghans and quilts shredded, polyester pants and tops tossed and wrinkling. He can't take a step without breaking something. Bo lifts his foot to discover a blend of wooden splinters and springs. When he recognizes the clock hands and carved bird, his gut sinks.

The urge to run is still strong, but his urge to fix things has never been stronger. He wants to glue the cats together and restitch the blankets.

Maybe fixing Dyson isn't as hard as he thinks?

Maybe it's worse? Something inside him says to shut the door and leave town.

WEDNESDAY, 9:17 AM

Garrett Queen stands before the Casino doors and waves goodbye to the government motorcade.

His nerves shake for caffeine and quiet.

That First Lady kept him awake for nearly two days straight, but did toss a lot of cash into the casino. Every time things got tidied up and he prepared to hunt his bandaged foe, a secret service agent knocked to say the President's wife wished to try her luck again. Each time Queen would rub his eyes and swallow another pot of coffee while the First Lady clutched a lucky rabbit's foot and made mudslides vanish at an alarming rate.

"There's going to be so much damn attention tomorrow," she said, placing chips last night. "It'll look fantastic."

"Well, Dyson sure could use some positive publicity," he said, as the silver ball and wheel spun in opposite directions.

"Oh, Gary," she said looking right at Garrett. "I meant it'll look good for the President. But I suppose your little town could look good. I was worried you folks would seem sort of *responsible*. But I like your angle better. You're a glass-half-full fella. Either way, America will forget Clearwater ever happened." She lifted a glass. "And I'm a glass-is-totally-empty girl. Ahem, *Stockton*."

"What? How could Dyson be responsible for a satellite falling?" Garrett opened wide with a yawn as the ball stopped.

The pair shared a confused moment as the secret serviceman replaced her glass with a cold, fresh mudslide. "Listen, Gary, I'll be honest. I think you have the wrong idea about what's happening. I didn't realize until just now you didn't know about the, you know . . . " She took a drink, glancing at the wheel. "Hey, seventeen black, pay the lady!"

Hours later, letting the gentle morning heat touch his skin, Garrett Queen prepares to support his wife the best he can. He smiles. "What a woman." He returns to the casino. "Muscles," he calls to the sleeping pit boss on the office floor. "Congratulations, you've been promoted. You're in charge while I'm gone."

Garrett grabs her blue suit before running to the car, stopping in front of the dent in the hood. He inspects the spot and shakes his head. His fist clenches until it goes sunset red. He punches the mummy-shaped dent.

He leaves the parking lot with the black fumes of burnt tires.

WEDNESDAY, 9:20 AM

Every car door slamming, every bird chirping, every child giggling makes Dixon anxious. Dyson's lone attorney pops his knuckles constantly, his neck twitches, and his ears ring as the gas tank fills. A stack of bright green papers, several reams tall, flutters on the car roof. The leaflets take flight and tumble down the sidewalk into the sunlight.

Five more gallons and he'll be ready to run. "It doesn't take a great lawyer to know what you'll get for murder. Even by musket," he says, watching the pump's numbers spiral up. "Just go into hiding for a few years. When the heat cools, you and Stephanie will be together again. Do criminals really call it 'heat?' Maybe she'll think you're more of a man now. Yeah, I bet so."

The pump kicks off with a full tank, and Dixon sighs with calm.

As the attorney twists the gas cap, a young woman walks by the station. Long stem legs, high rising shorts, and a haircut only college girls can pull off. "Maybe you need a ride," Dixon whispers, holding an imaginary conversation. "It's a hot day . . . Where am I going? I don't know, wherever. Maybe New Orleans. Maybe LA. Maybe Peoria. Sky's the limit, but we gotta split, babe. Why? I'm wanted by the law, that's why. Get in."

This seduction continues as the woman grows smaller in the distance, walking away.

"On second thought," he says. "No, you can't. You're a good husband, you're not a cheater. You're not a murderer, either. You are a good guy. One of the few. Don't listen to everyone else."

Pulling away, the young woman in his rearview, Dixon waits for traffic to pass with a tail of flopping papers shedding from his roof.

Dixon's escape is cut off by a cheerful voice traveling like a poisonous dart.

"Wendell!" Stephanie calls from the sidewalk, moving quickly, waving an arm. Her dark hair is a mess, her light skin is sunburned pink. Her wide hips look like a car bumper in sweatpants. "Where have you been, sweetheart?"

"Stephanie." His voice lifts bright. "I've been looking everywhere for you. You're not mad at me?"

"Wendell." Her head tilts, confused. "Why would I be mad, honey?"

"About . . . about . . . you know, everything."

Her gentle hand enters the open window and brushes her husband's cheek. "I'm so proud of you staying behind with the fire department. I heard you were out saving lives. I don't even remember what we were fighting about."

"Me neither," he lies.

"I went by the house. It's all still in one piece! C'mon, I'll hop in, we can go together. I'm not going to let you out of my sight." From the passenger seat she clutches Dixon's hand harder than ever. He loves it.

WEDNESDAY, 10:00 AM

In downtown Dyson, a Gerald Rosinski look-alike bounces across rooftops. A fake mustache catches the breeze and threatens to zip away until its owner presses the fur down again. He is three stories up, walking across a long thin plank spanning the gap above an alley. Adding to the spectacle, he is carrying two garbage sacks of plastic fruit.

"Easy, easy." One foot gently drops in front of the other as the board sinks and makes noises that cause lives to flash before eyes. "Left, right, left." Troy Gomez moves steady but fast.

It's a relief when his feet touch the rooftop and he deposits the bags. He stops to peer down at a newspaper skipping across the gutter. Main Street's sidewalks are disappointingly empty. Cars honk in the distance, news choppers swirl above, but Main Street has nothing. "Thank God for Dixon and those flyers." Troy looks back and counts twenty sacks of fruit piled across the rooftops.

There is another rope dropping into another alley. A minute's worth of tugging and pulling hauls up the treasure: more sacks of fruit. Each rooftop requires several for his plan. The more bags, the more amazing this parade. The more amazing the parade, the more amazing Dyson will be. The more amazing Dyson becomes, Troy estimates, the more amazing his life will be.

The wind threatens to send his hat into orbit. He scrunches the bowler and slides it between his belt and pants. The last thing he wants is to screw up this costume and upset Marci again.

"Troy, you can't do that," she told him earlier as the sun rose. They'd spent hours repairing the floats. "Gerald's head looks like a broken watermelon."

"I'm doing my best," he said, barely able to form words he was so exhausted. Papier-mâché floats don't take well to fireworks and flames. Rosinski's face was cooked Cajun, pockmarked, and lopsided. "Alright, it looks . . . off. But we can't let that stop us. We've come too far."

"I'm just saying, the nose could be straighter. He had a really cute nose."

"Look, I've been busting my ass all night while you two work on those stupid costumes. Don't you think that's a lot for one person?" Gene, applying paint to the float, took a subtle step backward.

Marci's eyes were dark and aching. "Oh, I see now. Maybe you should get Dixon or Packy to help. Don't even *think* about asking me." He saw a shirt tag sticking up as she walked off.

"Packy is bagging fruit and loading it into the truck. That's *important*. Dixon is using the copier at his office. It takes time to print a thousand flyers. That's *important*." He took a weak swing at apologizing. "I can't pull them away. I'm just saying I'm a little tired . . . Marci . . ."

The rest of the morning Pearl and Marci spoke so quietly he couldn't hear. They shifted tight, angry glances. He pushed the I LOVE DYSON float to the opposite end of the warehouse to work alone. When he finished, the letters, a dozen feet tall, resembled the crude handiwork of field doctors.

Hours later—atop Dyson's decomposed rooftops—a burst of pride overcomes Troy as he hauls up plastic fruit. "Teamwork, that's what it was all about really. We had a great crew, all focused. We couldn't have saved Dyson without one another," he says, imagining what he'll tell reporters one day when they look back at the moment his town turned around and shoved its way out of the casket. "It's not unlike the Stones recording *Exile on Main Street*. Sure, they didn't get along, but that tension produced something that will last for generations . . . We weren't all on heroin, though."

Grinning, "Tumbling Dice" playing in his head, Troy walks to the building's opposite edge and settles the flimsy plank three stories above the alley. He hauls twice as many garbage sacks as before—tightroping to the last building on his route.

He gives downtown a second glance. The buildings are in so many states of grey and brown and yellow disrepair. They remind Troy of a mouthful of decayed teeth. But that's only temporary.

He has the answer. It sort of makes him Dyson's dentist. Troy likes that title much better than factory manager.

Halfway across the alley, the plank bows deep and a lightning bolt of panic crackles in his head. With the sound of wood snapping, Troy Gomez's bubbly optimism disappears.

Troy doesn't count the windows as he falls hard toward the cement. Gomez's life doesn't blend into a montage as the ground zooms closer. His body just twists and flails for an invisible ladder.

There is precious little to grasp as air whips past his ears.

His bones smack the ground. His eyes bang closed with the force of marbles in an empty can. The impact crushes air from both lungs.

Lying on his back across bags of flattened fruit, the oxygen returns, and all sorts of strange, broken noises belch from his body.

There's no telling how long he stays like that. Minutes for sure, maybe longer.

"Troy, why are you crying?"

Gomez lifts his eyes to find Bo's sad face looking down. He's holding some ridiculous cat.

"Why are you lying in an alley?" he asks.

Tears and snot glaze Troy's face and gum his fake mustache, which miraculously stayed put during the fall. Gomez doesn't like this sudden lack of control. He hates the black, scummy thought nestling into his brain. "I can't . . ." the tears roll, " . . . do all this myself."

Wind flaps plastic sacks in the silence.

"I wish I could help," Bo says. "But I have to take off." He is holding the cat to his chest, stroking it. "You're absolutely right. You can't do anything by yourself. You're talking to the king of that thinking."

Slowly, painfully, Gomez sits up. "That's not what I need to hear."

"Sorry. I'm done giving people hope."

WEDNESDAY, 11:31 AM

Cody's confidence drops into an uncharted circle of Hell as the midday sun peaks. The shady spots around Christmas Park's perimeter are packed with visitors. The majority of people, however, are trapped in its treeless center, beneath the pounding heat.

"Cody Kellogg, WDSR, can I ask a few questions?" He plugs the microphone into a woman's face. Her cheeks are sunburnt and her lungs pant.

"Who? What? No, beat it." She swats at Cody. Long black hair clings to her sweaty face. She looks—much like the rest of the crowd—on the verge of collapse. "If you want to help, get me some water or some food. I love our troops just as much as the next girl, but this is getting ridiculous."

"Troops? Please explain to the folks at home."

"Oh, for God's sake." She whispers, "Don't you reporters have any dignity? You're all walking around pumping us for sound bites when all we want to do is show our respect and get the hell out of this shit hole."

This is the second or third interview Cody has had like this. Must be sun poisoning. Maybe other reporters are spoiling his deal? A spiny ball of anger travels through him, picturing journalists with designer suits and network television affiliations. Those big shots have claimed all the good space under the trees. Interviewees line up if only to escape the brutal sun.

Cody spots a woman in her twenties, shading herself beneath an American flag. He dances through the crowd and arrives just as a network reporter starts chatting with her, pointing to his cameraman. That little ball of anger trips some dangerous, red doomsday button within Cody.

"Hey you bastard, that was my interview." Cody shoves, but doesn't move the reporter.

"Excuse me, miss." The tall, handsome man in a brown suit turns and stares down at the wrinkles and crooked teeth of someone clearly not cut out for television. "Who are you?"

"Who do you think? I'm Cody Kellogg. *The* Cody Kellogg. This is my town and my story. Vamoose. I'm tired of city people taking what they want and leaving."

The man gives a warm smile. "Funny. You got me. Is this like improv comedy? Can I give you a topic, like . . ." he pauses. " . . . zero gravity butcher shop. Ok, go, act out a scene."

"I'm a reporter. You're standing on my land, son." His voice goes as quiet as cocking a gun. "Time to leave."

"Did the guy from CBS put you up to this?" The reporter shrugs to the girl under the flag. "This is cute. Fetch me a bottle of water and a turkey sandwich. I'm dying here."

"Ohhh, me too," she grumbles. "So thirsty. So *hungry*."

At any other point in Cody's life this would have been a green light for the old Memphis Shuffle. The Memphis Shuffle involves kicking a guy in the shin so he's off balance, then a couple of fists to the skull.

Cody is eyeballing the trajectory for his foot and the guy's shin when an opportunity sprouts in Cody's thinking.

Cody has had a few truly brilliant moments in his life, but this one glows like his finest.

"Sorry, big guy. My mistake." Cody tips his hat and takes a few steps. He starts broadcasting to himself, the microphone dangling at his side. "Ladies and gentlemen, I hope that chorizo hasn't gone bad . . . How many hours has the old refrigerator been off, exactly? That's the million dollar question."

Kellogg is deep in thought when a voice in the crowd kicks him in the shin and takes a few swings at his nose. "Cody, Cody!"

He doesn't see her, but recognizes Donna's bark.

"Wait. Get back here. I go live in a few minutes." Cody blends seamlessly into the crowd. "We need to do our *interview*. What about the Virgin Mary statue?"

WEDNESDAY, 11:59 AM

Men, women, and children gather around a small stage in the shade of the monstrous oak. Thousands of green leaves fan the crowd. The people fan themselves, too—a sea of flapping white funeral programs. After bagging the fruit, Packwicz was sent to find Dyson locals. The parade desperately needs volunteers. Packy, overwhelmed by the crowd, climbs a tall silver slide for a better view. All he can see are the backs of thousands of strangers' heads. The entire crowd wears black and waits patiently.

"Ladies and gentlemen," a speck atop the stage speaks into a microphone. "Please welcome the First Lady of the United States of America."

The audience is silent. The noise in the trees—sandpaper dancing across wood—replaces applause. *What gives? These people came to Dyson to help, right? They're all acting like Kennedy was shot again.*

A bright pink speck crosses the stage and pauses.

Packy looks at the faces in the crowd. Each is exhausted, skin raw and shimmering with sweat. He is touched so many people would suffer for Dyson. He assumes this pink dot will give orders and explain how everyone can bring Dyson back to life.

He notices six portraits—double the height of the pink speck—lined along the rear of the stage, ringed with patriotic bunting. The portrait subjects' crisp military greens remind him of the day he joined the army decades ago. He recognizes the men and women in the photos as the National Guard drunks from the Kreskin Inn.

This strikes Packwicz as a little odd, but he decides Dyson needs help no matter how it arrives.

"Thank you for your patience, ladies and gentlemen," the First Lady says. "As you all know, a tragic event happened here only a few days ago."

Packy stands and relaxes. Dyson is ready to be saved. He takes pride in this success. He loosens a strangling grip on the slide's guardrail.

"Six brave soldiers, while on assignment to evacuate this quote-unquote community, died in the line of duty. We've all watched the tributes to our fallen heroes on the news and heard about their courage. So we are here to pay respects to that American spirit today, and I thank you."

At once, Packwicz sees all the American flags. All around are hundreds of red, white, and blue-painted faces. Finally, Packy realizes those are six caskets wrapped tight in Old Glory onstage. *This isn't a rally to save Dyson.*

The pink dot dabs its eyes with a tissue. "But first," her voice hums through the dead humid air while Packy shimmies down the ladder. "I'd like to introduce a friend of mine. A patriotic woman who met these soldiers and can tell you personally how their bravery inspired Dyson. Please welcome Mrs. Donna Queen."

The pink speck shakes hands with a blue speck, yellow hair blowing every way possible.

That voice slashes razors down Packy's spine: "Donna *Urinating Bear-Queen*, just like my ancestors. Just like the fabulous new casino with Vegas-style gambling right here in Dyson."

Packwicz can't turn away.

"I could go on and on about heroism. I really could." Donna's excited voice clashes against the mourning mood in the park. "But I thought, perhaps you'd rather hear it in song. A song that I wrote . . . with no help . . . from, you know, anybody."

The crowd remains silent. The quiet hush of the trees is the only sound.

"Please welcome Dyson's own Small Town Songbird, Chief Bert Grover." Donna raises her hands, clapping. She stoops back to the microphone. "Also, I'll be available for questions later. No thanks to Cody Kellogg."

A brown speck crosses the stage. His throat clears and he tugs up the belt. Packy looks at his neighbors and shares their confusion. For a flash, the rustling leaves stop and a tense quiet swallows the audience.

The silence doesn't last.

If Packy's eyes were closed, he would swear this is a beautiful recording from long ago. An a cappella opera. Simply a naked voice as thick as Dyson's humidity. The Chief blends those words into something so pitch perfect Packy's flesh tingles:

Donna Queen, Donna Queen
Greatest hero we've ever seen
Urinating Bear, Urinating Bear
That proud Indian was her ances-tor.
When the satellite came a-crashing down
And there was no light in Dyson town
One brave soul lit the way and spoke up loud
God bless you, Donna
You taught us all to be so proud

A collective blood vessel bursts. Boos and water bottles and shoes hurl toward the stage until the singing stops.

Packy hunts for a way out through the audience's raised fists and four-letter slurs. He shoots a quick glance over his shoulder and sees Chief Grover on his knees, head buried in both hands. He pauses a beat and thinks to reach out to his friend, but doesn't.

At the edge of the park, where the crowd thins, Packwicz finds a man holding a badge to people's faces and yelling. "Stop booing. I'm a deputy. Please show some respect for our Chief."

Skeet gets shoved into the grass by one angry visitor rushing toward the stage.

Packy helps the farmer back to his feet. "Skeet, you alright?"

"Leave me. Get out before you get hurt."

"Troy Gomez needs you on Main Street."

"Main Street?"

An errant elbow jams into Skeet's back.

"You rather stick around here?"

WEDNESDAY, 12:19 PM

Marci hauled all the Rosinski costumes from the factory to the Museum.

"Pearl, get your butt down here," she says, holding a phone between shoulder and ear, making last minute adjustments to a cuff. "This thing starts soon. We can't have a parade without floats."

"I'm working on it. There've been some complications." Pearl sounds frantic. Marci wishes she had a pint of ice cream for her sister. "So I'm guessing this means the crowd must be pretty big. Is there enough room on Main Street to pull through? Try and keep the crowds on the sidewalk, okay?"

"Uh-huh." Marci squints out the window, into the powerful daylight. Downtown Dyson is just as empty and abandoned as ever. "Yep. Tons of people."

"Gene and I are working as fast as we can. Frankly, if he'd stop doodling in his little notebook things would go a lot faster."

"Just hurry, but drive careful. Bye." Marci inspects the costumes again, haphazardly mended together and scarred. "Horrible floats, burnt outfits, and no audience. Not even one volunteer to wear this crap." She massages neck stress with both hands. "And it's your fault." Her foot stamps.

Marci works out the muscle kink for another minute before his response formalizes. "Don't you dare blame me, my love."

"You lied, Gerald," she says, straightening a mannequin's hat. She closes her eyes.

The man of her dreams moves close. "I'd say, technically, you lied . . . to yourself."

"Did you hear Troy yell at me? What an asshole. God, I always fall in love with total headcases. And this stupid parade isn't *beautiful* like you promised. It's a pile of shit." Her voice rises. "So right now, you're the last imaginary person I want to see."

"Calm down. Look at all your hard work. Even if this fails, you've put your heart into something important. You've never dedicated yourself like this. You're growing up, dear."

"What are you saying? What does all this mean?" She takes a seat in the Twenty-First Century Fruit exhibit and crumples her face into her hands.

"Why does it have to mean anything? I always thought half the fun of getting somewhere was the journey."

"You died on a journey to Tahiti."

"Touché."

"Was it fun lying about how rich you were and ruining all these lives for stupid gold fruit?"

"No, it was not. Forget I mentioned anything. I just came to cheer you up. Let you know I think this parade will surprise you. But now, eh, I don't feel so great about things. So long."

Marci tosses a spool and needle to the floorboards and escapes for the exit.

WEDNESDAY, 12:45 PM

The rooftops look like junk pickup day. Neat piles of opaque garbage sacks—reds and greens and yellows—are everywhere.

Main Street's faded Christmas decorations swing in the breeze. Bo is surprised he enjoyed finishing Troy's job. That resignation letter in his pocket kept telling him to bail fast, and it was persuasive. But Troy Gomez was also persuasive and filled with passion for the parade. Since Bo was sort of responsible for the festival, he decided to stick around. "I can always resign later," he told himself.

After dropping off all the fruit, Bo stumbles into a conversation back on the ground. "Wait, wait," Troy says, sitting in a pickup truck bed with his disfigured leg. "I've got a better idea. Let's wait and see what the mayor says."

"Don't ask me anything," Bo says, rounding the corner into the alley's shaded coolness.

"All these people are dying," Cody Kellogg reports. "The heat, the crowd—they need help." He pauses and takes off his hat, making a face. "Is that a cat?"

"Yeah," Bo says.

"I don't want to know."

Everyone stares with awkward glances. It makes him feel microscopic. He nestles Boots to his face, breathes in that wonderful smell, and becomes whole again. That cat couldn't have come at a better time.

"Anyway, people need help. It got me thinking. You see, I have all this chorizo sausage." Cody winks. "My uncle owns a factory. Did you know that, Bo?"

"Fascinating."

"Yeah, I have a ton of meat in my fridge. Figured I'd buy some drinks and have a cookout for all these poor saps. Do my good deed for the day." He watches the ground and shuffles his feet.

"And?" Troy slices through goodwill.

"Yeah, yeah, yeah, and take my pick of interviews." Cody uses his hat as a fan. "Sue me."

"That sounds like a nice thing to do. And a very professional use of that sausage," Bo says.

"Whatever." Troy is wound up, talking with his hands. "I don't care. Nobody is going to come to the parade. Look out there—the street's empty." He slows, bites his cheek a touch. "Shit, I didn't think failure'd bug me, but . . . forget it."

"Don't talk like that," Bo says. "There's still time. And tons of media."

"Hey, I'm standing right *here*," Cody protests.

"Forget it," Troy says, waving Bo away. "Packwicz just swung by. Said all these people came to town for those drunk soldiers. Some memorial. Dyson isn't getting saved by anybody."

"That explains a lot." A sinking overcomes the mayor. He can't turn off his heart so easily.

The cat is purring and that helps slow the sinking.

Cody's voice is ragged and hoarse. "Hey, you boys gave it your best. But sometimes the world is too much of a bitch. So why not make the best of it? Feed these bastards and let me at least salvage something for my career."

"Sure," Bo says. "You have my blessing. Make the best of a shitty situation, Cody."

"Thank you. I'll remember this when I'm back in Memphis."

"Go have a cookout." Bo removes a creased envelope from his pocket. "I have to take this to my office. It's been good knowing you guys."

"Wait." Troy gongs the truck bed with a fist. He looks to the other men, expecting them to see his brilliant plan too. They don't. "We have everything we need."

"Troy, man, it's over," Cody says.

"He's right. God knows I'm the last person to admit it," Bo says. "But we're out of options."

"Did your parents ever bribe you to do something you didn't want to do?"

"I suppose," Cody says.

"My parents died when I was young," Bo says.

"Well, then, you don't count," Gomez says. "Look, my old man used to trick me into doing my homework. I was nuts about building things, so he would promise me a new box of Erector Sets if I just finished my math or science or whatever. And it worked. I didn't even realize he was leading me toward engineering with the old carrot on a stick routine."

"This makes no sense."

"It's obvious. We have to coax them. We'll just *make* people watch our parade. Pied Piper-style."

"I didn't know you played the flute," Cody says.

"Very funny."

"Look, I have to go score some interviews."

Gomez grins, but breaks into agony after moving his leg an inch. "Okay, then. Cody, you go run around and report stuff. Do whatever you want. Just leave us the key to your apartment. I know just the guy to help with the sausage."

"I'm telling you, everything you want so bad is here. You already have it," Gene says. "Watch out for that bump. Slow down."

Pearl and Gene roll the truck down the street in first gear. They are towing the most important float in the parade. She drives slowly because the papier-mâché bust of Gerald Rosinski toppled and cracked its skull a few blocks back.

"You know," she says. "For a hippie dude, you have a big mouth."

"I'm not even sure how to respond to that."

"Look, all this free advice is easy for you to give." She doesn't slow down, not wanting to give the impression of being a pushover. "You live in a big city. You get to travel. You have a career."

"You call teaching Tae Kwon Do a career? You think I get retirement or sick days?" He laughs. "I used to have a career. I was actually in advertising. But now I'm scraping by. That's all a choice I made. Whether good things or bad things happen in life, I understand it's because I had the freedom to make those choices. If you want to be an actress so bad, move to New York. But you can also choose to stay here. Hell, it sounds like you've been choosing to stick with Dyson for years."

"No I haven't." Pearl's voice cracks.

"You just don't want to admit it," he says in slow, steady, fatherly tones.

"Shut up and quit scribbling in that notebook. What do you keep writing?"

"Zen diary. It's an Eastern philosophy thing. Helps center my chi. Right now I'm writing thoughts about seeing my childhood home, about nostalgic trembles under the skin. It feels nice. See, Pearl, you can always go back. Dyson's always going to be here."

"Will it?"

"Look around. Even a satellite couldn't kill it."

"What if people keep moving away? Then what?"

"Stop sign," Eugene says, very quiet.

The brakes squeal and the floats train wreck into the truck with horrible steel-on-steel hammering.

"Look what you made me do."

"Pearl, please relax."

"The float is probably ruined. But maybe that's what you want. Why would someone from out of town be so helpful? What is your angle?"

"Come on. That's obvious, isn't it?"

They stare for a moment until Pearl's phone rings. "I need some air." She jumps from the truck. Pearl worries about slapping this insensitive prick if she doesn't get some space.

Troy is on the line.

"Change of plans?" she says. "Don't tell me we're canceling this stupid parade. I've been driving across town with this annoying jerk—"

"No, no, that's not it. We just want you to drive down Main Street in the opposite direction."

"*Toward* the park?"

"Yeah, is that cool?"

"I'll have to make some really sharp turns, I don't know."

"I trust you. This parade is going to work, Pearl. People will have fun even if we have to twist their arms and make them love it."

WEDNESDAY, 1:16 PM

"Where's Chief Grover?" says Dixon, bent over, hands on knees. He is gasping for air. "I need Bert. Lock me up. Haul me away. Put me out of Stephanie's reach."

When he stands straight, that normally petrified hair is a sweaty thicket. His white shirt is pooled dark on his chest and underarms.

The alley's high walls block the sun. The brick sides ping with sounds from the park—the First Lady's distant, choppy speech. The garbage here is beginning to turn.

"Take it easy. Catch your breath," Bo says, patting Dixon's back.

"Nice to see you too, asshole," Troy says from the truck bed. The meat inside his pant leg pushes the seams with swelling and shattered bone. "Your wife's pissed? What'd you do, jackhammer her floor, too?"

"Worse than pissed."

"Worse?"

"Lock me up. That's the law. I know it by heart." Dixon pulls at his collar like little bursts of heat need to escape. "I'm a killer. You're witnesses."

"Stop freaking out. First, tell us where you disappeared to. We really needed your help." Troy leans forward and winces. "Did you at least pass out those flyers?"

"Not exactly." Dixon's face freezes with shame. "Now, don't be angry, but I was going to run away. Hide. Go on the lam. That kind of thing."

A cyclone of bright green papers blows down the sidewalk in full view of the alley.

"So let's get this straight," Troy says. His leg is so bad his fingers crunch into a fist to avoid tears. "You were going to run away because of the Murray Kreskin thing. But now you're back and you want to go to jail?"

"Jail, gas chamber, poisonous snake bite, I'll take what I can get. I need to get away from my wife."

"Your wife . . . who is, what did you say, worse than pissed?"

"Yes, worse. Much worse. She's . . . happy. I think when she saw that the house and I weren't harmed . . . let's just say Stephanie grew incredibly attached." His manners tighten. "I mean really attached. A second or two before I left town, there she was, hanging all over me. She only let go when I begged to use the restroom."

"That doesn't sound so bad. I'd be so lucky to have a wife who loved me."

"Oh, it was awful. Stephanie was talking about early retirement, spending every *remaining* minute together." He stops for a long moment. Bird chirps battle for airtime with the noise from the park. "I remembered real quick why I work sixty hours a week. All that tenderness and warmth, it doesn't leave me enough time to . . ."

"Hate yourself?" Gomez says.

"Decompress, thank you very much. I get itchy just thinking about it."

"What a shame."

"That's when I decided I need to take responsibility for Murray. So I crawled out the bathroom window like a gentleman."

"Well now, Wendell, I'm sure you're emotional. Take it easy," Bo says. "You were defending your life back at the factory." Bo's face is in peacemaker mode again, cat packed under his arm. "Right, Troy?"

"What are you guys blabbing about?" Cody's ragged radio voice interrupts.

"I'm a killer, Cody. Where's Grover. I need justice—"

"Take a deep breath, man." Troy points excitedly at Dixon. "Ah ha, see, Cody, I told you we needed another piece to your sausage puzzle."

He moves the leg slightly, with a wince. "I think we found him."

Dixon desperately grabs at the mayor's hands. "No, I need the Chief. I need judgment. I need a cold, clammy cell without wives."

"Sure, sure, sure. I'm positive someone would love to kill you, Wendell." Troy takes painful scoots toward the end of the truck and puts a hand on Dixon's shoulder. "But first, how'd you like to help us with this parade? We're having a tough time attracting a crowd, and we need a sort of . . ."

"Guinea pig," says Bo.

"You do owe me for messing up the factory floor. And, you know, the *other thing*."

Bo says, "He's looking for someone brave enough to do a very stupid thing."

"And, if by some strange coincidence you don't die, then we'll let you turn yourself in," Troy says. "Lock away the key and get you fitted for an electric chair. You name it."

"Really?" Dixon begins to cry.

"I'll beat you to death with a bag of rocks if that's what it takes," says Troy.

Relief overcomes the blushing lawyer's face. "Promise?"

"I'll make sure you die one way or another. Scout's honor."

WEDNESDAY, 1:30 PM

"Come on, sweetie," Garrett says, gently rubbing tears into shiny spots on Donna's cheeks. "Let's get out of here before that monster finishes her speech."

Garrett wraps his arms around his wife. She hasn't said a word since running across the stage, explaining the artistic meaning behind her song, and being escorted offstage.

The more the First Lady speaks—soothing the audience and chastising Dyson's unofficial hero—the angrier Garrett grows. He wants to straighten the First Lady out, maybe get revenge.

Any other time, the inferiority that lives inside Garrett would have seen him lash out. Instead, he doesn't move.

It isn't a secret service bullet or a prison sentence that keeps him backstage. Instead, it is feeling this strong woman crumble, knowing money and love and revenge can't fix an embarrassed heart.

He whispers, "I think you did great. These people, they're too selfish to realize."

Donna keeps shivering. "I wasted so much," she says through mucus gulps and hyperventilating breaths.

Wind finds the backstage area and coats them in cool buttery air in the shade of the drunken soldiers' enormous portraits. Fat green leaves cry to the ground.

"We didn't lose much money. Plus, the casino is doing great."

"Not that," she snuffles. "I wasted so much of my life on trying to help Dyson and where's it gotten me? You can make money back, but this . . ."

He sinks down with her. Even falling apart like this, Donna can hit nails on the head with a sledgehammer.

"I'm just going to let Packwicz do it."

"Do what, sweetheart?"

"Kill me. Go ahead. Why not? I don't care anymore. I deserve it."

"Don't say that." He squeezes tighter. "You're a good person."

"Am I?"

"Of course."

"How does anyone know who's good?"

WEDNESDAY, 1:45 PM

Packwicz opens Cody's apartment door. He's not surprised to have company. The shades are pulled tight, but that doesn't matter.

"You didn't eat all the sausage, did you?" he calls to the familiar silhouette across the darkened room. "I didn't think so. You have fancier taste than that."

His eyes adjust and wait for the mummy to move. It sits cross-legged in a chair with a magazine in its lap. The mummy's bandaged head gives a friendly shake.

"I need that stuff." He opens the fridge and a moist breath coughs out. The air is spicy with the fragrance of chili pepper and paprika. The sausage is still brown and plump and ready for eating. "Where've you been, anyhow?" He hefts the enormous roll of links into his arms. "I'm done jumping from buildings, in case you're worried."

Silently, the mummy has moved behind the fridge door. It holds a familiar plate of foie gras.

Packy smiles and readjusts the chorizo. He estimates at least twenty pounds worth. "No thanks. It's not my thing anymore. You should eat it. Don't let it go to waste."

The mummy cocks its head.

"I found something else to live for," he calls over his shoulder, running out.

WEDNESDAY, 1:52 PM

A clipping breeze cartwheels the Chief's hat down the street. With lips facing the sun's scorch, Grover decides he'll just sing himself to death. Everything hurts so fiercely—his chest, his stomach, the back of his skull, his limbs, even the reddening flesh across his face. At this rate, Chief Grover determines, it won't take long for his heart to simply quit.

"Why did you trust Donna? Why did you trust yourself?"

His aching legs only carried him a few blocks beyond Christmas Park before they melted to jelly candies. He never knew embarrassment could zap a body so violently. Grover simply collapsed into the street.

"I am ready to die," he says between suffocating breaths. "I am ready to die." Grover doesn't feel the elevator rise, but a gust of opera bursts from within—the end of Strauss' *Salome*, before John the Baptist loses his head.

With eyes shut tight, sunlight turns his inner eyelids brilliant orange. Death kicks his tires and checks under the hood. It is ready to take him for a test drive, but needs the key.

Needling sunrays cook the Chief's cheeks and forehead. The mighty bellow grows and pain stomps his body.

The words keep time with his pounding chest. Notes swirl and flutter and nosedive. His hands conduct weak gestures of pain and disaster. Grover nears the end of that aria and feels his pulse slow. It pumps droplets. He partially never expected this singing-to-death idea to work. But here it is.

Salome's final scene finishes with a note that could set off nearby car alarms. Grover takes a deep breath and lets the smell of grass and clean air fill his nose one final time. He loves that smell.

But the whipping wind brings a surprise. One that pauses death's shiny sharp blade just as it kisses Chief Grover's neck.

A counterpoint to John the Baptist's death, Puccini's *La Bohéme* and its songs of life and birth fill the street. The voice is sweet and tender and so familiar Grover chokes on tears. A woman's fluttering high notes and sweeping lower register electrifies his once-trickling heart.

Salty tears sting his raw, red cheeks.

That voice is powerful and close. It takes a few more bars to gather the muscle to lift both eyelids.

"Hey come on." A gentle kick meets his boot. "You love that song. What do I have to do around here?"

The wind braids Joyce's long black hair into a messy twist. She is lovely and here, unbelievably.

"You came back for me?"

"I came back to get some things from the house." She kneels to his level. "Then, I stopped by the park and saw what happened."

Grover groans, feeling suicidal just at the thought of his performance.

"Bert, that was so brave. I'm proud of you." She wraps warm arms around Grover's neck. "Don't listen to anyone. Anyone but me. I love you."

WEDNESDAY, 2:32 PM

"Dateline, Dyson," Cody says into a microphone, adjusting a mustache. "A microscopic town gearing up for the battle of its life. A small army of volunteers stand around nervously, dressed like a man who died seventy years ago, myself included.

"Some smoke cigarettes to take off the edge. Some make small talk about weather and gossip as they patiently stand atop Main Street's rooftops—a two-block stretch of boarded-up brick buildings that were once the active center of a thriving town. Some walk down on street level admiring the floats. Four homemade parade floats honoring what many consider this community's greatest gift to the world: imitation fruit.

"That, however, is misguided. Let me explain.

"Plastic apples are not its greatest gift. Not by a long shot, even though many here brag that the set of *South Pacific* in New York City was once decorated exclusively in Dyson plastic fruit.

"But, no, that is only its second-finest gift. You see, Dyson's spirit—a ragged togetherness and sense of history—is its greatest gift. When most people scratch their heads and wonder why anyone still lives in a no-horse town like this, here is the answer. A quiet sense of dignity on this level is something you cannot find in any city. A purpose in simply being that is far too slippery in other towns. Trust me, I've looked.

"The sun is brutal as we stand in brown wool suits, brown bowlers, and thick black mustaches. There are twelve of us dressed like Gerald Rosinski, the long-dead founder of Dyson's plastic fruit empire. We will walk in packs of four between each of the floats, wave to the crowd and toss penny candy. We are tense, but optimistic. It's not unlike the moment before the door opens at a surprise party.

"City Hall's plan to drum up much needed tourist excitement has gone almost perfectly.

"Well, not perfectly.

"Far from it, actually.

"While the preparation has come together beautifully, there's no crowd to watch the parade. But that isn't because the town is empty. Not by a long shot. Today, thousands of visitors have come to Dyson from all across the country. These men and women are only a few blocks away at the town park. These folks are unaware of the Rosinski parade, however.

"Even if there is no audience for this heritage celebration, you get the feeling Dyson's citizens would still be out here supporting one another. It brings this reporter chills.

"There is talk—rumor is more like it—that there is a plan to attract these thousands of out-of-towners. One parade official gave WDSR an exclusive interview just before going on the air.

"And, boy, folks. It's a doozey. Stay tuned to find out what, exactly."

WEDNESDAY, 2:38 PM

It takes a few laps around Christmas Park for the mourners to catch on. Whether it is the savory smell of grilled sausage or Wendell Dixon's loudspeaker announcing, "Free meat! Free water! Free fruit!," it works.

Dixon steers the pickup truck with one hand and holds the bullhorn in the other. Packwicz is in the truck bed, working the barbecue. An icy cooler filled with bottles of spring water rests at his feet.

"Packy, you didn't have to do this," Dixon hollers back. "We could have found some other sucker for this suicide mission."

"Nope. It's time I took control. It's time I stopped blaming everyone else. It's time," he yells, "for fate to kiss my ass."

The First Lady is finishing her speech about the brave, heroic, always sober National Guardsmen. She pauses mid-sentence, catching a glimpse of what Troy Gomez dubbed *The Meat Wagon*. Her voice slips. "Oh, Christ. I need a mudslide."

Thousands of sun-chapped faces—sweaty, tired, and starving—turn toward this truck as it belts out some disrespectful racket. Who in their right mind would disrespect the dead in such a way, they wonder, as savory curls of smoke spread across the audience.

Packy, between Dixon's advertisements for freebees, hears a chorus of groans like mummies shaking cemetery dust from burial suits. The sight of several thousand horrific, sunken, bloodshot eyes does not eliminate this theory.

"Free meat!" Dixon repeats. "Free water! Dyson loves you!" He takes a dry gulp. He senses the scuttle of rocks under his feet that will soon cause an avalanche. "Free fruit!"

"Here they come," Packwicz shouts. "Dix, this is more exciting than when I was elected. We're kicking fate in the balls. Can you feel it?" The ex-mayor's face looks instantly younger. Barbecue tongs shoot victory-style into the air. Packy's apron is stained with the dark juice of grilled meat. The sausage sizzles with more promise than any meal before it.

"Packy." Dixon sounds shaky. "They're coming. Get ready."

A thin tail of bodies forms behind the truck. That tail quickly grows fat. Soon, sunburned fingers claw the truck's sides and graze Packy's pants. He lifts a hot sausage off the grill and grenade-hucks it into the mob.

Meat bounces off hairlines and onto the ground.

The crowd, packed shoulder-to-shoulder, now fills the street for an entire block. A small hole in the mass clears where chorizo drops, reminding Packy of a hurricane's eye on television radar. Within that center desperate men and women fight for scraps.

Sweaty hands clutch at the tailgate and parched mouths hang wide. Voices leak from bleached lips, but in some slurred tongue only other exhausted patriots understand.

Packwicz has seen this before. Not this type of dead-eyed madness, exactly, but its cousin. When he was mayor he learned how slowly change comes. Whether it was physical change like the months and months spent repairing a water line under Gulliver Street, or the psychic change in people. It wasn't just Dyson, Packy figured. It was an epidemic across the country. Nobody wants to change and yet nobody is happy, he once concluded while whittling behind his desk. And even when people do change, it takes something with a hook—change has to look like a Vegas show—for people to start turning their ship a few degrees.

He wanted a series of property tax levies and financial breaks for businesses thinking about relocating to Dyson. That would have brought in a nice stream of money to keep the town prosperous. Nobody listened. Everyone complained about how Dyson was falling apart, but nobody wanted to change the way they did anything. Until, almost as a joke, he suggested Christmas City.

It took something that absurd and unrealistic to eek out change in people. Packy wasn't serious about turning his town into a year-long North Pole, but it got citizens interested in government. It slowly brought about that psychic change Dyson so desperately needed. However, when Mayor Packwicz tried to dampen everyone's enthusiasm for purchasing a thirty-foot snowman, and instead give tax incentives to this brake pad manufacturer considering Dyson as a new home, it was too late.

The idea of some foolish tourist trap became Packy's baby to the people so resistant to change. He was a hero for it at first. Then, once they did change, everyone blamed him for its failure.

Packwicz hasn't seen a crowd of people with that stepping-into-the-light look on their faces since then. Standing on a truck bed, barbecuing meat, he sees it in this starving horde. They are changing because of a bright, shining, off-kilter spectacle—the only kind of change people in this country want.

Here is the change that'll finally put Dyson back on its feet, he thinks and chucks another link.

"Give it some more gas, Dix." Packy bangs the truck roof. "These animals wanna treat me like a hotdog." Packy whips water bottles at their heads, peeling hungry bodies off the truck. Small, dehydrated riots spring up for a cold sip.

Dixon is happy to see the plan working, but it doesn't seem like retribution. He feels cruel and still a little dead. "Hold on, I'm one-armed up here."

The truck speeds and forms a gap between its bumper and hungry mouths. Chorizo missiles cut through clean blue sky. An aerial assault of cured meats.

Along the route, men in black suits hide behind trees. One pops out of the nativity scene, whispering into his coat sleeve.

"Pearl, I'm not trying to be rude," Troy says, holding himself up on the truck's doorframe. "Without your help we wouldn't have a parade, but . . ." he can't say the actual words. He's spent so many years telling people what a cancer Dyson is, that his lips can't articulate his love for the town. This place means so much.

"What are you doing with my sister?" she looks down at his face, saggy with exhaustion, his goatee mussed and fading grey a bit, eyelids crushed tight in the sun.

A rusty sign for the former hardware store hangs just over Troy's shoulder, its chain squeaks in the wind.

"Marci," he says. "I really like her. I'd love to, you know, be with her. But, Bo and all. Plus, I sort of lost my temper earlier." His thumb pounds a neurotic beat on the truck door that would make Charlie Watts proud. "Look, the last couple days have been miserable. I just want to drive this float in the parade and sleep for a week."

Pearl watches his face a while longer, then turns on the bright lights of her smile. She crawls from the cab and helps him in.

"Thank you. This means a lot to me."

"I know it does." She slams the truck door and leans through the window. "Good luck. I'll be watching from up there."

Troy slides his haggard leg under the steering wheel, relieved to find an automatic transmission. The quiet street grows loud with fuzzy radio traffic. It's Dixon's bullhorn. A jerk of adrenaline swims through Troy, and his hands clamp on the steering wheel, knuckles faded red.

The Meat Wagon turns onto the street, heading directly toward him. Troy knows all that hard work is going to pay off the moment the first staggering, hungry body rounds the corner.

He turns the key.

"Just keep walking," Garrett whispers, tugging her closer.

They are trapped in a mob. It reminds Donna of that small bowling alley fire a few years back. Several hundred people pressed chest-to-back, stumbling toward the exit.

The same strangers that booed and stripped her pride down to its primer march without noticing them. "So hungry," some say. "So thirsty," others mutter, hoarse.

Looking around, Donna whispers to Garrett, "Who cares what they think? Why was I so upset?" That crushing expression from the park has largely disappeared from her eyes.

Garrett knows what his wife means. "Look at them. Just going wherever." He stands on his toes, but only sees more bobbing heads up ahead. "Crowds'll follow anything."

"Honey," Donna says. "I've been thinking: this isn't any way to live. I like helping people. I need to do more of that and less helping us. I'm wasting a gift."

"Maybe you're right."

They stop for a kiss, which is tough to do as dozens of sweaty bodies shoulder past. One hungry person sniffs Garrett's shoulder, but decides not to bite when it doesn't smell like chorizo.

Another dark pair of eyes focus on Garrett. The owner of those black pits adjusts the bandages wrapped around its head before marching onward. Garrett doesn't notice since Donna started using her tongue.

"The scene is incredible, ladies and gentlemen," Cody speaks softly into a microphone. His Herbert Morrison moment has arrived.

"I am atop the old Savings and Loan building. This community, though struggling to survive, has found the strength to celebrate its most famous resident, Gerald Rosinski, the plastic fruit magnate. The Gerald Rosinski Imitation Fruit Festival has begun.

"I was supposed to be part of the parade," he says, itching at the fake mustache, "but decided it was more important to bring you the story.

"So, believe me when I say this is no ordinary gathering. This parade is a surprise to the thousands of visitors in town. We're talking *Candid Camera* meets the Macy's Parade, folks."

He pictures a flaming zeppelin gently crashing to the ground. Under the hot sun, a thick queue of city visitors spreads through Main Street, slowly colliding with the parade a block away. The two parties inch closer and closer.

"The scene here on the rooftop is intense. Dozens of Dyson citizens are standing still, holding white garbage bags full of plastic fruit, waiting for a signal. Some are smiling, some stiff-jawed, some just curious about what the heck they have been mysteriously recruited to do."

Cody hangs over the ledge and inhales. A bulge of pride pauses the broadcast, knowing this wouldn't be possible without his brilliant sausage bribe back at town hall.

Packwicz tosses one final link to the crowd. The squirming mass claws and fights. Cody feels accomplished, the same satisfying rush as being promoted to the drive time slot in Memphis. Back then, his future felt unstoppable. His career seems headed in that direction once more.

"Here we go. What is going to happen when these visitors discover such a proud community's parade? We'll know in about one minute."

In the middle of a tender hug—one that eased Grover's muscles and loosened the migraines of loneliness—he and Joyce are interrupted.

"I said no *flubs*," Agent Eggleston says. The harsh sun draws black map lines across his face. Years of worry and stress, guarding first ladies, lying about NASA, and heading who-knows-how-many covert operations, has beat him in a way Grover didn't notice before. "What would you call all this?"

"What? What's the matter?"

"You think you're so funny. You've got the world by the dick, huh?" Eggleston's medicinally sharp aftershave attacks the air as he rests his hands on his hips. There is a gun and a badge hanging from his belt. "Not me. Not this dick, bub."

Grover unwraps from Joyce and stands eye-to-eye with Eggleston. He breathes through his mouth. "Take the First Lady and leave. We have enough problems without you. If people don't like my singing—" he tests the waters of confidence. His wife clasps both tiny hands around the Chief's palm for a boost. "Then I don't care. I like my singing."

"Who gives a rat's ass about singing? The First Lady mopped the floor with your singing. Singing is the last thing on my worry list. I'm talking about this idiotic parade."

"Parade?"

"Oh, a guy who has the world by the cock doesn't need to cooperate, right? Well, just know that if you don't call it off it in the next . . . " Eggleston knocks his head back and hums as he calculates, " . . . in the next *minute*, I'll stop it. And you won't like my way of stopping things." Eggleston trots back to a waiting car.

Skeet waves the Meat Wagon into the alley and slides a wooden barricade behind it. Dixon and Packy turn off the engine and join him.

The pounding of drums and warbling unison of marching band horns fill the air.

"It's going to work. I have a good feeling," Dixon says, watching the gap between the enormous Rosinski head. The first wave of hungry, blind visitors grows smaller.

"I mean, what exactly are we accomplishing here?" Skeet regrets saying that. It came out wrong. He sounds mean and cynical, but is actually just curious. Skeet has been wandering the streets, mourning his city's history, asking a lot of "What if" questions.

"Your guess is as good as mine," Packwicz says. "But I'm moving to higher ground." He reaches for a fire escape ladder.

Part of Skeet is proud, watching Dyson come together and create a new history in the ashes of the old. But he's also jealous that nobody asked him to help. Sure, he was presumed dead, but Skeet thinks he was still owed an invitation. He worries that no one will even know about his sacrifice and accomplishment over the past few days.

These walking corpses certainly won't. The front row begins to show signs of life. Heads shake out cobwebs, sunglasses flip off to see if their vision is playing tricks, hands hold up, trying to stop this oncoming truck creeping their way.

Similar reactions spread viral through the ranks, and Skeet feels the mosquito buzz of accomplishment.

"That was then, Packy. We can't worry about the past. Things change. Everything comes to an end. You know?" he says, realizing Packwicz has already shimmied up the ladder.

Visitors fill the sidewalk, just like they planned, forcing them to be a parade audience. One young woman reminds Skeet of his wife, Janet, before she died—red-faced, pained, sad.

Skeet is alone in so many ways.

"Marci! It's working," Bo's voice climbs heights. His resignation letter doesn't beckon anymore. "Look! They're lining the sidewalks. They can't miss Dyson now, can they?"

The rooftop group clutches garbage sacks, waiting. Bo almost didn't notice Marci, holding the bag by her head, hiding.

"Here we go. Are you ready, do you feel the excitement?"

"I'm fine, really." She is quiet, but sharp enough to draw blood. "When you walked away from us, when we needed you most back at the factory, it was okay. Congratulations. Now you can strut around and take all the credit. I hope you and Dyson are very happy together."

A hot charcoal smell of the barbecue still hangs.

"I'm sorry. I needed time to think." Bo smiles. Marci obviously doesn't get the big picture. "Sure, this was my *initiative*. I supplied you and Troy the financial support. But this is a team effort. We all came together for this success. I'm just so proud everyone—"

"Save it," she says. "If you'll excuse me, I'm waiting for Troy to give us the sign."

"Marci." He latches onto her bare shoulder. Bo is falling from a very tall tree, grasping at branches. "Are you mad?"

Bo watches the Gerald Rosinski float slowly push visitors toward the sidewalk. Her lips mouth silent encouragement. Her hand rubs a green flag the same way she nervously rubbed Bo's hair during election night results.

"Marci? Sweetheart?"

"Bo, it's over. You . . . I don't know where to begin. You're a decent guy but you are a lousy boyfriend. You're worse than lousy. You . . . I promised I wouldn't get worked up like this."

"It's okay. I deserve this. I understand."

"You made me feel like less of a person. You made me feel like my opinion didn't matter, like I didn't matter, and that's bullshit."

"I'm sorry."

"I matter, Bo."

"You do. Absolutely."

"My happiness matters."

"You're right. I blew it. I've always known it, but I guess I just didn't want to say it."

She never takes her eyes off the street. "We're over. It's not working."

His cheeks fill with color. "Was it Rajula? I'm sorry."

"The reporter?" She bunches the green flag. "I don't follow?"

"Alright, you win, I admit it." He steps closer. "I cheated on you. I lost you when I cheated, and I'm sorry."

"Jesus. You're awful." She takes a moment to look at him. Marci's freckles grow heavy with all the sun. Her eyes bright. "You lost me when you won that election, we just didn't know it."

"I can make it up to you, if you'll let me."

"It's okay. That news would have felt like walking in space a week ago. But now, *eh*. I'm not so impressed. Funny how fast that kind of thing changes."

"Beat it," someone calls on the rooftop. "Out of here, now."

"You want to spend the night in jail?" a female yells. "Scram."

Bo turns and finds a small group of men and women in black suits on the rooftop. Each carries a long black plastic case. One flashes a badge.

"Whoa, excuse me," Bo steps up and extends a hand to the man he recognizes. "Agent Eggleston, what's going on here?"

"You need to vacate the property."

"Wait, let's talk this over. What are you doing up here? What're those?"

"Guitars. We're starting a band. Now leave before arms get broken."

"Too late," a man in a black suit says. Chris, the city sanitation worker lies sobbing, holding an arm disfigured at the elbow.

Bo glances down. The black cases are too small. "I'll have to see some official paperwork before anybody budges an inch."

Bo is a few inches taller than Eggleston. He looks down and feels a tiny foothold of authority.

A truck honks and Marci screams. "Now, now, now!" She hoists the green flag and snaps it back and forth.

For two blocks in every direction Dyson's rooftop volunteers turn the garbage bags upside down. A rainbow of plastic falls onto the street. Cheers erupt.

"What a sight, folks," Cody says. "New Year's Eve in July. The crowd below is being treated to one of the most spirited parades you'll ever see. The floats are as follows: a bust of Gerald Rosinski, a beautiful spray of fruit from his hat." Cody fills in the blanks of this disaster since the float lost its wheels thirty feet back, Rosinski's head rolling empty like a jack-o-lantern.

"Behind it is a small group of real-life Rosinskis tossing candy to the crowd." This too is fiction, since they only tossed about two handfuls before someone waved smelling salt under the crowd. The out of town visitors began screaming about "assault" and "calling their lawyers." Within seconds, the Rosinskis' mustaches were hunted like scalps.

"Oh, and the 'I Heart Dyson' sign that I told you all about earlier is magnificent and tall and colorful." It is, but some jester lit the heart on fire. Across the papery float, flames spread like cold sores through a dormitory.

"And finest of all is the tickertape of plastic fruit. The crowd below is being gently showered by thousands of plastic apples, bananas, oranges, and grapes. A cornucopia."

Nerves scissor through Cody, watching Dyson get a wrecking ball in the belly. Journalistic instincts say to report the carnage and chaos below, but something won't let his friends' work die. "This is what small town pride is all about. How wonderful." He cuts off the microphone, feeling a sobbing bubble work up his throat.

The crowd moves in dozens of directions. The smell of burning papier-mâché overtakes the air. The Hindenburg has caught flames and he can't turn away.

Cody summons Herbert Morrison and finds some strength to report for a few more minutes, expanding on the lovely detail of the smiling faces, the dancing children, the beautiful harmony between all.

"Mr. Razzle-Dazzle?" someone says a few steps away. "The Cody Kellogg?" A gentle woman in a sharp suit smiles. "We can't stop listening to your brave broadcasts. My name's Sonora Rodgers, director of KGFR. Some people say we're the biggest radio station in America. Ever heard of us?"

"Ahhhh." He sniffles and rubs tears with his fingers. "Yeah, I think so." Of course he's heard of them. "Out of Cincinnati, right?"

"Try New York City." She glances at the chaos, but refocuses on Cody. "Do you have a second? Mark Grauman, your old producer, said we should chat."

"No, please, I don't want to hurt you." Troy stops the truck. "Aren't you enjoying yourself? It's supposed to be fun."

At first the crowd took to the sidewalks. The parade plan gave Troy thrills of success, but he should have known something was wrong from the silence.

No one spoke—not the crowd, not the Rosinskis, nobody. The turning, humming idle of truck engines and the soft smack-slap of a few thousand feet bounced off the damaged brick storefronts.

A tense bubble of quiet wrapped around downtown Dyson. Troy held his breath, just praying to reach the end of the block. He honked twice, sending Marci the signal. Then the fruit rained down.

"Wow," he whispered as a Crayola box of color fell on the crowd. This was the perfect, special moment he'd been planning. All those sleepless hours at the factory, doing the job of ten workers, finally paid off. A shiver of delight ran down his spine. "Beautiful," he said as apples and bananas and pears and grapes gently clicked to the ground in the hush.

The revolt started softly. Someone said, "Hey, what's the big idea?" and a few "Ouch"s, but quickly, as necks turned upward and began swatting away the candy-colored gifts, big city patience wore away. Apparently, not everyone appreciates being surprised by FruitCo's generosity.

"So wait, there's no more free food?" was the last comment Troy heard before trouble erupted.

Now, he realizes this was a mistake. The truck window shatters, and angry hands reach through crumbling safety glass.

"I broke my leg for this," he cries. "I did this for you." At this moment, Troy wishes he'd spent more time in church, as he says some sort of prayer before being ripped in half.

Sweaty pounding fists leave dirty smudges on the windshield. The truck rocks violently. "I'm really sorry," he screams as clutching hands scratch his arms and neck. "I thought you'd like it."

Troy folds his fingers together and finishes that ad-hoc prayer. Throughout the horror, visions of Marci creep through his mind. Thoughts of her freckles and delicate lips do more to comfort that wildly beating heart than any Hail Mary.

Why did you yell at her? Why didn't you apologize? His eyes are tight, and repentant thoughts of Marci pixilate in the darkness.

The crowd noise, a choir of angry grunting and metallic snapping, rises several decibels.

"No, no. Please don't."

The door suddenly clears of arms for a breath or two. Troy isn't fast enough to stop one set of pink fingernails as a hand powers through the hole in the window and flips the lock.

The door opens onto a sea of pushing men and women, all with an irritation in their eyes he's only seen after incredible traffic jams. "I'm sorry," he whispers.

He gives up and steadies himself for death.

Marci's panicked face bursts into the cabin. She stands on the doorframe and kicks backward. Bones crackle. "Come on." She grabs his wrist and yanks. Her nails are pink. "Get out of this truck before they kill you." Their eyes connect, and amongst the hellish chaos, he smiles.

"I couldn't leave you," Marci says.

Later in life, after they are grandparents, Troy will apologize for not saying something more dashing when she rescued him. Instead of marveling at Marci powering through a mob of angry city folks, Troy just drops his jaw and mumbles: "M-m-my leg."

Marci spends about a quarter of a second digesting his medical condition before yanking his body through the door. She kicks out another couple sets of teeth and throws Troy across her back.

"Best ballplayer I ever coached," Dixon tells Packy above the Savings and Loan building.

"This ain't basketball, and I'm keeping my distance." Packy edges back toward the fire escape, scaring off blackbirds.

The kung-fu expert stands over the bodies of four men and a woman in dark clothes. Their guitar cases are broken open, revealing sniper rifles in various stages of assembly.

Eugene rubs blood from his knuckles.

Chief Grover climbs to the top of the ladder and begins warning about Eggleston. "You're a little late, Chief," Dixon says.

"I see." He is panting and red-faced.

"Eugene just sort of . . . I don't know what you call it. Kicked their ass."

"Thank God." He points to Eggleston. "That man is crazy."

They stare at this strange sight atop the building. Below them the sound of havoc is still strong and random.

"Hey, since you're up here . . . well, I have a confession," Dixon says, waiting for Grover's tired face to turn. "Murray Kreskin's at the factory. He's dead. I did it."

Grover's face twists. "What?"

"Kreskin's dead. It's my fault." He holds out his wrists, awaiting cuffs.

"Wendell, are you feeling alright?" The Chief uses his hat as a fan. A clear trickle of sweat pools at his sideburns.

"Never felt worse, actually."

"Maybe you should see Dr. Goldberg. You didn't eat one of those funky sausages Packwicz was tossing around, did you?"

"No, Bert, it's *guilt*. I'm a murderer. It's . . . come on. Why aren't you a little more concerned?"

"Wendell, have you been living under a rock?"

"Living under a satellite."

"Hilarious."

"It's the truth, Bert, I was a witness," Bo says. He stands beside and makes a long shadow over the lawyer.

"So, first that reporter is trampled, then Ed Lee over at Edna Rutili's, now Murray is dead, too?" Grover raises eyebrows.

"Hey, wait, Ed Lee at Grandma's?" Gene says.

"I told you I'm dangerous . . . Murray and I ripped that place apart looking for that stupid treasure . . ."

"Poor Rajula." A webbing of blood vessels, nervous and purple, come to the surface of Bo's face.

"Now what's really going on here?" Grover says. "We need to sort this out. Don't anyone move." He looks down, searching for Joyce, remembering what it means to sing with the love of his life.

"Listen, fatty, I know the law better than even you. I am guilty. Take me to jail." Dixon reaches for Grover's belt, latching the handcuffs.

He swats Dixon away. "No need for name calling."

"Get mad, damn it. You couldn't find a clue if it was inside a jelly doughnut. I'm a dangerous criminal. A criminal *genius*, maybe. And all I want is to go to jail and serve my time. Maybe also never see my wife again. So stop being a pussy and do something about it."

Color and life drain from Grover's face.

Dixon sticks out his chin. "Come on. Slug me. Knock me cold. Please."

"Okay, if you say so." He rubs his eyes and speaks slowly. "Go down to the station and wait for me. I have too many messes to sort out on Main Street."

"You're serious?" Dixon says. "I don't pay taxes to not have you physically abuse me. I'm a murderer—do something cop-like. Don't you have one of those wooden clubs?"

Grover massages the bridge of his nose, slowly, painfully. "You can . . . I don't know . . . cuff yourself to my desk if that makes you feel better."

"Bo?" Eugene calls across the roof, checking one of the secret service men for a pulse. "What's coach talking about? What happened at Grandma's?"

"Sounds to me like Mr. Popular here was the one who ransacked Grandma's house," Bo calls. "I saw it, the place is wrecked."

Atop the brick building, everyone's hair whips with the breeze. They are at tree level and the greenage rustles with the vacancy shared by each resident's heart.

"What?"

"That, I can explain," Dixon's face darkens and he backs up quickly. "It all started because my idiotic insurance wouldn't cover our house in case of a satellite. And then my lunatic wife threatened—"

"You're the bastard that broke everything?" the mayor says. "The kitties, the walls, the family pictures. Everything. You and Murray Kreskin."

"Is this true?" Gene says.

"Yes and no," he stammers. "Did I mention I can't have kids? I'm really a victim of society here—"

"Listen," Gene rests a hand on his brother's shoulder. "You wouldn't be looking for renters, would you?"

"I was actually thinking about leaving town for a while, but—"

"I want to help rebuild everything. Sloan and I are starting a family; I'll need a good house and a safe place to raise kids."

"Here?"

"That house is all I've been thinking about. Sloan's into it, too."

"But your inheritance . . . it's, well, it's not there. It's destroyed."

He pulls out the Zen diary, keeping it closed, but clutching it tighter. "I've been thinking about starting fresh."

"So, I'll be an uncle? Uncle Bo. I think that could be cool."

"Point is," Gene says, "I wanted you to know that I'm not being an asshole before I do this."

"Do what?"

Dixon is poking Chief Grover's stomach. "Hey, hello, murderer here. Are you illiterate like Kreskin? M-u-r-d-e—"

With that, Gene slides the Zen diary back into a pocket and nose punches Wendell Dixon. A heavy bone snap fills the air. The lawyer collapses.

The crowd of visitors fully thrashes downtown Dyson. Rocks through windows. High school band members kicked and punched. Fire consuming all the floats, making hearty black spirals.

From the bullseye of this chaos, a single voice rings loud and strong from a figure covered head to toe in old bandages. "This is so *boring.*"

"I'm sorry, dear listeners, I can't keep hiding the truth. Dyson's peaceful display of public pride has gone horribly wrong." Cody peels off the mustache and sops up forehead sweat. "For what seemed like hours, citizens fended for their lives. Promoting small town achievement quickly became a title bout to the death.

"However, just as quickly as it began, the fury and smashing stopped. Strangers quit destroying the fruit bowl float in mid slash. In a depressingly slow shuffle everyone simply walked to their cars, leaving the shattered remains of Dyson.

"When interviewed, most didn't give reasons for quitting. However, this reporter witnessed one small child tugging on his mother's dress hem, saying, 'Can we go home yet?' The mother said yes, and they walked off."

He shuffles through a ream of notebook paper, scribbled with quotes. "One rioter claimed: 'I thought little towns were supposed to be cute?'

"'Where's the old-fashioned diner?'

"'Where's the antiquing?'

"'Where are the homemade candles? This stupid town and this stupid riot are hell on my blood pressure.'

"What does this say when people don't have the attention span to finish a riot? Lack of attention is not something the hard-working, albeit misguided, citizens of Dyson need worry about. Especially in terms of their civic pride. And I, for one, have seen something today that will stay with me. So long, ladies and gentlemen."

Coiling a microphone cable and looking at the wreckage, the DJ is surprised. Pearl Krupp sneaks up on Cody and offers him a bottle of water. "Hey," she says.

"Thanks, I'm so thirsty." The coolness is a relief to his dry throat. "Where'd you disappear to? I haven't seen you since before *you know what*." He points to the sky.

"I told you, I couldn't be part of it. I actually got talked into helping with floats," she points down to the street.

"You did a good job. It looked nice until all hell broke loose."

"Thanks." She takes back the water.

"I should have walked off with you," Cody says. "Those TV guys, they were a bunch of jerks."

"They barely blinked when Rajula died."

"Monsters."

"Hey, who was that lady you were talking to? The one in the suit. I was across the way, on top of the bar."

"Ha. You mean the one person not destroying everything?"

"Duh."

"Sonora Rodgers. She offered me a job in New York."

"Get out! Congratulations." Her eyes plump.

"Yeah, pretty cool. Guess I'll be taking a stab at the Big Apple or whatever people call it."

Pearl removes her shades and cleans them with a shirttail. She holds the water in Cody's direction, but he declines a second helping.

"Listen, I'm just going to come out and say this." Pearl bites her lip and thinks about stopping, but remembers Gene's advice. "Do you need a roommate? You and I always got along." Cody's eyes are large, not sure where this is going. "I want to move to New York, but I just can't do it by myself."

He laughs and takes another water slug. "Do you know how expensive Brooklyn rent is?"

"No."

"It's a lot. I think their mayor even needs a roommate. You got a deal."

Packwicz sits, dangling his feet over the old savings and loan, taking in the eerie calm below. A shoelace hangs, worn and grubby.

"A pit boss, huh? Watch over the casino, make sure nobody's cheating, give the dealer his break, run the show." A sheepish look begins. "Kind of like being a mayor, only smaller."

He pictures the tour Garrett gave of the Urinating Bear Casino. He'll wear a suit every day and have a gold name badge. Pay's not bad, which means he can move out of Bo's apartment. Smart plan since it's missing a ceiling and all.

"Yeah," he says, looking over his shoulder at the angelic grain elevator, rising above the tree line, stretching toward Heaven. "I think I could get into that."

Garrett Queen finds a fire extinguisher in WDSR's office and runs back to Main Street. After smothering another fire, he spots Donna's Hero Mobile. The wheels are stripped and the hood is up, revealing an empty shell where the engine once hung.

Garrett pokes his head inside. The seats are pried out, white stuffing spread around the cabin. Wiring lies by the fistful across the dash. "Animals," he says.

He extinguishes a few more nearby fires, little ones comprised of trash and melting bananas.

"Holy mother of God," he says, noticing something at his feet when the pale extinguisher gas clears. It is half-buried under destroyed plastic fruit. "Maybe things aren't so bad after all." There's that old radio, the one with the big orange tuning bar. "I've been looking everywhere for you. I don't think Donna'd mind too much if we put you in the Mercedes." Inspecting the radio for damage, he trips over something solid. The red metal extinguisher gongs to the pavement.

Garrett, splayed across the street, claws to a sitting position. "You son of a bitch," he cries.

This wakes the mummy. The pile of bandages moves slowly after having been trampled.

"Get up and fight, you bastard." Garrett's fists are rotating. "Who's your insurance provider?"

The mummy shakes its head and looks around. Garrett stands overhead, punching the air.

"I demand a new hood."

The mummy scrambles to its feet, pointing to an invisible wristwatch, and hikes its thumb over a shoulder.

Garret's face softens. In a flash, the mummy retreats, just like everyone else when things get too boring. It runs surprisingly fast for something dead. Garrett's foot is firmly planted on one end of the bandages. He watches with curiosity as it untangles, running down the block.

Main Street is paved with trampled plastic fruit. Dirty reds, disgusting oranges, tainted yellows, and bruised purples have been stomped flat until the asphalt is hidden.

Bo beats the last flame from the "I Heart Dyson" float and rubs ashes from his face. "Not the sandwich board. Come on," he says, surveying his town's decay.

Downtown Dyson seems to sag more than before. The Christmas City's wooden Santas and reindeer are in splinters. The wind seems to die, but smoldering floats fill the air with bonfire smoke. Brave birds sit on phone lines and chirp.

The picture window of the Dyson Drop is a sheet of cracked ice. The door slumps inward on broken hinges. A thin, dark trickle of pinot noir streams onto the sidewalk where it meets a toppled and charred sandwich board.

The scene wrings his eyes until tears wash down blackened cheeks. Seeing his town destroyed didn't do it. Losing Marci didn't do it. Hearing the horrible news about Rajula didn't do it. But this sandwich board activates a painful spigot within the Mayor and takes several minutes to run dry.

He knows it's not the sign causing all the heartache, just the final straw that broke his back.

"Some people," Bo says with heavy disappointment, "have no respect." He kneels and wipes dark gunk from the board with his shirt. The store name is illegible. The mayor takes a long breath and props the sign up, nudging it as close to three feet from the building as he can. "This might not have been the best way to rescue Dyson," he says with a sigh.

"I'll say." Donna Queen walks up. Her voice is playful, friendly. He doesn't tense like all those times before. She is probably going to jam a knife into his heart, but it doesn't matter anymore. He welcomes the relief of defeat.

"Fair enough. I deserve that." He shrugs. "Part of me thinks a huge exploding satellite . . ."

"*Wouldn't have been the worst thing in the world?*" she says gently.

The mayor rubs ashy grit between his fingers, nodding. "Couldn't have said it better myself." The two stare down the street as friends from around Dyson tape broken windows, sweep up bags full of plastic fruit, and seem to genuinely help one another.

"So, I guess this means you're not dead?"

Bo chuckles.

"Congratulations?"

"Feels like I should be dead, but no. Maybe it's just my career."

"Packy told me he'd, well—that you were dead."

"I know. Packy told me the whole plan," Bo says.

Donna makes a deflated sound. "That was stupid. Thank God you're okay. I know you don't believe me, but I feel awful about it. It was this . . . I don't know, moment of weakness. I would take it back in a heartbeat. I understand if you never want to . . . you know . . . talk to me . . . *something-something-something.*"

"It's cool. I'm not mad. I just needed some space. I'm very confused right now." He picks up sidewalk litter. "You know, I really thought I was helping the town. I mean, I felt something deep inside that told me I was right and everyone else was wrong."

"I wouldn't know that feeling." Donna grins.

Bo shoots a dismissing eye-roll. "But it occurs to me now that I was focusing on the wrong things. Not like you."

"Really?" She locks onto the mayor's eyes. "Really?"

Bo waves her off. "Hey, was that you beating a mob away from the Gibbons twins with a high-heel shoe?"

"I might have. It's all a blur." Donna looks down. One foot is bare and caked with filth. Shaking her head, she takes a harder look at the scene. Something catches her eye among the burnt muck and plastic fruit.

"That was awesome. Good for you."

"Doesn't take a hero to beat someone with a shoe."

"I don't know. I . . ." He stops when Donna moves quick to the ground. "What's that?"

Kneeling, she unearths a small, grimy bottle. "Oh, thank God," she says, squirting a clear dollop of sanitizer onto her palm. "Interested?"

Bo stares for a moment, remembering its cleansing cold zing. "No, I'm good," Bo says, wiping filthy hands on his pants.

An exhausted cheer sounds down the block. Apparently the flames on the last float have been extinguished. The west sky and setting sun look so lovely. He laughs. "I have good news for you."

"Why do I find that hard to believe?"

"I think you *are* a hero," Bo says with a generous smile. "That was really brave."

"Thanks. That's sweet of you to say."

"Everyone in town was brave today."

"Couldn't agree more," she says as they shuffle through smashed plastic, enjoying the warmth of a blossoming truce.

Donna picks up a blue high heel, tries jamming her toes into it without a fit. She looks at the shoe a moment, wondering how it got here, and then tosses it.

"Hey, Donna, listen," he says, quiet and professional, laying an arm on the millionaire. "It's pretty obvious there's a lot I don't know. If Dyson's going to recover, I'll need all the help I can muster."

"Probably," she says plainly.

"I was thinking there might be room in my administration. Your insight could be a huge help."

"Co-Mayor?" A faded imitation of the foreclosure stare forms. Her eyes aren't so brutal, though. Almost looking sweet, the mayor thinks. She looks eager.

They share a genuine laugh.

"How about, like, deputy mayor today. Tomorrow we'll let you rule the world."

"Hmmm. Yeah. I never tried baby steps before. That might be the way to go," she says.

For a few minutes they gather fruit and don't speak. It will be days before Main Street is even passable. Every business is destroyed, and Bo doesn't know if anyone will even come back. The ten million necessary to keep operating seems like a much smaller problem suddenly.

"God, look at the mess," she says. "People aren't going to forget the Fake Fruit Festival."

"What a mistake."

"Eh, I've seen worse."

"Yeah right," Bo says. "This makes our whole Lincoln obsession seem sensible."

"Honest Abe and his bowels never hurt anyone."

Bo laughs as they brush away more plastic wreckage.

"You have pets, right?" he says.

"Yeah. Yep. Couple dogs. A cat. Garrett's birds. We had a giraffe for a few years, God rest her soul."

"That's what I thought. Can you recommend a veterinarian?"

"Why?" Donna says.

"I'm suddenly a cat lover."

"That's a big change for you."

"I'm as surprised as anyone."

Dyson is once again a speck of pepper.

A spot of spice like this can grow to unthinkable size once in a while. And pepper can shrink back to microscopic doses. But it carries on.

Unlike its cousin salt, which is famous for blending, becoming an invisible portion of the larger whole, pepper does not hide. Pepper stands out no matter how it is used. Pepper never goes away. Like a grain of sand, a speck of pepper cannot simply vanish into the big picture. It may get smaller and harder to see, but its elements never completely break down.

And like a grain of sand, with the right attention and tenderness and a little irritation, it can morph into something unimaginably beautiful.

THANK YOU

Jeremy Morris
Jason Jordan
Matt Bialer
Cameron Pierce
Todd Summar
Owen King

PATRICK WENSINK is the author of four books, including the bestseller *Broken Piano for President*. His writing appears in *New York Times, Esquire, Salon, Oxford American, Men's Health* and others. In 2016 HarperCollins will publish his first children's book, *Gorillas A-Go-Go*.

He lives in Louisville, KY with his wife, son, and fragile ego.

www.patrickwensink.com

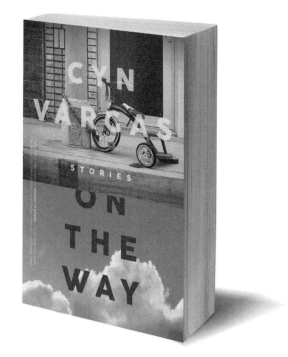

ON THE WAY
STORIES BY CYN VARGAS

"In these fresh, sensual stories, Vargas bravely explores family, friendship and irreconcilable loss, and she will break your heart nicely." —**BONNIE JO CAMPBELL**

Cyn Vargas's debut collection explores the whims and follies of the human heart. When an American woman disappears in Guatemala, her daughter refuses to accept she's gone; a divorced DMV employee falls in love during a driving lesson; a young woman shares a well-kept family secret with the one person who it might hurt the most; a bad haircut is the last straw in a crumbling marriage. In these stories, characters grasp at love and beg to belong—often at the expense of their own happiness.

CRAZY HORSE'S GIRLFRIEND

A NOVEL BY ERIKA T. WURTH

"Crazy Horse's Girlfriend is gritty and tough and sad beyond measure; but it also contains startling, heartfelt moments of hope and love." —DONALD RAY POLLOCK

Margaritte is a sharp-tongued, drug-dealing, sixteen-year-old Native American floundering in a Colorado town crippled by poverty, unemployment, and drug abuse. She hates the burnout, futureless kids surrounding her and dreams that she and her unreliable new boyfriend can move far beyond the bright lights of Denver before the daily suffocation of teen pregnancy eats her alive. *Crazy Horse's Girlfriend* thoroughly shakes up cultural preconceptions of what it means to be Native American today.

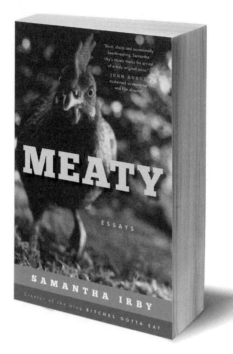

MEATY

ESSAYS BY SAMANTHA IRBY

"Raunchy, funny and vivid . . . Those faint of heart beware . . . strap in and get ready for a roller-coaster ride to remember." —**KIRKUS REVIEWS**

Samantha Irby explodes onto the page with essays about laughing her way through a life of failed relationships, taco feasts, bouts with Crohn's Disease, and much more. Written with the same scathing wit and poignant bluntness readers of her riotous blog, Bitches Gotta Eat, have come to expect, *Meaty* takes on subjects both high and low—from why she can't be mad at Lena Dunham, to the anguish of growing up with a sick mother, to why she wants to write your mom's Match.com profile.

ONCE I WAS COOL

ESSAYS BY MEGAN STIELSTRA

"Stielstra is a masterful essayist. From the first page to the last, she demonstrates a graceful understanding of the power of storytelling." —**ROXANE GAY**

In these insightful, compassionate, gutsy, and heartbreaking personal essays, Stielstra explores the messy, maddening beauty of adulthood with wit, intelligence, and biting humor. The essays in *Once I Was Cool* tackle topics ranging from beating postpartum depression by stalking her neighbor, to a surprise run-in with an old lover while on ecstasy, to blowing her mortgage on a condo she bought because of Jane's Addiction. Or, said another way, they tackle life in all of its quotidian richness.